VOICE OF LIFE

VOICE OF LIFE

THE SPOKEN MAGE BOOK 4

MELANIE CELLIER

LUMINANT PUBLICATIONS

VOICE OF LIFE

The Spoken Mage Book 4
First edition published in 2019 (v1.0)
by Luminant Publications

ISBN 978-1-925898-09-5

Luminant Publications
PO Box 203
Glen Osmond, South Australia 5064

melaniecellier@internode.on.net
http://www.melaniecellier.com

Cover Design by Karri Klawiter
Editing by Mary Novak
Proofreading by Deborah Grace White
Map Illustration by Rebecca E Paavo

For my brothers, James and Stephen,
who help me define family

ROYAL FAMILY OF ARDANN

King Stellan
Queen Verena
Crown Princess Lucienne
Prince Lucas

MAGE COUNCIL

Academy Head (black robe) - Duke Lorcan of Callinos
University Head (black robe) - Duchess Jessamine of
    Callinos
Head of Law Enforcement (red robe) - Duke Lennox of
    Ellington
Head of the Seekers (gray robe) - Duchess Phyllida of
    Callinos
Head of the Healers (purple robe) - Duke Dashiell of
    Callinos
Head of the Growers (green robe) - Duchess Annika of
    Devoras
Head of the Wind Workers (blue robe) - Duke Magnus of
    Ellington
Head of the Creators (orange robe) - Duke Casimir of
    Stantorn
Head of the Armed Forces (silver robe) - General Griffith of
    Devoras
Head of the Royal Guard (gold robe) - General Thaddeus of
    Stantorn

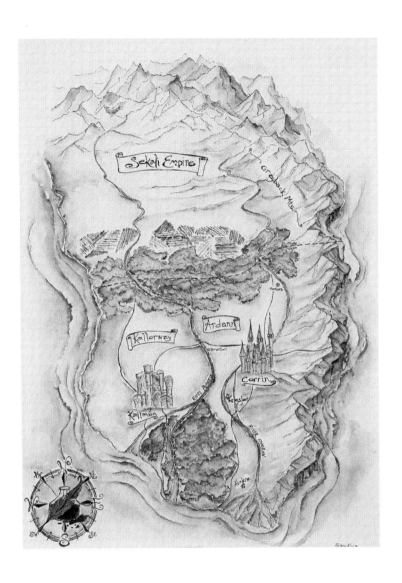

The gentle swell of music and bright colors of robes and gowns filled the room. I told myself I had no reason to feel out of place, but I didn't seem to be listening.

"It's not too late to turn around," Finnian said behind me.

"Don't sound so hopeful," I muttered.

He chuckled. "You know Coralie insisted I look after you while she's in Abalene. There's no way I'd be here otherwise. Not if I could possibly avoid it."

"That's funny," I said. "I could have sworn you've been talking about the Devoras chef for days."

"Well, your new father does have the best food at his parties, and I have to find the silver lining somewhere." His eyes wandered over to the long table covered in delicacies.

I winced. "Don't call him that."

Finnian grinned. "That's why we're here, isn't it? Your new, dear Papa."

I sighed. General Griffith, my new adoptive father, had visited the Academy in person to tell me he expected his children to grace his soiree with their presence. Since the twins were happily spending the summer between their family's estate and their Corrin mansion, I was no doubt the only recalcitrant one.

I hadn't turned up to any of the other parties and events he had hosted over the summer, and I had known my avoidance was too good to last. The general hadn't invited me into his family so I could hide away and shun them all. He wanted to show me off— or show off our new connection at least.

The press of people made my stomach roil, and a sudden headache sprang up behind my temples. The Academy was almost deserted over the summer break, and I wasn't used to such a crowd.

When I rubbed at my head, Finnian glanced at me, his expression changing to one of concern.

"Are you all right?" he asked, his voice low.

"There's just so many people." I straightened my back. "But I'll get used to it. I have to."

Like all mages, I could sense the presence of power. It swirled around many of the guests—the people, as well as the building itself, cloaked in a dizzying number of unidentified compositions. But I was used to that. The headache came from an entirely new awareness. One I didn't share with other mages.

Ever since I had reached out and ripped energy from Lucas and Araminta during the Battle of Abneris, I had been able to sense the energy inside every person. It pulsed at their life core, sometimes stronger, sometimes weaker, depending on their level of exhaustion. My awareness of the energy in those around me had sharpened and honed itself in the weeks since the battle. I had even grown used to it.

But I had also been hiding away in the Academy, avoiding large crowds. And now people pressed at me on every side. Even the commonborn servants who moved around the party carried energy in their center. And their energy felt exactly the same as what filled the mageborn, although the commonborn only burned their energy through regular exertion. Any drain to their energy from accessing power would be irrelevant—wiped out in the fiery death that would result from their lack of control.

The energy filled my mind, a discordant note that rang against the sense of power twining through the room. It called to me, reminding me how easily I could suck it into myself. But the thought always brought another hard on its heels. Thirty-nine hearts ceasing to beat at my command. My stomach heaved again.

I pushed the thought aside. Their deaths had not been the result of my new energy ability, and I had seen first-hand that it could be used to bring life as well as death. And in this moment, I didn't intend to take any energy at all. I just needed to find a way to push my awareness of it to the back of my mind—something I would never do without exposure to crowds. I sighed again.

"Come on then," I said. "Let's do this."

Finnian kept pace beside me as we walked into the room, both of us nodding politely at any familiar faces in the crowd. Finnian nodded a lot more than I did.

I had asked him to accompany me for that exact reason. He had grown up in this world, son of the Head of the Healers. He had attended so many parties like this one that they seemed commonplace and boring to him.

"Daughter." General Griffith approached me, his arms held wide in a welcoming gesture.

I pasted a smile on my face.

"Sir."

"And Finnian, good to see you're back in Corrin already." He nodded at my companion. Apparently Duke Dashiell's son met with his approval as an escort.

"I came back early this year," Finnian said easily. "I wouldn't want to miss all the social events of the season."

He didn't mention the real reason he had come back early: to see Coralie before she left to spend a few weeks with her family in Abalene, and to keep me company once she was gone.

"How goes it at the front?" I asked the general.

"Quiet enough to permit my absence," Griffith replied, his expression suggesting he found the lull in hostilities unnerving rather than relieving.

I began to ask another question, but he cut me off.

"I have several people I'd like you to meet." He turned to my companion. "If you don't mind excusing us, Finnian?"

Apparently the war wasn't an approved topic for an event like this. I filed the information away, and when Finnian headed in the direction of the food, I took a fortifying breath and followed in my new father's steps.

He introduced me to a parade of Devoras members, many of them senior in one of the ten disciplines. I would have been completely lost if the general hadn't given me a family catalog of sorts shortly after my official entry to the family. I had memorized it with some reluctance at the time, but I praised my foresight now.

The guests greeted me with varying levels of interest, some surveying me with obvious disapproval and others with equally apparent disappointment. I felt like apologizing to them all for being so obviously below expectation, but I doubted they would appreciate my attempt at humor. Finnian had already warned me to tread gently, at least with the older ones.

But others wore pleased, almost greedy, expressions as they surveyed me.

"We're delighted to have the hero of Abneris among our number," a man a couple decades my senior assured me.

From the general's introduction he was a wind worker. Thanks to my efforts with the family catalog, I knew him to be a distant cousin but a strong mage, rising rapidly through the ranks of his discipline.

I cast an uncomfortable glance at the general who knew more of my actions in the battle than most—although even he didn't know the full story.

4

"I didn't win that battle myself, whatever the rumors say," I told the wind worker.

The man shrugged. "The truth is hardly important in such a matter, now is it? It's the perception that matters. Between you and the general, Devoras is in high favor at court, thanks to that battle."

I blinked. "Oh. I suppose…"

Someone called for the general, and I took his departure as an opportunity to escape from the conversation.

"Regretting signing those papers yet?" asked Finnian, appearing beside me and offering a plate of food.

"I'm not saying I actually want to be related to any of these people," I murmured, "but…"

"Well?" He raised an eyebrow at me. "But?"

"Every one of those people just looked me in the eye and talked to me. And when they had questions about my studies or the battle, they asked me. Even the ones who obviously don't approve of me."

"Were you expecting them to hold back?" Finnian sounded confused.

"You probably never saw it—or maybe you never noticed—but it used to be that senior mages rarely asked me questions. If I was with someone like the general and they had a question about me, or about something I witnessed, they would have asked him. But every single one of them looked me in the eye and directed their questions at me."

I shook my head. "I had to fight for that respect at the Academy. And even with the general. And now, with a stroke of the pen, I have that respect from everyone. I might not like the reason why, but I was never going to be able to win over everyone individually." I looked at Finnian. "Is it weakness that I'm glad not to have to fight to be seen as a person anymore?"

"You have a voice that needs to be heard, Elena. It helps if people are listening."

A stirring near the door drew both of our attention as yet more mages I didn't recognize entered the large reception room. When I looked questioningly at Finnian, he said nothing, his brow furrowed as he watched them.

"Who are they?" I asked.

"I don't know. I don't recognize them."

I stared back at the new arrivals. Finnian knew everybody. Either these newcomers came from a minor family who rarely attended court—an unlikely possibility given their invitation to this event—or they weren't Ardannian mages at all.

I examined them more closely. They all had similar golden skin and black hair to Finnian's northern family, and they all wore robes. As the crowd moved slightly, giving me a clearer view, I noted the differences in their robes compared to the familiar Ardannian ones. High-collared, the garments bore golden embroidery that wound around their throats and the cuffs of their long sleeves. The sides bore long slits which opened as they walked, revealing loose trousers underneath.

The foreign mages stood close together, the almost solid knot of their energy combining with their excessive layers of compositions to press against me in the already crowded room. I swayed slightly and put a hand to the side of my head. My senses felt indistinct and confused.

A moment later my eyes fell on someone else who had slipped into the room in the wake of the unfamiliar newcomers. My surroundings slowed and then disappeared before reappearing in crystal clarity. Lucas.

I stared at him, unable for a brief moment to move. I wanted to run across the room and throw myself into his arms, but I knew better than to do anything so foolish. The sight of his tall form and familiar dark hair and green eyes brought a rush of homesickness greater than any I had felt before. I missed him. Had it really been so many weeks since I felt the warm grip of his hand or the strength of his embrace?

But at the same time, it had been forever. I hadn't seen him since our dramatic kiss in the entranceway of the Academy on our return from the front lines. He had been called to the palace after that, and the summer weeks had dragged on without his presence. I woke every morning to a disorienting feeling that something was missing. I told myself it was the chatter of a building full of students, but I knew it was only one voice I missed.

His family needed him at the palace was the official word—after his long absence at the front he had many official duties. But I understood what lay behind that—the immense pressure they were bringing to bear on him to marry a Sekali princess and save us all. A sacrifice he would probably have made gladly if it wasn't for me.

He had promised me he would fight for us. That he would not let anyone rip us apart. I could only imagine how that was tearing him apart now, the broken promise eating him up inside. But how could he let countless more die just so we could be together?

Staring hungrily at him now, I could read fatigue hiding behind his usual court facade. If only we could have an uninhibited chance to talk.

Slowly my feet carried me in Lucas's direction, Finnian forgotten behind me. I had nearly reached him before he turned in my direction and saw me. For a brief moment his face lit up, and then his mask slammed back into place.

I flinched slightly but continued until I stood before him.

"Lucas."

"Elena."

There was too much to be said between us. My mind went blank.

"I've missed you," I managed to blurt out.

His eyes softened slightly, but they looked more hurt than pleased.

"I've missed you too." His voice was a bare whisper.

His eyes flickered around the room, and then he spoke in a more normal volume.

"I heard you've remained at the Academy for the summer. You didn't feel inclined to move in with your new family?"

A hint of humor sounded in his words, so I managed a small smile.

"Strangely enough, I did not. The Academy is my home for now."

He nodded, and I tried to read the thoughts behind his eyes. Did he approve of my becoming a Devoras? I wanted to blurt out that I had done it for us, but people surrounded us on all sides, and I kept my words inside.

"Jasper graduated, and my…other family have moved here to Corrin," I said instead. I had wanted to say true family but remembered who might overhear us just in time.

He nodded. "I heard."

I glanced away. Of course he had heard. No doubt the royal family kept track of everyone connected with the Spoken Mage —hope of Ardann, hero of the Battle of Abneris. Had Lucas told them of my new ability?

But as I looked back into his eyes, I knew he hadn't. He was the one who had sworn all of us present to secrecy even before the thought had occurred to me. He might be forced by circumstance to sacrifice our relationship, but he would never betray me.

"I hope they're enjoying the city," he said, and it took me a moment to remember we were speaking of my family. How strange it felt to be exchanging trivial news as if we were merely year mates meeting again after the summer break.

"Clemmy loves it," I said. "They've found a tiny apartment, but we're hoping they'll be able to move to something bigger in a while."

I didn't mention that my allowance from the general was funding their new home. The sale from their Kingslee store had not been enough to cover the cost of a new shop in Corrin without an additional loan, and Jasper's steady salary as a palace official was required to help cover the repayments.

"I'm glad."

Something in me broke, and I leaned toward him, my voice filling with urgency.

"Lucas—"

He cut me off with a small shake of his head.

"I can't stay long, but I promised to attend this event with the Sekali Ambassador." His eyes moved to where the group of foreigners now talked to General Griffith beside one of the food tables. A tall, elegant young woman in a magnificent gown stood beside the general, and with a start I recognized Lucas's sister, Crown Princess Lucienne. I hadn't noticed her before, but she must have arrived with the Sekalis and her brother.

Lucas's presence had driven everything else from my mind, but I noticed now how everyone in the room watched the Sekalis, even as they pretended to go on with their conversations. The Sekalis, on the other hand, displayed no such curiosity, their attention either on the food or the general. Except for one, who watched Lucas and me.

I swallowed. "So they are Sekalis. I suspected as much, but the general didn't tell me they would be here."

"Perhaps he thought it might scare you off." He paused. "In truth—" His voice dropped. "I only came because I hoped you would be here. But now…this is worse than not seeing you at all."

My eyes flew to his, the pain I saw there making my own pain flare like the stab of a knife. But a calm, commanding voice interrupted us before I could respond.

"Brother, we need your opinion."

I curtsied to the crown princess while Lucas gave her a level stare. She returned it, her own holding steady. He looked away first, giving the slightest nod, and she turned to me.

"You must excuse us, Spoken Mage. We have many responsibilities."

I met her eyes. "I understand, Your Highness."

And I did understand the message she truly wished to convey to me. They couldn't let their potential new allies see any hint that Lucas might disrespect—or worse, reject—the proposed marriage alliance.

She nodded once and swept Lucas away. He met my eyes for the briefest second, his gaze laden with far too much to be exchanged in such a fleeting moment.

I watched as they were absorbed into the Sekali delegation, the general turning to include them both in his conversation. My heart throbbed. If only I could run straight back to my room at the Academy. I wanted to be done with this evening.

"Elena of Kingslee," said an unfamiliar voice behind me. "We meet at last."

"Elena of Devoras now," I said without turning around.

"So I've heard. Sister."

I twisted, taking in the tall young man beside me. He had dark hair and looked more like Natalya than her fair-haired twin, Calix, did.

"Julian." I had seen him before, but we had never met. The general's oldest son.

"Father said you would be here."

"And here I am. A dutiful daughter."

He gave a wry laugh. "Are you now? Natty's in Father's bad books at the moment, so that makes one of you."

"Is that why the twins aren't here? I thought all of us were required, but I haven't seen them."

"Their return from the estate was unavoidably detained," he said. "Or so I'm told. Perhaps Father didn't want to risk a scene by having you all in the same room along with our new friends." His eyes lingered on the Sekalis.

"I'm sure the twins know better than to be starting any scenes."

"Oh, Calix does, certainly. He's the truly dutiful one."

Amusement lingered in his voice and around his eyes. I watched him curiously as he regarded the crowd. The general had hinted that Julian didn't see the value in allying their family with me. Did that mean he sided with Natalya?

"You're not like I expected, I must admit," he said without turning to look at me.

"What did you expect? That I would be taller? Or breathing fire, perhaps?"

He chuckled. "From what I hear, you could, if you wished to. But I was expecting more along the lines of...coarse."

I knit my brows. "I suppose I'm meant to take that as a compliment."

He finally turned to look at me, a quirk on one side of his mouth. "You can take it however you like."

"How generous," I said dryly.

It occurred to me that I couldn't remember anyone mentioning what discipline the general's oldest son had chosen. He hadn't been at the front the previous year, so I could only assume he hadn't followed in his father's footsteps.

"Since we haven't met before, I take it you didn't choose the Armed Forces," I said.

He raised an eyebrow. "Thirty years into a war that might never end? I'm not so foolish."

"Or so brave," I muttered.

He snorted. "And I suppose you mean to choose it, do you?" His tone suggested he thought no such thing.

I glanced away, my face warming slightly. I had no intention of choosing the armed forces discipline.

"I can't imagine they'd want me after the Battle of Abneris," I said.

"Oh? And here was I thinking you were its hero."

I narrowed my eyes, examining his expression. Surely the general's son knew the truth of what had happened in the battle? His face held enough mockery to suggest he might, but not enough to confirm it.

"So what did you choose for yourself, then?" I asked, wanting to deflect the conversation away from me.

"When I'm on duty I wear a gold robe," he said, "and answer to the other general."

The Royal Guard, then. Their head, General Thaddeus, was a Stantorn, so perhaps Julian had seen it as the next best thing to serving under a member of his own family. I wished I could ask him about Thaddeus, but I didn't think he was likely to be a receptive audience for my concerns about the potentially traitorous leanings of the Stantorn family.

"I see my future in a palace, not a battlefield," he added. His eyes sparkled down at me. "I hear you do, too."

"I don't know what you mean," I said stiffly.

He laughed. "I'm sure you don't." He tipped me a mocking salute and strolled away, a lazy smile on his face.

I ground my teeth. I didn't like my oldest new sibling much more than the two I already knew. But I had to admit he was more interesting than either of them.

The conversation had distracted me from the sensation of power and energy that filled the room, but left to myself, it pushed at me again. The strongest blaze came from where the Sekali delegation stood, still clumped together, and I watched them, idly practicing picking out the different sensations.

As I reached the inner part of their circle, I faltered. Frowning, I stepped forward. Princess Lucienne glanced up and met my eyes, a clear warning in hers, and I stopped. But I didn't turn away from the group.

Most of their robes bore familiar colors, although we didn't know enough of their culture for me to be certain if the purple and blue and orange represented the same disciplines. Or if they even had disciplines at all.

But my attention focused in on an unfamiliar color in the center of the group. The man wearing the pale green robe was one of the youngest of the Sekalis present, although he was still significantly older than me. The shade of his garment bore little similarity to the darker forest green of the robes worn by our growers, but it wasn't the difference in his clothes that had attracted my attention.

I could sense his presence, as I sensed the people who stood around him, but he didn't feel like them. He didn't feel like anyone I had encountered.

CHAPTER 2

$\mathcal{A}$s if he felt the weight of my stare, the green-robed man looked toward me. I quickly withdrew my gaze, glancing blindly around the ballroom.

"Are you all right?" asked a quiet voice at my side, and I blinked and tried to focus on Finnian.

"Well enough," I managed to say. Silence fell between us for a moment before I blurted out, "Does that man seem strange to you?"

Finnian frowned. "Which man?"

"The Sekali with the pale green robe."

Finnian examined the man from afar.

"Not especially." He gave a small shrug. "He might have a touch more power surrounding him, but then all the Sekalis seem to be coated in compositions. They have the other times I've seen them, too. Not that it's any great surprise, given they didn't bring any guards with them."

I turned to him in surprise. "No guards? Not just here tonight, but at all? That seems bold."

"I suppose they figured their workings would offer them greater protection, and they're right, of course. They'd need a lot more guards than courtesy would allow them to bring to make a difference if we decided to offer them violence."

I looked back at the Sekalis. Or perhaps they didn't have guards in the Empire at all? The idea seemed crazy, but we knew so little about them.

"Why do you ask?" asked Finnian. He lowered his voice. "Do you sense something strange about him?"

"I've never felt anything like it," I whispered back.

"So he's not just low on energy? Maybe he spent the day composing?"

I shook my head. "No, I know what that feels like. You exhausted yourself two days ago, remember?"

He looked guilty. "Well I really wanted to try that composition, and I know I won't have the energy for it once classes start again."

"He has plenty of energy," I said. "It's just muffled. No..." I shook my head. "That's not right. It's more like it's...shadowed. Or something. It's hard to describe."

I could sense the energy coiled inside him, but not in the same way I sensed it in others. It was like a veil had been drawn across it, and only a hazy glow shone through.

Several academics who I recognized approached the foreign delegation and struck up conversation. Duchess Annika, Head of the Growers and a Devoras, apprehended Lucas and his sister. The general, meanwhile, detached himself from the group and approached us.

His eyes gleamed as he glanced back at the clustered Sekalis.

"You'll have to remind me to introduce you to the Sekalis later, Elena. I'm sure they would be interested to meet you."

"I'm not sure the crown princess would be so pleased about the introduction," I murmured, and he raised an eyebrow.

"Perhaps you're right." His good humor didn't fade however. "There's no need to push things when we're already honored enough by their presence. They haven't accepted every social

15

invitation they've received—not by far. I'm sure you'll have an opportunity to meet them at a later occasion."

I could almost see the calculation behind his eyes as he weighed up the advantages of increasing the Devoras family's links to the Sekalis versus the possibility of upsetting the crown.

"I understand they provided very little information about themselves when our delegation visited their lands four years ago," Finnian said. "Are they being more forthcoming now?"

The general glanced across at him. "It's early days still."

So, not really, in other words. How could we consider an alliance with a land we knew so little about? A land that had always kept its border firmly closed to us. But I didn't ask the question because I already knew the answer. After thirty years of aggression from Kallorway, we couldn't afford not to take the opportunity to gain such a powerful ally.

"Have they shared information about their disciplines, at least?" Finnian pushed.

"We know they have them, at least. And not so dissimilar to our own," the general said. "Although they call them branches."

I realized where Finnian's questioning was headed.

"Do you know what branch the pale green robe denotes?" I asked.

The general frowned. "It's hard to say with any certainty. Not one that seems to line up with any of ours. Mostly they wear the same colors as our own disciplines, but their growers wear brown. I heard Annika asking about the green robe, and the Sekali answer was typically vague. Something about new life. Why do you ask?"

I shrugged.

His eyes narrowed, and he glanced once at Finnian. But his reluctance to speak in front of a Callinos wasn't enough to completely hold him back.

"Only one green-robed mage accompanied them, and the one thing that has been apparent is that he is held in great respect."

He might not want to spell it out in front of my year mate, but his subtext was clear. Don't go poking around where it might cause offense and, by extension, embarrassment to the Devoras family.

"Perhaps they are a sub-group of their grower branch," I said, trying to keep my voice nonchalant.

The general looked at me a little suspiciously but let the subject drop, striding off to welcome another new arrival.

"Mysterious," said Finnian.

"Everything about the Sekalis seems to be mysterious," I said.

Part of me itched to try pulling energy from the green-robed man, but I resisted the urge. The general didn't know what type of diplomatic incident I had the capacity to provoke, but his instincts had apparently been right. I needed to be warned away.

I rubbed at my head. He didn't need to worry, however. I hadn't drawn energy from anyone since the Battle of Abneris. I was hardly going to start on a foreign dignitary cocooned in unknown protections.

"Getting tired?" Sympathy laced Finnian's voice. "Ready to head home?"

I sighed in relief. "More than ready." I couldn't get back inside the Academy walls quickly enough for my liking.

Our year mates began to slowly return to the Academy over the following days. This was to be our final year, and I wondered if their return felt bittersweet. After this year, we were all supposed to return to the front to complete our two year terms with the Armed Forces. Did they fear it? Or had our time there last year given the idea an unanticipated familiarity?

Sometimes I let my mind dwell on what my life would be if I just accepted the inevitability of Lucas's betrothal and put aside all thought of trying to bring about an end to the war. I highly doubted Griffith would be assigning me to the front. And not because I was now legally his daughter. He was one of the few who knew that my proximity to the battle lines had been the reason for the all-out attack now called the Battle of Abneris. He would no doubt assign me to some dull duty far from the battlefield.

And I could not be sorry. I still woke up screaming and sweating from nightmares. Sometimes my sleeping mind dwelled on the lives I had taken, the no-longer beating hearts. Other times it circled around the moment of weakness when I agreed to accompany the Kallorwegian crown prince back to his capital, thinking it the only way to save my friends.

No, I couldn't help being glad I would not have to face the war again. But that didn't mean I was free from the fear of graduation. I already dreaded being separated from my friends, of knowing they were in danger and I wasn't there to help protect them.

But I could hold out hope. An alliance with the Sekalis must bring an end to the war. Perhaps they would have to serve only weeks or months before a truce was declared. Perhaps we would all be released from our conscription duties in such a case, free to return to our families, or pursue our chosen disciplines.

I only wished I could imagine such a hopeful future without a lurking sense of dread. Without conscription, we would all scatter even sooner. The pain of separation from Lucas already sat in my chest like a rock. I couldn't imagine carrying that burden without the help of my friends' company.

And at least the two years with the Armed Forces would have direction. For myself I feared release from my term almost more. My year mates might look forward to life after conscription, certain of their future paths. I, on the other hand, couldn't imagine life beyond both the Academy and the Armed Forces, when I would have to find my own way.

Kingslee was no longer my home, or even the home of my

parents. And in the world of the mages, the Academy alone felt familiar. My parents' small apartment in Corrin had no room for another occupant, and I had no desire to live in any of the general's dwellings.

No, after the Academy, I could imagine only one place feeling like home. The one place that had been barred to me. At Lucas's side.

Which is why such images of the future were only an idle imagination. I was determined to change that future. I had vowed to find a way to end the war before graduation, and despite the many times I had struggled with the seeming futility of the attempt, I could not abandon my efforts. Not when doing so meant abandoning any hope of a future with Lucas.

If only I had any idea how to achieve such an end. I had hoped the summer would bring answers, but it had not. None that I liked, anyway. And the constraints of being stuck at the Academy had become abundantly clear.

Trainees from the other years trickled in as well, and I began to grow accustomed to the feel of their energy filling the building. I paid closer attention than I had done previously, but I felt nothing like the shadow over the Sekali's energy.

Coralie returned, although her initial attention was monopolized by Finnian. When she finally shook him off long enough to hear the story of the Devoras soiree, however, she asked if the Sekali could be ill.

"I suppose it's possible," I said, "although I've never felt a change in anyone's energy from illness. Well," I corrected myself, "not a change like that. Generally they just feel weaker. This didn't feel like his energy was depleted, more like it was...veiled."

"Veiled?" Saffron entered the living room of Coralie's suite on Finnian's heels. "What's veiled?"

I explained it all again, including Coralie's suggestion.

"What if he has a fatal condition of some sort?" Saffron asked. "One you've never encountered before?"

"It's certainly possible," I said.

"But why would he be included in the delegation if he was so ill?" Finnian argued, tucking Coralie into his side.

"The general did say he was highly respected," I said. "Perhaps he was too important to be left behind."

"Or perhaps they don't even know about it?" said Coralie. "It's not like any of their healers can sense his energy the way you can. Maybe he hasn't shown any symptoms that would warrant a diagnosis composition?"

"Has Beatrice returned from the front?" I asked. "Maybe I should see if she would consider taking me on a tour of some of Corrin's healing clinics? I could see whether anyone else feels the same way."

"Perhaps Acacia would take you around?" Saffron suggested.

"Maybe," I said. "I could ask her next time I see her, although I'll have to think of a good excuse for wanting to go."

We were still discussing it over breakfast the next morning, the day before classes commenced.

"You've been studying healing for three years now," said Finnian. "I think it would be quite natural for you to ask for a tour of some healing facilities while you consider which discipline you want to join after conscription."

"I imagine they'll all be falling over themselves to have the Spoken Mage choose them," said Saffron.

I shook my head but didn't actually raise any doubt aloud. She might even be right. I had come a long way from first year when the discussion among the discipline heads was whether or not they should execute me.

Two newcomers caught my eye as they strode through the doors of the dining hall. Natalya and Calix made a striking pair as they paused to survey the room as if they owned it. Apparently they had finally returned from the family estate.

We had finally worked our way up to the row of fourth year tables against the wall closest to the kitchen, and their eyes latched on to where we sat at the end of the row. Natalya threw Calix a look I couldn't read, and he shrugged in reply before they both moved in our direction.

I turned back to my friends. We sat at the top of the row while Weston and Lavinia—the twins' Stantorn friends—had claimed the bottom table when they arrived several days ago. Naturally we had chosen to sit as far away as possible from each other.

"I actually would like to see—" I started to say to Finnian, but my words sputtered to a halt when Natalya and Calix pulled out chairs and joined us.

"Morning," Calix said, by way of general greeting, before helping himself to food from the shared platters in the center of the table. Natalya silently followed his lead. My friends exchanged confused looks, but no one questioned them.

Lavinia and Weston, at the other end of the row of tables, looked our way with displeased expressions. I looked back at Calix who was munching away with unconcern while Natalya picked at her food. All over the hall, younger trainees glanced our way, leaning their heads together to whisper as they did so.

I grasped my fork, only to put it down again without taking a bite.

"Uh...so what exactly is going on?" I asked.

"What do you mean?" asked Calix. "You're our sister now, and family sticks together."

"Really?" I asked, focusing my attention on Natalya.

"Family sticks together." She grimaced slightly, looking like the words hurt her to say.

"Oh. Well, thanks. I guess."

Everyone ate a few bites in uncomfortable silence. Araminta paused behind Calix and looked around our table in confusion. I shrugged at her apologetically. Natalya and Calix had taken the last two seats—hers and the one that Clarence used to occupy. Its glaring emptiness had hurt at every previous meal, but I preferred his memory to my new table mates.

After a moment, Araminta took a seat alone at the next table along. I glanced across at Coralie and Saffron, but before I could suggest my other friends join her, a tall, elegant figure strode into the room.

Dariela didn't break stride at the sight of our new seating arrangements, although her face tightened. Passing us, she sat across from Araminta, and I smiled. I had almost forgotten how we had left things last year. Dariela might not be one of my group of friends, but by the end of third year we had developed an individual friendship. She had even sided with me openly over her previous mageborn companions.

I turned back to the twins. "This is just for today, right? A show of solidarity and all that, and then we can go back to our regular lives?"

"I certainly hope so," Natalya muttered, almost too quietly for me to hear.

"If you prefer it that way." Calix shrugged. "Makes no difference to us where we sit."

Natalya gave him a scathing look, but he ignored her.

"Yes, I most definitely prefer it that way," I said.

Calix shrugged, and Natalya looked relieved.

"And you can tell your father that if he asks," I added.

"*Our* father," Calix corrected me. I rolled my eyes and didn't respond.

A moment later my heart seized. The last remaining fourth year had arrived. Part of me had been tense and on edge all week, constantly waiting for Lucas to appear through a doorway or around a corner. But still his appearance caught me by surprise.

He took in our unusual positions in a single sweeping glance, his eyes lingering on me for the barest second before he moved on to take a seat beside Dariela. She nodded in greeting but didn't look at him, continuing her conversation with Araminta who seemed utterly bemused at the direction the meal had taken.

Lucas looked sideways at me, glancing away quickly when our

eyes met. I surveyed the room. Not a Sekali, or even an instructor, in sight. I hoped whatever strictures had kept Lucas from speaking freely to me at the soiree weren't going to apply at the Academy. Even if nothing else, I needed the chance to have a proper conversation with him.

He ate quickly, however, and left the room without a backward glance. Lavinia followed not long after, pausing by our table. Natalya stood and left the room with her, the Stantorn girl throwing me a poisonous look as they exited, as if she blamed me for attempting to steal her friend. Calix also finished his meal and bid me farewell, nodding at Finnian as well before wandering over to speak to Weston.

With his departure, conversation returned to my table, and my friends began to discuss the rumors that a grand gala was to be hosted at the Academy at the start of spring to celebrate five hundred years since the completion of the building. I left them to it, crossing over to greet Araminta and Dariela.

"Sorry about that," I said to Araminta. "We didn't invite them to join us, or anything."

She giggled. "No, I can imagine not! And I suspect I had better company for the meal." She smiled at Dariela before standing. "Excuse me, but I need to ask Saffron something."

I turned to Dariela who had stood at the same time as Araminta.

"Welcome back. I didn't know you'd arrived."

"Last night." Her voice sounded stiff, and she didn't meet my eyes.

"Strange to be back for our last year, isn't it?" I said. "I hope your travel went well." Perhaps she was tired after her journey.

"Perfectly well. I'll see you in class." She nodded at me once, and then strode from the room.

I watched her go, my mouth hanging slightly open. What had happened to our budding friendship? When I felt someone at my side, I turned.

"Well that was weird," I said to Coralie.

"Which part?" she asked, shaking her head.

Finnian slipped his arms around her waist and rested his chin on the top of her head. "I'm starting to get the feeling this is going to be another odd year."

I nodded, my eyes still on the door of the dining hall. "At least Lavinia and Weston still seem to hate me. So something at least is normal."

Finnian chuckled. "How utterly reassuring. And I'm sure you needn't worry—they're Stantorns which means they're obdurate down to their bones. I imagine they'll go on hating you forever. I'll be sure to remind you of it every time you get disheartened."

I rolled my eyes at him and trailed behind the others as we left the room. Lucas and Dariela appeared to be avoiding me, while Calix and Natalya sought me out. Everything had turned upside down since the last time our year was together, and I didn't like it one bit. Clarence's absence was change enough.

The bright sunshine paired with a cool breeze had convinced my friends to spend the morning in the Academy gardens. We lay on the soft grass and reminisced. Somehow they ended up trying to outdo each other by recalling our most disastrous or embarrassing classes. Of course most of them featured me. I had used more of Acacia's healing compositions than the rest of my year combined.

"Ugh," I said at last, waving my hand lazily in an attempt to make them stop. "Please don't remind me."

"We're only doing it for your sake," Finnian assured me gravely. "We don't want you to get a big head now that you're both hope *and* hero."

I gave a muffled groan and covered my eyes. "It's going to be an awful year, isn't it?"

"I don't think so," said Coralie quietly, and I groaned again, this time in an exaggerated and comical way.

"Saffron, tell me if it's safe to open my eyes. I don't know how much lovey dovey I can take."

Saffron laughed. "You're safe."

I sat up and saw that Finnian now lay with his head in Coralie's lap while she ran her fingers through his hair. I turned outraged eyes on Saffron who giggled.

"Traitor!" I said.

"Consider it exposure therapy—I'm pretty sure we're going to have to get used to them."

I groaned again and flopped back down. In truth, my mixed emotions didn't know how to feel about Coralie and Finnian. On the one hand, I got a happy thrill of my own whenever I saw the joy on their faces, and I was truly glad the Battle of Abneris had convinced my friend to give Finnian a chance despite her fears over his family's reaction. But if I was honest, I also couldn't see them so happy together without a pang. My own relationship didn't appear to be heading for such an ending.

Not unless I could somehow do the impossible.

CHAPTER 3

$\mathcal{I}$ chose to spend the afternoon in my suite, preparing myself mentally for the next day. The thought of classes sat uncomfortably, and I struggled to imagine what they would be like. Not because I anticipated any great change in our instruction. We had already moved to fourth year level strategy bouts in the arena, and I had been doing compositions beyond fourth year level for some time.

No, the change was in me. I had a new power, one I had barely begun to grapple with, and I wasn't sure what to do about it. I certainly couldn't imagine revealing it to Redmond—my Stantorn composition instructor—and asking for his help in refining it. It was almost equally difficult to picture such a conversation with Thornton, my combat instructor, despite the fact he and I were now officially related in some distant way.

The door to my sitting room opened, jerking me out of my thoughts. I hadn't heard a knock, but as soon as I saw who it was, my alarm fell away. Within three strides Lucas had the door closed behind him and me in his arms.

My tears poured out, springing from nowhere, and I buried my face in his chest. His arms tightened, and for a long moment we just held each other. When I finally looked up at him, I only managed to catch the green fire of his eyes for the briefest second before he pressed his lips down over mine.

But they had barely made contact when he pulled himself back, pushing me abruptly away and taking a step back. He ran a hand through his hair and drew a ragged breath.

"I'm sorry. I promised I would fight for us, and now here I am almost betrothed to someone else. I have no right to kiss you."

I took a step toward him, but he took another one back, holding out a hand to ward me off.

"Don't tempt me," he said, his voice still rough.

I took a trembling breath and put the small sofa between us, resting my shaking hands on its back.

"I understand," I said. "I understand why you have to…Why we can't…" I couldn't quite bring myself to say the words.

"I thought the summer would be long enough to find a way out. To convince my family…" He held up his hands and then let them fall in a defeated gesture. "I don't know what I thought. I guess I just hoped. When we arrived back and I discovered their summons, I was sure someone had poisoned them against you just as I feared. But I thought if I obeyed their summons and hurried back to the palace, I could find a way to change their minds. I didn't expect the alliance offer."

"And what choice do you have?" I asked softly. "We can't turn our backs on all of Ardann just so we can be together."

"I would," he whispered, and the burning look he gave me made my knees tremble.

But I locked them in place and met his gaze. "Would you? Really?"

He sank into a chair, his legs sprawled before him and his head in one hand.

"No," he said. "Of course, I can't. As much as I wish I could."

"I wouldn't love you the way I do if you could turn your back on your kingdom like that," I said, coming around the back of the sofa and curling onto it, my legs tucked beneath me. "And I daresay you wouldn't love me if you thought I could make that choice."

He looked up quickly at that, shaking his head. "No, I know you would never choose me over the rest of the kingdom. You're made of stronger stuff, and you've never been afraid of sacrifice."

My lip trembled and another tear rolled down my cheek, but I wiped it away.

"Well, this is our reality then," I said. "And we have to learn how to live with each other for the year."

He winced. "Yes, about that. I'm sorry I just barged in here, but I didn't want anyone to see me lingering in the corridor."

An angry flush burned through me. So we were to be kept apart even here.

"The delegation have asked an uncomfortable number of questions about you, and my parents have been at great pains to assure them that there will be no hindrance to the betrothal. They're too well-informed about us, and Mother and Father seem to think that if we spend too much time together here, or show any preference for each other, word will somehow get back to them. I've been strictly forbidden from, well, anything like this." He gestured back and forth between us and then around the room.

"So, normal year mates, nothing more," I whispered, and he nodded reluctantly.

"It could be worse," I said. "They could have forbidden us to speak at all."

He stared at me, his eyes roaming around my face, and for a moment silence fell between us.

"It's strange to think of you as a Devoras," he murmured at last.

I shook my head. "I keep forgetting myself. I certainly don't feel like one." I swallowed, and my voice dropped. "I did it for us, you know."

He groaned softly. "I thought as much as soon as I heard. It would have cleared up everything if it wasn't for this blasted alliance." He jumped to his feet and strode over to the window.

"If only we weren't stuck in this war," I said.

"Yes, this cursed war." He pounded his fist on the windowsill.

"Without the war, we wouldn't need the alliance." I sighed.

"I'm sure my parents would still wish for it," Lucas said. "But if it wasn't for the war, I would defy them and refuse. But as it stands…"

"I heard we still have time," I whispered. "That the details of the betrothal and treaty are to be worked out by the end of the year. That means we still have time to find another way. There is still hope."

Lucas jerked at my words, swinging around and striding quickly over to kneel on one knee before me. He took both my shoulders in his hands, his haste making him rough.

"That's my line, Elena. This is my problem to fix."

I stared back at him defiantly. "I'm the one with the special powers, remember."

"Don't you dare do anything stupid," he growled.

I worried at my lip. I had a bad track record in that department, so I wasn't making any promises.

"Maybe we can work it out together," I said. "Find a way to end this war."

He slowly dropped his hands, his eyes narrowing as he watched me closely. After a moment, he sat beside me on the sofa.

"As long as you don't get any foolish ideas about that Cassius." He almost spat the Kallorwegian crown prince's name.

"He did say—" I cut off my words at his angry expression. "Perhaps there is another way. If anyone can find it, surely it's us. No one else knows of my new powers, perhaps there's some way to make use of them, like you were always hoping."

Lucas took a slow breath. "I've been thinking about that all summer, but I can't think of any way for one of us to replicate it. Mages have been attempting to do so for centuries without success. There is something about the directness of your workings that allows what none of us can do."

My shoulders slumped. "We haven't even begun experimenting, though. Perhaps…" I sighed. "Do you think I should tell our instructors? Lorcan?"

Lucas was shaking his head before I had finished speaking. "No, it's too dangerous. You might have escaped the Armed Forces, but you're a Devoras now. General Griffith still has a hold over you."

"Do you still think he would wish me harm?" I asked. "Or want me anywhere near the front?"

Lucas sighed. "Honestly, it would probably be more dangerous for you without his protection. Far too many powerful people would love to make use of you already—the Kallorwegians dedicated their entire army to the cause. No. The great families cannot know how powerful you've become."

I nodded, secretly relieved. I wasn't ready to tell Lucas my certainty that the Stantorn family were traitors to the kingdom—not without proof. It simplified things that I didn't have to make an excuse for why I didn't want them to know about my new ability.

But I did need to find some way to train. Some way to understand my new power and its limitations. I had been handed a gift and a powerful weapon, and our kingdom might need it.

"I should be going." Lucas stood reluctantly. "There are still those among our year mates who would gladly report back if they got wind of my being in here alone with you. Not to mention the servants. I don't know how we can work together, but somehow we'll figure out a way to end this war before I'm bound to the Sekali princess."

I leaped up and wrapped my arms around his middle,

squeezing as tightly as I could. If this was our last chance to be real with each other, I needed longer with him.

But the moment was all too quickly gone. For one brief instant his strong arms were wrapped so tightly around me they lifted me off the floor, and then he was slipping back out the door.

None of us pushed ourselves as we strolled out of the dining hall and through the gardens the next morning. Thornton always spent the first week, at least, with the first years, and the junior instructors were notoriously less strict on punctuality. I felt no desire to hurry toward combat class. Even if the first lesson would be little more than a warm up and refresher on our sword skills.

After Lucas left the afternoon before, I had pushed myself too close to exhaustion working on a series of complex compositions. I told myself I truly believed I could get a covert working all the way to the Kallorwegian border from here, but if I was honest, I had been certain it would prove impossible. Deep down I knew I had used more energy than I should purely to push out the unhappy thoughts circling my mind.

My eyes lingered on Lucas's back as we walked. We might be forced to keep our distance, just like in the past, but at least one thing had changed. I no longer had to pretend disinterest. After our kiss in the Academy entrance hall at the end of last year, everyone at the Academy knew of our connection, and they must all know the reasons for our current distance. As long as we didn't act on our feelings, the Sekali delegation couldn't complain.

But the unimpressed face of the instructor waiting in the training yard drew my attention back to the class.

"You're all late, and Thornton isn't going to be pleased," she snapped.

"Thornton?" Weston frowned. "He's never with the fourth years on the first day."

"Never is a strong word, trainee." She looked down her nose at him. "You might be a fourth year, but don't start thinking you know everything there is to know about the Academy."

I exchanged a worried look with Coralie. The last thing I needed was more surprises in combat. My classes were supposed to be the one easy thing about this year.

"You're all to report to the arena for your first class," she said.

"The arena?" Natalya asked.

The instructor narrowed her eyes at her. "That's what I said. And you're already late, so I suggest you all get moving without any more talk."

Finnian raised an eyebrow but kept his mouth shut, breaking into a light jog that we all followed. I kept up with the group easily until I noticed Saffron hanging at the rear. Dropping back, I kept pace with her.

She hardly seemed to notice me, her eyes—large in her gray face—focused on the arena in the distance.

"Are you all right?" I asked.

"I keep remembering it," she said. "The attack in the gully, and then the battle. I see them all the time in my sleep." She swallowed and finally looked at me. "I never asked you. Was he in pain? Clarence, I mean."

My pulse throbbed in my ears, although my breath came easily at our fast walk.

"No," I whispered. "It happened so fast. There wasn't anything I could do to help him."

"Oh." Saffron placed a hand on my arm. "No, I didn't mean..." She took a breath. "I guess I'm just afraid that I'll freeze up if I face battle again. Even battle in the arena, where I know it isn't real."

"I think you'll be fine," I said. "It's the sounds and the smells that get you, and the illusions from the compositions that we command in the arena don't have those." I glanced at her sideways, hesitating. I suspected her real fear wasn't about what might happen in the arena.

"And beyond that," I said, "I think you'll find that when the time comes, you'll do what you have to."

Saffron gave me a tentative smile. "I hope you're right."

The rest of our year mates had already disappeared inside the arena, but we maintained our slower pace as we approached the entrance. Neither of us was in a hurry for what awaited us inside.

Saffron was half a step behind me when my feet hit the arena floor. I registered no more than a rush of movement before a force hit me from the side. As I was lifted into the air, I managed to thrust blindly at Saffron, pushing her stumbling back out into the Academy grounds.

I hit the dirt with enough force to rob me of air. I struggled to take a breath, my mind and body panicking at my double incapacitation. Without breath, my power was as useless as my body. My attacker, a man in rough leather clothing, aimed a kick in my direction. I rolled, narrowly avoiding his foot as my lungs continued to scream at me.

My world narrowed, other sounds falling away, as I focused on the man. Just as I finally drew breath to speak a composition and shield myself, a second set of arms grabbed at me. They hauled me from the ground as I struggled to form the mental picture I needed to complete a working.

The second man made no effort to beat me, instead attempting to sling me over his shoulder. I had no idea how this could be happening here and now, but I recognized the situation. This wasn't the first time someone had tried to abduct me.

My body responded before my mind could catch up, twisting away from him as I drove my elbow back into his stomach. He

33

grunted but didn't let go, his companion approaching me from the other side.

I pushed off against the man holding me, trying to get enough momentum to bring my feet back in a crippling kick. But the first man grabbed me around the knees instead, hauling my legs higher into the air. I took a deep breath, but the second man tightened his grip around my lungs painfully, pushing the air back out again. Black dots began to dance across my vision.

The man holding me jerked, his grip loosening as a weight pulled at him from behind. Smaller arms appeared, hanging from around his neck, dragging him backward and down. Now he was the one struggling to breathe.

I sucked in air, but I couldn't seem to get enough. I wouldn't manage a long composition, so I needed to make it a powerful one. But what if it wasn't enough? I never should have exhausted myself so foolishly.

Without thinking, I gasped out, "Drain." My power instinctively latched onto the familiar feeling of Saffron, hanging off my captor's neck, and a rush of energy filled me. I renewed my struggles, flailing wildly with new strength. One of my feet collided with the first man's face just as I managed to shout, "Separate!"

The four of us sprang apart, our bodies sailing through the air in different directions, hurled by the force of my power. The shock made me cut off the river of energy flowing into me, but I had already received more than my fill.

As the ground rushed toward me, I whispered, "Shield," overlapping a sense of both Saffron and me.

Invisible cushioning sprang into life around me just in time to soften my collision with the arena floor. I lay there for a moment, panting for breath, before I rolled onto all fours and then scrambled to my feet.

Both of my attackers still lay prone, moaning. Nothing had broken their fall.

Saffron sat, one hand pressed to the side of her head. She

appeared to have bounced off a section of arena seating but looked unharmed. Her eyes were fixed on something deeper inside the arena, however, and I swung around, alert for further threats.

Instead I saw my nine remaining year mates and Thornton watching us. The other trainees all wore some level of shock and confusion on their faces. But our instructor looked impassive.

"Your reactions were a little slow," he said. "Especially yours, Saffron. And you should carry defensive compositions on you at all times, even if you aren't expecting any arena bouts. That's something to work on for next time."

He looked at me. "Elena, you need to develop better strategies against an opponent who succeeds in catching you by surprise and winding you. You would have been in trouble without your friend's assistance."

I stared at him for a moment before Saffron and I exchanged a disbelieving look.

"Are you telling me that was part of combat class?" I asked.

"Of course," he said. "How else could two commonborn attackers get to you here, inside the arena? And with all of us watching?"

He was right that it had made no sense. After my abduction in first year, Lorcan had improved the protections on the Academy. Access was now only possible through the main gates, and the head himself monitored everyone who passed through them. But I had barely been able to draw a breath the entire time. I hadn't had extra brain space to give the matter much consideration. My gaze fell on the two men still twitching on the ground, and then crossed over to Saffron. She was only just shakily rising to her feet, her face pale.

A sick feeling filled me as the low pulse of her energy stabbed at me like an accusation. I had reacted on instinct and fear, and I had taken too much of her energy. I hadn't set the proper limitations, and if it hadn't been for my second composition severing the connection, I could have bled her dry.

And all, it turned out, for a training exercise. A swell of anger threatened to overpower me.

"A training exercise? But I could have—" I bit off my next words. I couldn't say anything about what I had nearly done to Saffron.

Instead I turned my attention to the injured men at my feet. Ignoring both my instructor and my year mates, I dropped onto one knee beside the man with blood all over his face. I winced at the sight of his broken nose and began murmuring the binding words.

"That is unnecessary," said Thornton behind me. "Naturally they will be healed. Acacia awaits them in her rooms."

I turned to glare at him, but even as I did so, I modified my composition, reducing it to mere pain relief. The man sighed as my power washed over him and moved toward his companion. They both fell still and took several deep breaths.

I would have preferred to heal them completely, but I knew Thornton would reprimand me for wasting the energy. And he would be right. It was an unnecessary drain if healing compositions had already been set aside for the task.

"Sorry about the nose," I said to the man, offering him a hand.

He slowly heaved himself to his feet without using it, shaking his head as he did so.

"They didn't tell us we would be attacking the Spoken Mage," the other one muttered.

"Never mind my face, My Lady," the one with the broken nose said, ignoring his companion. "You put up a good fight which is what you was supposed to do."

The two lurched out of the arena, disappearing toward the Academy. I turned back to Thornton.

"What if I had killed one of them!" *What if I had killed Saffron?*

"You're not the killing type," he said calmly. His eyes surveyed the whole group of trainees. "You have all seen first-hand that in true combat you cannot predict the moment or method of an attack. Real life doesn't look like our pretty exercises in the arena. This year I will be changing things. Expect the unexpected. When you graduate, you will be as prepared as humanly possible for the outside world."

An intense light filled his eyes, and I swallowed. This was about Clarence.

In Thornton's mind, the worst had happened—one of the trainees in his care had been killed in combat. Not a graduate released into the world, but one still under his tutelage. And apparently he had decided to take our training to new levels as a result.

I took a step toward the rest of the group and winced, my hand flying to my side. Now that the rush from the attack was fading, I could feel the throbbing pain from where I had landed after the first attack.

Lucas stepped forward, his hand catching my elbow and holding me up. When I sucked in a sharp breath, he cursed quietly and let me go. Withdrawing a parchment from his sleeve, he ripped it before I could protest, flicking his fingers toward me.

Sweet, healing power poured over me, and I couldn't help the soft sigh that slipped from my lips. I closed my eyes and took one long breath before opening them again to glare at him.

"That was a lot of power. More than I needed. You shouldn't have wasted it on me."

He frowned. "Who knows what internal injuries you might have had." He glanced toward our instructor. "I tried to intervene. So did Finnian and Coralie. But it happened before any of us realized, and Thornton threw up a shield to hold us all back and incapacitate any compositions we might send your way."

I smiled, the gesture easy now that my pain had disappeared, every ache wiped away by his working.

37

"It's not your fault. And honestly, I've had worse beatings in this class."

Lucas's face twitched, and I belatedly remembered one of my more severe injuries had come from him.

"Thank goodness for healing compositions, hey," I said, trying to cheer him up.

"Did your power connect you to Saffron?" he asked in a low voice. "It was hard to tell with the way she was hanging off your attacker. But I thought…" He glanced once at her. "And she looks awfully tired now."

I turned away from the questions in his eyes, unable to admit to what I had done.

"Elena…" His voice trailed off as he glanced across to where Natalya and Lavinia watched us.

"I'm glad you're both all right," he said, watching as Saffron approached Finnian.

Finnian looked nearly as black as Lucas had done when he first approached me—the angry glares he was directing at Thornton out of character for him—so I headed in their direction as soon as Lucas stepped away. Sickness pooled in my stomach, fueled by guilt and fear for what could have been. I needed to apologize to Saffron, but I couldn't do it here. And in the meantime, I needed to distract Finnian before he punched someone.

"So," I said, making my voice as bright as I could, "looks like it's going to be a fun year."

Saffron chortled weakly, and Finnian's face lightened.

"It actually was sort of fun," she said. "In a weird way. Did you see the way I bounced off that railing? Thank goodness you're quick with your compositions, Elena."

Another stab of guilt at her words morphed into confusion as she gave me a significant look I couldn't read. Thornton called for our attention, and as the trainees around us moved, she leaned close to me.

"You were right. When it came to it, I could act, after all."

"And I'm very grateful you did. I was in trouble until you arrived."

Her face brightened. "I didn't do much."

"But it was just enough," I said. "And I repaid you by—"

"Hush!" she said. "Don't speak of it. You did what you needed to, thinking we were both under threat. I understand."

"Saffron, I'm sorry. Really."

"You have no need to be. It's nothing a good sleep won't fix."

I bit my lip, but Thornton sent a quelling stare in our direction, and we both fell silent. Saffron might be willing to let me off the hook, but that didn't mean I was going to let myself off so easily.

I had been right not to risk using this new power since the battle. And obviously I needed to keep it that way. Some things were too dangerous to be played with.

CHAPTER 4

To my relief, Redmond had no surprises for us in our first composition class of the year and blathered the whole time on theory, so Saffron wasn't called on to compose. I watched her closely, and she had regained some color by the time we were all making our way to the library to sign up for our chosen discipline studies for the year.

All of my friends, even Saffron, intended to sign up for armed forces studies again, and I could understand why. But I had reached my fill of destruction. I longed to try my hand at creation for once.

I didn't intend to sign up for actual creator studies, however. Building design didn't strike me as particularly alluring. But Saffron planned to try grower studies as her second discipline, and I had decided to join her.

"You know, it's not too late," Coralie said, as we approached the library doors. "You could still decide to join Finnian and me in healing studies with your other choice."

She had tried creator studies in third year but was returning to healing. I had accused her of doing it to impress Finnian's family, given his father was Head of the Healers, and she had acknowledged it without shame.

"I wouldn't do it if I wasn't interested, though," she had said. "We saw so many interesting advanced healings at the front. And I'm not going back to creating. I'd much rather rebuild a leg than a house."

Finnian I suspected of having no such interest in healing. He was merely following Coralie and attempting to please his father. He and Coralie had decided to wait to introduce each other to their families until graduation, and he no doubt wanted his family in as good a mood as possible when that day came.

"No, I've made up my mind about my second discipline," I told her, as we entered the library. "All of Saffron's stories about wind working last year were interesting. I want to give it a try, even if she's not continuing with it. Plus, Araminta's going to join me."

Araminta nodded before sighing. "My only hope of passing is to keep trying new things so I can stay a beginner the whole way through."

I nudged her with my shoulder.

"Don't say that! You've improved enormously since first year."

She shrugged but managed a smile. It was true she had improved, but I still understood her fear. Araminta remained the weakest trainee in our year, and the final year exams were the only ones rumored to be truly difficult. The consequence of failure, of course, was incarceration. No one who could write but was unable to safely control power could be allowed to roam through the kingdom freely. Even mages were not exempt from that.

Few mages had ever failed the Academy—most of their mageborn prison mates were those who had misused their power—but Araminta was unusual. She had confided in me in second year that her mother was a commonborn, which explained why she could only call on minimal levels of power and only with weak control.

Walden waited for us in the library, eight sheets of parchment on a table in front of him. My friends spread out, writing their names on the relevant lists for their chosen studies. A handful of third and fourth year names preceded us, and more trainees trickled into the library behind us. The second years wouldn't start until the second week of the year, since it would be their first introduction to discipline studies.

"Ah, Elena!" Walden beamed at me. "Lovely to see you as always. And where may I place your name this year?"

As the only trainee unable to write, I would need Walden to do the actual scribing for me.

"I've decided to branch out this year," I told him. "I'm going to try growing and wind working."

"Ah! It's always a good idea to try something new." He spun the relevant parchments around to face him and leaned over them. "I had rather hoped you might try law enforcement, you know."

"Law enforcement?" I asked. "I'll admit, I didn't even really consider it." Although now that he said it, I wondered if I should have. The truth composition—one of the only law enforcement workings I had ever tried—had already proven extremely useful to me.

"It's often overlooked, I'm afraid," Walden said, finishing with the parchments and spinning them back around. "But I myself was considering joining law enforcement before I realized my true calling was in a library."

He smiled as he gazed around at the rows of shelves. "I must admit that even in my own distant trainee days, I was more likely to be found here in the library than conducting extra training in the yards outside. The combat instructor at the time despaired of me a little, I think. He was an older mage and is sadly no longer alive to see how well my love of this place has served me."

He looked back at me, the smile still lingering on his face. "But even so, I sometimes think there must be something very satisfying about striding the streets, bringing order and justice to the kingdom."

I had always thought I could do the most good for common-borns as a healer, but he was right. Law enforcement would be a powerful place to work for change. But I had already made my decision, and I wasn't going to second guess myself now.

"I attended the Academy with Duke Lennox, you know," said Walden, naming the Head of Law Enforcement. "But we are very distant cousins, and he comes from a stronger branch of the family, so I'm sure I would not have been challenging his rise through the ranks if I had decided to join him with the Law Enforcers."

"Head librarian at the Academy is a senior position," I said, "I'm sure you underestimate yourself. Not that I'm complaining. My time here would have been a lot more difficult if you had joined law enforcement."

Dariela approached the table, not looking in my direction. Carefully she wrote her name down on the lengthy armed forces list, and then her hand hovered above the grower list. I tried to tell myself it was my imagination that her eyes lingered on the last name on the list. Mine.

A heartbeat passed, and then she stepped to the side and wrote her name on the creator list. When she looked up and saw Walden and me standing to one side of the table, her face flushed slightly. But she merely nodded and moved further into the library.

I watched her go, my stomach churning. What had happened to our fledgling friendship?

"Her parents are extremely exacting," Walden said in a gentle voice. "She's under a lot of pressure."

I managed a tight smile for the librarian, knowing he was only trying to comfort me. As Ellingtons, Dariela's parents must be some sort of distant relations of his, so presumably he would know. But he hadn't been there at the front to see the beginning of our friendship, so he couldn't understand the change now. Rather than attempt any explanation, I bid him farewell and went in search of my friends. They, at least, had not changed their opinion of me over the summer.

~

Classes fell into a familiar routine. Black robed academics from the University sometimes sat in on our composition classes, as if they had suddenly realized that I was soon to be out of their reach—taking my unique type of power with me. I welcomed their presence, since they provided a point of interest in an otherwise tedious class.

Redmond clearly despised their presence, but Lorcan had ordered that they were to have free access to me, and we had some interesting conversations on the various theories behind the usage of power. Sometimes I got so caught up in them that I had to watch myself unless I slipped and mentioned something about my new ability. And sometimes their conversations made me long to try out exactly what I could do with it. But I firmly tamped the instinct down. There was no way to experiment with it without involving someone else. Without stripping them of something central to their essence.

Many of my visitors came from the Callinos family—no surprise, perhaps, since both the Academy Head and University Head hailed from Callinos. I tried to be as friendly as possible, eager to show them that my becoming a Devoras had not been intended as a rejection of the Callinos family. Given I had not had a single private conversation with Lorcan the entire summer —a stark contrast to the previous one—I suspected he disapproved of my accepting the general's offer.

Jocasta and Walden encouraged those of us studying growing

to choose a small section of the Academy gardens to claim as our own. A couple of the third years had started on their second year of grower studies, and they had returned to their patches from the previous year. Already impossible blooms filled their sections to bursting, and I started to be able to recognize which parts of the gardens were tended by commonborn gardeners and which were the play areas of mages.

The afternoons spent in the gardens putting our studies into practice soon became my favorite part of the week. Growing required a certain level of manual effort, alongside the compositions, and I found I enjoyed having my hands in the dirt, working to produce something alive and beautiful. It reminded me of the days I used to spend alone in the woods, searching for rare herbs my parents could sell in their store.

After a month, Saffron was seriously considering joining the growers after her two years with the Armed Forces. I could understand the appeal, but I knew that healing would draw me back. Still, I would learn as much as I could in this year, and maybe one day I would have a house with a large garden.

Thoughts like that always caught me off guard, beating at my heart with frightening force. A small house with a large garden was a future without Lucas, and I wasn't ready to resign myself to a life without love. Even if defeat pulled at me in quiet moments, reminding me that each week brought us closer to an alliance with the Sekali Empire but no closer to a different sort of end to the war.

When Lucas and I could find odd moments to snatch a few words, we threw ideas at each other faster than we could absorb them. But none of them stood up to debate. And the seeds that had begun to sprout inside me over the summer—of the utter foolish conceit of the task we had set ourselves—only continued to grow. Who were we to think we could end a war the whole kingdom had been trying unsuccessfully to win for over thirty years?

Our most common place to steal a moment was in combat class which had been gripped by a new level of chaos. When the second and third years fought in the arena, we continued our regular arms training, but as the most senior trainees, we had been assigned three sessions in the arena a week.

We spent one session doing command exercises with the illusory soldiers from third year. But for the remaining two, Thornton had returned us to fighting each other. When I challenged him as to why he never called my name for a bout, he actually apologized, a response which almost floored me.

"It is wrong that you never have the chance to train," he said. "And I am considering…"

I raised an eyebrow, but he didn't continue the sentence.

"It's not fair to the other trainees to pit them against you. You too far outmatch them. But I would like you to begin observing the bouts with me in a junior instructor role. It will allow you to achieve maximum learning from observing their fights."

I had to be content with that and, to my surprise, I enjoyed the process. Analyzing each performance and working out advice for improvement based on individual strengths turned out to be absorbing. Occasionally I got so carried away, I even gave excellent advice to Natalya and Lavinia. And once Weston surprised us both by thanking me for a particularly ingenious suggestion. But the culmination of the role came when Thornton took me aside after class one day.

When he finally released me, I was grinning as I ran to catch up with my friends. Finnian regarded me suspiciously.

"What's going on? You look terrifyingly gleeful."

"Not now," I told him, glancing at Natalya who watched us with narrowed eyes. "I'll tell you all later. But this is going to be fun."

The next morning we all settled into our usual places in the arena. But before Thornton could issue instructions as to the day's bouts, Coralie's fist punched the air.

The night before, when they were strategizing in my room, she had insisted that she be the one to give the signal. Parchments flashed out all around me before her hand had even fallen back to her side, and the sound of tearing filled the arena.

I scrambled from my place and dashed higher up the tiered seating to give myself a better view as my friends attacked the rest of our year mates. Thornton had been very clear that my role was adjudication only.

With the advantage of surprise, the whole thing might have been over within seconds if it wasn't for the almost superhuman speed of Dariela. She must have been watching us because she had a shielding composition out just in time. Weston's came several beats behind, shoring hers up, as they scrambled into a huddle with Calix, Natalya, and Lavinia.

My friends had prepared for such an eventuality, however, and Lucas ripped a composition that made the arena seating shake, sending them all sprawling in different directions.

After that, battle was properly joined, and the ten of them scrambled up and down the seats, weaving around and through each other as they hurled combat compositions in every direction. I watched from the highest row of seats, safe behind a shield of my own working, and Thornton watched from the arena floor.

His and my role was to remove those deemed to have been incapacitated or killed by the battle. He rescued Lavinia, dousing the flames that engulfed her before her hair could go up, and shortly after Araminta joined them on the dirt floor so that Acacia could heal her injured arms.

Lucas battled Calix, wielding the extra advantage of higher ground, but his confidence made him sloppy. Dariela swooped in from behind and caught him with a binding composition.

I worked a releasing composition and then called for him to join me out of the battle.

"Sorry," I said when he clambered over the two rows between us. "I'm not allowed to intervene."

Hc shook his head. "No, it was my error. I should have known better."

He glanced at me sideways, and I suddenly realized we stood above everyone else, a small distance from the current hub of the battle. He had been defeated at the perfect moment and location to afford us an unusual moment alone. I narrowed my eyes at him, but he had returned to watching the action, not a trace of guilt on his face.

He moved slightly, following the action with his body, and brushed up against me. Hidden from those below us, his hand found mine and gripped it tightly.

Warmth rushed through me, and I had to force myself to keep my eyes on the fight.

"Thornton did well to give you this role," he whispered. "You're a good instructor."

"Not as good as you," I whispered back.

"I miss those days when we trained together."

"Me too." I sighed. "I miss you."

His hand tightened around mine. We had managed to exchange a few whispered lines the evening before when he had met with our friends in my suite for a strategy session. But the suggestions had been our most ludicrous yet.

"We can't do anything from here," I said. "And we don't even have any workable ideas if we found ourselves at the front."

"Perhaps your new ability could provide some solutions," Lucas murmured. "If only we could get away so you could try practicing it on me."

"Absolutely not!" I struggled to keep my voice low.

"We have to try something," he said.

I took a deep breath. "I think it's time we considered—"

"No," he said sharply just as Dariela came sprinting past us.

Two compositions from both Finnian and Coralie caught her square in the back, and I had to intervene before she bounced head over heels all the way to the arena floor. I declared her incapacitated, and she climbed up toward Lucas and me.

"You are not going to Cassius. He cannot be trusted. I don't care what else we have to do," Lucas managed to whisper before Dariela arrived, forcing him to fall silent.

His eyes continued to glare at me, however, until I relented and slowly nodded. He relaxed, looking back toward the last of the attack as Dariela looked between us with knit brows.

Both Calix and Weston stood with Thornton—I had missed whatever happened to them, distracted by Lucas. With Dariela also now removed from the bout, Finnian, Coralie, and Saffron easily overwhelmed Natalya. She shouted her surrender, and Thornton declared my friend's team victorious.

The three of us at the top of the stands hurried down to join the rest of the group as Finnian and Coralie embraced, and Araminta and Saffron slapped hands.

"Woo! We did it!" Coralie called to me as I joined them.

"With the element of surprise," Weston muttered. "See how you do when the tables are turned."

I suspected Thornton wouldn't do anything as predictable as an exact rematch—but then perhaps he would consider that the more unexpected move.

He had us all sit down and go over the bout in detail, discussing ways everyone's performances could have been improved. We finished in time for an individual bout, and I saw Thornton's eyes skim the class, pausing on Natalya before settling on Coralie.

"We have time for another bout," he said. "Between two of the survivors, perhaps. Natalya and—"

"Finnian," I said, jumping in.

Thornton frowned at me, and I tried to look confident and knowledgeable. After a moment, he nodded reluctantly.

"Yes," he said, "Natalya and Finnian. No doubt you have

already used the more effective compositions you carry with you. Consider this an…"

I tuned out the rest of his words, my eyes lingering on Coralie. Her core of energy had been worryingly low ever since we met up at breakfast, and the exertion of the recent mock battle had left her looking wan and tired. She might not have needed to compose on the spot, but she had spent the time clambering up and down over the backs of seats and physically tousling with our year mates.

"Thank you." She leaned in to whisper the words to me.

"What have you done to yourself?" I asked.

She screwed up her nose as she watched Finnian stride out to the center of the arena floor. "I might have stayed up half the night composing for the battle."

"Coralie!"

"Shush!" she whispered, her eyes on Thornton. "I'll make sure I'm better prepared next time."

"You'd better! Or just let yourself get hit early on. That's better than draining yourself dangerously."

"Yes, Mother." She rolled her eyes at me, and I shoved her in the side.

"I'm serious."

Her face softened. "I guess I didn't realize how drained I felt. Not until I saw your expression at breakfast when you got a good look at me." She dropped her voice even lower. "Do I feel strange?"

I shook my head. "Not strange. Not like that Sekali or anything. Just really weak."

Thornton called for the bout to begin, and we dropped the conversation, focusing on Finnian. We shouldn't have been talking about it around the rest of the year, anyway.

After class, as my friends congratulated themselves on their victory once again, Thornton pulled me aside.

"I don't like to be overridden."

I tried to think of an excuse for why I had shielded my friend, but he saved me the necessity by continuing.

"But on further observation, I can see that Coralie is not fit for a further bout. That was perceptive of you." He hesitated. "If you decide you have an interest in teaching, I feel sure Lorcan would find you a place at the Academy after your term in the Armed Forces is completed."

I stared at him. I had never seriously considered any discipline other than healing, but now I seemed to have options everywhere. But did I like teaching well enough to do it forever? However appealing I found the idea of returning to the only place where I still felt at home, I knew instinctively that my place wasn't in this insulated world, serving only the mageborn.

But I thanked him anyway. It was the best affirmation he ever given me. We had come a long way from first year when I disliked him nearly as much as I did Redmond, and he sat back and watched the other trainees abuse me. For so many mages, it had taken my becoming a Devoras for them to offer me any respect. But although Thornton was a member of Devoras himself, I knew it wasn't our new kinship that had swayed him.

In the end, it had been his passion for his job—for teaching the next generation and equipping us against the war to come— that had changed his attitude. His desire to do his task well, and to preserve life, had overcome any distaste for me as an individual. And I had now had ample opportunity to see the wisdom he possessed in his own sphere. We had each, in our own way, come to respect the other.

My friends' jubilation lasted all day, culminating at the evening meal when Finnian called Lucas over to our table before producing a large cake with the word *Victors* scribed across the top in icing.

"I did that myself," he announced proudly.

"You baked a cake? Yourself?" asked Saffron.

"Well, no, not the cake. Just the word."

Coralie laughed. "That doesn't count."

"Yes, it does," he protested. "It counts for something. It was quite tricky working out how to channel the power that one word of icing released."

"You sound ridiculous," I said. "You know that right? But honestly, I don't care who made it. The important thing is whether I get to eat some of it with you."

"Of course you do!" Coralie assured me. "You were the one to bring us the instructions, remember. And we strategized in your suite. That makes you one of us."

"You probably shouldn't have done that," said Lucas, his eyes laughing at me, although his face remained serious. "It wasn't exactly a neutral position for an adjudicator."

"Funny," I whispered to him as Saffron reached toward the cake with a knife. "I didn't hear you protesting my involvement yesterday evening."

"We all have our weaknesses." His eyes lingered on me.

I flushed and focused on Saffron who had hesitated, the tip of the knife hovering over the cake.

"What exactly did you do with that power?" she asked Finnian, a laugh in her voice. "Is the cake a giant composition? For victory? If I cut it will we win the war?"

Coralie laughed and told her to hurry up and cut us some slices, but I had to fight not to lock eyes with Lucas again at the mention of ending the war.

I found it hard to resist him when we stood so close—the reason I had agreed not to bring up Cassius after the bout. But we needed a chance to talk properly. Because with each week that passed, I became more and more certain that our only hope of ending the war lay with Prince Cassius and his band of dissenters.

Assuming, of course, they actually existed.

CHAPTER 5

*M*any nights I lay in bed, going over and over my conversation with Cassius in my mind. The fervent light in his eyes had made me believe he would depose his own father for the good of his kingdom. And surely his people must be as sick of this war as ours were.

He had said I could help him end the war. If I could somehow sneak into Kallorway, if I could get to him before his father's people found me...

And yet...I could still see that rock in his hand flashing toward me. How many Ardannians had he killed to get to me? Had he intended to kill me, too? The question all too often kept me awake into the night.

I had hoped that if I could expose the traitors, I could end the war without ever leaving Ardann, but no new clue had emerged. And after more than two years, I had to admit that proving the Stantorn treachery was beyond my capacity unless something new occurred to provide fresh evidence.

I knew the alternative Lucas preferred. He had quietly arranged for intelligencers to look for evidence that Cassius might be ready to betray his father. So far, they had found noth-

53

ing. But could that just mean the Kallorwegian prince was as effective at subterfuge as we needed him to be for any coup to work?

I knew Lucas wanted me to explore my new ability instead of thinking of Cassius. He had offered himself as my test subject, but how could I agree to such a thing? Even if it were practically possible.

I kept reliving the feel of Saffron's energy rushing into me, buoying me up as it drained her dry. The sight of her gray face haunted me. Surely such a thing was wrong.

But if it could save lives? If I could be more careful, not take too much energy? Surely I owed it the soldiers sacrificing their lives—both willingly and unwillingly—to try?

I needed someone to talk to about it. Someone with more wisdom and knowledge than me or my friends could possess.

General Griffith might be legally my father now, but I never even considered confiding in him. And I didn't trust Lorcan with the knowledge either. His desire to understand and find a way to use my unique power had always been too great. Which only left one option.

A week later, I had made up my mind. I suspected Lucas would disapprove of my telling anyone at all, but we rarely had the opportunity to speak in private, so I couldn't wait for his advice.

Winter had gripped the kingdom, and with it a spate of illness at the Academy. Saffron asked me to hand in her grower essay on the advantages and disadvantages of increasing the natural growth speed of plants at our next growing lesson. Acacia had ordered her to spend the day in bed resting after receiving a healing for her early flu symptoms. I hoped Saffron's absence would give me an opportunity to speak to Walden alone.

But when I arrived at the front library desk, Jocasta was the one collecting assignments. I handed Saffron's over reluctantly, trying to spot Walden among the shelves.

For a moment Jocasta didn't reach to take the parchment I offered, staring at it and then me in shock. In my distraction, it took a moment to understand her concern.

"Oh, this is Saffron's essay," I said. "I'll be ready to give my spoken presentation this evening as usual."

Jocasta relaxed and finally took the paper, adding it to the stack of parchments in front of her.

"I'm glad to see you expanding your horizons," she said. "Growing is a practical skill. My mother used to be a grower, and she still maintains a huge garden around our home down south."

She looked back at me. "We don't live in a big city, and there are always locals happy to work for my family in exchange for a year round supply of food from her gardens." Nothing in her face or voice suggested she was in the least ashamed of this indication that her family was less wealthy than most mage families, needing to barter goods to afford servants.

"There are plenty of people in Kingslee who would take that opportunity if we had any mage families in residence," I said.

"Aye, and there are many more who would starve if the growers didn't keep the kingdom's crops healthy and plentiful."

I shifted my weight to the other foot. "It's a noble profession."

"There are many injustices in the world," she said. "But we all play our part."

"Indeed," I said, giving her a tight smile.

She smiled at me wryly in return, seeming to find my discomfiture amusing. She had always found me wanting, but I had to give her credit that she had never seemed to envy the richer, more powerful mages who surrounded her at the Academy.

"Walden and the rest of the grower studies class are in the gardens today," she added, almost as an afterthought.

I nodded my thanks and hurried out of the library and around the back of the building. Hopefully I would have a chance to have a quiet word with Walden, after all.

The small group of trainees huddled around something in one of the furthest garden plots. Walden looked up as I approached.

"Ah, Elena, there you are." He looked past me. "No Saffron today?"

I shook my head. "Acacia's ordered her to rest."

"Too bad," he said. "She'll miss the flowering."

He gestured for me to join the small circle. They were gathered around a couple of small plants, each with heart-shaped, deep green leaves and three tall stems. Round knobs of tightly furled petals topped each stem. I recognized the plant from a drawing in one of the books Jocasta had recommended the week before.

"Oh!" I said. "I didn't realize we had any snow blossoms at the Academy."

Walden winked at me. "We didn't. These are my own recent additions. As you all should know, snow blossoms only bloom in the winter, and each flower only lasts for a single day. I have encouraged these particular blooms to flower on time for our class. So, any moment now…"

I leaned forward with the other trainees, watching for any change in the petals.

"There!" one of the second years cried. "That one is moving."

Sure enough, the petals on the three flowers of the left-hand plant had begun to loosen. We all watched with bated breath as they unfurled. Layer after layer of fragile white was revealed, their bases stained with a splash of startling red.

The flower hadn't fully opened before the other plant also began to unfurl. We all watched it transfixed. I felt eyes on me and looked up into Walden's smile.

"Spectacular, isn't it? A rare and startling bloom for a number of reasons. Which is why I chose it for our demonstration today." His eyes ran over the group. "Can anyone pick any difference between the plants? Any difference in the flowers?"

I looked back down at them but could discern no difference

of any kind. The two looked remarkably identical. The other trainees all slowly shook their heads.

Walden chuckled. "No need for such hesitance. I designed them to be identical, so I would hope you couldn't. But we will return shortly for further observation."

He gestured for us to follow him as he led us on a short tour of that section of the garden, pointing out various plants and discussing the work that had gone into them by the Academy gardeners and previous students. As the lesson neared a close, he led us back toward the snow blossoms.

"So," he said as we circled the two plants, "can you tell a difference between them now?"

No one responded since it was clearly a rhetorical question. The plant on the left had already visibly wilted. Two of the blooms had fallen off to lie on the cold, hard ground, and the stems looked brown and dead.

"I thought snow blossoms were perennials?" I asked. "It shouldn't have died after the first blossoming, should it?"

"Pull it up for me," Walden said in reply.

I knelt and grasped the base of the plant, pulling firmly. My hand shot into the air as the greenery and remaining dead flower pulled effortlessly free. I rocked back onto my heels and looked at the plant in my hand.

"It doesn't have any roots," said one of the younger trainees.

He was mostly right. A couple of thin tendrils trailed below the main part of the plant, the only thing that had been anchoring it to the soil.

Walden nodded. "I planted the seeds for that plant only last night. Its rapid growth is due entirely to my power. If the snow blossom had grown naturally, it would certainly have lasted to bloom again many times. I believe most of you have studied healing before. You are hopefully beginning to under-stand that in some ways plants are not so very different from the human body. Unless we wish to sustain it indefinitely with

57

our power, a plant must have time and fuel to grow properly. We can stimulate its growth, and protect it from pests and weather, but if we push it to grow too fast, it will not result in a strong and robust plant. Crops grown this way are deficient in nutrients, and the plants will quickly wither and die, as you have seen."

"A mage might grow such a flower to decorate a ballroom," an older trainee pointed out.

"Indeed, such displays have their uses," Walden said, "and I hope the essays you have all just submitted will have explored those in full. But there is nothing like a practical demonstration to bring home the disadvantages."

He knelt beside the second plant and pulled it firmly from the ground. It resisted its removal, clinging to the soil until a final tug released it. He held it up for the trainees to see.

"Grown in three weeks, this plant has a much healthier root system. My power pushed it to grow faster than is natural, so it was weaker than a natural bloom, more susceptible to weather and blight. But, if it managed to survive, over time, it could have become as strong as a regular flower. A grower must judge that fine line between enough power to help a plant, but not so much as to fatally injure it. And that balance will change from plant to plant and in different situations. The more you learn about each type of growth and its natural characteristics, the easier it will become to correctly judge each situation."

Several of the trainees leaned forward to better examine the second plant, but I hung back. Walden dismissed us, and the others moved away, talking quietly as they made their way back toward the dining hall.

"It seems like a waste," I said to Walden as he gathered the two plants for the compost heap.

He gave me a questioning look.

"It would have continued to grow and bloom." I gestured at the plant that still held three beautiful flowers.

Walden looked down at it and then back at me. "It has served its purpose well enough."

"Yes, I suppose so." I sighed.

When I continued to linger, he raised an eyebrow at me.

"Is there something on your mind?"

I glanced around, but the others had moved out of earshot and no one stood near us.

"Yes. I want to talk to you about something. I'm hoping you can help me answer a question."

"Oh?"

I didn't say anything, and he caught on quickly.

"Perhaps somewhere more private?" He glanced up at the Academy building. "It is nearly time for the evening meal. I generally take it in my office. Perhaps you would like to join me there once you have eaten yourself?"

I nodded, and we walked together back toward the Academy entrance. In the entrance, he waved me off in the direction of the dining hall.

"Now you've raised my curiosity," he told me with a chuckle, "don't go forgetting to appear."

I assured him that I would be there as soon as possible and hurried toward the food.

"You can strip others of energy? As much as you like? From anyone?" Walden stared at me. "Has the power no limits?"

I shifted in my seats. "I…I don't really know, to be honest."

His voice dropped. "Could you…drain someone completely?"

"I think—" I paused, not wanting to say it out loud. "I think so. Obviously I haven't tried it," I hurried to add.

"No, no indeed. Of course not." He sat back in his chair, his fingers steepled, and his eyes glazed over as he stared at a spot on the wall beside me.

I shifted uncomfortably in my chair but waited for him to speak. Walden had been the one to help me as I learned to access my power in first year. He had seen more of my unique ability than most, but I had never seen him shocked like this.

Slowly his face transformed, a fervent light filling his eyes. He dropped his hands and leaned forward.

"Elena! My dear girl! This is remarkable. Beyond remarkable! Unlimited energy. This is what mages have been searching for since the beginning of power itself."

"But is it right to use it?" I asked. "When it comes from other people?"

"Ah." He leaned back again, his excitement shuttered. "A worthy question indeed. One that requires consideration."

"Yes." Now I was the one leaning forward. "Lucas and Araminta both told me to take it from them, but Saffron did not. I took it without her agreement or even knowledge. Though she must have felt it. And she, at least, would have known what was happening. I took it from her on instinct, to save myself, and that scares me. What if I had taken too much?"

"Hmmm…" Walden surveyed me with a wrinkled brow. "But you did not, did you? And if I understood your earlier description correctly, you did it not just to save yourself, but to save both of you. It was merely using your combined resources where they would be most effective."

"Do you really think so? I've been afraid that I'm only telling myself that to excuse it away."

"Motivations are always important," he said. "And yours seem to have been pure in this instance."

He saw my look of uncertainty and continued. "Of course, motivation is not everything. Execution is important as well. And to my mind that is the reason why you must practice with this new gift. You must learn to understand and properly utilize it. If you reach for it only by instinct, when in desperation, you are far more likely to end up making a misstep. Whereas, if you set limits for yourself, rules, so to speak, then you will know when and how to restrain yourself."

I thought about his words. "You mean I'll know how much I can take without harming the other person?"

"Exactly." He beamed at me. "And the more you practice, the more you will be able to limit yourself without thought."

"That makes sense," I said slowly. The pressure across my chest eased. "And if I had known what I was doing, instead of draining too much from Saffron, I could have skimmed only the smallest amount of energy from everyone present, so that no one person bore the full burden."

Walden's eyes widened, a strange look on his face. "You could do such a thing?"

"I think so?" I shrugged. "But that's what you're saying, isn't it? I need to train, to understand my limits." I gave a wry smile. "Really, I should have taken the energy from our attackers. I could have achieved two purposes at once. But in my panic, I latched onto the familiar energy of my friend."

"Familiar energy?" Walden asked.

"I might have forgotten to mention that bit," I said. "I can sense everyone now. Sense their energy. And I spend so much time with my friends that they've started to feel familiar." I grimaced. "It's hard to explain."

"Utterly fascinating." Walden shook his head slowly. "The wonders of your power only increase. But that should be of great assistance to you. You will be able to sense whether you are drawing too much energy."

"I think so." I frowned. "Although if I intend to take only a little energy, it might be difficult to sense. It's not the most granular thing."

Walden rubbed his hands together. "But that's the purpose of experimentation! What fun would it be if you already had all the answers?" His eyes twinkled at me, and I reluctantly smiled back.

I could understand his enthusiasm. He had always loved the

pursuit of knowledge. But he didn't understand the sickening feeling of knowing you had drained a friend's life force to protect yourself. I couldn't deny the truth of what he said, though. If I had this power—and I could not remove it now—I would be safer if I understood it. I'd already demonstrated that I was in danger of using it regardless of any good intentions.

"I am happy to be of any assistance I can be," Walden said. "But it occurs to me that perhaps a healer would be a more effective assistant in this matter. It is they who most closely study the human system and the limits of energy. Perhaps Acacia is the best mage for the occasion." He hesitated slightly. "If you don't mind sharing this information with her, that is."

I smiled in gratitude at his instinctual understanding that I wished to keep this ability a secret.

"I'll consider it…" I met his eyes. "I want to keep knowledge of this as limited as possible."

"Of course, I understand. This is—" He shook his head. "It's revolutionary! But I believe you can trust Acacia. She is a first cousin of mine and a good healer, even if she's not as strong as she might wish."

I nodded. "I agree. But I need to think about it."

I stood, planning to leave, but Walden gestured for me to wait.

"Do you think you could demonstrate it for me? On me, of course."

I wanted to refuse, but the weight of his fascination shone through his eyes, clearly outweighing the hesitation that sounded in his voice. Walden had helped me when no one else would, and now he was volunteering himself as my first test subject. My body hummed with nerves, but I didn't like to refuse him.

"I suppose I could try. Just the smallest bit." I considered. "I've never actually tried doing it with binding words and proper limitations. I can…" My voice trailed off as I considered the words I wanted to use.

Once I was ready, I called up the words I needed into my

mind's eye. I spoke the binding words before outlining every possible limitation I could think of to minimize the power I would draw from him.

I paused for half a breath. "End binding."

Walden had also stood, coming around his desk to stand in front of me, although the extra proximity wasn't necessary. He waited with anticipation clear on his face, but the expression slowly faded. His brows knit.

"I didn't feel anything. Did it work? Maybe you took too little?"

I shook my head and grimaced. "No, nothing happened. You should have felt my power connecting us as well as the energy draining out." I bit my lip. "I don't think it works with the binding words. I suspected that might be the case, and I guess this just confirms it. I think the connection between us has to be absolutely direct. It only worked in the past because I was able to do two-word compositions without bindings."

Walden frowned. "How fascinating. It raises all sorts of questions about our understanding of binding power into compositions. I would have thought—" He cut himself off with a shake of his head. "But that is not relevant to the immediate question. Can you try it without bindings?"

I pressed my lips together and then reluctantly nodded. Closing my eyes, I pictured the words I needed, taking my time to form them clearly and overlaying as much meaning as I could within the simple phrase.

When I opened them, I took a deep breath and said, "Take energy."

This time Walden flinched as my power rushed out to latch onto him. I had tried to encapsulate the sense of a limited drain into the wording, but as soon as I felt the first tendrils of his energy flowing into me, I tensed and slammed down on my power, cutting it off with a gasped, "Stop!"

"Amazing," Walden whispered, shaking himself out slowly. "I

could feel it that time." He paused and frowned. "Not that I feel any more tired than I did before. You can't have taken much."

"Of course not," I said. "I don't want to exhaust you."

A distant look filled his face. "I wonder…Would I have felt it if I hadn't been warned? I felt your power, certainly, but I might have missed that if we were in a crowded place filled with workings."

"I could feel your energy draining into me along the flow of my power," I said. "Surely that's a sensation you couldn't miss?"

He wandered back around to his seat. "I felt no such sensation. But then I have never felt someone's energy as you say you do now." He paused and looked up quickly. "Not that I mean to suggest any disbelief. I don't doubt you."

I frowned. "I suppose that makes sense. I could never sense energy before either. And I didn't used to feel myself using my own energy except that I would feel tired afterward. So I suppose it would only be the connection of my power someone else would feel."

"We must try it again," Walden said with enthusiasm. "But take more this time. Enough to make a difference."

I frowned. "I don't want to—"

Walden cut me off with a chuckle. "Not too much, of course. I'd rather not spend the next couple of days prone. But it is late in the day, and I will be heading for my bed soon. I can afford to feel some measure of fatigue."

"I suppose…" I said reluctantly.

I carefully recreated the working, taking even more time to ensure I did it correctly. The jolt of my power connecting with his core nearly made me reflectively cut it off, but I steeled myself and continued.

I watched him, looking for any graying of his face, or sagging of his shoulders, but it was the sense of his energy that I monitored more closely. As soon as it began to noticeably shrink, I cut off the drain.

He slumped back against his seat, his eyes wide.

"I can feel it now," he said. "Not that I felt the energy leaving me exactly. But I feel noticeably more tired than I did before." His wide eyes latched onto me, and he shook his head.

I flushed. I didn't like the way he looked at me, as if I had changed everything. As if more was now riding on me than I was willing to carry.

"No more experiments tonight," I said quickly. "You're tired enough. But I'll think about what you said about Acacia."

He nodded, standing and coming around to place a warm hand on my shoulder.

"Thank you, Elena, for placing your trust in me."

I smiled and bid him farewell again before hurrying out of the room.

CHAPTER 6

*A*guilty elation still filled me the next morning. I had done it. I had harnessed the power and used it without causing any great harm. It had been hard to sleep with the extra energy coursing through me, and I had ended by composing a number of workings just to tire myself.

Part of me wished I didn't feel such fascination with my new ability, but the rest of me itched to try it again. And sharing the development with Walden had lifted an unseen weight.

My mood dropped again, though, when Dariela brushed past me without acknowledgment, taking a seat alone at one of the middle tables as she had taken to doing. My other friends had noticed her change of attitude, of course, but none of them could account for it. And the one time I had asked Dariela about it directly, she had responded with such indifferent confusion that I had hastily retreated from the conversation.

I tried to turn my mind from the unexpected fickleness of Dariela to the question that had occupied me since I woke up. Should I tell Acacia about my new ability?

All day I looked for an opportunity to have even a moment of private speech with Lucas, but nothing arose. In combat I was called on to adjudicate a number of individual bouts at Thornton's side, and in composition a small group of University mages shadowed me all lesson. In the library, Jocasta gave a lecture on wind working, and Araminta stayed glued to my side as she always did in sessions that focused on our shared wind working studies. I would have to make the decision without the benefit of Lucas's advice.

An uneasy feeling gripped me whenever I thought I had decided on telling her. Not that I had any great mistrust of Acacia as an individual, but a gnawing feeling that too many people already knew ate away at me. But I liked Acacia, and she had shown a genuine desire to help people—regardless of who they might be. If there was a chance she could help me now…

I sent Araminta to the dining hall ahead of me and lingered outside Acacia's office. With everyone else at dinner, this was my perfect opportunity. Her door stood partially ajar, and it swung open silently when I pushed on it.

The healer stood at the far end of her rooms, one of my year mates beside her. I froze. Acacia said something to Dariela too quietly for me to hear before she noticed me standing in the doorway. She smiled but a beat too late, and I could have sworn she stiffened before doing so.

"Elena, welcome," she said, and Dariela swung around to look at me.

"Sorry," I said quickly. "I didn't realize there was anyone else here. I'll come back later." I stepped back out of the room.

"I'm leaving anyway," Dariela said.

"No, no, it's nothing urgent." I took another step back.

"It's fine, come in," said Acacia, her smile still in place.

I shook my head. "I didn't realize you had someone with you. It will wait."

I walked away down the corridor, my heart pounding far more than was necessary. I had been an object of too much interest for too long not to recognize the expressions of people caught talking about me. And although I kept telling myself such thoughts only demonstrated an utter arrogance and self-absorption on my part, I couldn't shake them.

My hands shook slightly. Part of me wished I had stayed and demanded answers from Dariela in front of Acacia so she couldn't try to weasel out of an explanation. But the rest of me knew that leaving had been the right choice. If I had stayed, I would have needed to explain my presence, and now that I had seen Dariela consulting with Acacia, I couldn't imagine doing so myself.

Footsteps sounded behind me, and a quick glance over my shoulder told me Dariela's tall legs were closing the gap between us as we both hurried toward the dining hall. I lengthened my stride.

Dariela's energy felt low, and I tried to remember what compositions she had completed in class to so deplete her. Before I could recall, two new spots of energy distracted me. These ones burned at full strength, but they seemed to be positioned against the wall of the corridor between Dariela and me.

But I hadn't passed anyone since leaving Acacia's rooms.

My steps faltered, and I spun, looking behind me with confusion. Dariela's steps slowed as she looked at me warily. As if in response to our movements, a yell sounded in the enclosed space, and two people erupted from the seemingly clear wall.

"Shield!" I shouted without thought, power rushing to form a barrier around me. But nothing—either magical or physical— came to assault me.

Dariela, on the other hand, was knocked backward to the ground as one of her hands disappeared into a hidden pocket within her robe. In the time it took my confused mind to see what was happening, she had retrieved a small curl of parchment and ripped it in half.

Power surged around her just as the two men attacked again. They collided with the invisible wall around her and staggered back. One withdrew a sealed piece of parchment from his pocket, the ends marked in a light red.

I frowned at the color as he ripped it, sending a shaft of pure power at Dariela's shield. The force hit with enough strength to collapse it.

Commonborns equipped with color-coded compositions attacking a trainee within the Academy? My brain couldn't compute what was happening. I had been abducted here once, but Lorcan had assured me security had improved since then. And why would anyone want to attack Dariela anyway?

I shook the thoughts aside as the two men rushed forward, forcing Dariela to abandon her attempts to retrieve a second composition and fend them off by hand. I could work out what was going on later. For now, she needed my help.

I opened my mouth to speak a composition only for a hand to grip my upper arm and pull me back a couple of steps. I staggered, trying to keep my balance, and the hand let go before I could begin a defensive maneuver.

Spinning around, I confronted my combat instructor. My arms, which had been raised ready to block an attack, dropped to my sides. As soon as I saw him, standing there calmly, realization flooded my mind.

"Do not get involved. This is not your test," Thornton said calmly.

I glanced over my shoulder at Dariela who was too busy keeping the two men at bay to notice the new arrival.

"A test? Here? Really?" Inside I was kicking myself. After my own experience, I should have realized, even if we weren't inside the arena.

"I told you all to expect the unexpected. Weston has already fought off a similar attack." He frowned. "And Lavinia has been overpowered. Each was then requested to keep the attack quiet, so that others may be similarly surprised. My only error in this case, is you. I didn't expect you to be here."

He gave me a level look. "I cannot have you interfering in these tests. And not only for the purity of the exercise. I chose to test you in the safety of the arena due to your excessive strength. The others, however, do not need the same safety measures, and Lorcan would not be pleased to discover I goaded you into combat exercises outside the protection of the arena shield."

A thud sounded, and one of Dariela's attackers collapsed to the ground, disabled by a blow to the chest. Dariela took the opportunity to fall back a short way. Her hand flashed into her robe as she did so, producing a parchment. The power that rushed out when she ripped it enclosed the two attackers, holding them motionless.

She stood in place for two panting breaths before straightening and glancing quickly around. Her eyes fell on Thornton and me, and she froze, enlightenment racing across her features.

"Just a test?" she gasped out.

Thornton nodded, and she flicked her fingers toward the two men. The one still standing sank down onto the ground, breathing hard, at the release of her power.

For a moment we all stood looking at each other.

"I was going to intervene," I said to Dariela. "If Thornton hadn't stopped me."

"Indeed," said Thornton. "And I trust you will not attempt to do so if you find yourself near one of my tests again."

Dariela looked torn, and I couldn't decide if she was about to thank me or berate me for assuming she needed help. In the end she did neither.

"But how will I know for sure it's a test?" I asked Thornton.

Thornton gave me a flat look. "If commonborn louts attempt to attack a trainee within the Academy, you may rest assured it's a test."

"Who you calling a lout?" muttered one of the men so quietly I only just heard it.

I flashed him a grin, and he grinned back at me, despite the bruise already forming across one eye.

"You may go," Thornton said to me. "Dariela, a word regarding the exercise."

I hesitated a moment. Dariela's energy, already low before the attack, was teetering on the edge of exhaustion now. Should I say something?

But Thornton waved his hands at me impatiently, and I remembered Dariela had just been with Acacia. Clearly she would seek help if needed. The two might even be related since they came from the same family.

I hurried toward the dining hall, hoping some food would still remain. I slid into my usual seat just as the servers began clearing the communal trays from the tables. Coralie shook her head at me.

"Really, Elena! You don't want to miss out on food."

But even as she said it, she moved a full, untouched plate from in front of her over to me.

"Here. I saved this for you. I've already finished."

"Thanks." I gave her a grateful smile as I began to shovel down the food.

Inside a battle raged. Should I tell them about their upcoming tests? Clearly Thornton wanted them kept a surprise, and perhaps he was right. Perhaps tests like that would help keep them alive in the future. It didn't feel like the work of a friend not to say anything at all, though. I glanced across the table at Saffron.

"You carry defensive compositions at all times now, right?" I asked her.

She eyed me warily. "Of course."

Finnian grinned at me. "Tossing up the idea of attacking her, are you, Elena?"

I rolled my eyes at him. "I'm just saying it pays to be prepared." I gave each of them a serious look. "At all times."

Finnian raised both eyebrows. "Do you know something we don't know?"

"I'm just saying, be prepared."

I expected him to make another joke, but his face remained serious this time, his eyes sliding across to Coralie beside me.

"I, for one, always am," he said.

"Good," I said before steering the conversation in other directions.

Winter deepened, and first Araminta and then Finnian found a quiet moment to tell me they now understood my warning. From Araminta's expression, she hadn't passed the test, although she assured me when I asked that she was unhurt. She made it clear she didn't want to discuss it further, and I didn't push the matter. It was hard enough for her being bottom of the class—especially when I used to be down there with her and now surpassed everyone.

Calix surprised me by pulling me aside in the corridor one day and describing the attack he had just successfully defeated.

"Apparently they're going to test us all," he said. "So be ready."

I stared at him, not bothering to correct his misapprehension about my testing. "Why are you telling me? Didn't Thornton ask you to keep it a secret?"

"Oh, have you already been tested?" Calix frowned. "You should have warned Natalya and me."

I continued to stare at him, not quite sure what to say.

"We're family now, Elena," he said in a disapproving tone. "Family looks out for each other. Father would be highly disappointed to hear you left Natalya and me in the dark."

"Honestly?" I said. "It didn't even occur to me to tell you."

He shook his head, so I hurried to add, "I didn't tell my friends, either, if that's any consolation."

He looked at me for a moment and then sighed. "I suppose I should have known you wouldn't understand how these things work. But next time?" He paused. "Remember that family means more than friendship."

He gave me a curt nod and strode off down the corridor, leaving me blinking in surprise. I understood his words. I would always be there for Jasper and Clementine, no matter what. But it was a little hard to imagine applying that instinct to Calix or Natalya. Or Julian, who I barely even knew. If I failed to show enough loyalty, would the Devoras family disown me?

If Lucas was tested, he didn't tell me about it, but I didn't waste any concern on him. I doubted Thornton was game to send surprise attackers after a member of the royal family. And even if he did, Lucas was always prepared. I suspected he had kept a collection of defensive compositions on his person long before he could create them himself. Ardann wouldn't leave a member of its royal family vulnerable.

I did, however, find a moment to whisper to him about my experiments with Walden. He looked intrigued, but also displeased.

"Does it really strike you as a good idea to go around siphoning energy from senior members of one of the great families?" he asked. "Even with their permission? If word of your ability does get out, that's not going to look good."

I stared at him. "You wanted me to practice on you!"

He shook his head. "That's different. I would never tell anyone."

I frowned at him, but he pulled away as several of our year mates moved into earshot, and we had to leave it there. Clearly he was concerned about word spreading. Perhaps it was a good thing, then, that I had been put off telling Acacia.

When I thought about it, I had to concede his point, though. Walden wasn't a good test subject. When I told Walden as much, he suggested I use someone else, but I wasn't about to drain my friends when classes already required so much from them. And I wasn't willing to experiment on anyone else without their knowledge. I had been used as a test subject before without my permission, and I didn't intend to do that to anyone else.

As the days shortened toward the darkest, coldest part of the year, a new distraction took my thoughts away from my efforts to train. A rumor swept through the Academy that the Sekali delegation had expressed interest in the prince's training and had requested a tour.

All of the trainees were curious to see more of our mysterious northern neighbors, and Damon even told me that most of the servants were buzzing with interest in the supposed visit.

"Is it true?" Finnian asked Lucas one day, leaning back in his chair at the beginning of composition and speaking across Coralie and me. "Is the delegation coming to the Academy?"

Lucas nodded. "I believe so. They have requested a tour."

"And what does the royal family want from us?" Finnian asked. "Should we appear as strong as possible? The bright future of Ardann and all that?"

He flexed his muscles and winked at Coralie who snorted.

"If there are any young ladies among their number, I give you permission to charm them," she said. "I promise not to be jealous if you bat your eyelids in their direction."

Lucas coughed, clearly hiding a chuckle, his amused gaze catching on mine for a minute. I grinned back, wishing the light-hearted moment didn't send a stab of pain through me.

If only it could always be like this. Me, my friends, and Lucas. Finnian would be good for him—teach him to take life a little less seriously. Together we would have had an amazing final year at the Academy.

"Unfortunately, the members of the delegation are a little too old for your charms, Finnian," said Lucas.

"You've never seen me charm any grandmothers, then," Finnian assured him seriously.

"I think Lucas is trying to ask you not to create any diplomatic incidents," I told him. "Who knows what the Sekalis find charming?"

"Well, Lucas will have to learn soon enough," said Calix, entering the room late and taking the seat next to the prince that usually sat empty. He raised and lowered his eyebrows suggestively at Lucas, whose face immediately closed off, resuming its usual court mask.

The smile dropped off Finnian's face, and Coralie glanced quickly at me. Thankfully I was spared whatever might have been said next by a significant throat clearing from Redmond. Our instructor glared at Calix until he took his own seat, and then began his lecture.

I didn't hear a word, all my attention focused on keeping my eyes on my desk. They seemed determined to look right, toward Lucas, but I could feel his eyes already boring into the side of my head, and I wasn't sure I could meet his gaze without tearing up.

Thankfully Redmond was teaching on an element of written compositions that didn't apply to me because I barely heard one word in ten. I dreaded the delegation's arrival—their presence made the upcoming marriage alliance all too real. But at the same time, I was consumed with curiosity. Would the mage in the pale green robe still feel muted and strange? Would he look ill? With everything else going on, I still hadn't found a chance to ask for a tour of the city's healing clinics to see if I could find anyone else who felt the same way.

Two mornings later I walked into the dining hall to a widespread air of excitement. I had no sooner slid into my seat than Coralie announced the reason why.

"The delegation is here. A group of second years saw them going into Lorcan's office."

"The entire delegation?" I asked.

"I don't think so," said Finnian. "Apparently there are only seven of them here, and more than that are in residence at the palace."

"Seven is plenty," said Araminta, sounding glum.

I glanced over at her, and she grimaced.

"I just know I'm going to embarrass Ardann."

"Don't be silly," I said. "They're not here to assess us."

"Aren't they?" Saffron asked quietly, and we all fell into an uneasy silence.

I suspected she was right, and they were here to assess one of our number, at least. And despite my selfish desires, for the sake of our kingdom and everyone else I loved, I couldn't wish for Lucas to make a bad impression.

Glancing around the dining hall, I realized he was absent.

"I suppose Lucas is with the delegation?" I whispered to Coralie.

"I think so." She gave me a look of such sympathy that I quickly turned away.

My eyes fell on Saffron who was watching the door as if she expected the Sekalis to join us for breakfast.

"Do you think we'll meet them?" she asked.

"I don't know. Princess Lucienne didn't seem too keen on the idea of my meeting them at the Devoras party," I said. "Even the general didn't try to introduce me, despite my new family status."

"I can imagine the palace is doing their best to pretend you don't exist," Coralie said.

Finnian looked from her to me. "Pretending Elena doesn't exist? No doubt. The Spoken Mage, on the other hand…" He frowned thoughtfully. "Somehow I imagine that's not so easy to do."

A server arrived to clear our table, and I realized with a start that half of the trainees in the hall had already left. We all hurriedly stood and made our way out of the room.

"Everyone seems to be in a rush today," Finnian said dryly. "I can't imagine why that might be. You'd think something interesting was going on."

We exited into the large entrance hall just in time to see the delegation enter it from the other side, Lorcan at their head. He looked up and saw me, and his stride faltered for the briefest moment before he ushered them toward the main doors.

I watched them move ahead of us, my eyes lingering on Lucas who walked next to the oldest Sekali, listening respectfully to something he said. I thought he hadn't seen me until his eyes flashed up at the last moment, meeting mine for the briefest instant with such longing and regret that it took my breath away.

I stumbled down the stairs and out into the grounds, not really listening to my friends' whispers as they discussed the Sekalis. But a cheerful voice hailed me, calling me by name and demanding my attention. I picked Walden out from among the Sekalis, and he gestured for me to come forward and join them.

I quickened my pace with equal measures of anticipation and reluctance. As I came closer, I realized Walden walked beside the Sekali in the pale green robe. His energy still felt muted and strange, although it was almost hard to tell beneath the blaze of power that surrounded him.

Away from the crowded, power-filled atmosphere of the party, it was even more obvious that Finnian had been right. The delegation had come with layer on layer of compositions to protect them instead of commonborn guards. I itched to do some workings and see if I could decipher what protections they had hedged themselves with, but I knew better than to even think of trying such a thing.

I reached them just in time to see Lorcan cast a disapproving look at the oblivious Walden. Clearly I had been correct in thinking that the royal family had given instructions to try to keep me from too much close contact with the visitors. Too bad no one had informed the librarian.

The oldest of the group turned from Lucas with interest at

my arrival, and Walden introduced me. The group halted, and each Sekali bowed from the waist, murmuring, "Spoken Mage. We are honored," as they did so.

I squirmed and went to protest, but a swift look from Lucas stopped me, and I remembered I had seen them greet many of the mages at the party with the same bow. When Lucas flicked his eyes down and back up, I quickly mirrored their movement, murmuring that it was I who was honored to meet them.

My response seemed to meet with their approval, but before they could address me further, Lorcan stepped in.

"Elena, you should hurry to catch up with your year mates or risk being late for class."

He gestured toward my friends who had passed us, watching with interest out of the corners of their eyes.

"And you, too, Lucas," he added.

As we moved away together, I heard him murmuring to the older man who Walden had introduced as Chen. "They must have time to prepare…"

"That sounds ominous," I said to Lucas quietly. "Are we going to be doing some sort of display?"

His court mask remained in place, but he glanced sideways at me.

"My parents wanted to keep them away from the Academy, but they were persistent in their requests to visit, and we don't want to risk offending them. No one's given me any details, but given we had to accommodate the visit, I believe my parents want some sort of display of power. Something to make me look strong and make Ardann look like a desirable ally and partner."

My heart sank. I didn't like the sound of that.

"I don't care what's at stake, Elena," Lucas whispered suddenly. "I won't fight you, if that's what they ask."

I turned fully to stare at him. I hadn't even thought of that.

"Do you think they would?"

His bearing didn't change, the mask still in place, but I could see the tension in his shoulders.

"Not if they have any sense. Because I'll refuse, no matter what's at stake. There's only so much I can take."

I bit my lip. "No. If it comes to that, I'll refuse. Better me than you."

He turned his head quickly before looking back toward the arena.

"I don't want any repercussions falling on you."

"It's better for Ardann this way," I said tightly. "And we're doing all this for Ardann, aren't we?"

Lucas nodded, reluctance clear in every line of his body.

"Very well. If you insist. For Ardann." This time when he looked at me, his gaze lingered for a second longer, its fire burning into me. "But one of these days my sense of duty is going to hit its limit."

I forced myself to stand straight, not to buckle beneath the intensity of his gaze and his words.

"Then for the sake of the kingdom, let us hope it lasts a little longer." My voice dropped. "Because if it fails, I'm not sure I'll have the strength to do what's needed."

CHAPTER 7

"*E*lena and Lucas," Thornton said, calling my name for a bout for the first time since the year began.

My eyes flew to Lucas's back, but he kept his own straight ahead, his fists tightening as he slowly stood. Thornton ignored our obvious reluctance, speaking again before I had the chance to protest.

"If you will please stand to my left. The rest of you, please assemble to my right."

Lucas frowned and then glanced toward me. I hurried down the steps of the tiered seating to join him.

"What's going on?" I whispered before remembering he didn't know what was coming any more than I did.

He ignored my question, his attention focused on Thornton.

"Any moment now our guests will arrive," Thornton said. "They wish to watch our fourth years engage in practice combat." His eyes lingered on Lucas. "We wish to give them a proper display and uphold the honor of our kingdom." He paused while his stern gaze roamed over the nine trainees on his right.

"To that end, we will begin a new style of bouts. I had intended to introduce this new element to our training next week anyway. You will no longer only bout as individuals but will instead engage in a series of group bouts with varying allies and opponents. You have already had a taste of this with the surprise engagement from the other week."

"It feels a little unfair," Coralie muttered, eyeing Lucas and me standing alone.

Despite her quiet volume, Thornton caught the words. He raised a single eyebrow.

"I agree, and I would not have chosen to begin with such an unfairly weighted exercise in the normal course of things. But today is about more than just your training, and other considerations are at play." He glared at them all again. "And so I expect you to conduct yourselves admirably despite your disadvantage."

Finnian tried to hide a snorted laugh. "Well, that's put us in our place," he whispered, earning an extra frown from Thornton.

"Now is not the time for jokes," he said, but cut himself off when Lorcan appeared with the Sekalis in tow.

Welcoming the new arrivals, he indicated for them to take the seats we had previously occupied.

"The training bout you are about to witness will take place between these two groups." He swept his arms out to indicate us all. "Trainees are not permitted to dangerously wound or kill their fellow trainees, but they are otherwise without limits."

I raised both eyebrows and glanced nervously at my friends. No limits? So we could use as many compositions as we liked? Thornton had been serious about this being unlike our usual practice bouts. I hoped the others had come well-stocked because I knew Lucas would have.

He turned to me, his face serious and focused. He hadn't wasted any time worrying about the other team.

"We're seriously outnumbered here which is going to be our main disadvantage," he said quietly.

Out of the corner of my eye I saw the others form a large

huddle, their usual divisions forgotten in the short unity of purpose. I tried to make my mind focus on potential strategy.

"They're going to come at us hard, and from all angles," I said.

He nodded once. "Which is why we need you on defense. I don't have any shields that will last long against a nine-mage onslaught."

My surprise must have shown on my face because he amended his words.

"Well, I have a couple of strong shields on me, of course, but they come from General Thaddeus. I can only use my own compositions in training."

"Oh, of course," I said.

It made sense. Not only would it defeat the purpose of training for him to use the defensive compositions supplied by the Royal Guard, but it might leave him vulnerable in case of a true threat. I didn't like the idea of him depleting his own supplies, though. The idea that he might be left with no defenses other than those supplied by Thaddeus—a Stantorn—made me uncomfortable.

He stepped closer, and my heart rate picked up. I glanced back at the stands of seating and then at the rest of our year mates who were now spreading out—I had plenty of potential causes for the acceleration. I looked up into his eyes and saw the faintest hint of a smile in them and around his mouth.

"This is going to be fun," he breathed.

I shook my head. "You're crazed," I muttered, but I could feel the smile on my own face too.

"We need to stay close," he said, speaking quickly. "Minimize the area you need to shield. If we go back to back, we'll be able to keep eyes in all directions."

I nodded, but he gave me a stern look.

"Don't go rogue on me and try to take them out yourself. We're a team, and it's only a training exercise. So let me know if you see something coming your shield can't handle."

I winced, remembering his reprimand after the gully attack. He was right, I wasn't a great team player. If I thought my friends were in danger, I tended to just act.

Except this time I was the one attacking my friends.

The rest of our year mates had ranged themselves in a line, still on Thornton's right. Their hands all lingered near sleeves or pockets, clearly poised to reach for a composition as soon as Thornton gave the word.

I took a deep breath and spun to put myself back to back with Lucas. My mind raced through all the different ways I could approach the shielding as I readied the word in my mind's eye. I lifted onto the balls of my feet, my body quivering in readiness from the surge of energy and anticipation racing through me.

I wanted to win, but I didn't want to exhaust myself. I'd learned my lesson on maintaining reserves last year, and it wouldn't do Ardann any credit if I had to be carried from the arena when this was over.

Thornton had crossed over to speak to Lorcan, but I could see his eyes on us, both sides now positioned for the bout to begin. I didn't have long.

Layers. I needed layers. It would give me more flexibility. I kept the single word I needed in my mind, while I adjusted the limitations that I placed over it.

Thornton called for us to begin, and my words came out as a whisper, my focus too internal to put energy into volume.

"Shield." Power rushed around us as I changed the sense of limitations in my mind. "Shield." Another wave of power cocooned us, and I pivoted again within my mind. "Shield." I barely got the third word out before power smashed into my shield, rocking me backward. Lucas stood firm behind me and I regained my balance.

I had been too distracted by my desperate attempts to work quickly to take in anyone else's movements. But now I took a moment to survey the arena floor. Our year mates had surrounded us in a loose circle. They stood at a distance, but already I saw a gap in their ranks.

A quick glance at the stands showed Acacia ministering to a still-smoking Natalya.

"One down," I said to Lucas, as I heard him rip another parchment. A strong gust of wind swept through the arena, sending Finnian, Coralie, and Dariela on my left tumbling to the ground.

But he had no time to send a follow up while they were distracted. A bellow from the other side sent both of our heads whipping in that direction to see Calix charging Lucas with his sword held in front of him. Weston followed silently a step behind, Lavinia flanking them. All three angled toward Lucas, ignoring me—perhaps because he was the one who had been lobbing fire and wind at them.

My last shield—the one against all physical attack—would stop them in their tracks. But at what cost to my energy?

"Drop," I whispered, releasing that shield but retaining the others. Lucas was the best fighter in our year, he could hold them off. And my shields against magical attack and life-threatening physical blows remained.

Lucas took two steps away from me, giving himself room to maneuver, and my shield stretched, following him. The clang of steel against steel sounded, and I gripped the hilt of my own sword harder. Everything in me wanted to turn to help him, but if I did so, it would leave our backs unguarded. And their team still had five more mages in play.

Saffron ripped a parchment, and a small patch of grass just outside my shield sprang into flames. I ignored the tiny blaze, keeping my attention on the others. Finnian also had a composition in his hands, and when he ripped it, a gust of wind shot from him straight toward me. When it hit the flames, it fanned them, some of the tongues of fire leaping free of the grass to dance through the rushing air.

I suddenly remembered a half-overheard conversation

between the cousins from the week before about the possibilities of coordinated attacks. Would my shield consider the wind or the small spots of flame dangerous enough to block? I didn't wait to find out.

"Shield fire," I gasped out in time for the flickering spots to crash against an invisible wall. The wind, less dangerous on its own, hit me full force and sent me staggering backward two steps. I nearly collided with Lucas who only just dodged me.

Weston's sword lunged toward Lucas's chest, colliding with my shield which turned it aside, sending it sliding up his arm instead. It tore Lucas's sleeve, leaving welling blood behind. In my distraction I had forgotten the sword fight behind me. Outnumbered, Lucas would have been struck down without my shield.

The energy drain was already starting to wear on me, and it could have been worse if the wind hadn't hit Calix and Lavinia as well as Lucas and me. We needed a new plan.

I had hardly regained my balance when Coralie and Araminta both sent power snaking toward us. Whatever its purpose had been, my shield blocked it, draining yet more of my energy. I needed to act fast.

I spoke quickly, my words tumbling out and almost tangling together as I hurried through the binding words.

"Rock the earth beneath the arena floor, everywhere except under us—"

"What are you doing?" Lucas panted over the top of me, keeping his eyes on his attackers who had all regained their feet. "You're supposed to be on defense."

I ignored him, keeping hold of my power as I pulled up the next lot of words to finish the composition.

"—until a large rock has emerged from the ground over there. End binding." I pointed my finger at a break in the circle around us caused by Weston and Lavinia joining Calix.

The earth began to rumble, and our eight year mates all lost their feet, tumbling down as a large spear of dark gray rock tore the ground open, thrusting up into the sky. Lucas didn't need me to explain what I'd done.

He took off running a step ahead of me, the oasis of calm earth following us as we threw ourselves toward the rock, placing it at our backs. I panted, my head spinning from the expenditure of power. At least I had been able to call real rock from the ground and didn't have to maintain its existence with my power.

Calix regrouped, calling for Finnian and Dariela to join him, but now Lucas and I could face them together. And with the rock at our backs, they couldn't all reach us at once.

Weston struck at Lucas who blocked the blow, his sword flashing to block a second one from Calix a moment later. I grunted as my own blade took the force of Finnian's thrust, my hand trembling as energy drained from me to protect me from Dariela's blow.

For a minute, I could do nothing but fend off as many blows as I could. But Lavinia had fallen back to join Coralie, Saffron, and Araminta, and the four of them threw composition after composition at us.

Lucas glanced at me sideways, between blows. He was holding his attackers off better than I was, reducing the drain on me, but I still wasn't going to last much longer. We would have to surrender, or I would be drained dry.

For a second, I considered skimming some of my attackers' energy, but I tamped down the instinct. Even without the issue of consent, the middle of battle wasn't the time for such experiments, especially given our audience.

Two blows fell against my shield in quick succession as Lucas faltered in his defense, taking precious seconds to pull out a composition. A blast of raw power swept outward, widening to collide with all eight of our year mates.

It pushed our closest attackers far enough back that Lucas could safely lean over toward me.

"I've been testing their shields. I think I can break through all of them at once, but it won't take them long to get them back up again. Do you think you can incapacitate them all if I do it?"

I didn't have time to answer before our attackers charged forward again, but he must have read the agreement in my eyes. I saw both his hands plunge into his robe and managed to shout, "Shield," before the first blow fell, calling back up my third shield against all physical attack in time to protect him.

I dropped my own sword, collapsing to the ground to avoid the blows aimed at me. I needed to be ready.

Lucas stacked three parchments on top of each other, ripping them all at once. I felt the rush of shapeless power, three separate surges that battered against our year mates almost simultaneously. Araminta's, Coralie's, and Saffron's shields dissolved from the first wave, Natalya and Calix's from the second, and Weston, Finnian, and Dariela's from the third. As soon as I felt Dariela's fizzle out, I screamed, "Bind them!"

My power poured out, streaming toward each of them individually. Finnian, Dariela, Calix, and Weston—standing closest—went down first, their arms and legs clamping to their side under invisible bindings.

Saffron and Natalya staggered and fell, and Coralie dropped a moment later, an untorn parchment fluttering to the ground beside her. But Araminta still stood. She had lost her original shield first and had moved faster than any of the others, managing to retrieve and rip a new one before my power reached her.

My power strained against her shield, racing around her, looking for a weakness, and my vision spun. My knees might have buckled if I wasn't already on the ground.

"End Araminta's," I gasped out, cutting off the part of my

composition that sought to bind her before I bled even more power. It was already taking too much to hold the others.

The extra stream ended abruptly, and I remained huddled on the ground panting. Lucas moved toward me, but I shook my head, my eyes widening.

"What are you doing? Araminta's still standing!"

He jerked and took off running, racing past the prone figures of our year mates, several of them straining against their bonds as he passed. Araminta ran too, trying to stay ahead of him as her hands fumbled for another composition. But his longer legs soon caught up to her, and he leaped forward, tackling her to the ground.

As soon as she was pinned, clapping broke out from the stands, and Thornton declared the end of the bout. I instantly cut off my remaining compositions, flopping back to lie flat on the ground. I closed my eyes and groaned before remembering our audience.

I opened them again in time to see Lucas offer me his hand. I grasped it and let him help me to my feet. But as soon as I was standing, I pulled my hand free so our observers would know I was still standing on my own.

I let my eyes run over my friends first, checking none of them were harmed. All of them had regained their feet, although Coralie was bent over, retrieving her unused composition.

"Really?" Finnian, who had also been watching Coralie, turned to grin at me. "You couldn't have let us win? For the sake of our pride. Nine against two, you know."

"Ardann first," Lucas muttered, but he was grinning back at Finnian.

"Yes," said Finnian dryly, "it was nothing but pure altruism that pushed you to win."

"What can we say, Finnian?" I managed to muster enough energy for a chuckle. "We're just the giving types."

Coralie and Saffron reached us, and Finnian slung an arm

around each of them. "Good effort, girls. We lost, but we lost nobly."

"Did we?" Saffron shook him off when Thornton glared at them. "My bruises don't feel noble."

I winced. "Sorry about that."

She smiled at me. "It wouldn't be combat without a few bruises."

We reached the instructors and Sekalis just as Araminta joined us.

"Well done, Elena!" Walden beamed at me. "No surprises that you carried the day."

"His Royal Highness also performed admirably," said Lorcan coolly.

"A most interesting display." Chen stood and bowed again. "We thank you for your generosity."

My brow wrinkled, and I looked between him and Lorcan. Did he mean our expending power to give them a demonstration bout? I decided the safest option was to bow and say nothing.

At the deepest point of the bow I wobbled and might have lost my balance without Lucas's subtle steadying hand on my back. I threw him a grateful look when I was upright again, but his attention remained on the visitors.

"Interesting, indeed," said Thornton, turning the word from a compliment into an insult. "It seems the rest of you can learn something about shielding from Araminta."

She flushed with pleasure at the small measure of praise, and I wondered if it was the first Thornton had ever given her.

"Well done," I whispered to her. "I don't know if I would have lasted much longer, so you nearly had us."

Coralie nudged her. "And you were worried about embarrassing Ardann."

Araminta shook her head. "I'm not sure surviving the longest is a particularly impressive achievement."

Chen, who appeared to be the head of the delegation, looked

as if he intended to speak to me, but Thornton dismissed us, and I hurried away with the rest of my year mates except for Lucas. I could feel Sekali eyes on me as I left the arena, but it only made me move faster. The safest way to not say the wrong thing was to not say anything at all.

As we came into the entrance hall, I swayed slightly, pressing a hand to my head. I had used more of my reserve energy than was sensible.

"You should have a nap," Coralie said. "I'll help you up the stairs. And we'll save you some lunch."

I glanced toward the door to the dining hall before sighing and nodding.

"I should if I'm going to make it through composition."

She held out her arm, and I leaned on it gratefully as we climbed the stairs. At least we had a great deal less of them to climb now that we lived on the fourth year floor. Coralie dropped me off at the door of my suite.

"Are you sure you can make it into bed on your own?" she asked.

I rolled my eyes. "I'm tired but not that tired. I'm not going to collapse."

"See that you don't." Coralie laughed. "I don't want to have to carry you down to Acacia's rooms."

I gave her a light shove and closed my door. But I hadn't made it as far as my bed when I remembered Walden had earlier asked to see me over lunch. I groaned and trudged back down again.

Back out in the corridor, I picked up my pace, hoping to catch back up to Coralie and let her know where I would be. But as I stepped out onto the stairs, she had already made it to the entrance hall. It was otherwise deserted, the rest of our year mates having long passed through into the dining hall.

I opened my mouth to call to her, but before I could do so, two men came sprinting across the large open space, one of them tackling her to the ground. I froze, my tired brain scrambling to make sense of what I was seeing.

A moment later realization came. This must be her test. Anger boiled through me. What unfair timing. She hadn't had any chance to restock compositions since our bout. How many did she have left?

The man who had tackled her groaned and rolled to the side, and she emerged, disheveled but apparently unharmed, to face off against the other. His fist punched toward her, and I mustered the mental image I needed for a shielding composition even as I hurried down the steps.

"Elena!" Lorcan's voice, coming from the far corridor, made me pull up just as my feet hit the floor of the entrance hall.

I turned slowly to find Thornton and Lorcan, now free of the Sekalis, approaching.

Thornton gave me an unimpressed look before moving on to observe Coralie's efforts to fend off her attackers. I glanced toward her in time to see her block another attempted blow, dancing back as her hand flashed into her robe.

"Elena!" Lorcan's commanding voice called my attention back in his direction.

He gestured imperiously for me to precede him toward his office, and with a final glance back at my friend, I followed him.

CHAPTER 8

*N*either of us said anything until we were both seated inside his office with the door closed. He drummed the fingers of one hand against the desk, eyeing me with a weary expression.

"I believe Thornton has already spoken to you about interfering with the tests of other trainees."

I winced. "I just—" I paused. "We just had the bout. I didn't know how much she had left."

His expression didn't lighten, and I sighed.

"It's Coralie. I couldn't just walk away."

His fingers stopped, and his brow creased.

"Your year is one of the most exceptional we have ever had at the Academy. And I don't say that only because of you or even the prince. There is a reason for it, as you probably already know. Most of your parents' generation were recalled to the front the year you were conceived, occupied with fighting back an intense Kallorwegian offensive. Only those too important to be spared remained behind, free to continue with their lives—and to think of babies for those so inclined. Coralie might not come from one of the stronger families, but her parents are intelligent. Back then her mother was involved with a crucial project for the seekers. Coralie has plenty of sense to make up for any lack of strength. And she has a flexibility of thinking many of her peers lack."

He gave me a significant look, and I knew he was talking about her friendship with me. I hadn't known her mother used to be a Gray. Had she thought it an awkward thing to mention to me when I visited their home?

"I understand it's difficult for you," Lorcan continued, "but you must learn to let your friends stand on their own feet. You won't always be there with them, and they need the chance to receive as much training as they can get now. Even if that means failing at times." He gave me a look. "Not that Coralie looked as if she was failing to me. Trust your friends, Elena."

I looked away, uncomfortable beneath his gaze. Was that what I had been doing? Not trusting Coralie? I squirmed as the truth of his words hit. She hadn't needed me to intervene, and it had been arrogant of me to think I needed to do so. Especially given I was far more exhausted than her after our bout.

"You're right." I took a deep breath. "I should trust them."

Lorcan gave me a quizzical look. "Such ready acceptance! You astound me."

I looked at him quickly and caught the twinkle in his eye.

"You've come a long way since you first sat in this office, Elena. I find myself wondering what the Academy would be like if you had never arrived." A smile inched across his face. "And the strange thing is that I find myself completely unable to imagine it."

"I'm not sure if that's a compliment or an accusation."

He chuckled. "A little of both, perhaps. But I was not on my way to look for you because of Coralie's test."

"You were looking for me?"

He nodded. "Just for a quick word." He paused, his face turning serious. "Your...connection with the prince is hardly a secret. And Their Majesties would prefer not to remind the

Sekalis of it. The enthusiasm of my library head aside, I was not intending to introduce you to them."

"I didn't—"

He waved a hand to silence me. "I know you have done nothing to put yourself in their way. And I'm inclined to think the contact was inevitable. You are not just the prince's choice, you are also the Spoken Mage. We could hardly expect them not to be curious."

He said it casually, but my cheeks still flushed to hear someone else refer to me as Lucas's choice. If only he was actually free to choose.

I tried to focus on Lorcan's words. "You want me to stay away."

He sighed. "As much as you are able. If we are lucky, you won't cross their paths again anyway."

"I can certainly promise not to seek them out."

"I can ask no more," he said before dismissing me. As I left the room, I could hear him muttering to himself that the Academy would be a quieter place next year.

He had said the Academy had changed because of me. I didn't know if that was true, but I knew I had changed unrecognizably because of it. Leaving was hard to imagine.

I hurried down the corridor lost in my thoughts, hoping that I could still make it into the dining hall in time to eat. When I crossed the entrance hall, all signs of the attack on Coralie had disappeared. Was she eating already or with Acacia in the healing rooms?

I took another two hurried steps before pulling up short. Lucas, leaving the dining hall alone, also stopped. I moved, and he moved, and suddenly we were standing much too close. A smile played around his eyes as they roved over my face.

"We make a good team," he said.

"The delegation is gone, I suppose?"

He stiffened and moved the tiniest fraction away from me. "They have returned to the palace."

I bit my lip. I'd said the wrong thing.

His eyes followed my action, lingering on my lips, and I gulped. He swayed toward me, stopping himself a mere breath away.

"How am I going to escape this marriage, Elena? We are foolish dreamers both to think we have any hope."

"But what would we do without hope?" I whispered, my insides contracting at the pain on his face.

"Grow up." His voice sounded hard, and I flinched, although I knew he meant the words for himself.

His face softened slightly, and he lifted a hand to my face, cupping my cheek with his palm. "You deserve more than any of this."

The chatter of trainees sounded behind us, and we sprang apart. I looked toward them, my face warm, and when I looked back, he was already half way toward the stairs. I watched him go, sadness welling inside me although I refused to let any tears fall.

Lucas said he needed to grow up. But that suggested he was a child, and I wasn't sure Lucas had ever had the luxury of being young.

Midwinter approached, somehow only my second one in Corrin. Like last time, my year mates and I all received gold-embossed invitations to a royal ball at the palace. Only this year it wasn't to be like their usual Royal Midwinter Celebration. Those were usually more intimate affairs, held in honor of Lucas and his birthday.

But this year we had an unprecedented delegation present, and the royals were hosting a huge gala. They hadn't quite invited every mage in Ardann—as they did at Midsummer—but every member of the great families had been invited. And every one of Lucas's year mates.

"They couldn't leave us off the list since they'll still be celebrating Lucas's birthday," Coralie said, smiling down at her invitation.

"I'm sure they would have liked to leave me off." I struggled to keep my voice light. Memories of last Midwinter kept trying to intrude, and a royal ball was the last place I felt like going.

"Not even royals can do whatever they please," said Finnian. "You're the prince's year mate, the Spoken Mage, a Devoras, and General Griffith's daughter. There was no scenario where you were being left off the list."

Coralie glared at him. "Elena is more than aware that royals are not free to do as they please," she whispered. "Remember!"

I turned away quickly, pretending I hadn't caught her words. She was trying to be kind, but hearing it aloud only made the sting worse. Some things couldn't be softened.

On the following rest day after the invitations arrived, a pounding on my door roused me from sleep far too early. Groaning, I staggered through to the outer door of my suite and pulled it open, already grumbling.

My words cut off mid-stream when I saw who had woken me. I blinked several times, but the figure of Natalya didn't disappear.

"Hurry up and get dressed," she said. "We have shopping to do."

I raised both eyebrows, and she sighed.

"Somehow you've managed to look vaguely respectable for the last three Midwinters, but you're a Devoras now, and we don't leave things to chance. And since Mother is gone now, that means the responsibility falls to me."

I had never heard Natalya mention her deceased mother, and even the general had made no mention of her during our adoption discussions.

She narrowed her eyes. "Don't look pityingly at me. Mother wasn't exactly the maternal type, you know. She never came into Corrin, and we always spent at least half the year here, so it's not exactly strange for us to be without her. And I'm fairly sure half the estate breathed a sigh of relief when she passed."

"I—" I couldn't actually think of anything to say, but Natalya just rolled her eyes, brushing past the awkward moment.

"You're family now, remember? No secrets." But she bent an accusing eye on me, as if she knew I still harbored some of my own.

"So…we're going shopping…now?" I asked. "Can't it wait?"

She gave me a disparaging look.

"The seamstress will need time to actually sew the dress, remember." Her expression made it clear she felt the seamstress would have a difficult task in making me look presentable.

I took a deep breath and reminded myself this was Natalya. Her low opinion could hardly hurt me at this point.

"If we're going shopping, I'm bringing Clemmy." If I had to spend time with my Devoras sister, I wanted the sister I actually liked there as well. Clemmy would love helping me pick a dress.

"Clemmy?" She frowned at me. "Oh, that's right. Your real sister. Bring whoever you like, just don't be late. I'll meet you in the shopping district in an hour."

She didn't wait for my acknowledgment, turning on her heel and disappearing toward her own suite.

Reluctantly I threw on some clothes and hurried toward my family's new apartment. Clemmy greeted me with great delight, and my mother plied me with breakfast while I tried to herd my sister out the door.

"We're going to be late," I said, grabbing a roll from my mother's hand and blowing her a kiss. "It's just not worth arguing with Natalya."

"She's not going to try to pick you something horrid, is she?" Clemmy wrinkled her nose.

I swallowed my mouthful. "I don't think so. Her family pride seems to outweigh her hatred of me. Just."

Clemmy snorted, and then giggled, and suddenly I was laughing too.

"She sounds like a lot of fun," Clemmy said as her chortles subsided.

"Oh, a whole bunch." I grimaced. "Just ignore anything she says, all right?"

Clemmy bounced up and down. "Oh, she won't bother me. Did you see that?" She pointed toward an intricate blown glass figurine glowing in swirls of amber and emerald.

I pulled her down the street. "We can stop on our way back. There's no time now."

She let me pull her along, gazing with wide eyes through the windows of the expensive mage shops. Despite my hurry, Natalya was waiting for us part way down the street, her arms crossed, and her foot tapping.

I opened my mouth, but she cut me off before I could speak.

"You're a member of Devoras now. We don't apologize."

I didn't attempt to point out the illogic of this given her complaint about my tardy arrival, instead taking comfort in Clemmy's suppressed giggle. She didn't seem inclined to take Natalya too seriously.

"You're going to look amazing!" Clemmy crowed as she looked at the dresses in the window of the shop Natalya had chosen. "You should try on that one." She pointed at an emerald green ball gown.

"That's not how this works," Natalya said flatly, and pushed open the door.

I smiled at Clemmy, to soften her words, but my efforts to muster any true enthusiasm felt false. Last year Finnian had made sure Lucas and I were a matching pair. This year I needed to blend into the wall. I had my instructions, and I had made my promise to Lorcan. I would do my best not to be noticed.

The seamstress greeted Natalya with respect, and with a few words my Devoras sister managed to convey the entire situation. The woman instantly transformed, treating even commonborn Clemmy with the utmost respect.

I must have looked a little bewildered because Natalya explained it in a bored voice as soon as the seamstress disappeared into the bowels of her shop.

"She wants the prestige of dressing the Spoken Mage." Her words carried the faintest hint of bitterness beneath the boredom.

"Natalya, I don't want to upstage anyone, I promise. I didn't—"

"Let me guess?" She cut me off. "You didn't ask for any of this? Well, neither did I. And yet, here we are. You're family now, whether I like it or not. And family matters to me. It matters to my father and my brothers. But that doesn't mean we're suddenly going to become friends. We're here to do a job. Let's get it done as fast as possible, and then we can be back about our separate ways."

Clemmy looked across from the other side of the room, her eyes wide, but to my surprise, I smiled. It was strange the familiar things that brought me comfort.

Natalya looked at me suspiciously, so I tried to tone it down.

"Fine by me," I said. "I can promise I'll never mean you any harm. And I'll do my best not to disgrace your family. If you can say the same—" I paused and gave her a meaningful look, "and mean it—that's more than enough for me."

Natalya looked at me for a long moment and then nodded once. "You're family now. It doesn't matter how I feel about you, I won't work against you, if that's what you're worried about." She gave a humorless laugh. "And it's not as if it mattered which of us Lucas preferred in the end, did it?"

I turned away, not wanting her to see the pain on my face. I believed her when she said she would never work against me again, and I didn't think she had meant her final words to be hurtful. They had merely been a truthful reflection on our situation.

Which, of course, was exactly what made them so painful.

"Ignore her," Clemmy whispered when I crossed the room to stand beside her. "She's just jealous because you're one of a kind."

I glanced across at Natalya. She had hated me from the first, and when I arrived at the Academy there was nothing about me that could have made her jealous. No, it was more complicated than that. And so much had changed since then. In so many ways we had both grown up. Being in a war tended to have that effect —I had never been the only one with nightmares.

But I had become the Spoken Mage. And Lucas had moved far beyond her reach. It was entirely possible that being my sister would end up being the most notable thing about Natalya's life. She would use that without hesitation. But she would also never forgive it.

Her father had bought us an uneasy truce when he brought me into her family, and I would have to be content with that. I reached over and gave my true sister a squeeze. I didn't need Natalya to like me when I had Clemmy.

As soon as we had finished with the seamstress and made our final orders, Natalya hurried away. Clemmy and I turned back southward, and I tried to think what might cheer her up. She had been disappointed that I refused the bright materials she preferred, settling instead on a russet satin in a conservative design.

"You know this is the first Midwinter I've had any money to buy gifts for my friends," I said. "Would you like to help me choose some?"

Clemmy whooped and grabbed my hand, pulling me toward the glass shop we had seen earlier.

"So, I'll take that as a yes?" I smiled.

"Only if you help me choose something for Mother and

Father in the markets afterward." She grinned back at me, and I shook my head.

"Let me guess, I'm going to be the one paying for it?"

Clemmy's grin widened. "Of course. You're the mighty Devoras, right?" She winked at me while I groaned.

I pulled her into a quick, sideways hug. "What would I do without you, Clemmy? You've always kept me anchored."

She hugged me back. "I love you, too, Elena. Whoever and whatever you are—as long as you pay for the presents because I've spent all the coin Mother gave me on berry pies at the market."

I laughed. "Thank you for such unswerving loyalty."

She rolled her eyes. "You've got Jasper for that."

I swatted at her, but she danced away from me and into the store.

I rose early on Midwinter morning so I could eat the morning meal with my family. My mother had insisted I bring Coralie along since her own family were home in Abalene, but I hadn't held out much hope she would accept the invitation. Not when Finnian's family were in the capital for the Midwinter ball.

But to my surprise she accepted.

"We already agreed to wait until graduation to meet our families," she had said. "And Saffron's mother didn't come down. He thinks it will go better with his mother if his aunt is there as well."

She said it all quite matter-of-factly, but I could detect the lurking doubt behind her equanimity. This was what she had always feared—not being good enough to be welcomed into Finnian's family.

But she seemed nothing but cheerful on Midwinter morning, and my family's small apartment shook with laughter and merriment. When we left to return to the Academy and prepare for the ball, she dragged Clemmy with us, much to my sister's delight. And Jasper walked beside us as well, on his way back to the palace.

"Not that I'm to attend the ball as a guest, of course," he told me as we strolled along, our bellies too full for hurrying. "But there's plenty to be done at the palace. I—"

He cut himself off and glanced sideways at me.

I raised an eyebrow. "That sounds awfully mysterious."

He smiled and shook his head. "Ask me about it tomorrow."

"Even more mysterious."

From everything he had said the few times we crossed paths at our family's apartment, he seemed to be enjoying his role as a palace official. But a sadness lingered behind his cheerful front, and I noticed that he never spoke of Clara. I resolved that I would find a chance as soon as possible after Midwinter to take him out for a meal. I could hear his mysterious news and make him finally tell me what had happened between him and Clara when they graduated.

He left us at the Academy gates, continuing on to the palace where he had a room. But Clemmy's enthusiasm soon lifted my mood, carrying me through all the ball preparation.

"I wish you were coming with us," I told her when we finally stood ready, but she only shook her head.

"What would I do at a ball full of mages? Our part of the city is going to have its own festivities, you know, and I'll have far more fun there."

"Wisdom beyond your years," I said, pinning her in a hug and kissing her on the head.

But Coralie laughed at me. "You're forgetting. It's the young who always know where to find the best party." She winked at Clemmy.

"You know, I think you were right, Elena," Clemmy said, ignoring us both. "I couldn't understand why you wanted to pick boring brown for your dress, but it suits you. It's got the same rich, almost golden tone that shows in your eyes. And the simple style makes you look…" She frowned, searching for the right word as both my sister and my friend surveyed me with narrowed eyes.

"Rich and important," Coralie supplied. "It makes you look rich and important. Everyone else will look overdressed by comparison."

"That wasn't my intention," I said, frowning at myself in the mirror. "I just liked the material."

"Well it likes you, too," Coralie said with a cheeky grin. "Now hurry up, or we're going to be late."

CHAPTER 9

*I*nside the ballroom doors, looking over the room from the top of the four shallow stairs, I drew a deep breath. It was just as I remembered it. The white marble, the red velvet runner, the wine-red drapes over the long windows, the gold touches everywhere. I glanced up at the gold chandeliers that floated impossibly in the air above the dancers. I could feel the power that cushioned and held them in intricate detail that had escaped me last time I was here.

Without instruction, my eyes flew to a set of long glass doors that I knew led out onto a quiet balcony. Or they had once done so, before it collapsed with me on it. I imagined the creators had rebuilt it since then, though. If I pushed past the drapes and escaped out into the cool night air, would Lucas follow me, as he had done then?

But I knew better. Too much had changed.

My eyes sought him out, standing next to his parents with Chen beside them. The Sekalis wore the same robes I had seen them in previously with the high collars and slits. But the embroidery at their throats and cuffs winked with expensive jewels.

Our own royal family easily matched their magnificence, Queen Verena making up for her lack of height with the widest, most elaborate golden gown I had ever seen. It was a stark contrast to the slim, blood-red dress of her tall daughter beside her, both somehow looking more impressive for the contrast.

Like his sister, Lucas was back in his red uniform, the gold sash across his chest and the gold circlet in his hair. Only his boots were black this year.

I fisted my hands in my simple skirt. He wore the same haughty, distant look I remembered from first year. Then it had repelled me, whereas now it made me long to run to him and tuck my hand inside his—to remind him that there was one person, at least, who didn't require him to wear a mask.

But Coralie had already started down the stairs, and I followed behind her, obediently heading away from the royal family and the Sekali delegation. We found Finnian standing near one of the long food tables, but he didn't seem to see me. He only had eyes for my friend, who had outdone herself in a flowing dress of the palest pink which perfectly set off her complexion.

"Coralie," he breathed, stepping forward, hands outstretched ready to pull her into his arms.

She blushed and sidestepped.

"Not here, remember," she whispered at him.

"How can I remember when you look so stunning?" he asked in a plaintive voice, and I laughed.

He glanced over, noticing me for the first time.

"Back me up here, Elena!"

"No, you don't," said Coralie, zipping to my side. "Elena was my friend first. Plus, us girls need solidarity."

I shrugged apologetically at Finnian. "Sorry. She speaks only truth."

"Dance with me, at least," he said to Coralie. "I'll keep us away from anyone in my family, I promise."

I frowned at him as Coralie accepted his hand with a roll of her eyes. I was fairly certain he was genuinely trying to reassure her, but I suspected he would have done better to boldly announce he couldn't wait another moment and was going to introduce her to his family immediately.

My eyes strayed back to the royal family. Had it really only been months since I was contemplating the possibility of being introduced to them as future family? Those happy weeks were hard to remember now.

"Sister." Julian stepped up beside me, nodding his head in greeting.

I held back a groan. Instead of royalty as family, I had gotten the twins and Julian.

"Julian," I said, not bothering to nod. "Don't you have more important people to bother…uh, I mean, talk to?" I wasn't in the mood for charged small talk, especially with him.

Julian didn't seem in the least put off by my lack of welcome.

"Father pulled some strings for me, so here I am, repaying the favor."

I stared at him, my heart sinking.

"What's that supposed to mean?"

"You'll find out soon enough." He didn't look at me, his eyes on the royal family across the room.

Something in his words reminded me of Jasper's earlier pronouncement. My eyes followed Julian's, latching onto Lucas. Did he know something I didn't? I was too far away to read any subtle play of emotion across his face, though.

"I'm starting to get the feeling there's something big going on that I don't know about," I said to Julian.

He smiled down at me. "Patience, young sister, all will be revealed soon enough."

I raised an eyebrow. "They're making an announcement tonight? At the ball?"

Julian's smile widened. "Father told me you were perceptive. Perhaps I shouldn't have listened to Natty when it came to you."

"Oh, haven't you heard? Natalya and I have declared a truce. I think."

He laughed. "For all her protestations, at heart she's as loyal to the family as her twin." His eyes glinted mockingly. "She knows where her best interests lie."

"And you don't?" I frowned as I examined his face, trying to understand what lay behind his mocking, wry manner.

"Oh, my blood bleeds Devoras just like the rest of them," he said lightly. "I'm here right now, aren't I?"

My frown deepened. "Yes, why was that again?"

He grinned. "Nice try, sis, but you'll just have to wait and hear with everyone else."

I frowned at him. If the royal family were making some sort of announcement tonight, I couldn't see what it could have to do with me. Jasper certainly hadn't given any indication that I should be nervous. And yet, Julian claimed he was here beside me under coercion.

A deep chime sounded through the ballroom before I could consider it further, and the dancers slowly stilled, everyone turning to the platform inside the doorway. The double doors had been closed, and the royal family now stood there, Chen beside them.

"Thank you all for sharing in our Midwinter celebrations," said King Stellan in a booming voice. "And a special welcome to our Sekali guests."

He turned and bowed to Chen, although I noticed he didn't bow as deeply as the Sekali did in return.

"We are honored," said Chen, his vowels less rounded than an Ardannian's, but his words clearly heard on the other side of the ballroom.

"A happy birthday, also, to our son, Prince Lucas, who will turn twenty-one at midnight." He smiled and clapped a hand on his son's shoulder. Lucas's expression didn't change, but the crowd applauded for him, and he nodded in their direction.

"As you all know," King Stellan continued, "we are currently negotiating a potential treaty with the Sekalis, and toward that end, I would like to take this moment to make an announcement."

Julian smiled, and I tensed.

"Prince Lucas will be part of an Ardannian delegation which will travel to the Sekali Empire to finish negotiating and seal the alliance. They will leave in a matter of weeks. We look forward to news of their success, and a bright future for both Ardann and the Empire."

No. No no no no no. We had until the end of the year. We were supposed to have until the end of the year!

King Stellan bowed again to Chen, who bowed back, lower than ever. The hiss of many whispers had broken out across the room at the king's words, but when the two men straightened, a small cheer replaced it.

Both of them smiled and nodded, their eyes roving over the crowd. I watched them, my mind reeling. Both of them looked pleased, although I didn't know either of them well enough to guess what might lie behind their expressions.

Chen's eyes seemed to meet mine across the room, lingering for a second. But then they moved on, and I concluded it was a trick of the distance. I was tucked away in a far corner of the room.

Chills raced through me, panic chasing them around my body. The king had said weeks. Weeks, and then Lucas would disappear.

I turned slowly to Julian.

"And there you have it," he said.

My mind focused in on him. "You knew about this." It wasn't a question. "And let me guess—the strings the general pulled were to get you on the delegation."

He raised an eyebrow. "Perceptive, indeed."

"Not perceptive enough to know what any of it has to do with me," I muttered.

He said nothing.

"Why do you want to go?" I asked.

He gave me a surprised look. "A chance to see the fabled Sekali Empire whose border has been closed to us for hundreds of years? Wouldn't you want to?"

I shook my head. "I have quite enough problems here in Ardann. I don't need to deal with an empire on top of them." I didn't add that the proposed marriage alliance had killed any desire I might have had to connect with the Sekalis.

"But what an opportunity," Julian said. "The one previous delegation—from the year before you started at the Academy—is the only contact anyone has had with the Sekalis in generations. Who knows how much similarity their land still bears to the ancient records we have from before they closed their borders? We know so little about them."

He seemed to warm to his topic. "Who knows what power and profit might be waiting for us? When this alliance goes through, those present scoping the situation and making connections will have a decided advantage."

"That sounds like very Devoras reasoning," I said. "I would have thought your father would be fully behind you rather than your having to call in a favor."

Julian's face tightened slightly. "Oh, Father wants someone in the family along, certainly. But who said I would be his first choice?"

He looked behind me.

"Ah, Father. There you are."

"Greetings, my boy," said General Griffith cheerfully. "And to you, Elena. You look lovely. I must remember to congratulate Natalya."

I took a deep breath and refrained from telling him that

Natalya had barely tolerated my choice of material and design—finding them boring and unimaginative, even if acceptable for the family honor. A wild notion that perhaps he could stop this delegation flitted through my mind, but I equally quickly discarded it.

The general's face only confirmed Julian's words. The members of Devoras saw great opportunity in this development. And I could only imagine the general's glee if this alliance succeeded in giving us access to the Sekali armies.

"General. Spoken Mage." A foreign voice behind us made me turn to see Chen bowing to us.

Where had he come from? He must have hurried straight from the platform to here. An uneasy feeling swirled in my stomach. Could he have been looking at me after all?

"Greetings, Ambassador." I bowed, as did Julian and the general.

Julian, at least, made the gesture with ease. Had he been practicing in preparation for his trip to the Empire?

"I was hoping to have a chance to speak with you tonight, Spoken Mage," Chen said.

I wanted to blurt out, *You were?* But I managed to hold onto the words. He continued, not seeming to take offense at my silence.

"Word of your unique abilities has made it even as far as our illustrious capital. And His Imperial Majesty, the emperor himself, has expressed interest in seeing a demonstration of your power such as the one I was fortunate enough to witness at your Academy."

"Oh," I said, "that is very kind."

Over his shoulder I caught a glimpse of Queen Verena talking furiously to Lorcan and looking in my direction. But what was I supposed to do? The ambassador had sought me out. I looked around for my friends, hoping to find a polite way to extricate myself from the conversation. But Griffith and Julian had closed in on either side of me, blocking my view of anyone I might use as a reason to excuse myself.

"We would like to invite you to accompany the delegation as a guest of honor," Chen said, capturing my full attention.

"I…" My mind whirled, suddenly blank of all useful thought. "But I'm a trainee…at the Academy. I can't go to the Empire."

Chen didn't seem in the least perturbed by my words. "I understand the prince is also a trainee but that special arrangements have been made with your Academy Head. I am sure they can also be extended to cover you. You needn't fear failing."

The slightest wrinkle around his nose conveyed a strange sense of disgust, although I couldn't be sure if it was for the concept of failing or for something to do with our academy system. Perhaps mage training was handled differently in the Empire.

"I—"

I wasn't sure exactly what I intended to say, but whatever it was, the general cut me off.

"My daughter would be delighted to accept your most generous and flattering offer," he said.

"Your daughter?" Chen looked mildly surprised. "I had heard the Spoken Mage was commonborn."

"I am," I said, at the same time as General Griffith said, "My adopted daughter, that is."

"Ah." Chen nodded. "In that case, I thank you and look forward to welcoming the Spoken Mage to the Sekali Empire." He bowed yet again.

I opened my mouth to protest, but Julian jabbed me in the side. I glared at him and tried to regather my thoughts, but the ambassador was already gone.

"Before you start protesting," the general said calmly, "I am your father. So, yes, I have every right to answer for you. Just as I would answer without hesitation for any one of my children— something that is well understood in the Sekali Empire where no one would question the ruling of their clan head. That much we learned from our one previous delegation."

"It's a great honor to our family," Julian said. "You are the only person they have individually requested. They did not even insist on the prince himself being personally present. That was Their Majesties' decision for the expediency of the alliance. The Sekalis don't seem to feel the same time pressure we do."

"You knew about this. Both of you," I said, infuriated.

"Of course we did," said the general. "I am Head of the Armed Forces and sit on the Mage Council. I know a great many things you, as a trainee, do not. Their Majesties would have preferred not to include you, I know. I think they were hoping if they kept you apart, Chen wouldn't have the opportunity to issue the invitation, and the Sekalis would let the whole thing go." He shook his head.

"Then why are you encouraging it?" I asked.

He lowered his voice. "Times are changing. This alliance is unprecedented. You can be sure that it will affect the balance of power among the great families back here in Ardann, one way or another. Their Majesties did not forbid your accompanying the delegation—they could hardly afford to do so and risk offending the Sekalis—and so I mean to see that none of the other families have a chance to steal a march on Devoras. You are our greatest asset, and if I cannot have you at the front, then I will not hesitate to use you elsewhere."

He waited a moment, as if daring me to protest, and then strode away.

"I would have expected you to leap at the chance to go." Julian examined his nails rather than meet my eyes. "Since Lucas is going."

I glared at him. "Go or not go, I prefer to make my own decision."

"You're playing at court now, Spoken Mage. Nothing is ever that simple."

I sighed and rubbed a hand across my eyes. He was right, of course, and I knew it. Just like I knew that becoming a Devoras might have consequences like this. I had judged it worth it at the time, and I couldn't take it back just because Lucas was no longer available.

And I did want to stay near Lucas. I just didn't want to go to the Empire with him. I wanted to find a way for him to stay here.

"Either way it doesn't much matter, does it?" I asked wearily. "It sounds like I'm going whether I want to or not."

"That's the spirit," said Julian, amusement in his voice. "And don't worry. Your big brother will be there to look after you."

My eyes flew to his in sudden concern before I remembered that the description now fit him.

"It sounds like you'll be there to make sure I fall in line with Devoras interests," I said sourly.

His eyes continued to laugh at me. "Isn't that basically the same thing?"

I shook my head and left him without a farewell, weaving through the crowd toward the doors. I had barely arrived, but I'd already had enough of this evening. Near the exit I crossed paths with Lorcan. He hailed me, but I didn't give him the chance to talk first.

"Is it true?" I asked. "You've agreed to release Lucas from the Academy?"

Lorcan frowned. "Not release him. Such a thing is not permitted. I have merely agreed that he can complete his remaining fourth year studies at an external location. Your year has plenty of experience with that. An Academy instructor will accompany him, and he will return for the final exams." He shook his head. "Naturally it is not an ideal situation, but these are unprecedented times."

"Well the instructor will need to take on two trainees, I'm afraid."

Lorcan looked at me sharply. "What do you mean?"

I nearly said that the general was making me go but decided at the last minute that it would be disloyal to my adoptive family to phrase it like that. And for all they drove me crazy, I had willingly chosen to join them.

"Ambassador Chen has issued me a gracious invitation. One it proved impossible to refuse."

Lorcan swore quietly. "I was afraid of that. And since we've worked out a means for Lucas to attend, we can hardly use the trainee excuse for you."

"So we would return for exams?" I asked. Perhaps that meant the actual wedding was still to be put off until after graduation.

"Yes," Lorcan said, his voice gentle. "I believe Their Majesties will suggest an Ardannian tour for Lucas's bride."

Of course. How foolish of me. Marriage didn't prevent exam participation. I tried to keep my face void of expression, hating how easily Lorcan had read me. Someone called his name, and I used the opportunity to slip away and out the door.

I had made it down the flight of stairs and into the vast entryway when a familiar voice called my name. I slowed and stopped, fighting to calm my rushing emotions before turning to face Lucas.

"Why didn't you tell me?" I kept my voice low so the footmen who lined the space wouldn't hear me.

"I didn't know. I swear it was as much a surprise to me as it was to you." His voice turned bitter. "My parents knew I would have fought it, so they kept it from me until it was too late." He ground his teeth. "I was supposed to have until the end of the year."

"I'm going as well," I said.

"What?" He gripped my arm, his voice rising.

I glanced toward the closest footman, and he lowered it again.

"What do you mean, you're going?"

"Exactly that. Ambassador Chen cornered me and issued an invitation. And my dear adoptive father accepted on my behalf."

Lucas looked furious, but I'd had time to calm down.

"Maybe this is a good thing," I whispered. "Maybe this will give us a chance to find another way."

"To end the war? What can we do from the Sekali Empire? They have no involvement in it."

"No, but maybe we can find another way to win their support. Other than a marriage alliance." He didn't look convinced, so I leaned closer. "It doesn't matter what you said before. We have to have hope. I have to hold onto hope."

"I love that about you, you know," he said. "Your persistence. Your perseverance despite all odds." He shook his head. "But we don't know exactly how things will go in the Empire. And I don't want you caught up in the middle of it."

I sighed. "Well clearly no one is interested in asking either of us. So we'll just have to watch out for one another."

He closed the gap between us, resting his forehead against mine for one all too brief second.

"There's no one I would rather have watching my back."

"Nor me," I murmured, and then he pulled back, voices sounding on the stairs.

He gave me a formal half-bow and disappeared back toward the ballroom. I stayed where I was, the mages exiting the palace looking at me curiously as they passed through the entry.

Perhaps this would all work out for the best? Perhaps away from the Academy we could find the answers that had so far eluded us.

"Elena!" A loud whisper startled me back into movement.

I looked around in confusion.

"Over here!"

This time I pinpointed the location as well as the voice itself. Hurrying across the large space and into the side corridor, I didn't speak until we were both some distance from the servants on duty for the ball.

"Jasper! What are you doing here?"

"I live here remember?" He grinned and pulled me into a hug.

I sank into it for a moment, wishing I could forget everything else in this brief taste of family and home. But reality quickly intruded, and I pushed back.

"Don't try to tell me your rooms are right inside the entryway. I'm sure they're buried in some back warren somewhere."

"I was waiting for you." He didn't look in the least repentant. "You heard the announcement?"

"That's what you were talking about earlier today, right?" I asked. "The delegation to the Empire? I suppose it's causing all kinds of work for you palace officials."

An excitement filled his eyes that made me vaguely uncomfortable.

"For some of us more than others," he said.

I eyed him. "What's that supposed to mean?"

"I talked to my superior and volunteered." He sounded exultant. "And I was chosen. I'm going as part of the delegation, Elena!"

My heart sank, and my mind instantly flew back to Julian's words. Had he meant Jasper all along? It seemed both of my older brothers were to travel with me.

"Why would you volunteer, Jasper?" I whispered. "We still don't know much about the Sekalis. It might be dangerous."

"Perhaps." Jasper brushed away my concerns. "But it will certainly be fascinating. And you're going, aren't you? I took this position to help protect you, and here's my opportunity."

"How do you know that?" I asked. "About me, I mean?"

He rolled his eyes. "Those of us officials who've been closely involved with details for the visiting delegation have heard all the gossip on this new expedition."

I frowned. "You've been closely involved with the delegation? But surely you must be a junior official? You only started the job this year."

"I probably shouldn't be, it's true," he said. "But you know they call us all southern savages, right? The Sekalis, I mean?"

"Of course." It was one of the few things most Ardannians knew about the Sekalis.

"Well, they don't seem to view the commonborn the way Ardannian mages do. So I think Their Majesties wanted me assigned to the delegation to demonstrate their enlightened views on commonborns, or some such thing. Most of the officials here are mages on assignment from the various disciplines. The only other commonborn official here at the palace is an old man, set in his ways." He shrugged. "Whatever the reason, I wasn't going to turn down the opportunity."

I bit my lip. "You were supposed to get a well-paying job with a merchant family, marry Clara, settle down, and have some beautiful nieces and nephews for me to spoil," I said. "Not throw everything away to protect me!"

He smiled, but the expression didn't look entirely happy. "In truth, I would have volunteered even without you. This is too good an opportunity to miss. There is so much to learn about the Sekalis and their empire. It's already obvious they view life differently from us."

I shook my head. "You're as bad as Julian!"

"Julian?"

I sighed. "The general's oldest son. But I take it back. At least your motives are pure."

"Ah yes, he's to be part of our delegation as well, isn't he?"

"Jasper," I said. "What happened with Clara?"

"Nothing you need worry about," he said quickly.

I put my hands on my hips. "I'm your sister. I can worry if I want to. What happened?"

He shifted uncomfortably before giving a deep sigh.

"It's not as if I ever had any great desire to be a merchant, you know."

117

"But you did—do—have a desire for Clara. Don't try to deny it."

He wouldn't meet my eyes. "I'm not saying she didn't argue against my taking a position as an official. She did. But she understood in the end that I needed to do it for you, if not for myself. And she was never arguing because she cared what position I held for her own sake."

I frowned, trying to piece it together. "Her family, then?"

He nodded, still not meeting my eyes. "They were wealthy merchants once. Her grandfather also attended the University. But her father didn't win a place, and their fortunes changed. They believe they were cheated by a mage family. They have… strong feelings about the mages."

"And you chose to come and work for the mages instead of helping a commonborn merchant family like them," I said, realization dawning. "Basically, you're a traitor."

"More or less." He blew out a long breath. "Clara might have defied them and married me anyway, but I didn't ask. She's working for them, of course, helping them turn around the family fortunes, and she's not drawing a salary until things improve for them. I couldn't ask her to step away from that. And my salary as an official isn't enough to support us on its own. Not while our own family is still getting established here."

"Oh Jasper," I said, my voice soft. "And so, once again, you put everything of yourself aside for the sake of our family. I could ask the general for a larger allowance."

My heart sank at the thought, but I steeled my resolve. Jasper had already done more for our family.

"No, don't," he said quickly. "Mother and Father wouldn't like it. You're already helping so much, and I know they're not entirely comfortable taking the Devoras money that's meant for you. But they'd still be stuck in Kingslee without it. In a few years they'll repay their debt for the new store, and then I can save for myself."

"Will Clara wait for you?" I asked.

Jasper looked at the ground. "I hope so."

I sighed and wrapped my arms around him again. "Let's just focus on this visit to the Empire. If we both come back from that in one piece, then we'll sort this out for you. One way or another."

CHAPTER 10

$\mathcal{C}$oralie, Finnian, and Saffron confronted Lorcan the day
after Midwinter to demand that they be included in the
delegation as well.

"We're not going to let you and Lucas have all the fun,"
Finnian had informed me as they hurried off in search of him.

"How did it go?" I asked when they reappeared in the dining
hall.

"He laughed us out of his office," Saffron said glumly.

"I appreciate your loyalty, really I do," I said. "And I wish you
could come, too."

For my own sake, I did wish it. Although part of me was glad
they were staying safely in Ardann. Too many people I cared
about were going already.

"I haven't given up yet," Finnian said. "Not entirely at any
rate."

He refused to give us any more detail, saying he didn't want to
get anyone's hopes up if he couldn't deliver. But two weeks later
he gave us early warning of an announcement from Lorcan to the
fourth years. As the senior trainees, and as a learning exercise,
the whole year was to accompany the returning Sekali delegation

and outgoing Ardannian one as far as Torcos, nearly on the northern border.

"I offered to house the whole year at our estate just outside Torcos," Finnian explained. "It's not as good as going all the way into the Empire, but at least it will allow us to be together a little longer." He glanced sideways at Coralie as he spoke, assessing her reaction.

"We're going to stay with your family?" she asked slowly.

He crossed over to take her hands, looking uncertain—an unusual look for him.

"I know we said we'd wait until graduation," he said quietly. "But I don't want to wait so long. I want them to meet you now. Saffron's mother will be there, so you can meet everyone at once, like we talked about."

A faint flush colored Coralie's cheeks. "You don't want to wait?"

Finnian ran a hand through his hair. "I know my family is intimidating. And I guess I'm nervous about scaring you away, but there's no point to waiting when I've made up my mind."

Coralie assumed an expression of fake outrage.

"I'm not so cowardly, I assure you."

Finnian chuckled, but I could see him trying to weigh the truth behind her humor. Her face dropped into a serious expression, and she leaned forward to kiss his cheek.

"I'm not saying it's going to be easy," she whispered to him. "All I can promise is that I won't run from it. As long as you want me there, I'll be by your side."

"Forever then," Finnian said, nothing but serious intent in his face and voice.

I turned away quickly to give them some privacy as he pulled her into his arms. Saffron sidled over to me.

"This could be an awkward trip," she whispered, and I stifled a laugh.

"Do you think they'll accept her, in the end?" I asked.

She bit her lip, looking thoughtful. "I'm not saying Coralie's concerns aren't valid, but Uncle Dashiell would never disown his only son. And I think Finnian underestimates just how much he's his mother's world."

"I thought that was exactly what they were afraid of?" I asked.

She nibbled on her lower lip. "It might make her more exacting at first, perhaps. But he seems resolute, and in time, he'll carry the day. I'm sure of it."

"Which will leave all the pressure on you, of course," I murmured. "There's nothing else for it. You'll just have to marry Calix."

She burst into giggles, causing Finnian and Coralie to break apart and turn toward us.

"What are you laughing about?" Finnian asked suspiciously.

But his expression only made Saffron laugh harder, so he swept us all out to dinner ahead of him. As we passed through the doorway, I leaned over and whispered to Saffron.

"Seriously, though. He's my brother now. I could put in a good word for you."

She burst into fresh laughter, causing Finnian to mutter darkly all the way to the dining hall.

The days before the delegation was to depart raced by at frightening speed. Our instructors seemed determined to make up for the time we would lose on the road and gave us more assignments than ever. And, on top of that, Walden gave the fourth years a series of lessons on the Sekali Empire. It turned out he had been part of the original delegation the year before we started at the Academy since each discipline had been permitted to send one mage.

"The most direct route to the Sekali capital would take us too close to the Kallorwegian border," he told us. "And on top of that, with no previous traffic between the Empire and the southern kingdoms, no roads of any significance bisect the northern forests that cover the length of the border. They are old forests, thickly grown, and nearly impassable for a group of any size. As a result, our delegation will take the same circuitous route we took four years ago."

"I remember you coming through Torcos then," Finnian said.

Walden nodded at him. "Indeed. Your family were generous in their hospitality, if I recall."

"So we will travel up the North Road to Torcos," Weston said in a bored voice. "Hardly a novel journey."

"Regardless of the excitement of the road itself," Walden said with a disapproving look, "I hope you will all take the learning opportunity presented by the close proximity of the Sekalis."

He smiled in my direction. "But it is true that the real excitement will come for Lucas and Elena once they depart Torcos. From Torcos, you will take the river through the forest and past the southern farmlands of the Empire. From there you will take a Sekali road west to the capital. It is a vast land and a fascinating journey."

"From what I understand, they didn't exactly give you open tours of their capital on your last visit," Natalya said.

"Sadly, that is true," Walden said. "We remained in the large palace complex for the entirety of our stay, and no one but the top imperial courtiers were permitted to speak to us. But naturally this delegation will be different, and we look forward to much more open dialogue between our two lands once the alliance has been sealed."

Lucas sat like a statue, saying nothing, and Walden seemed to be carefully avoiding looking in his direction.

"We did, however, learn something of their court customs which will be of use to you when interacting with the Sekalis. They value formality, seeing it as a sign of respect, and they greet each other with bows, regardless of rank."

That much at least I had observed for myself.

"Their mage families are organized into eight clans," he

continued, "and each owns vast swathes of land, managing the commonborn who live there."

"Do their clans align with their disciplines, then?" Araminta asked.

Walden shook his head. "Their branches of power—as they call them—are assigned based on ability and temperament."

"Assigned?" Lavinia asked. "You mean they don't get to choose?"

"No, each must serve where they are most suited," Lucas said, speaking up for the first time. "For the good of the Empire."

A familiar concept for him, if not for Lavinia.

"For Sekalis," Walden said, "honor appears to be paramount. By serving well and achieving prestige in their assigned branch, they win honor for their clan."

Walden had actually been in the Empire, while the general had not. Perhaps he knew more of their branches.

"I heard their growers wear brown," I said. "Do you know what branch the green robe represents?"

He frowned at me, stroking his chin. "They have both forest green and pale green robes, and they appeared to be connected in some way. I believe they represent some extra discipline beyond what we have in Ardann."

"The Sekalis tend to meet direct questions with vague answers," Lucas said. "I never received a clear explanation of the green robes."

"Nor I," said Walden. "And I only ever observed them fulfilling bureaucratic functions. They are a vast and populous place. Perhaps it is a branch for weaker mages who fulfill roles as officials?"

I sat back, disappointed. Their answers gave me no clues about the mysterious energy of the green-robed Sekali.

But I had little time to dwell on the question as we finished all the final preparations for the delegation. An official summons from the palace took me out of classes for an entire day, but my nerves soon turned to boredom when I found myself locked in a room with a team of seamstresses.

Jasper had met me at the front gates, explaining that I was accompanying the delegation in a somewhat official capacity as Spoken Mage, and that the crown was therefore to provide my wardrobe.

"Which can be safely interpreted as Their Majesties wishing to ensure you make a good impression," he had said cheerfully as he left me in the fitting room. "All of the mages in the delegation have received new robes, and all the officials new uniforms—all from the royal funds. But you are a more tricky problem since you are not going as a trainee, and therefore won't be wearing your white robe."

But just as I was in danger of nodding off standing up, the door opened without ceremony, and a tall, commanding figure entered the room. All of the seamstresses immediately stopped their work and stood before giving deep curtsies.

It took me a moment longer to recognize the crown princess, and when I started to sink awkwardly downward, she waved a hand to stop me.

"No, please don't. You'll end up pricking yourself."

"Thank you," I said with relief, since I could hardly move in the material currently pinned around me.

"I had a free moment and thought I would check on your progress." She paused, and at some silent cue unseen by me, the seamstresses all hurried out the door, leaving me alone with the princess.

We surveyed each other, awkwardly on my side, and with keen interest on hers.

"We haven't met. Not properly," she said.

"I'm Elena, Your Highness." I took a deep breath. "And I wish we could have met under other circumstances."

She inclined her head slightly. "I always wished for a younger sister." Her voice sounded wistful. But a moment later, she straightened, and something sharp and glittering entered her eyes.

"I hope you know that none of this—" she made a vague gesture with her hands, "—is personal."

"I know, Your Highness."

"If the situation had been otherwise, I, for one, would have welcomed a different sort of alliance." She spoke softly, but her words still carried steel. "The crown can always use fresh, strong new blood. Change is good for us, though we may not appreciate it."

I examined her face. It was easy to believe her words—she spoke with strength and conviction. And it only made the current situation more painful, thinking about what could have been.

"But the situation is not otherwise," I said.

"No." She looked me directly in the eyes. "You have spent time at the front lines. I can only hope you understand Ardann's need, and the role we must all play. We need this alliance."

For a taut moment silence stretched between us as we each weighed the other.

"I know, Your Highness. I will do nothing to weaken Ardann."

She nodded once, slowly, and then seemed to droop a little.

"I had hoped Lucas, at least, might be happy."

I said nothing, because there was nothing to say, and she bid me farewell. As soon as she left the room, the seamstresses poured back in, resuming their work. But I didn't hear their chatter for a long time afterward, as I replayed my conversation with the princess in my mind.

My official wardrobe was delivered to the Academy two weeks later, the seamstresses having worked at a feverish pace. The dresses were lovely, similar in understated style to the one I had worn at Midwinter. And I noted that none were in anything that could possibly be construed as royal colors.

Saffron, Coralie, and Araminta all admired them with sufficient interest, each putting forward guesses as to what sort of entertainments the emperor might host for our benefit.

"I wish I was coming with you," Coralie sighed, sitting on my bed and surveying the garments spread on every available surface.

"Not me," said Araminta from the doorway. "I can't afford to miss potentially months of lessons. I'll need all the study I can cram in if I'm to pass final exams. You know they're the only ones they make truly difficult."

Saffron shook her head. "You underestimate yourself, Araminta. You've come a long way since first year. The exams are designed to weed out anyone who lacks control of their power. You won't fail just because you have less strength, and you're much more confident now."

"I hope you're right," Araminta said. "But I still think it's best if I don't go jaunting off for half the year."

"Half the year." Coralie moaned. "Will you really be gone so long, Elena, do you think?"

"I have no idea." I began to gather the dresses up. "I don't think anyone does. It depends how the negotiations go. All we know is that we'll definitely be back for exams."

"That's so far away." Coralie flopped back onto the bed. "What am I going to do without you?"

I laughed. "Don't be so dramatic. You've got Finnian now, you don't need me. And Saffron and Araminta, if you need an escape from his manly charms."

Coralie rolled over and buried her face in my covers. "As long as I don't horrifically embarrass myself in front of his family causing him to lose all love for me," she said in a muffled voice.

Saffron pulled her arm and dragged her back up.

"You're as bad as Araminta. No one is failing. No one is losing anyone's love. I promise my family isn't that terrifying."

"Not to you." Coralie sighed. "The most embarrassing thing is thinking about the contrast. *My* family is going to fall all over him. They already love him from when he visited for my birthday two summers ago."

"Well, don't worry about that," said Saffron. "There's nothing Finnian loves so much as universal admiration."

I snorted, and Coralie threw my pillow at my head.

"Hey!" I chased them all out of my room. "We all have packing to do, remember."

But as they filed out, I had to resist the urge to call them back. I would miss this. Sitting around, laughing and chatting with my friends. I had thought I had another half a year, and I wasn't ready for it to end so soon.

The fourth years met the rest of the delegation on the North Road, outside the city. I had hoped Walden's experience in the Empire might mean he was assigned to be Lucas and my tutor, but apparently he was too important to be spared for so long. Instead we got Jocasta.

Lorcan accompanied us, too, along with a squad of soldiers, to escort the other fourth years back to the capital once we parted ways in Torcos. The soldiers rode on horseback while the trainees and our instructors traveled in carriages as usual.

We didn't tarry at the meeting place, so I didn't have a chance to get a good look at the rest of the delegation, or even to confirm Jasper's presence. Although I did see Julian ride past the window of our carriage at one point.

Only when we stopped for the evening at a large wayside inn did I see that Beatrice had been selected as the healing representative on the delegation. I embraced her without thinking, and she accepted the gesture with a warm smile.

"Elena! It is lovely to see you again."

"I'm sorry," I said, quickly stepping back. "It's just nice to see a familiar face."

"Don't apologize," she said. "We are practically becoming old friends, you and I."

"Where's Reese?" I asked, looking around for her younger cousin. I had never seen her without him somewhere in tow.

"He does not accompany us on this occasion. His expertise is needed at the front, unfortunately. Only I could be spared."

I frowned. Beatrice might be a Stantorn, but I would never suspect her of wishing harm on anyone. Reese, on the other hand, had been the mage in attendance when one of our intelligencers got murdered before imparting crucial information. He was one of my lead suspects. I didn't like the idea that he had been left at the front, free from Beatrice's supervision.

"Yes," Beatrice said, unaware of my suspicions. "It's a great pity for him to miss such an opportunity. But I have the most experience with research and development of new healing compositions, so Dashiell decided I must be the one to go. We are hoping the Sekalis might have knowledge and healing techniques unknown to us."

"Well I, for one, am glad to have you along," I said. Whatever suspicions I might have of Reese, there was nothing I could do about them from here.

"Elena!" Jasper called my name, and I turned to greet him. "What an adventure!" He looked more excited than I had seen him since his graduation.

A surge of gratitude filled me to find myself surrounded by so many friendly faces on such an intimidating journey. I smiled at Jasper, and he slung an arm around my shoulders.

"Tell me, do I need to launch into protective older brother mode?" asked a drawling voice from my right.

I glared at Julian, but he ignored me, approaching us with a lazy smile.

Jasper stiffened beside me, dropping his arm. I expected him to ask what Julian meant, but he gave a small, tight bow to the mage instead.

"Lord Julian of Devoras, I presume?"

It sounded strange to hear the general honorific for mages on his lips. Especially directed toward Julian. My brother might be a prodigy, and he might have lived beside mages for four years, just as I had, but he had never been accepted into their midst. I pulled him upright.

"You're my brother. He's my brother. I'm sure we don't need all this formality."

He straightened, his shoulders still tight, and gave Julian a direct look.

"Do we not, Your Lordship?" The challenge in his voice was clear despite his respectful words.

Julian hesitated, his eyes flicking from Jasper to my face.

"No, I suppose we do not," he said at last, and I let out a breath I hadn't realized I was holding.

With a nod that felt more mocking than warm, he strolled away again.

"Watch out for him," Jasper said quietly. "He's clever and ambitious, for all he doesn't seem to take things too seriously."

"Julian I can handle," I said. "It's the Sekalis that worry me." And the Kallorwegians. But I didn't add that. Jasper knew nothing of my determination to end the war, and I intended to keep it that way.

A sudden thought struck me.

"Do you have to ride in a particular carriage?" I asked. "Because if not, we have room for one more in ours. And there's something I want to tell you."

He chuckled. "Considering it's you, that sounds dangerous." He hesitated. "But are you sure your mage friends won't mind?"

I shook my head. "It's just Coralie and Finnian and everyone. You met them all in Abalene, anyway."

He agreed readily at my assurances, and the next morning when we all assembled to continue our journey, he slipped into our carriage. My friends all greeted him with enough warmth to put him at ease, and I wasted no time launching into my reason for inviting him to join us.

"There's something I need to tell you," I said. "It's not something I could exactly talk about in our parents' apartment, or at the palace...It's about my ability. You've spent more time studying than any of us—studying academics at any rate. You might have some insight none of us would think of."

He frowned. "Is something wrong?"

I wrinkled my nose. "Not wrong, exactly..."

Some time later I finished the tale, and silence fell in the carriage. Jasper stared at me with an expression I didn't entirely like. I didn't want my own brother to be in awe of me.

"Unlimited energy?" he whispered. "You've cracked the secret of unlimited energy?"

I glanced at my friends before nodding.

"Elena, that makes you the most powerful mage who's ever lived." His round eyes continued to stare at me.

I shifted on my seat. "Only in terms of raw power. I still can't regrow a man's leg like Beatrice. Or...or design and build an entire building like most of the creator discipline. And half of our year can beat me in a straight sword fight."

Jasper shrugged off my caveats.

"It's still incredible," he said.

"Well, it could be," I admitted. "If I could find a way to practice and to properly study it."

"Oh, is that your issue?" he asked. "That's easy, then. You can practice on me."

CHAPTER 11

"What?!?" I jumped in my seat, bumping against Araminta on my left. "I'm not going to practice on you!"

But when I looked around the carriage, no other shocked or outraged expressions greeted me. Jasper looked matter-of-fact, and my friends a mix of thoughtful and excited.

"Why not?" Jasper asked. "You did say that commonborns have energy, too, right? I don't exactly need it for compositions."

"But you need it for regular life—walking around, and doing your work," I argued.

"But you want to learn about skimming just a little off the top, not draining someone into exhaustion. And my work doesn't exactly involve manual labor, or anything."

"You know, he's right," Finnian said. "It's a rather perfect solution. And he can tell you what he senses from his end as a non-mage. That would be interesting information."

"Why don't you try it now?" Saffron asked, leaning forward with interest.

"What is wrong with you all?" I asked, but without much feeling. They seemed agreed that it was a valid idea, and wasn't this the heart of what Lorcan was saying to me? I needed to stop trying to protect everyone around me when they didn't need to be shielded. My brother might not be a mage, but that didn't make him weak or a victim in need of my protection.

"All right," I said, slowly, building the composition in my mind. "Take energy."

I kept my eyes on my brother, and as soon as I felt my power connect to him and begin to tap into his energy, I said, "Stop."

My friends looked between me and Jasper as everyone silently considered us for a moment.

"I felt power connecting you," Araminta said at last, "but that was it." She looked around at the others. "Did any of you feel anything more?"

Finnian, Saffron, and Coralie all shook their heads.

"How do you feel?" I asked Jasper.

"Exactly the same." He regarded me suspiciously. "Did you actually do anything?"

Finnian narrowed his eyes at me. "It was an awfully quick working." He turned to Jasper. "Do you feel exhausted? Or even a little more tired than you did before?"

Jasper swung his arms as much as he could in the limited space. "I feel exactly the same. I think. I mean, I don't exactly have a precise way to measure my energy levels."

Finnian turned to me. "You're the most able to monitor energy levels, Elena. Are his lower than they were before? What about you? Can you feel the extra energy?"

I chewed on the inside of my cheek and squirmed.

"You didn't take enough to make a difference to either of you, did you?" said Coralie. "You should try again—and don't cut it off so quickly this time."

I looked over at Jasper, and he rolled his eyes at me.

"I can take more than that, Elena."

I winced. "Sorry. I'm still working this out. It's not exactly a comfortable feeling draining people I love of their energy."

His face softened. "No, I'm sorry. We shouldn't give you a hard time. The whole point of this is training, after all. Try again."

This time I did the same thing I had done with Walden, monitoring his energy and waiting until I could sense a change in it before I cut off my working.

"How do you feel now?" I asked.

He rolled his shoulders. "Mostly normal. But I did feel it that time."

"So you could actually sense it?" Finnian looked fascinated.

"Not anything specific," Jasper said. "If I hadn't known Elena was doing it, I would never have guessed anything had happened. It feels like…" He paused, thinking, before a smile spread across his face. "It feels like that moment in the middle of the afternoon, when the day's tiredness suddenly crashes over you all at once, and you start to think longingly of sweet cakes."

Araminta laughed. "I know that feeling."

"I might have noted it," Jasper said. "But I wouldn't have thought anything of it."

Finnian looked across at me, his eyes wide, but I shook my head slightly, and he said nothing. I knew what he was thinking, and I wasn't ready to hear the words aloud. If I perfected this ability, I could skim a small amount of energy from every commonborn I encountered. They wouldn't be able to sense my power, and it wouldn't harm them—but it would provide me with a limitless amount of power. The larger the army that came against me, the stronger my power would become.

"We'll leave it at that for now," I said quickly. "I want to know how you feel later in the day, Jasper. Let me know if the energy drain affects you at any point."

"Yes, Mother," he said, his eyes laughing at me across the carriage.

We had made it well past half way the day before, and a shout went up from the front of the riders, although we hadn't yet stopped for the midday meal.

"Is this Torcos already?" I asked.

Finnian stuck his head out the window and whooped. Pulling back into the carriage, he grinned at Saffron.

"Home, sweet home."

She smiled and peered out the window herself. "Not quite." She turned to the rest of us. "Uncle Dashiell and Aunt Helene's estate is on the other side of the city, so we'll have to travel a bit further before a warm fire and a meal, I'm afraid."

I leaned over her to peer out the window myself. The wheels rolled over cobblestones now, and buildings had sprung up on either side of us. The rushing of the river sounded over the clatter of the horses and carriages, although the road hadn't yet brought us into view of the water. The journey had been leading us gently downhill for some time, and the air had lost its biting chill.

"It's warmer," I said, breathing deeply and appreciating the lack of bite in my throat and lungs.

"Not warm enough," muttered Coralie, and Finnian slung an arm around her shoulders and pulled her against his side.

"We can't all come from the river delta," he said cheerfully.

She smiled at him, but it had a tremulous quality.

The houses and buildings were all built of a rough gray stone, giving the city a uniform look. People lined the streets, gawking at us as we rode past, and I quickly pulled back from the window. Not that any of them would recognize me, but I didn't like the feeling of being watched like a curiosity.

"Your subjects have gathered for your return," Coralie said to Finnian.

Saffron snorted. "He wishes. I think they want to see the Sekalis. It's strange living up here near the border but never seeing a sight of them."

Every one of the Sekalis had chosen to ride, which meant the townsfolk would get the opportunity they wanted. They were easy to pick out, too, despite most of the northern locals having the same golden skin and dark hair as the Sekalis themselves. On horseback the slits up the sides of their tunics were more obvious, and the embroidery on their robes glinted in the winter sun. They carried themselves differently, as well, their backs ramrod straight, and their attention always ahead, despite riding through an unfamiliar land.

The houses continued right up to the edge of the wall, visible briefly as we rumbled through the city's northern gate.

"All of this is Uncle Dashiell's land now," Saffron said quietly, and Coralie tensed, her eyes on the window.

We traveled on for a short distance further before turning off the main road. The paving remained even and smooth, however, the road comfortably wide enough for a carriage.

I had been wondering how Finnian's family would house us all, but when we passed through a new set of gates, they weren't much smaller than the ones into Torcos. Behind the walls, Duke Dashiell's home more closely resembled a village than an estate. The enormous manor house at its center had been constructed from the same rough stone as both the buildings in the city and the smaller buildings in the estate grounds, but its size alone distinguished it.

"All of the new healing recruits come here for a time," Finnian said. "The commonborn healing assistants as well as the actual healers. So we're used to hosting a crowd."

"I wrote to Mother that we were coming," Saffron said as we all piled out of the carriage. "And she said she'd already decided to spend the winter here." She turned to look at me and Araminta. "My family has a home in Torcos, but we've always spent more time out here at Uncle Dashiell's estate than we do in our own house."

"Finnian!" A voice pierced through the hubbub of our arrival, and an elegant older woman appeared, with eyes only for her son.

"Mother." He strode forward and wrapped her in an embrace.

After a moment she drew back. "And these are your friends?" She turned to us with a smile on her lips.

Finnian glanced at Coralie and paused for the barest second. "Is Father home?"

"Yes, of course," she said. "He wouldn't miss such distinguished guests. He arrived two days ago and has been readying the estate for your arrival."

"I see. Well hopefully I'll get a proper chance to talk to both of you later, despite the chaos."

Her brow crinkled slightly, and she looked at him with penetrating eyes, but he was already turning back to us.

"Yes, these are my friends. Other than Saffron, obviously, this is Araminta, Coralie, and Elena. Oh and that's Jasper, Elena's brother."

"Saffron, darling." Helene kissed her niece's cheek before turning to me. "And the Spoken Mage." She put out her hand, and when I placed my own into it, she warmly grasped it with both of hers. "It is a pleasure to host you here. I have heard a great many interesting things about you."

"Mother don't embarrass me," Finnian said lightly, his eyes flickering to Coralie. I knew what he was thinking. She was the one his mother should have been gushing over.

Helene seemed to pick up on the tension in the air because her eyes settled consideringly on Finnian. But she said nothing other than to invite us all inside.

Tucking her hand into Finnian's arm, she pulled him along beside her, leaving me to walk with Coralie. My friend gripped my arm, her hand painfully tight.

"It's so huge!" she whispered. "Somehow I didn't expect it to be so huge."

"You'll get used to it," I whispered back.

Duke Dashiell had been occupied with Lucas and the Sekalis, but he broke away to greet his son before giving nearly as warm a welcome to Beatrice.

"It's good to see you," he said to her. "I was afraid we wouldn't be able to prize you from the front lines."

"I do as my duke commands," she said with a wry smile. "Although I think you underestimate my curiosity in this instance."

The duke smiled at her. "Well, we have your usual chamber prepared for you."

"I offered to have you all share my rooms," Saffron said to Coralie, Araminta, and me. "The house will be filled to the rafters, so I figured it was the safest option or who knows where they would have put you?"

She showed us the way to a small but elegant set of rooms furnished in rose satin. A number of pallets had been lined up on the floor, and I collapsed onto one of them, stretching myself out.

"It's good to be out of that carriage."

"Not for long in your case," Saffron remarked, dumping her heavy travel cloak on her bed.

Araminta laid claim to the furthest pallet, and I waited for Coralie to take the one beside me. But she didn't appear.

I popped back upright and found her staring unseeing at the door, her breaths increasing quickly toward hyperventilation.

"Coralie!" I rushed over and pulled her to sit on Saffron's bed. "Breathe slowly. Come on, now."

"Did you see?" she asked. "His mother barely even looked at me. She was probably hoping he would fall in love with you."

"If they can't see how amazing you are, then they don't deserve to have you in their family." I glanced over at Saffron who hovered nearby with a concerned expression. "No offense, Saffron."

"Oh, I'm not worried for my sake," Coralie said. "But they're going to be so angry with Finnian. And you saw how they greeted him. It's going to be just like I always feared. I'll drive a wedge between them, and—" She broke off and pressed her eyes shut, taking a slow, deep breath.

I looked at Saffron who gazed back at me with equal concern, neither of us sure what to say. Araminta climbed over from the other side of the bed, squeezing in next to Coralie.

"It will be good for him. And them," she said.

Coralie's eyes sprang back open. "What do you mean?"

"I've seen what love looks like—real love," she said. "Because I see it in my parents' eyes when they look at each other and when they look at me. But I've also seen its absence. My father's parents nearly disowned my father for who he chose to marry."

Coralie frowned, but Araminta pressed on. "I know what it looks like, and it's obvious Finnian's parents truly love him. They want what's best for him, that's understandable. But love can be like shackles, too. When he chooses his own path—in defiance of their desires—that will be the true test."

She reached out and gripped Coralie's hand. "Their love will stand the test, I'm sure of it, and it will emerge stronger than ever. Finnian will thank you one day for showing him that his parents will love him no matter what. And they will thank you for showing them that Finnian can take his own path without being separated from them."

She grinned. "And then, one day, they'll realize what a fantastic daughter-in-law they've received, and be truly grateful."

"That will probably happen the moment you give them their first grandbaby," Saffron said with a wicked grin, and Coralie managed a chuckle.

"I think we're getting a bit ahead of ourselves. But I hope you're right."

"We are," Araminta said with feeling. "Believe me—I might not be a strong mage, but I know a great deal about complicated families."

Coralie gave her a quick hug, and I threw Araminta a grateful look. With a mage father and commonborn mother, she must have a more complicated home life than any of us. Would her words have proven true for Lucas and me as well, if the Sekalis had never proposed an alliance? But then the royal family didn't follow the usual rules.

When we joined everyone else in the vast formal dining hall, we encountered Helene before we found Finnian. This time her attention centered solely on Coralie.

"Coralie," she said, her tone hard to read. "Of Cygnet, I believe?"

Coralie nodded. "My family live in Abalene."

"So I have just heard." Helene weighed her with her eyes. "It seems you have caught my son's interest. I think it would be best if you joined me for tea tomorrow."

"Thank you, that would be lovely." Coralie's poise belied her earlier panic.

Helene nodded at us all and swept away.

"So, tea." Coralie let out a long breath and looked at Saffron. "Is that a good or bad sign?"

Saffron wrinkled her nose. "Neither, to be honest. Aunt Helene never makes up her mind about anyone without tea being involved."

"An excellent quality, if you ask me," I murmured, and Coralie laughed.

"I'll take it as a good sign."

"There you are!" Finnian appeared from the crowd, his attention on Coralie. "I spoke to my parents."

"Yes, we gathered," said Saffron. "Aunt already found us."

A gong sounded, calling us all to the long table. Duke Dashiell sat at the head of the table, his wife on his right and Lorcan on his left. Lucas sat at the foot, the Sekalis around him, and for some reason I had been placed at Lorcan's left, across from Finnian who sat beside his mother.

"You have rank now," Finnian whispered to me as our friends headed for their seats in the middle of the table.

When I gave him a doubtful look, he grinned.

"I'm not saying anyone knows exactly what it is, but you do

have it." His face fell into a more serious expression. "Don't forget it when you're in the Empire. You're not going as a trainee, but as the Spoken Mage. If you want respect, you must demand it."

I bit my lip but nodded and took my place without protest.

My stomach growled as soon as we sat, and for a while I gave the food my full attention. But as the meal began to wind down, I noticed that Dashiell's gaze seemed focused on the distant middle of the table. Following his line of sight, I could easily guess who was holding his attention.

I looked down into my plate. I wished there was something I could do to help my friend, but this was one drama that had nothing to do with me.

Lorcan, between the duke and me, must have noticed the same thing.

"She's a good student," he said quietly to the duke. "Clever, like her mother, but even more flexible in her thinking. The world is changing around us, Dashiell. Life won't be the same for our children as it's always been for us."

I felt the weight of his gaze, and kept my eyes firmly on my food, lifting another forkful to my mouth.

"Flexibility is a quality that will stand her in good stead," he finished.

The duke sighed, the sound heavy and weary.

"Forgive my insensitivity," he said, "but tell me, old friend... Would you be where you are today if things had not turned out as they did?"

Lorcan drew in an audible breath, taking several long moments before he answered.

"I cannot know what might have been, so let me answer a different question. If the choice had been mine, I would not have hesitated to choose her. Even knowing what my accomplishments might otherwise be."

Dashiell froze for a moment, his eyes on his son now, and then he nodded slowly.

"Your counsel is always wise."

He rose from the table, signaling the end of the meal, and others began to drift away also. I remained riveted in place, going over their words in my mind and trying to puzzle out their meaning. Had Lorcan once been faced with the same choice as Finnian?

"I spoke of my accomplishments," Lorcan said, as if continuing the conversation although the duke had already left.

I looked up quickly, and he gave me a half smile.

"I suppose I meant becoming Academy Head, but in truth, I suspect you are my greatest accomplishment. I think the history books will remember me as the Head who enrolled and protected the Spoken Mage."

I said nothing, unable to think of anything to say.

"It is something of a sobering reflection, if I am honest. But then, I suppose there are far worse things to be remembered for." He swirled the glass of wine in his hand. "And with that in mind, you are probably wondering about the duke's question."

"I—"

He held up a hand and smiled. "Don't bother trying to deny it. Curiosity is ever a hallmark of youth.

"When I was a mere trainee myself, I loved a fellow trainee from a minor family, much like your friend, Finnian."

"Did your family refuse to accept the match?" I asked.

He glanced at me with raised brows. "My family? I do not know. I never had the chance to introduce her to them." He paused. "She was killed in our first year at the front."

I sucked in a breath. "Oh! I'm so sorry. I didn't..." I let my words trail away, realizing there was nothing I could say.

"This was well before your time, and I have lived a great deal of life since then." He leaned forward abruptly, spearing me with his gaze. "But you never forget. It never goes away. Some things shouldn't be lost."

I stared at him, my brows drawing together in confusion, but he pushed himself back from the table and stood.

"All of you trainees can take the afternoon off. I will not conduct any training sessions for your year mates until you have departed with the delegation tomorrow morning."

He strode away, leaving me sitting alone, breathless. Had he been speaking of himself and his lost love? Or of Finnian and Coralie? Or did he speak of Lucas and me? Surely as Academy Head, he wasn't advocating our sabotaging the alliance?

Locked in conversation with Lorcan, I had missed my friends and had to find my way back to Saffron's rooms on my own. After three turns I found myself in a small sitting room that didn't look in the least familiar.

I sighed and turned back toward the door, ready to find a servant and ask for assistance. But before I could leave the room, Lucas appeared, closing the door firmly behind him.

I stared at him, wondering if my intense thoughts of him had drawn him to me.

"What are you doing here?" I asked.

"I was following you."

He took two long strides forward and pulled me into his arms, cutting off my response. Hard and fast, he pressed me against him and lowered his lips to mine.

CHAPTER 12

*H*eat raced through me, and I trembled, rising onto my tiptoes, driven by my desire to be closer to him. When he pulled away, tears streamed down my cheeks.

"Oh, Elena." He scooped me up into his arms and crossed over to a nearby sofa, sitting with me on his lap. "I shouldn't have done that."

I clutched at his jacket and sobbed harder.

For a long minute we just sat there, and he let me cry, pressing the occasional kiss against my hair.

"I really am sorry," he said when my tears eventually eased. "But this might be the last chance I ever have to do that." His hands tightened convulsively around me at the words.

"I was so sure we would find a way," I whispered. "But we're not going to, are we?"

He trembled slightly, the movement only perceptible because of the way he held me close.

"I wish I could tell you I'd thought of a way. But I haven't," he said. "I've failed you."

"No," I said. "You've done what's right, no matter the cost to you. That's never a failure."

He pressed his face into my hair. "But you're sharing in that cost. I never wanted that."

"I know you didn't."

We sat there for a long time, saying nothing, just being together.

"I'm going to train with my new ability," I said. "With Jasper."

He stirred, pushing me back a little so he could see my face more clearly.

"And it works just the same even though he's commonborn?"

I nodded.

"It's good to know that if anything goes wrong with the Sekalis, you'll have the strength you need to fight your way home," he murmured.

I frowned. "Are you expecting something to go wrong?"

"No," he said quickly. "But it never hurts to be prepared." He dropped his voice to a whisper. "If I can't have you, I at least want to know that you're safe and happy somewhere."

"But how can I be happy without you?" I whispered back, and he groaned.

"Don't say that. Please don't say that."

Voices sounded from the corridor, and we both fell silent until they passed by. Lucas stood, placing me back on my feet.

"I don't know what the Sekalis would say if they discovered we were alone together. But I'm fairly sure they would consider it a dishonor to their princess. We can't do this in the Empire."

"I know," I whispered.

But still our hands clasped tight together as we moved to the door. We paused in front of it, looking at each other without speaking. And then he took my face gently in his hands and placed the softest of kisses against my mouth.

The moment stretched out, saying what our words could not, and then he slipped out the door and was gone.

$\sim$

When my carriage rattled out of the duke's gates the next morning, I didn't look back. Jocasta was riding with me this time, and I didn't want her to see me cry. I knew I would be returning to see my friends again, but somehow the goodbyes had felt weighty and significant, as if we wouldn't be the same people when we met again.

Phineas of Stantorn, a senior member of the Royal Guard, led the delegation. As someone who was a relative of the royal family, through the queen, he made a logical choice. Especially since he had dedicated his life to the protection of the crown and spent many of those years representing the Royal Guard as a palace official. But I couldn't shake the feeling of unease that the alliance hinged on a Stantorn.

"We won't be in here long," Jocasta said, her eyes on the window. "The road intersects with the river soon." She looked across at me. "Have you ever traveled by boat?"

I shook my head. "I'm looking forward to it, actually."

"I get seasick," Jocasta said in a matter-of-fact voice.

"On a river?"

"On any water."

I grimaced. "Don't you come from the southern coast?"

She smiled slightly. "There's a reason I chose to seek a position in Corrin."

"And here you are having to ride on a boat again. I'm sorry."

She gave me a confused look. "I'm not here for you, Elena. Or for the prince," she added as an afterthought. "I'm here for the incredible opportunity for learning. The boat ride is merely a necessary evil."

"Oh. Of course. I didn't mean…" I trailed off awkwardly.

She shook her head, amusement on her face. "Relax, Elena. With me, at least, you needn't worry about offense." She regarded me thoughtfully for a moment. "I know you and I have never been close, but you're in deep waters now. And I want you to know that if you need someone to turn to, you can trust me."

"Thank you," I said, surprised.

Jocasta continued to watch me, and I had the uneasy feeling she could see right through me and knew I was struggling to imagine using her as any sort of confidante.

"Like I said, we've never had any particular connection," she said after a moment. "But that's precisely why I'm making the offer now. If there's anything our nearly four years of proximity should have shown you, it's that I don't want anything from you. I don't know how this trip is going to turn out, but it's obvious that one way or another it's going to be of great import to our kingdom. And, like it or not, you're a part of that."

"And you don't think I'm equipped to be? You think I'll need help?" If she said not to watch my words with her, then I would take that offer.

"I think you're young," she said. "Make of that what you will."

I considered her for a moment.

"Thank you. I'll take that into consideration."

"Do." She chuckled and looked back out the window. "Oh, look, the river. How excellent."

I laughed at her dry tone and peered across the carriage to see out her window. The Overon River was narrower up here, but still wide and deep. It would easily carry a large enough boat. Except for the fact that we needed to travel upriver.

"I hope Duke Magnus sent some of his best, or it's going to be a long trip," I said.

"He did," said Jocasta, moving toward the door as the carriage stopped. "I already checked."

Sure enough, two senior wind workers I didn't recognize took command, distributing us around the unadorned wooden barge in the most ideal positions for weight balance. I lost Jocasta in the shuffle but gained Jasper.

His face glowed with excitement, and he turned it into the wind.

"It feels good," he said.

"What? The water?"

"No," he smiled, "being finished with study and ready to live."

The wind workers tore the first compositions and an unnatural wave sprouted beneath us, propelling the boat forward. Jasper gasped, swayed, and gripped the railing so tightly his knuckles turned white.

"Are you all right?" I leaned in close, but he gestured for me to back off.

I did so just in time for him to throw the top half of his body over the railing and lose the contents of his stomach into the water below. When he finished heaving, he weakly wiped his sleeve across his mouth and slumped down.

"So…" I said. "That living thing?"

"Highly, highly overrated," he croaked.

I tried to suppress my laugh.

"Oh, go on and laugh," he said without looking in my direction, and my chuckle broke out.

"I think I heard we only have about ten hours of this to go," I told him.

He groaned and sank onto the wooden planks. "Wake me when this is over—if I'm still alive, that is."

I shook my head and leaned against the railing, watching the riverbank flash past. The movement of the boat thrilled me, my stomach making no protest. Apparently I should consider myself lucky.

In some places the wide trunks of ancient trees came down almost into the river itself, while in other places stretches of level, grassy ground lined the bank. I saw no sign of any humans, though, and could easily believe the forest was as impenetrable as we had been told.

When I grew bored of watching the riverbank, I worked a series of compositions to test the workings of the wind workers. I treated it like an Academy exercise, crafting my own compositions to give me information about theirs without interfering with their functionality.

In the process I realized that every other mage in our delegation had now shielded themselves, so I spent some time crafting one for myself. I would want to maintain it indefinitely once we crossed into the Empire, so I couldn't have it drawing too much power. The shielding function alone shouldn't draw enough to be noticeable unless it was called into use, but I wanted it to do more than just shield. I wanted it to also monitor any compositions that interacted with me in a way that didn't threaten physical harm, and to break down their purpose, as well as maintaining a latent awareness of the power in my general vicinity.

When I had finally crafted it to my satisfaction, I tweaked the actual composition to extend it to my brother. He had come on this delegation to protect me, but it was I who needed to protect him.

I had no way to know when we passed the border. I wasn't entirely sure anyone had a way to tell. But when the trees finally petered out and fields spread before my eyes, I knew with certainty we had entered the Sekali Empire.

The wave that had propelled us upstream slowed, pushing us gently against a simple wooden dock. The members of both delegations stirred and began to file off the boat, some of them looking nearly as green as Jasper, although I hadn't seen anyone else lose their breakfast.

"How's Jasper?" Lucas asked me quietly, appearing from nowhere amid the movement.

"Alive," Jasper said from where he still lay on the wooden planks. "Barely." He cracked his eyes open, his whole body jolting when he saw who had joined us. Somehow he pulled himself to his feet and managed a shaky bow.

"My apologies, Your Highness."

"It's good to finally meet you, Jasper," Lucas said.

Jasper looked between the prince and me. "And…and you, Your Highness."

"Shouldn't you be out leading the way?" I gestured vaguely toward the gangway.

"Perhaps," Lucas said quietly, but he didn't move. "That wasn't here four years ago." He looked at the dock. "They've built it just for us, I think."

"A sign of good faith, perhaps," Julian said from behind us. "That they truly do mean to open the border between Ardann and the Empire." He nodded at Lucas. "Your Highness."

Lucas nodded back. "Julian. It's been awhile."

"I just came over to check that all was well with my sister."

Jasper, still unsteady on his feet, stiffened at the word. I slipped a supportive shoulder beneath his arm, and he relaxed again.

"Admirable," said Lucas dryly before finally heading toward the shore.

"Let me guess," I said to Julian as I helped Jasper move forward. "You want us to leave the boat together as a reminder of our connection for whoever has come from the Sekali court to greet us."

"You know, I'm going to have to admit to Father I was wrong," Julian said. "And I hate doing that."

"What's that supposed to mean?" Jasper asked with panting breaths between each word.

"I'm afraid I showed an unusual lack of foresight," Julian said. "Not having had any interaction with our lovely Spoken Mage myself, I doubted whether she would be an asset to our family."

I muttered something extremely rude which only made Julian laugh, with the result that we looked like a picture of family amiability as we stepped onto the riverbank. Lucas had already been swept away, but officials still remained to greet us.

Less power blazed around this new collection of Sekalis, but between them, our own delegation, the boat, and the residual compositions in the river, the area hummed with power. Between all the bowing, I had a glimpse of a variety of colorful robes—including both more pale green ones and some in a darker forest green I hadn't seen before—and a number of commonborn guards in a uniform that included a long tunic of heavy leather. Before I could get a closer look, however, Jasper, Julian, and I were thrust into a comfortable carriage.

Jasper immediately positioned himself in a corner and leaned his head back, closing his eyes. The door opened again, and Jocasta climbed in before a shout rang out, and the carriage began to roll forward.

I scooted over to the window and peered out. A long row of mounted soldiers rode on either side of the string of carriages. Each carried a long wooden pole with a small yellow flag on the end that snapped in the light breeze. No doubt our cavalcade made an impressive display, although I also noticed that sharp looking spearheads tipped the poles above the flags. Decorative but also practical, then.

"Jocasta." Julian gave my instructor a lazy smile.

"Julian. Why am I not surprised you managed to worm your way onto this expedition?"

"Because I was always your favorite student?"

"Hah!"

Julian grinned at his old instructor. "So, you're here to ensure Elena and Prince Lucas continue their training, I hear."

Jocasta glanced over at me. "I think we all know that Elena and Lucas are beyond the need of any training I can give them. And they're not exactly in danger of failing their final exams. I'm here for optics, and nothing more. All mages must study for four years under the tutelage of the Academy—so here I am."

This was news to me. So we weren't to have lessons? My eyes caught on Jasper who had recovered sufficiently to open his eyes, and who was now gazing at me with a loaded expression. He had found me the night before to tell me that he felt no ill-effects of my energy skim. I didn't need him to use words now to understand what he was trying to say. My official lessons might be over, but I had training of my own to continue.

I gave him a slight nod, and he shut his eyes again, leaning his head back. The rest of us also fell silent as we gazed out the windows at the passing landscape. To the north, I could see the beginning of gentle rolling hills, while to the south, the road bordered field after field of ordered grains. If I ignored the leather-clad guards and the yellow flags, it didn't look so different from home.

We traveled for only a couple of hours before stopping for the night. I had expected that we would be hosted either in the grand estate of one of their clans, or in a large roadside inn. Instead we were ushered into a large, utilitarian wooden building that most closely resembled a military barracks.

"These wayhouses are maintained by His Imperial Majesty for the use of all official travelers," a Sekali in a forest green robe informed us.

No one in the delegation complained, although most of the Ardannians had only endured such spartan conditions during their time on the front. According to Jasper, the Mage Council had deliberated for some weeks about who to send but had eventually concluded that the course least likely to give offense was to follow the example set forth by the Sekalis themselves. We had therefore come without guards, the group made up entirely of mage representatives from the different disciplines, the only exceptions being Lucas, Jasper, and myself.

When I emerged to eat the following morning, I ran into Beatrice.

"Elena, good morning." She greeted me with a smile, but the expression quickly fell into a look of concern. "Are you all right, my dear? You look tired. Did you not sleep well?"

"Oh, no, I'm fine," I said, although her words made me realize I did feel unusually fatigued.

Narrowing her eyes, she turned from me, her gaze making a direct line for my brother who already sat at one of the long tables consuming a bowl of porridge.

"Be careful about overextending yourself," she said when she looked back at me. She placed a gentle hand on my arm. "We have no reason to fear the Sekalis mean us harm."

I flushed. So she had felt the string of power that connected me to Jasper.

"I know we don't, and I'll be careful," I promised her before hurrying in Jasper's direction.

The journey itself had been more tiring than I anticipated, and my exercises exploring the wind worker compositions meant maintaining two shields had more of an impact than I liked. I was nowhere near exhaustion or burn out, but my steps had an extra lag, and my mind felt heavy and weary. Beatrice was right that this was no time to overextend myself. And with my new ability, there was no need for me to do so.

I would let Jasper decide for himself about his shield—one small way in which I could stop needlessly sacrificing for my friends and family and let them have a say in my decision-making. Sliding into the seat next to him, I lowered my voice to a faint whisper.

"Would you feel safer with a shield?"

He looked at me sharply. "Should I feel unsafe?"

I shrugged. "Not for any specific reason that I know about. But we don't know much about the Empire. And everyone else has shielded themselves."

He frowned. "I suppose I can understand that. And I'm not saying I like feeling exposed and vulnerable..." He abruptly put down his spoon. "You're shielding me right now, aren't you?"

I nodded and glanced around to see that no one had approached too close.

"I am, but I don't know if I can keep it up on both of us when I'll have other compositions to perform. Not without feeling

153

constantly tired—a less than appealing prospect given we could be here for months. So, I was thinking…"

"Yes," he said quickly, his eyes cautioning me against saying too much out loud. "Yes, I would be more than happy to do my part. And it will be excellent training for you, as well."

I murmured, "Drain slowly," under my breath, but the rush of energy that flowed into me was still too fast, so I cut it off.

"What about 'glacially'?" Jasper suggested, and I rolled my eyes.

"That's not how it works. I don't need fancier words. I need more precision in my—" I stopped myself. "Never mind. I'll try again."

This time I spoke more slowly, interposing the mental concept of a glacial pace. But I wouldn't give Jasper the satisfaction of actually speaking the word aloud.

"Drain slowly," I whispered, and this time the flow trickled in, balanced against the flow of power that held his shield. It wouldn't be enough if something actually challenged the shield, of course, but I still had plenty of power to draw on.

Could I link them? Somehow work the two compositions in conjunction so that if the shield required more power from me, my draining composition would take more energy from Jasper? It would need limits, though. If we did face danger at any point, things might start happening too fast for me to monitor his energy levels. Still…

"Don't forget to eat," Jasper said, standing up with his empty bowl. "There will be time enough to explore every possibility later."

I grinned up at him. He knew me too well.

I ate quickly, distracted. And all too soon, I found myself back in the carriage and facing a full day on the road. We stopped at another wayhouse for the midday meal, and yet another when the sun began to set.

Beatrice found me as soon as Jasper and I entered the large dining room.

"Ah, there you are." She peered at my face. "I just wanted to check on you and make sure you're doing all right."

"Oh yes, I'm feeling much better," I said.

"Oh good." She smiled. "Did you manage to sleep in the carriage? I never can, and it always seems ridiculous how exhausted I feel after a day of sitting doing nothing."

"Oh yes, it's more tiring than you'd think," I agreed. "I'm afraid I'm not too good at sleeping upright either."

"You aren't?" She peered at me and then glanced across at Jasper, no doubt still able to sense the way my power surrounded him. A look of confusion crossed her face.

I kicked myself mentally. I felt significantly more awake than in the morning, thanks to the steady trickle of Jasper's energy, but I should have hidden that from Beatrice.

"Elena!" Julian called for me from across the far side of the room, and I gratefully took the excuse to escape, Jasper trailing along behind me.

He stood with a number of Sekalis in different colored robes. The one in the pale green robe, a different man from the one who had been part of the delegation to Corrin, stood a half step ahead of the others, and he led them all in bowing to me and murmuring polite welcomes.

"This is my sister, Elena. The Spoken Mage," Julian said. "I sat with them at lunch, and they expressed an interest in meeting you," he added as an aside to me.

"We are greatly interested in your unique ability," the green-robed Sekali said. "We have never encountered such a power in the Empire."

"And neither have we in Ardann before now," Julian said. "She's one of a kind." He put an arm around my shoulders and squeezed, as if we truly had the affection of siblings, and he was proud of me.

"I hope when we reach our capital, you will permit us to study you," the Sekali said.

I hesitated, and Julian quickly stepped in.

"Of course Elena would be more than happy to do some demonstrations for your emperor and your academics. But if you wish to conduct any tests on her, that is a more complicated matter. We would need to know your intentions and discuss the matter with the head of our delegation. I'm sure you understand."

"Certainly, certainly," the man said, before bowing again and directing us toward the food.

"I'm telling myself you were trying to protect me, not control me," I said to Julian as we took seats together at one of the long wooden tables. "But I'm not entirely succeeding."

"You aren't her keeper," Jasper said with venom in his voice.

I nudged him with my foot. I had never heard him speak like that to a mage, and I didn't want him making enemies for my sake.

Julian looked at Jasper with a cool expression and then turned to me.

"I'm neither protecting nor controlling you, if you must know. The Sekalis respect age and authority. You might be powerful, but you're also young and have no official position. They will not expect you to be free to make your own choices on such matters. They would no doubt think it foolish of us to allow such a thing." He glanced at me between mouthfuls. "And Ardann does not want to appear weak."

Jasper shoveled in his food as quickly as possible, keeping his eyes away from Julian, but I ate more slowly, considering his words. If I had sat back and let those older and more authoritative than me direct my life, where would I be now? Dead, quite possibly.

But, on the other hand, we had traveled through the Empire now for more than a day and had passed through several villages. The buildings—like the fields—had been neat and well-kept, and the people looked prosperous enough, moving busily through their day with calm focus. Their ways might be different from ours, but those ways seemed to have served the Empire well. Still, I was glad to know I would be returning to Ardann soon enough.

The chicken in my mouth turned hard and flavorless, and I could barely swallow it down. I would be returning to Ardann, but what of Lucas?

I surreptitiously examined the Sekalis eating at the tables around me, trying to imagine Lucas as one of them. As I looked, however, a frown slowly gathered on my brow. If my friends were right, and the mage with the strangely muted energy was dangerously ill, then a great many Sekalis must be equally in danger. And I must have been distracted indeed not to notice it before. All around me I could feel others just like him, including commonborns.

CHAPTER 13

By the time we emerged the next morning, I had noticed that the soldiers all had the muted energy, along with a small handful of mages. In this group, at least, it was only those wearing one of the two shades of green.

I hadn't had a chance to talk to Jasper about it, however, and his mind was clearly elsewhere as he glowered across at our carriage and at Julian who stood beside it talking to a Sekali.

"Does he have to travel with us every day?"

"He's my brother, too," I said. "Officially. And he's not someone you want as an enemy."

Jasper narrowed his eyes. "He's using you."

I looked down the row of carriages. Now that I had noticed the strangeness of so many of the Sekalis' energy, I couldn't stop noticing it.

"Perhaps," I said, distracted. "But then I'm using his family, too, remember? My allowance. My position at court."

"You don't need them. You're better than them."

I finally turned and gave Jasper my full attention.

"Maybe I don't need them, but they're helpful to me. Enough

of my life is a battle, Jasper. I don't always have to take the hard way."

He sighed. "No, of course not. I just hate the way he..." He let his words trail off.

I put a hand on his arm. "Just remember he's here because his father pulled strings for him. You're here because you earned your place as one of the only commonborn palace officials."

Beatrice walked past, and I gave his arm a quick squeeze before stepping away from him.

"Sorry, I just need to catch—" I hurried off after the healer without finishing my sentence. "Beatrice!" I called, and she stopped for me.

"Good morning, Elena. How are you feeling today?" She watched me with a quizzical look, her eyes flashing back and forth to Jasper, who stood where I had left him.

"I'm fine, it's the Sekalis I'm wondering about."

She frowned. "What do you mean?"

"Are they healthy? Can you sense anything...*strange* about them? An illness perhaps?"

I had lain awake half the night wondering about it, and in the dark hours had begun to worry that it might be some sort of contagion unknown in the south. If so, we were all in danger, surrounded by it now as we were.

Beatrice blinked and then looked around at the various Sekalis on foot or horseback.

"I...I don't know. I haven't noticed anything unusual. None of them look particularly unhealthy." She looked back at me. "Naturally I haven't done any diagnosis workings."

"No." I deflated a little. "No, of course not."

She took one of my hands in both of hers. "Are you sure you're all right, Elena?"

Lucas walked past us, his eyes catching on our strange posture as he moved toward the front carriage. Beatrice gave my hand an extra squeeze, and I flushed.

"I'm fine, truly I'm fine. I don't feel tired at all today. I just…" I took a frustrated breath. "I just feel something strange about them. The ones in the green robes. And the soldiers. Have you noticed anything different about those ones?"

"You *feel?*" Beatrice let my hand drop, her expression confused. "You mean you think there's something strange about the way they're acting?"

I shook my head. "No, they seem perfectly normal."

A strange look crossed her face, and I realized I must sound insane.

"Never mind," I said quickly. "I must have imagined it."

"Did you?" She sounded thoughtful.

I mumbled a farewell and hurried toward my carriage, Jasper joining me.

"What was that all about?" he asked.

"Later," I said as I climbed into the carriage and took one of the corners.

"Good morning," Julian drawled, but no one answered.

"A cheery group today," he said after a moment, and leaned his head back into the corner of the carriage and began to nap. Or to pretend to.

I was glad to be spared the need to talk. I had acted without thinking, and now who knew what Beatrice was thinking? I would need to be particularly careful around her from here on.

We passed more villages as we drew closer to the capital, and in each one I examined the villagers who I could spot from the window. All of them had the same shadow over their energy, although in one I glimpsed two groups of mages, only a couple of them bearing the shadow, and in another a young mother walking with her children drew my attention.

A young boy leaped about, chattering at the woman, and I

could feel the shadow over his small core of energy, as it lay over hers. She had a young girl in her arms, however, not yet old enough to walk although she sat up straight, gazing at the world around her with wide eyes. She felt just like the young children I had encountered in Ardann. Was it something that set in with age then? A weakness or an illness that took time and exposure to catch?

The other three watched the villages we passed with almost equal interest, even Julian rousing himself whenever one came into view. The buildings all looked sturdy and well built, and the people well-fed and prosperous. Some of the villages even approached the level of towns. And with each one we passed, the anticipation for our arrival at the Sekali capital of Yanshin built.

In the mid-afternoon we reached another river. I knew from maps that it was the same River Abneris that marked the border between Ardann and Kallorway further south, but it was hard to think of it as such.

Here the water broadened for a short stretch, becoming shallow enough that we could ford it without a bridge. It took a while for all the carriages and horses to cross, however, and I took the chance to take a look at the road ahead. In the distance, I could see high walls and what looked like red tiles.

"I think I can see Yanshin," I said.

"That sounds right," Jocasta said. "It isn't far past the Abneris."

Not long later, we rolled through vast gates of solid timber which stood open ready for our arrival. I had expected our progress to slow to a crawl once we entered the city, as it always did in Corrin, but we continued at a steady pace. The surface beneath the wheels changed to smooth stones, but other than that, I wouldn't have guessed we were inside a large city.

Peering out the window, I saw people stationary on the sides of the road and in some of the windows, but we didn't appear to be competing with any traffic.

"They cleared the roads for us," Jasper said quietly, peering out the window on the other side of the carriage. "As a mark of respect?"

Julian leaned forward to look at a large building on our side of the road, and I also stared at it, but it flashed past too quickly for me to take in its purpose.

"Either that, or they don't want to give us time to examine their city," Julian said, his mouth grim. "The last delegation were kept cloistered in the palace, were they not?"

"What do they have to hide?" Jasper asked.

Julian looked across at him, and a shiver ran through me at the oddness of seeing identical expressions of wary concern on their faces. There wasn't much that united my commonborn and mageborn brothers.

"That is the question, isn't it?" said Julian.

No one answered.

Even moving at pace, it took us a while to make it to the center of the city where a vast palace housed the Sekali Emperor and his court. Unlike Corrin, I had noticed no specific distinction between zones of the city as we moved deeper in. It seemed the poorer parts inhabited by the commonborn must be located away from the main road, perhaps around the outer walls. The buildings were built from smooth gray stone, with many archways and flat roofs of red tile, elevated only by a steep peak running along the center of each roof.

When the carriages at last rolled through a second set of gates, I discovered that the imperial palace was not a single building, as I had been imagining, but a vast complex. Pitched roofs spread in many directions, often stacked up several stories high.

"It's like a city within a city," Jasper breathed.

"Some university graduate should write a book about it when we get back," Julian said casually. "Our libraries could do with some information about the Sekalis."

I glared across at him, but I could hardly call him out for the jab when Jasper had shown himself to be equally disparaging of

Julian. Sighing, I turned my attention back to the palace. They would have to sort it out between them, I had other things on my mind.

Yet more Sekali officials had gathered at what looked like the primary entrance, once again with a rainbow of robes on display. As we climbed out of the carriage, I craned my neck, trying to get a glimpse of the fabled emperor, only to be informed that we would meet him at a grand banquet that night.

I examined each of the officials, my brow creasing as I did so. I expanded my attention outward to the whole courtyard. The Sekali delegation who had been with us thus far, returning home from Ardann, had melted away, but the space teemed with people.

"My Lady?" I blinked and realized someone addressed me.

In fact, an individual servant had appeared for every member of the Ardannian delegation. With a deep bow, the older woman in front of me indicated that she was to show me to a guest suite.

"She stays with me," Jocasta said.

The servant glanced between us, traces of dismay on her face.

"But, My Lady, we have prepared a suite to honor each of our guests. The Spoken Mage has been assigned one of the largest."

"Excellent," Jocasta said calmly. "We'll take that one then. But we stay together."

The woman rubbed her hands together and then bowed again.

"Very well, My Lady. As you wish it."

Even more servants appeared to take possession of our belongings, so we strolled along behind her unburdened.

"So am I too important to be left unguarded, or too young and naive to be left unsupervised?" I asked Jocasta in a low voice.

She chuckled. "Both?"

I rolled my eyes but couldn't resist smiling back.

The servant led us through a maze of passages, passing through several internal courtyards, open to the air. They all held bubbling fountains that flowed into intricately designed ponds and elaborate gardens.

"It's beautiful," I told her.

She smiled and bowed. "Thank you, My Lady. The imperial palace has a team of a thousand gardeners. The gardens are the finest in the Empire."

"A *thousand* gardeners?" I stared at her wide-eyed.

"His Imperial Majesty loves his gardens," the woman said.

I glanced at Jocasta who had raised both brows. No wonder Ardann needed this alliance. The Sekali Empire must be vast and populous indeed.

At last we reached our suite. The large, airy rooms were decorated in yellow and red, and the servant promised that a second bed would be fetched and placed in the enormous dressing room.

"I can't imagine what they thought I would do with all this space on my own," I whispered to Jocasta when the Sekali crossed over to the outer door.

"Be impressed, I imagine," she said.

The woman stopped at the door and gave another deep bow.

"I have been assigned to your care for the duration of your stay. If you should need anything, anything at all, do not hesitate to ask me."

"What's your name?" I asked.

"Mei, My Lady."

"It's nice to meet you, Mei." I bowed. I was getting enough practice that the movement might soon come naturally.

"I am most honored," she said. "And I will be back shortly with ladies to assist you in dressing for this evening."

As soon as she had backed from the room, I turned to Jocasta.

"I don't like that they've separated us all and spread us out."

"I don't think we're too spread out, actually," she said. "I was following our path here, and it was circuitous. And just before we entered the suite, I saw Lucas being shown into the one next door."

"Next door?" Some of my unease lifted.

Jocasta shrugged. "I think that was a tour of sorts, designed to impress and overwhelm us. We all probably got led here via different routes."

I sank onto the bed. "Well, it worked."

"You'd better gird yourself," she said. "I imagine it's only beginning. This grand fete tonight will probably be eye-opening."

Mei reappeared much more quickly than I had been expecting, four young servants in tow. Each greeted us with deep bows and beaming smiles, and I resigned myself to losing the remaining afternoon hours to preparation for the evening.

I had hoped I might have the chance to talk to Jasper, or even Lucas, alone, but clearly that wasn't going to happen. Certainty in my early observations had grown throughout the day, confirmed by what I sensed in the palace courtyard.

The mages wearing green robes—either forest green or pale green—all had the shadow over their energy. The mages wearing the other colored robes felt exactly like all the Ardannians. And all commonborn bore it, except for that young girl I had seen, and a couple of babies I had spied on the streets of Yanshin.

I watched the women surreptitiously as they helped to unpack and lay out our gowns along with the various tools they would use to style our hair. Nothing about them seemed remarkable in any way, and they certainly didn't act weakened or ill.

I was eager to have the opportunity to share the realization with someone because the longer I mused over it, the less it made sense. The divisions seemed to disprove the infectious disease theory. Unless the locals were aware of the issue and had segregated their roles accordingly? But that made no sense. Why would all of the commonborns and only a small segment of the mageborn be affected?

As Mei guided us to the evening's festivities, I continued to check each person we passed. I found no one who didn't match the pattern.

Elaborate paper lanterns, small balls of power at their center, no doubt fueling both their glow and their ability to float in the air, led the way into the center of the palace. As we approached the audience chamber where the banquet was to be held, we joined with the rest of the delegation.

I found myself beside Lucas and managed to whisper to him.

"If we can possibly get a chance, there's something I need to tell you."

He looked at me in swift alarm.

"What's wrong? Are you unwell?"

"What? No, no. I'm fine. Do I look unwell?"

He relaxed, his eyes gleaming appreciatively as they swept over my elegant gown.

"Not at all. I just saw you talking to Beatrice earlier, and she looked concerned."

I grimaced. "I think she might suspect I'm going mad. I wasn't as discreet as I should have been. But that's what I need to talk to you about. There's something strange going on here."

The earlier alarm sprang back into his eyes, but Phineas beckoned for his attention, eyeing me disapprovingly, and we had to let the conversation drop. The head of the delegation that had just returned from Ardann, Chen, appeared in front of the chamber doors. The green-robed, younger man from the delegation stood beside him. I had never caught his name or position, but my few encounters with the Sekalis had confirmed the general's opinion that the others in his delegation treated him with respect, despite his age.

"His Imperial Majesty waits with eagerness to welcome you," Chen said. "Please remember that it is not permitted to turn your back on His Imperial Majesty, nor to address him without first being spoken to. And we do not speak his name. To speak the name of so great a personage would show dishonor."

"Thank you for your wisdom," Phineas said with a respectful bow. "We are eager to meet him also."

The doors creaked, pulling slowly open, although I couldn't see who moved them. An enormous chamber was revealed, lined with immense red columns and filled with glowing, floating paper lanterns. A large crowd of robed Sekalis filled the space, glasses in their hands provided by servants who moved through the guests with trays.

Small creeks of pure, golden light wove around and through the guests, carrying large water lilies which floated on the light as if on water. Large, colorful butterflies, unlike any I had ever seen, fluttered throughout the crowd.

An involuntary sound of astonishment and admiration swept through the Ardannians, and the Sekali in the green robe smiled before gesturing for us to advance up the center of the room toward the distant throne.

Lucas strode beside Phineas at the front of our group, while I remained toward the rear. My nerves had started to make themselves known, but they couldn't entirely distract me from the spectacle of the room.

"Are they real?" I asked, as a butterfly almost as big as my hand fluttered past my face.

I had been speaking mainly to myself, but a Sekali accompanying our group replied.

"Mages developed the strain many years ago, and mages continue to be required to maintain the exacting environment they require to hatch. But, yes. They are real."

"They're beautiful." I shook my head. Mages in Ardann used power for decoration and adornment, but not to this extent.

My eyes strayed toward our destination. An enormous gilt throne stood on a platform at the head of the room, a smaller seat beside it. The chairs dwarfed their occupants, a man and woman several decades my senior. Just behind them, three young women stood on the platform, their hands folded in front of them, their eyes downward. They were arranged in height order, the youngest still a child. The three imperial princesses. Which of the older two was Lucas's future bride?

The whole family, even the youngest princess, wore elaborate robes in the Sekali style, the silver and gold thread of their embroidery glittering, the jewels sprinkled through the designs winking in the light of the lanterns. Their robes were yellow, the first yellow robes I had ever seen, and given the color of the guards' flags, I assumed it must be the imperial color. Their energy glowed inside them, strong and healthy.

We all stopped and bowed en masse. Lucas gave only a shallow bow, as befitted royalty, but the rest of us bent so low that I feared I might tip over. I straightened just in time.

"Welcome mages of Ardann," the emperor said in a strong voice, giving us a stately nod. "I hope you will enjoy your stay in our great empire."

"Thank you, Your Imperial Highness," said Phineas. "We look forward to a fruitful visit." He began to introduce each member of our delegation, each person bowing again after their name was announced.

The emperor sat unmoving for most of the process, a slight twitch in his eyebrows at my commonborn brother's introduction indicating more interest than he had shown for any of our senior mages. Only for Lucas did he actually speak, bidding him an individual welcome.

Whether by accident or design, Phineas introduced me last.

"And finally, Elena of Devoras, more widely known as the Spoken Mage. I understand you would be interested to see a demonstration of her abilities during our stay."

The emperor leaned forward, examining me from top to toe.

"The Spoken Mage," he said. "We are honored indeed by your presence in our court. Tonight we have a demonstration of our own for all of you. But tomorrow I hope you will indulge my curiosity."

"I would be honored to do so, Your Majesty," I said and then wondered if I should have let Phineas speak for me.

But the emperor seemed satisfied, smiling and sitting back again.

"In that case, let the festivities begin in earnest." He spoke louder, his words carrying down the room, and somewhere a gong rang out.

Immediately servers appeared with large platters laden with finger food and began to circulate among the guests. A silent server offered a platter to the emperor who made a selection before turning to say something to the empress in an undertone. Phineas gestured for us all to move away from the thrones, and we did so promptly, no one evincing any desire to linger.

"Well, that went fairly well," I heard Phineas murmur to Lucas.

"And the negotiations are to start tomorrow?" Lucas asked.

Phineas nodded an acknowledgment. "Although there is no need for you to take part personally. The emperor will not, nor any of his family. This is a matter for the bureaucrats, Your Highness."

Another gong sounded, and a ripple of anticipation swept through the crowd. Everyone pressed back, away from the central section of the room.

Five mages in wind worker blue entered the room, marching forward in perfect unison toward the cleared center. When they reached it, four peeled away to stand at the front of the watching crowd while the oldest of them remained in place. I stood too far off to see any details of the parchment he withdrew from his robe, but it looked like he had retrieved more than one. The sound of tearing filled the air.

For a moment it seemed like nothing was happening, although power rushed out from him in all directions. And then Jasper nudged me, pointing off to our left between two columns. One of the small creeks of golden light had lifted into the air, carrying the waterlilies with it, and had begun to snake toward the man.

Another soon followed and another, until the air in the middle of the room was full of dancing streams of light. The man began to flick his fingers in the direction of different sections of light, and the rivers pulsed where he pointed, flaring up for a moment as rich musical notes sounded through the room.

His fingers moved faster, dancing now like the light, and the notes cascaded over each other, creating a beautiful melody. The music crescendoed, signaling the streams to explode, tiny sparks of light fountaining into the air or descending like a waterfall. I raised my hands ready to clap, but neither the light nor the music died away, merely dropping before beginning to build again as the streams of light flashed, transforming into birds of pure energy with long elegant tails and broad wingspans. They began to make their own dance to the notes, weaving between each other through the air.

I could feel the power required to fuel the wide-reaching performance, and it shocked me.

"So much power," I whispered to Jocasta beside me. "He must have been prostrate for a week to complete a composition such as this."

She shook her head. "This isn't just one working, it's many. Didn't you see he had a whole stack of parchments? Although only one man is conducting, I'm sure all of those who just entered the room contributed compositions for it."

I examined them more closely.

"Are you sure?" I asked. "It must have taken an enormous amount of precision to patchwork the different workings together so seamlessly."

"As you said, this is too much power for a single mage. We already know they have a more communal mentality here in the Empire—this is most likely meant as a demonstration of how they can use that strength."

She turned back to the performance, angling her body away from me to signal she didn't wish to be further distracted. The birds transformed again, bursting into showers of sparks that reformed into small dragons.

A light touch on my arm made me start. Lucas had sidled up to me unseen while the rest of the room was held enthralled by the display. We drifted backward through the crowd until we stood inside a small alcove in one of the walls. I could still see flashes of light from the performance, but the crowd partially obscured it. No one looked our way.

"You needed to speak to me?" Lucas asked.

"Yes." I shook myself, trying to marshal my thoughts.

"Something about the Sekalis?" His eyes darted around the assembled crowd.

I leaned closer. "It's their energy. I thought maybe they were sick, but Beatrice hasn't noticed anything. And I've been watching more closely since then. It's all the commonborn, and all the mages with the green robes. Both shades."

"What do you mean?" He frowned. "Their energy is sick?"

"I don't know. Maybe? It just feels wrong, different. Like it's… shadowed somehow."

"Shadowed?" He stared into the distance.

"I felt it back in Ardann first, with the green-robed mage who accompanied their delegation."

His eyes swung back to me, intent.

"In Ardann? You never said anything to me."

I gave him an apologetic look. "There was only one of them, then. It seemed more like a curiosity than anything of great significance. And we haven't exactly had a lot of opportunities to talk."

He sighed. "You've been practicing?"

I nodded. "With Jasper."

"Good."

His eyes suddenly darted past me, latching onto something in a dark corner of the room where a small side corridor entered the main chamber. I spun to follow his line of sight, sucking in a shocked breath.

A servant bent over a small table. A long parchment rested on the flat surface, and the girl examined it closely. As we watched, she glanced over her shoulder, surveying the crowd. We were out of her sight, tucked into the alcove, and no one else watched her. Pulling a pen from her tunic, she pressed its tip toward the paper.

CHAPTER 14

*L*ucas and I both reacted at once.

"Stop!" he yelled, thrusting one hand into his robes and the other back, sweeping me behind him and using his body to shield me within the alcove.

I ducked beneath his arm, keeping my eyes on the girl.

"Shield!" I screamed, and power poured out from me.

It raced across the short distance and enclosed the servant. I could only hope it would be enough to contain the blast.

Those close enough to hear our shouts turned, confusion and disapproval on their faces. If my shield failed, they would all be dead. Without hesitation, I gasped out another word.

"Drain."

My power raced across the crowd, searching for any unshielded source of energy, drawing small drops from many places. Lucas seemed to have anticipated my action before I had even thought of it myself. Ripping a parchment, his power swept out, not shielding but pushing back the crowd, creating a ring of empty space around the servant girl. And ensuring no one would notice my own strange working brushing against them.

But a breath passed and then another, and nothing happened.

No explosion. No fire. The servant girl had dropped the pen, staring wide-eyed at the commotion around her, but I could see two full words on the parchment.

"I don't understand," I whispered.

Lucas stood rigid beside me, his eyes focused on the girl, wide and disbelieving.

The ripple of disruption spread, flowing through the crowd, and murmuring sounded, a counterpoint to the final climax of the music. As the ending notes rang out and the light display finished, the streams sinking back into their original positions, Phineas thrust through the crowd toward us.

I had dropped my shield, and both Lucas and I stepped forward, approaching the girl. Seeing us together so far from the others, Phineas frowned, but Lucas didn't give him time to speak.

"Do you see those words?" He pointed at the parchment. "That servant wrote them. We saw her."

A gasp sounded from the Ardannians who had arrived in Phineas's wake.

"Impossible," he said. "There was no explosion." He looked between me and Lucas. "Did you contain it somehow?"

Lucas shook his head. "Nothing whatsoever happened."

Chen appeared from the crowd. "If you will please come with me. The emperor would like to speak to you."

"Good." Lucas's voice sounded hard. "We would like to speak to him also."

Chen led us through the murmuring crowd and past the now empty thrones. A door in the wall behind them led us through to a smaller, more intimate audience chamber. The empress and princesses had disappeared, but the emperor awaited us there in an elaborate wooden chair. We stopped before him.

"You have made a disturbance at my banquet," the emperor said, his voice flat and without emotion.

"We sought only to protect your people from what appeared

to us a threat," Lucas said. "It seems you have not been entirely open with us."

Phineas stepped forward. "We do not wish to question the way you choose to run your empire, Your Majesty, but is it possible you use mages as servants?"

I could hear the incredulity in his voice.

The emperor briefly met Chen's gaze before speaking.

"Such an allocation of roles would not be an effective use of my citizens' differing abilities."

"So that girl we saw writing is not a mage?" Lucas asked.

"No, she is not." The emperor paused, and we all waited in silence, trying to absorb the meaning of his words.

"Every Sekali, regardless of their birth, is able to read and write," he said. "We do not permit any of our citizens to remain in darkness as do the southern kingdoms."

"It is not a matter of *permitting*," Lucas said stiffly.

"Perhaps," the emperor said. "You and the Kallorwegians have squandered your opportunity in blood and death."

"We are not the aggressors," Phineas started, but the emperor cut him off.

"I do not speak of your current conflict. It is small and insignificant in the history of your kingdoms and this peninsula."

I stiffened. It wasn't insignificant to Torkan, or Tobias, or Clarence. Or to their families.

"What do you speak of then?" asked Lucas.

The emperor gestured and servants sprang forward, placing large cushions throughout the room. When they had withdrawn from the room, he gestured for us to be seated on them.

"Please, join me."

Phineas hesitated, but Lucas sat smoothly, and the rest of the delegation followed.

The emperor began to speak, his voice falling into the cadence of a storyteller.

"The Sekali civilization is old. And for a long time our development was stunted by the same shackles that still bind the south. With so many of our population unable to read or write, the mage clans had to carry them on their backs."

Jasper glanced at me, and I only just refrained from rolling my eyes at him. We knew all about such a system, and the mages took as much as they gave.

"And so our mages searched without ceasing for a solution to this dilemma. And, at last, the greatest of us discovered the answer. He was the first to wear the honored green robe, as he gave birth to new life for the Empire."

"And what sort of life would that be?" Phineas asked, his brow creased.

"He discovered a composition that would block a person's ability to access power, thus rendering their written words no more than ink on a page. A permanent block."

"Permanent?" Lucas sat up straight, and I could almost see the thoughts racing through his brain, the unbelievable potential of this information.

"Yes," the emperor confirmed. "It does not matter how much they write, the act does nothing to unleash power of any sort. It is as if a wall blocks their personal connection to power—or perhaps a cocoon is a better image. They are entirely enclosed, blocked forever, free from the connection that would unleash so much destruction. We call it sealing."

"And why did you not share this composition with us?" Phineas asked.

"It is not a simple solution," the emperor said. "There is a side effect. It cannot be done by solely tying our power into parchment in the way we traditionally do compositions. It must be designed as an open composition—one that, when released, draws power directly from the mage who works it."

Phineas frowned. "Such workings are dangerous, it is true, and we discourage their use, but they can be done safely. Are you saying this working drains the mage dry?"

The emperor shook his head. "No, it does not kill the mage. But it means the mage must be present for the working. We set up careful shields around the halls where the compositions are worked, to give the working boundaries, but the mage themselves must be inside."

I frowned, confused, but I could see from Jasper's face that he already understood.

"The mage's access to power is also blocked," the emperor said. "Permanently. It is not a working to be taken lightly."

A rustle swept through the mages around me, but I sat rooted in place, my mind whirling. Jasper could read and write. And his Clara. Clemmy, my parents, Leila. Perhaps all of Kingslee. I could do that for them. But if I did so, I would never speak a composition again.

"How...how many?" My voice was quiet, but it brought silence.

The emperor leaned toward me slightly, his eyes gleaming.

"That depends," he said.

"On what?" Lucas asked, also watching me, concern on his face.

The emperor resettled himself. "It depends on the strength of the mage. Commonborns are gathered together in large groups inside our shielded halls in their second year of life, and a mage in their eighteenth year enters with them to work the sealing that blocks them all. Between sixteen and eighteen, those mages have trained with a single purpose: to extend their strength and efficiency so they may seal as many as possible."

"But not all your mages," Lucas said. "I feel power all around us."

"No, certainly not all," said the emperor. "Only those from the most honored of our clans. Only those who wear the green robes."

I blinked several times, robbed of speech. It all made sense now. The veiled energy. The pattern in who possessed it.

177

"So both colors of green robes are sealed mages?" I asked, still in shock.

"No." The emperor shook his head. "The forest green robes are worn by our administrative branch—commonborns who have passed a series of exams and won places in the administration of the Empire."

"A branch made of commonborns? Wearing mage robes?" One of the older members of the delegation spoke for the first time, outrage roughening his voice.

After everything we had just heard, of course he would choose to fixate on that.

"They are the best our kingdom has to offer, rigorously selected for their intelligence and skill," the emperor said coolly, and the mage subsided.

I glanced across at Jasper. If he had been born a Sekali, he would not only be able to read and write, but he would have won himself a position of honor and prestige and the right to wear a robe like a mage. I could see the same awareness in his eyes, changing everything.

"Even if one mage can seal many, how do you have enough mages for the purpose?" asked Lucas, his face serious as he weighed each aspect of this revelation.

"For two reasons," the emperor replied. "Although the mage's power is blocked, his bloodline remains. His children are full mages, just the same as if he had not been sealed. We have two mage clans dedicated solely to sealing our citizens. They are awarded great honor among us."

I could see the mages around me casting each other uncomfortable looks. No amount of honor would convince them to sacrifice their own power to enable commonborns to read and write.

"But how many are we talking?" Lucas leaned forward. "How many mages would it take?"

"More than you have," said the emperor.

Lucas sat back, disappointment in his eyes.

"And that is why I say that you southern kingdoms squandered your opportunity. And that is why my Empire long ago closed our borders against you."

"Our history teaches it," Chen said. "But it is hard to believe."

"No," the emperor said. "Never disbelieve the folly of men."

"And what folly are we guilty of specifically?" Lucas asked, his voice level once more, his emotions locked away.

"Here in the Empire we have many more mages than you. And not just because of our greater population. Proportionally we have a higher number. Once you were the same. Back in ancient times when you were united. A strong southern kingdom who enjoyed open trade and traffic with the great Sekali Empire."

The emperor's eyes narrowed slightly. "And then you splintered. Internal conflict led to the creation of a second capital at Corrin, and half the kingdom broke away."

"Are you saying the united kingdom was Kallorwegian?" Phineas asked, incensed.

The emperor regarded him. "It was neither Kallorwegian nor Ardannian, but Southern. But its capital was at Kallmon, if that's what you mean."

Muttering sounded around me, but I ignored it. Even if this was true—and it did seem hard to believe—it didn't matter what had once been. We had been two separate kingdoms for many centuries now, and Osborne had no right to deal out death for the expansion of his power.

It did provide some explanation, however. The words of Prince Cassius, burned into my memory, sounded in my head again. *He believes you Ardannians stand in the way of the rightful Kallorwegian possession of the entire southern half of the peninsula.* It seemed that somehow King Osborne had heard this story.

"You warred among yourselves for years," the emperor continued. "You sent teams of mages to battle one another, and they were consumed in the process, their bloodlines lost forever."

Lucas's eyes met mine. *Breach teams.*

"And why do our own history books not tell of this united southern kingdom?" Phineas asked. "Or the history books of Kallorway? I remember in my youth when we could still travel to Kallmon and access their libraries as freely as our own."

"That loss of history was the spark for us to close our borders," the emperor said. "Your ancestors, consumed by civil war and division, acted to destroy those records that might remind their people you were once brothers. The records that might speak for peace, for understanding of your enemies. They sought to ensure that the hearts of those around them would never turn back to their previous kinsmen, and they re-wrote history to serve those ends. It was inevitable that in the generations to come, the truth would eventually be forgotten. When the Empire saw what was happening, we withdrew and closed our borders. No good could come of such a thing, and we did not wish such violence and destruction to spread here."

"Destroyed all records?" Jocasta asked faintly, looking as if her librarian's heart was about to stop from shock and horror.

Was such a thing even possible? If Osborne had found out the truth of the histories without help from the Sekalis, then I suspected it had not been. But if the Kallorwegian throne had preserved true records for all this time, what catalyst had led Osborne to act on them now?

"I would like to see some of your own ancient records for myself," Lucas said. "To confirm your story."

Anger flashed in Chen's eyes at the suggestion that his emperor might be lying, but the emperor raised a hand to calm him.

"You may do so whenever you wish," he said to Lucas. "Now that you know of the sealing composition, we have nothing further to hide. It is no doubt for the best anyway."

"But this new knowledge does us little good," Lucas murmured.

"It is true that you no longer have the mage numbers to both protect, build, and feed your kingdom and also seal your commonborn populace," the emperor said. "But what you choose to do with the information we have now provided is up to you. Our mages will provide you with copies of the sealing composition if you desire it."

"We would appreciate that," Phineas said.

"I think that is enough for one evening," the emperor said. "It is not the beginning I had hoped for your visit, but we will move forward in the morning."

Phineas stood and bowed, shaking slightly. "I will be ready to convene for alliance discussions as previously planned."

Chen stood also. "As will I."

The rest of us also rose, bowing to the emperor and filing from the room. Since the Sekali dictates required us to walk backward so as not to turn our back on the emperor, I was able to see the way his eyes lingered on me until the door closed behind us.

I slept fitfully, tossing and turning as my mind turned over the enormity of what the Sekalis had told us. Some of the delegation had grumbled after we left the emperor's presence, unwilling to believe something so radical.

But Lucas had silenced them. He had used his observation of the servant girl as his reason, but his eyes flicked to me, and I knew he had another reason to believe the emperor. The same reason I did.

Before ever we had been told anything, I had sensed the way something blocked off some essential part of both the commonborn and the green-robed mages. Cocooning them, as the emperor had said. And Beatrice knew it, too. She hadn't said a word since the revelation, but as we made our way back to our suites, her eyes followed me.

When I rose early the next morning, slipping out of the suite to walk through the nearby gardens, she was waiting for me.

"You knew," she said, as soon as we crossed an arched wooden bridge and stood in a small oasis of green. "You said it to me, at the wayhouse. You asked if something was wrong with the green-robed mages and the commonborn. So tell me, Elena, how did you know?"

I kept my eyes on the pond beside us. I liked Beatrice. And I thought I trusted her. But she was a Stantorn. So how much did I really trust her?

"Elena?" she asked, a hint of steel in her kind voice. "I'm not letting you go without an answer."

I saw a vision of a commonborn leg re-growing before my eyes and shook off my doubt. She didn't deserve it.

"It turns out my unique ability doesn't end at speaking compositions," I said. "It turns out I can tap into other people's energy as well. And now that I've learned how to do that, I can sense everyone's energy. I could sense the sealing, although I didn't know what it was."

"You can access the energy of others." Her voice sounded faint. "Anyone?"

I nodded uncomfortably. "Unless they're shielded against me."

She didn't immediately produce an extra shield, and I appreciated it.

"And the prince knows." She didn't make it a question. I nodded anyway.

"So that's why he accepted the emperor's story so readily. He already had the confirmation from you."

"Yes," I whispered.

"You can access unlimited energy," she repeated, seeming to struggle to take it in. "The possibilities..." Her eyes glowed. "You could heal anything, no matter how complex or deep-rooted."

The thoughts of a healer.

"Or bring death, in equally unlimited supply," I said, my voice serious.

The glow on her face dimmed. "Of course," she said. "And we're in the middle of a war." She passed a hand over her face before glancing around the garden. "But perhaps not for long."

"Perhaps," I said without enthusiasm.

She shot me a sympathetic look but said nothing. A long moment of silence passed.

"I hope you can understand why I'm not telling people," I said at last. I shifted on the seat to face her. "Will you keep my secret?"

Beatrice hesitated and then sighed. "Of course I will, Elena. I can't see any good coming of making it general knowledge." She looked at me, concern in her face. "But that's a heavy burden for you. What do you intend to do with it?"

I suppressed a sudden urge to cry in response to her sympathy. "For now, I'll keep training and learning how to use it. I need to be able to use it seamlessly, so I never run the risk of reacting without thinking and hurting someone."

"That is an admirable goal. And I now understand how you managed to regain your energy on our first day in the carriages. I thought it strange at the time. Who did you take energy from?"

"Jasper. Since I was expending it to shield him in the first place."

"Ah, of course."

We fell silent again although I kept shooting her looks.

"What is it?" she asked eventually.

I swallowed. "You've spent so much of your life helping others. Commonborns even. When you heard about the sealing composition...did you consider..."

"Did I consider going home and working it?" she asked. "Sealing as many commonborn as I can?"

I nodded.

She heaved a sigh. "For a fleeting moment. But the thought

183

quickly passed. I have been given a gift, Elena, and I use it to the best of my ability to help others. It is simple truth to say that I have saved countless lives. In the Empire they may have healers enough, but in Ardann we do not. It would be squandering my gift to throw it away in such a fashion."

A band around my chest eased. "You don't think it's selfishness to want to cling to your power when others have none? When others can't even read or write?"

She placed a gentle hand on my shoulder.

"That entirely depends on what you do with that power, now doesn't it?"

"Elena?" Jocasta's voice called through the leaves. "Are you there?"

I squeezed Beatrice's arm gratefully and stood.

"Yes, I'm here. With Beatrice."

Jocasta emerged. "Oh, thank goodness. I didn't know where you'd gone." She nodded at the healer. "Morning, Beatrice."

"Morning," Beatrice replied.

"I don't suppose either of you are part of the alliance negotiation team," she said. "So I was thinking perhaps we should search out their library. Read the truth of this history for ourselves."

Beatrice also stood. "That sounds like an excellent idea."

The Imperial Library turned out to be a comfortingly familiar place, and being there helped settle and balance me. We encountered several more from our delegation—all of those who had attended to pursue the interests of their discipline rather than for the negotiations, in fact.

Even Julian was there, lounging in a window and watching the people who moved about the library.

"I wouldn't have picked you as much of a reader," I said, stopping beside him.

"I'm generally to be found in the most interesting place I can manage. And since they don't want me on the negotiation team, here I am."

"How the mighty have fallen," I said, my mouth twitching.

"Peace, young one," he said. "History is changing before our eyes and leading us who knows where. It is exciting enough for me."

My amusement dimmed. "Well, I'm glad someone's finding it exciting."

His expression shifted as he focused intently on my face.

"Don't tell me you're considering sealing yourself for a handful of commonborn?" He didn't sound amused anymore.

I didn't reply, and he sat up straight.

"That would be foolish in the extreme. I can see I was right when I told Father you would need a keeper."

I raised an eyebrow. "I thought you were here for yourself, and I was the favor repaid?"

He gave a mocking smile. "Haven't you ever heard that family is complicated?" The humor dropped from his face. "You have a gift unlike anything we've seen before. And from what I hear we are still far from understanding it. To throw all that away so a few commonborn can read and write?" He shook his head. "Unthinkable."

"I wouldn't expect you to understand," I said. "I'm sure such a thought never crossed your mind."

He paused for the briefest moment. "No, it didn't. And it should never have crossed yours."

I sighed and left him there, not wanting to argue the point any further. Deep in the shelves, I trailed my hand along the books and scrolls, remembering what I had thought my first time in a library, what wonders had been opened to me when I learned to read. And I held the power to give that gift to an untold number of others. Could I withhold it? Did I trust myself to meet the balance Beatrice had described?

"Elena." A familiar voice made me halt. Of course Lucas would be here, meeting me among the shelves.

He stepped toward me, stopping less than an arm's length away. But he didn't reach out and neither did I. The distance remained between us, fraught with a thousand conversations bound by other shelves and other books.

"He's right, you know. Julian," Lucas said at last.

"You heard that?"

He nodded.

"But you of all people should know that they're not just a 'handful of commonborn'. They're your subjects. And they're my family."

He looked away from me. "As a ruler, I know that I must consider the good of all, and not just a small number of individuals. Your power is even more important than Julian knows. You cannot recklessly throw it away."

I longed to step forward into his arms, to let him convince me, but this was not our shelves, it was not our library. I could not run to him for comfort here. And I could not let myself give in too easily to what I selfishly desired to be true.

"I know it never crossed Julian's mind," I said. "But equally I know that it must have crossed yours. You think always of the good of the kingdom."

"Not always," he whispered, and I turned my head away from the pain in his voice. Our moment of rebellion had been brief.

He drew a breath. "It occurred to me, of course. But the emperor is right when he said we don't have the numbers. And we cannot give up healing and farming and fighting in exchange for reading. No matter how much we might wish to."

I sighed, unable to argue with his words.

"And how many would even wish to?" I murmured.

He did not argue with me, either.

CHAPTER 15

The next day Phineas gathered the entire delegation in his suite.

"Negotiations are now underway," he said. "But it is apparent they will take some time. I have sent an urgent missive to King Stellan with the information we have just received. None of you are to communicate about it outside of this delegation until we receive his orders on how we are to proceed."

"We will proceed as we have always done," said the mage who had been shocked by the idea of commonborns wearing robes. "Personally, I'm not convinced this story is even true."

Phineas bent a disapproving stare on him. "Regardless of your feelings on the matter, you will not let any whisper of such a sentiment be heard outside this room. The last thing we need is to offend the Sekalis any more than we already have. Remember we need this alliance a great deal more than they do."

"But it's ludicrous," the man protested. "Whole clans where every member willingly blocks their own power? I find that hard to believe."

Several others nodded, their faces skeptical.

"But that's why it must be whole clans," said Jasper. "I'm sure they're conditioned from birth to believe this sealing is their purpose and duty. Surely you've seen the differences in how the Sekalis think? They have been raised from birth to believe the collective good more important than their individual desires, and to believe that bringing honor to their clan is their greatest achievement. And you can see how the mages honor those who wear the green robes."

He looked around at the assembled mages. "Just as those of us in Ardann have been raised to believe that only mages can safely read and write, and that the right to rule is therefore theirs."

The implication rang through the following silence. *It is possible to think in another way.*

I would have appreciated such a speech from anyone else. But instead I turned cold to hear my usually circumspect brother speak so boldly to mages of power and influence. Nothing else so strongly demonstrated the power of ideas to bring change. Whatever these mages thought, Ardann could not go on unchanged.

But they would not thank him for pointing it out to them.

For a moment there was silence, tension heavy in the air, and I tried to think of something to say to defuse it. I cast a desperate glance at Lucas, but it was Julian who stepped forward.

"My brother speaks the truth," he said.

A few eyebrows raised at his stretching his relationship with me to cover Jasper as well, but I could have embraced him for it. General Griffith's son claiming kinship with a powerless commonborn spoke as loudly as my brother's words, and it meant he was no longer the only target.

"You all traveled the same road I did," he said. "You saw the villages we passed. At the time I thought perhaps we had been purposely shown the most prosperous part of the Empire. But I now suspect we would find every village in a like manner, no matter where we traveled."

He spread his arms wide. "Look around you. Sekali is a prosperous place, with wealth—both of riches and of power—that we only dream of in Ardann. Could such a thing be the result of using all the resources open to them? What heights could civilization reach if reading could be shared with all? I, for one, intend to give the matter a great deal of deliberation. And I shall certainly not be doing anything to offend such wealthy and powerful people."

"You raise an excellent point," said Phineas, clearly grateful to bring the conversation back to where he had left it. "And you may all consider not offending the Sekalis to be a royal order." He glared around the group until he received nods from everyone.

"You may go," he said, and the group broke up. But as I turned to leave, he spoke again. "Not you, Elena. I need to speak to you."

I halted, as did Jasper, Julian, Lucas, and Jocasta. Phineas eyed them for a moment before sighing and ignoring their presence.

"As you are aware, the emperor is most keen to see a demonstration of your power. We have told him tomorrow afternoon."

"What sort of demonstration is he hoping for? What do you want me to do?" I asked.

"Apparently he would like to request the compositions himself," Phineas said.

"No doubt he wants to ensure you can't have regular compositions somehow prepared in advance to fool him," Lucas said.

My stomach began to churn. "Just how many people are going to be observing this demonstration?"

"We told him it would be a private audience with only a few of his top mages and advisers," Phineas said. "And he accepted that stricture remarkably readily. In truth I thought he would want to make you a spectacle for his people."

"Perhaps that is still to come," said Jocasta.

"Perhaps," Phineas acknowledged.

I glanced at them uneasily. The emperor had a lot of people. This could be a long visit.

When I finally left the suite, I matched my stride to Julian's.

"Thank you," I said. "For speaking up for Jasper."

He looked down at me. "I didn't do it for you. Didn't I already say that change is coming, and I mean to be at the forefront of it?"

I grinned, not perturbed by his words. "I seem to remember you saying family is complicated."

He rolled his eyes and then chuckled once, clapping me on the shoulder before strolling away. My chest filled with warmth as I watched him go. I had said it without thought, and for the first time I had truly meant it. Julian had somehow become family.

I had seen a storm brewing between my two brothers on this trip, but instead the opposite had happened. Jasper had spoken up for himself, and Julian had stepped up and supported him. Perhaps there was a true place in the Devoras family for me, after all. Perhaps I really did have room in my life for two older brothers.

Maybe in some way, we had all gained relatives rather than me standing alone between them, pulled one way and then the other.

～

The next day Mei led me in an entirely different direction from the formal audience chamber that had housed the welcome feast. We passed down many corridors and through what seemed like endless courtyards and gardens. Jasper walked with me, excused from the alliance negotiations to accompany me. I only hoped that was the real reason, and not that he was being excluded because of his words the day before.

He seemed calm, however, taking in everything we passed with a far more analytical eye than me. The Sekalis who crossed our path all stopped to bow to us, regardless of their status.

"Does it make you uncomfortable?" I whispered to Jasper,

glancing over my shoulder at the most recent group to have thus greeted us.

"It seems to be their way," he said, but his eyes rested on me thoughtfully.

"So they do this when you walk around on your own?"

He hesitated.

"They don't, do they?" I said.

Reluctantly he shook his head. "Not unless we are actually introduced or have some reason to converse. But they show you extra honor as the Spoken Mage. That's natural."

"Is it, though?" I frowned around me. "Our borders have been closed for centuries. I wouldn't have expected the average Sekali to even have heard of me."

"Strength and power are heard far and wide," he said.

Mei stopped ahead of us and gestured to an open door.

"The emperor awaits you."

We thanked her and proceeded through the doorway. As soon as we entered the room on the other side, she closed the door behind us. I spun, startled at the surge of power that blazed behind me.

"Be at peace," said Chen from the other side of the room. "It is merely a shield built into the structure of the room. It operates in the same way as your Academy's arena."

I looked around and realized we had been shown into a training room of some kind. A single row of benches ran down each wall, and the emperor and Chen sat directly across from us. Otherwise the room was empty.

I glanced at Jasper. "Is Lord Phineas not to attend?"

"He leads the negotiations," Chen said. "I assured him his presence here wasn't needed."

No doubt Phineas hadn't liked that. But there was nothing I could do except proceed with the demonstration as instructed.

Jasper and I crossed to stand in front of the emperor, bowing low. He still glittered, his yellow robe adorned with fine embroidery and jewels, but a more practical cut gave it a simpler look.

"I would like you to know," the emperor said, "that if it had not come out the other night, I would have taken this opportunity to inform you of our custom of sealing commonborns in the Empire."

Neither Jasper nor I said anything, but unease turned my nerves into a raging inferno. I wasn't here as an official part of the negotiations, and I wanted no private conversations or confidences from the emperor. What reason could he possibly have for offering them?

"But I get ahead of myself," the emperor said, seemingly unaffected by my silence. "First the demonstration."

Chen produced a blank piece of parchment and an elaborate pen.

"First, if you would write—"

"I cannot," I said, cutting him off and then bowing low to try to mitigate the rudeness. "I am commonborn, and though I can speak compositions, I cannot safely write without bringing harm to us all."

"Interesting." The emperor nodded, and Chen whisked the parchment and pen away.

Out of the corner of my eye, I saw Jasper watch them go with a longing expression. It pulled at my heart. If I chose to do so, I could give him the gift of words.

"We will continue straight to spoken compositions, then," the emperor said, and my mind sharpened, thoughts of Jasper falling away.

The parchment had been a test. And after three years at the Academy, I had some experience of tests. I could do this without bringing shame on my kingdom.

I had expected him to want to see something big, something showy. But Chen walked a few steps away from us and upended a bag of rice, the grains falling to the ground, bouncing across the smooth floor in all directions. Some were the usual white, but mixed among them were an equal number of black grains.

"Separate out the white grains into one pile and the black into another," Chen said.

I nodded, taking a moment to consider how to frame the composition. It appeared they wished to test not my strength, but my finesse. I chose my words and ran through them silently a couple of times to be sure I had them straight.

Then I spoke the binding words, ensuring that I used a clear, measured voice for the sake of my listeners.

"Gather the white grains to the left, and the black grains to the right," I said, visualizing the words in my mind. "End binding."

Power flowed out of me, sweeping across the grains, spreading to the furthest reaches of where they had fallen. Sliding across the polished floor, the grains flew together, the white streaming to one side while the black moved to the other.

Gathered together, they formed themselves not into shapeless piles but into the elegant shape of two lily blossoms. One white. One black. My power had obeyed not only my words but the extra instruction I had overlaid on top of the simple sentence.

When the last grain stopped moving, the sense of my power faded away, its task complete. I turned to the emperor and bowed.

"As you requested," I said.

He looked from the rice to me to Chen.

"The reports of your prowess are not exaggerated," he said. "I congratulate you. Tell me, are all fourth year trainees in Ardann as advanced?"

I thought of Lucas, and then of Araminta.

"Some are, Your Majesty. But it is true that my unique situation has forced me to advance my training in some areas in order to stay abreast of my year mates in combat."

The emperor sighed. "Ah, yes, combat. The favorite pastime of the southern kingdoms."

"Ardann does not seek conflict," I said, trying to pick my words carefully. "But we will defend ourselves when attacked. As I am sure the Empire would do also."

"We must all be ready to look to our own defense, it is true," he said.

I shifted slightly, refraining from looking over at Jasper. I didn't like the tone of the emperor's comments. We had come all this way looking for allies in our war, yet the emperor seemed to dismiss the matter.

"Let us proceed," the emperor said.

For an hour, Chen continued to bring forward complex tasks for me to complete. Gradually the effort began to wear on me, but they made no attempt to attack me or to challenge my shield, and none of the tests required any great expenditure of power. It was a far cry from the sort of testing I had most commonly encountered in Ardann.

At last, they declared it over, and Chen indicated that Jasper and I should take a seat on the ground at the emperor's feet. We sat awkwardly, our legs crossed far less elegantly in our Ardannian robes than Chen achieved in his Sekali one.

"You may perhaps wonder," the emperor said, "why I have promised openness with you, and why I called the two of you here today unaccompanied."

I glanced at Jasper. So it had not been the Ardannians who sent him away from the negotiations.

"Naturally a barrier must lie between our august selves and the primitive southerners. But among our own people, we may speak freely."

Jasper and I both stirred, exchanging another quick glance.

"I understand it is news to you to discover that you are Sekalis," he continued calmly. "But our suspicions were confirmed by a number of tests conducted by my trusted adviser on his arrival in your capital." He nodded toward Chen.

Jasper stiffened, and bile raced up the back of my throat. In some ways the Sekalis were just like the Ardannians.

"I felt no such testing," I said, unable to entirely keep the caustic note from my voice.

"Certainly such a test would have been perceptible to you," the emperor said, still calm. "So it was conducted on your brother."

Jasper made a low sound in the back of his throat but didn't speak.

"Occasionally," the emperor continued, "a member of one of our sealed clans finds the sacrifice of their power to be a burden too heavy to carry. In those instances, to prevent from infecting their clan members with their own sorrow, and to avoid the reminders of power that abound around them, they choose a life of solitude in our southern forests."

I frowned. Choose or were forced into it?

"We believe that one such sealed mage found her way across the border and into the section of trees which you know as your northern forests. Eventually she must have worked her way far enough south to meet and breed with one of your own people."

My grandfather's grandmother. We had assumed our grandfather's grandfather had strayed across the Kallorwegian border to find his bride, but perhaps it was she who had strayed. And not from Kallorway.

The emperor met my eyes. "You are a Sekali, Elena. And it is from us that you gain your ability to access power."

Jasper sucked in a breath, but I didn't look at him, already struggling to process the emperor's pronouncement.

It was all too likely he was right—to an extent. But a single mage four generations back was too distant to grant me the ability to safely control power, as evidenced by my parents and by Jasper and Clemmy. The emperor might wish to lay claim to the credit, but he did not know of the strange composition my parents had used to conceive me. My apparent Sekali blood had only provided the seed that the strange circumstances of my birth had transformed into my unique ability. Even Jasper, who shared in my strange origin, had received an entirely different ability—a mind that didn't need to access power to be exceptional.

"We may have one portion of Sekali within us," I said. "But we are many more parts Ardann."

"The emperor, in his graciousness, is willing to accept you as Sekalis, despite this flaw," Chen said.

I could see the cynical twist to Jasper's lips. Of course he was willing to accept us—given I had extraordinary abilities.

"Naturally you will remain here, among your people," the emperor said, as calmly as if commenting on the weather.

I barely bit back a startled exclamation, robbed for a moment of coherent speech.

"The Ardannians are our people," Jasper said when I remained silent.

The emperor continued on as if he had not spoken.

"Naturally we will send for the rest of your family as well, since they also bear our blood. And the four of you will be sealed at the next available ceremony, as is our way. You will find that here in the Empire we respect our commonborn—especially those of great talent, such as yourself."

Jasper's mouth, which had been opened to protest further, slowly closed, an altogether different look coming into his eyes.

Did they truly give commonborns equal respect? Was that why their delegation had included no guards or servants? Because they didn't wish to expose them to our southern prejudice? My mind raced, trying to understand the breadth of the emperor's intentions.

"You wish to have the Spoken Mage working for you?" I asked.

"We wish always to advance the good of our Empire and her

people," he said. "You are strong, perhaps the strongest child of Sekali. We believe you could seal many—far more than an ordinary mage."

The light died from Jasper's eyes.

"You wish to seal Elena?"

Chen leaned forward, displaying eagerness for the first time.

"We wish to test her power. And not only to see how many she might be able to seal. Her power works differently, and it is possible that she could somehow work the sealing in such a way as not to block her own power."

My whirling thoughts sputtered, falling away. Could such a thing be possible?

"If Elena could complete the working without blocking her own power, it would release a great many of your mages," Jasper said. "But there would only be one way to know for sure. And if it didn't work, her ability would be lost forever. Surely even you cannot want that."

"It is of no consequence," said the emperor. "The Empire's life is not measured in years but in centuries. If our experiment fails, we shall know not to conduct it on her children. Or," he paused to correct himself, "not on all of them at least. At times some experimentation is necessary before achieving a worthy outcome."

"All of them?" The words squeaked out of my mouth before I realized I had spoken.

"You shall receive great honor by serving the Empire in such a manner," Chen said.

Jasper stood abruptly. "Just to be clear. This service you speak of is breeding as many spoken mage children as possible to further serve the Empire?" He used the emperor's own word from earlier—breeding—but it sounded wrong on his lips.

"We each serve as best we are able," the emperor said.

I surged to my feet and placed a restraining hand on his arm. I could see the angry rejection in his eyes, but I had learned the wisdom of circumspection, and I had never needed it as badly as I did now—alone before a foreign emperor, but for my brother.

"Your news is overwhelming to my brother and me," I said. "We will need time to consider it."

The emperor inclined his head. "Time we have in abundance."

I kept my whirling confusion and anger tamped down as best I could, dropping into a full bow and dragging Jasper down as well. Tugging him with me, I rushed us both out of the room, almost tripping over my feet in my efforts to move quickly without turning my back on the emperor. I didn't stop when we were free of the room, propelling Jasper through a number of corridors and gardens before I let him pull me to a halt.

"I...Did you...You heard..." Jasper spluttered to a halt. "What was that?"

"That," I said grimly, "was the reason the Sekalis insisted I accompany the delegation. And the reason they showed interest in you as well, I'd warrant. You're the enticement they're dangling in case the prospect should be less than appealing for some reason."

I could hear my own sarcasm thick in my voice, but as I gazed on Jasper's face, I couldn't deny the pull of it. My brilliant brother free to pursue his genius to its fullest extent. Was it my turn to sacrifice for him after all his years of sacrificing for us?

"It wasn't like you to speak up like that in there," I said. "What happened to the brother who survived four years with the mages at the Academy and always counseled me to hold my tongue?"

"He wants to breed you like a prize cow!" Jasper exclaimed.

I knew I should tell him to keep his voice down. And I knew the seriousness of the situation we now found ourselves in. But for some reason giggles bubbled inside me, bursting out of my mouth although I tried to suppress them.

"Surely a prize mare, at least," I managed to squeeze out between giggles.

He stared at me like I'd lost my mind, and perhaps I had.

"You need time," he said, running a shaking hand through his hair. "Gracious, *I* need time! But we have to think of something. They're hoping you can work sealing compositions over and over, thus taking the role of two entire clans into one person. I can understand the attraction of that. But it's a big risk to take with a unique ability—even when they don't know the full extent. Given the risks it won't work, they seem extremely unconcerned about what they could be throwing away."

His face tightened. "I'd be excessively interested to know just how many dissatisfied sealed mages are fleeing for the forests— and if those numbers have been increasing lately."

His words instantly sobered me. "You think maybe the sealed clans are unhappy about that and are putting pressure on the emperor to find another solution?"

He shrugged. "Either that or some of those mages are deciding to run *before* they turn eighteen and seal themselves. That would disrupt the whole system. It might explain why the emperor decided to open his border and invite a delegation a few years ago. Perhaps he thought it was time to check if the southern kingdoms had made any progress on the issue of commonborns in the centuries of separation?"

"And of course, we hadn't," I said with a sigh.

He looked at me with a shadow in his eyes.

"Oh, but the emperor did discover a helpful new tool by opening the border. You. And I don't get the impression he's too used to hearing the word no."

"Don't mention this to anyone," I said, grasping his hand urgently. "Not until we've had a chance to think it fully through."

He nodded. "Who would I tell? You're the one with all the important friends."

I winced, and he slipped an apologetic arm around my shoulders.

"I didn't mean it like that," he said. "Just that I won't say anything."

"Perhaps…" I spoke slowly. "Perhaps it is not something to be instantly dismissed. You could have your power sealed, Jasper."

He swung me around to face him, looking me directly in the eyes. "I made my peace with my fate years ago, Elena. Don't throw away everything you've built just for me."

I nodded slowly, but I didn't speak any promises.

CHAPTER 16

J slept little and picked at my food at meals, the emperor's shocking pronouncements running around and around in my head. But one day became another, and he made no effort to meet with me again, nor to press for an answer.

I knew when I eventually approached him it would have to be with caution since I could think of no way to turn him down without risking a diplomatic incident at the very least. I would need help from Lucas and the diplomats to attempt it.

But I couldn't tell any of them until I knew for sure what I wanted to do. Because I had no doubt that they would have strong opinions on the matter, even if I couldn't be sure which way they would fall. No doubt they wouldn't want to lose my strength and ability—back in Ardann I was a symbol of hope, and if Cassius was to be believed, in Kallorway a symbol of fear. But the might of the Sekali Empire outweighed any one person, however strong. What if I was the cause of overturning the alliance?

And so I waited, and the days rolled on. I had plenty of time to work on my own personal training, and before long I had successfully worked out a way to tie the rate of Jasper's energy drain to the outgoing power of his shield composition.

The scare at the welcome feast had finally broken down my remaining hesitations, and I also taught myself to skim a large crowd, taking only the smallest drops from each person. Collectively, the drops filled my well, keeping me buoyed up and strong no matter how much I trained. I couldn't take energy from a mage shielded against the encroachment of power, and it seemed safer to avoid mages altogether, in case they sensed my power connecting with them. But there were enough commonborn around the palace that it didn't matter.

Even so, and despite my inner turmoil, the days began to drag. The Ardannians ate the midday and evening meals together, and I heard murmured updates about the negotiations. They weren't going well, mired in endless minutiae from all accounts.

"I hope you have been making more progress on learning some of their skill at healing," I heard Phineas say to Beatrice one night. "Because the negotiations seem to make no progress at all. It is two steps back for every one step forward. Not what we expected at all." He rubbed a hand across his face. "Looking back, I can see that all Chen's pronouncements in Corrin were couched in vague language. Now that it comes to discussing concrete terms, our way forward seems to be far less smooth than we anticipated."

Beatrice frowned. "Now that we know their biggest secret, they have shared with us more freely than they did during your last visit. And they have some interesting approaches to healing. But there is much to learn. Too much for one visit. We must secure that alliance."

"We are doing our best," Phineas said, but he sounded tired. "Today we somehow got bogged down discussing crop rotations of all things. The Sekalis have developed some new system, and their food production and population are booming as a result. Our grower representative was greatly interested, of course, but what any of it has to do with the alliance is beyond me. Sometimes I fear they are purposely stalling."

Jasper sat across from me, and our eyes met. If an increase in food production had led to a boom in population, I doubted it had been those at the top of the social tree who had been affected. No doubt they always had plentiful access to food, regardless. And if it had only been the commonborn numbers that expanded, that might be the root of the problem that had driven the emperor to Ardann in the first place. All those new toddlers, needing to be sealed. Perhaps he even had pressure on both sides from fleeing mages as well.

I couldn't talk about it with Jasper over the meal, but I could read the same thought on his face. It wasn't him I most wished I could talk to freely, anyway. But Lucas and I had even less opportunity to talk now than we had at the Academy.

I crossed paths with him at the end of the meal, however.

"I hear the negotiation isn't going well," I said to him softly.

He gave me a tormented look, and I wished I hadn't brought it up. We must be the only two people in Ardann who hoped for the alliance to fail nearly as much as we hoped for it to succeed.

Phineas appeared from nowhere, and we sprang apart guiltily, although we hadn't even been touching. As Phineas led Lucas away, I heard him murmuring that the negotiations were proving difficult enough without the prince giving the Sekalis an excuse to question his commitment to the alliance and the honor of their princess.

No wonder Lucas barely even looked in my direction at mealtimes. Even friendship was barred from us now.

His face lingered in my mind, the aching sorrow of his eyes lodging inside me. Friendship would never be enough, so even if I ended up remaining in the Empire, we would always have to maintain this distance. My head could think the words, but my heart wept and railed against them. Whichever way I turned, I saw only risk, with little hope of reward.

~

When the negotiations continued to remain mired down, and my own position continued to vacillate, I knew I needed to seek advice. But neither my old brother, nor my new one, could be trusted to be objective. And Lucas least of all.

Jocasta's words to me in the carriage came back. She had shown wisdom in her counsel to me in the past. If anyone would be objective, it was her.

That night, in our shared sitting room, I told her everything of my conversation with the emperor. She asked no questions, despite the shock on her face, letting me relate the whole encounter without interruption.

"So," I said at the end of the tale, "what do you think I should do?"

"For your own sake or for the good of the kingdom?" she asked.

I frowned. "In truth, I can't make up my mind on either, let alone decide which one weighs more with me."

She laughed, the unexpected sound filling the small room.

"Oh, Elena, I don't think it has taken you weeks to decide if you wish to block your power and start producing babies like a brood mare. You've always carried the weight of too many on your shoulders. It seems to me the real question you're wrestling with is what would be best for your family. And then whether their benefit conflicts with what would be best for the rest of the kingdom."

"Well, obviously," I said, struggling to understand her point.

She shook her head. "Somehow, against my better judgment, I can't help liking you, Elena. If anyone was to be gifted with such great powers, you were a good choice."

"Against your better judgment?" In spite of myself I smiled.

She chuckled again. "Trouble follows you which is why I've

done my best not to get involved. Life is hard enough without inviting more difficulties."

She had spoken openly, so I did the same in return.

"That's why I came to you. For objectivity, since we're not friends. Although I can see in hindsight that you have always steered me well."

She looked across the room, her eyes glued to a blank patch of wall. I waited, giving her time to think and trying not to guess at every minute change of her expression.

"I have watched you struggling for nearly four years now, Elena," she finally said. "It has seemed to me that you fought to gain a position in Ardann that would ensure freedom and security for yourself and your family. An admirable goal." She paused. "So tell me—will becoming a Sekali and bringing them here grant you all that freedom you crave?"

My brow creased as I watched her closely.

"It will give them the freedom to read and write. To expand their minds," I said. "You are a librarian, Jocasta. Surely you of all people understand the value of the written word?"

"Words are powerful, it is true," she said. "But in more ways than one. Who knows better than you that it is our voice that is most powerful of all? Written or spoken, we need our unique voices to be heard. All of us. Do you think any of you will be free to have a voice here in the Empire?"

"Do we have a voice in Ardann?" I countered quietly.

She looked at me, her face hard to read. "A commonborn Devoras with the love of a prince? I would say your voice has already brought much change."

"But maybe not enough," I said, thinking of Jasper who spent his days so close to vast troves of knowledge that remained barred to him.

"You are still young," Jocasta said, and Julian's words flashed through my mind. *Change is coming.*

If we stayed in Ardann, my family had a chance at a full future. But if we moved to Sekali, I had none. I only had to consider how my family would vote if they were given the chance to weigh in to know which path to choose. If, indeed, I had a choice.

"But what of the alliance?" I asked.

Jocasta sighed. "That I cannot advise on. I'm here as a tutor and a librarian. No one would pick me to be a diplomat."

"So I have to talk to Phineas." I didn't look forward to the conversation or to admitting how many weeks I had kept quiet.

"Or Lucas," Jocasta said. "For all his young years, he is experienced in this arena."

I bit my lip. Lucas would like it even less than Phineas. But after everything we had been through, he deserved to hear it from me. I glanced sideways at Jocasta.

"Will you help me get a moment alone with him?" I asked.

She nodded. "That much I can do."

It took her nearly a full day to maneuver an appropriate moment, but the next afternoon she led him into a small study room that opened off the library.

"I have some texts for you to study," she said as he followed her through the door. "They might be of use to you in your final exams."

He looked bemused, but he followed without demur. As soon as he saw me, though, his expression changed, his eyes flashing from Jocasta to me.

"Elena needs to speak to you," Jocasta said. She pointed at a second door. "There is another room through there. I will wait here and guard the entrance for you."

Lucas hesitated for a moment, looking like he wanted to question her, and then he glanced again at me and strode through the indicated doorway. I followed close behind, shutting the door behind us.

"Elena," he said, "I can't—"

I held up my hand. "This is important. I promise. Whatever you think this is about, it's not that." I paused to take a deep breath. "The emperor believes my non-Ardannian ancestor was a sealed Sekali mage. He is claiming that I and my brother are therefore Sekalis and must remain in the Empire. He wishes me to work a sealing composition in case the differences in my ability allow me to work it without blocking my own power."

"What?" Lucas's voice thundered in the room, and I looked toward the closed door before glaring at him.

He took a long breath through his nose, visibly working to control himself. I took the opportunity to hurry on, cringing inside as I said the words.

"And regardless of whether it seals me or not, he intends for me to remain here and produce children for him. As many as I can."

I had thought Jasper angry at the suggestion, but it was nothing to the rage that transformed Lucas's face. He closed the distance between us, grasping me by both arms and looking down into my face.

"The Sekali Emperor wants to lay claim to you and breed you like some animal?" All of his muscles stood taut, trembling from the tension, the movement passing down his arms and shaking me slightly.

"I will not allow it," he said. "I don't care how powerful he is."

"Lucas," I said, suddenly afraid. "Calm down. We have to think about this rationally. This could ruin everything. Destroy the whole alliance. We had hoped to win an ally against the Kallor-wegians. We cannot afford to gain another enemy instead."

Lucas abruptly let me go, striding up and down the short distance of the room.

"Forget the stupid alliance," he muttered angrily, "it's not as if we're making any…"

He froze as if stabbed, his whole body going rigid, and then he swung slowly around to face me.

"I was part of the delegation four years ago," he said. "When we were kept cloistered and not taken seriously. We hoped an alliance might come of it, but there was no talk of one then. When Chen arrived at the end of last year, my father thought the previous visit must have inspired their interest. That I must have made a good impression." He shook his head. "But four years is a long time to wait to follow up, don't you think?"

"What are you saying?" I asked.

"What changed in those four years? Nothing—except for one big development. You. My parents tried every trick they could think of to keep you from being included in this trip. But Chen insisted. And we could understand their curiosity, their desire to study your power. We would have felt the same way, and we wished to keep their good will."

He slammed a fist into the stone wall.

"They played us for fools," he snarled. "This whole thing has always been about luring you into the Empire. It must have been. In Ardann we thought we would have this alliance drawn up within days, and yet it has been weeks, and I couldn't tell you if we were any closer to success than we were on the day we arrived."

He looked over at me. "I don't think they ever intended to marry their precious princess to a southern savage at all."

My eyes widened. Some of the emperor's remarks came back to me in full clarity. His disdain for southerners, and his remarks about war seemed all too ominous now.

"But what about the war?" I asked. "What about Kallorway?"

Lucas looked pale and shaken. "I don't think he ever intended to help us with Kallorway."

I sat down hard on the lone chair in the room. No alliance

meant no marriage. It meant Lucas was free. But what good would it do us if the emperor meant to keep me here? And if he had really gone to such elaborate lengths to bring me here, surely he did not mean to let me go.

I stared up at Lucas. "What are we going to do?"

~

When Phineas returned to his suite after the day's negotiations, he found us waiting for him. His consternation soon turned to shock and concern. And I couldn't help but notice how his eyes lingered on Lucas. It didn't take much effort to guess his thoughts. If the Sekalis didn't want an alliance with Ardann, if they had no interest in the delegation outside of me, was the prince safe here? The older man had spent more than two decades in the Royal Guard, charged with protecting the royal family and the Ardannian throne.

"It is possible they want both," he said. "An alliance and Elena."

Lucas shook his head impatiently. "Then why prolong negotiations? Surely a completed alliance would only incline Elena to view the Empire more favorably?"

"Perhaps." Phineas's eyes dwelled again on Lucas.

"The question is what do we do now?" I asked.

Phineas rubbed the side of his face, staring fixedly into the small fire that burned in his suite's large fireplace.

"I must press more aggressively in negotiations. We must force them to reveal their hand. If they do not want an alliance, we need to know it." He drew in a long breath.

"And we must be ready to flee for our lives if necessary."

"So you agree she must say no?" Lucas sounded relieved. "If they don't want an alliance, we all flee."

Phineas turned his gaze to me. "That is not such a simple matter. Would the emperor let us go peacefully in such a circumstance? If he insists she stays, we are hardly in a position to countermand him."

Lucas caught his arm in a firm grip. "We are not sacrificing her for the rest of our safety."

Phineas sighed. "We can certainly hope it doesn't come to that. But if the choice is Elena alone or us all—including Elena? Well that is no choice at all. I know my duty."

I knew he wasn't thinking of his own safety when he said it, and it took out any sting I might otherwise have felt at his willingness to leave me behind.

"So, what should I do?" I asked.

"Wait. For now," he replied.

After so many days of uncertainty, another day of waiting should have been easy. But I moved restlessly from book to book and place to place, unable to settle. What was being discussed behind the closed doors of the negotiating chamber?

I wasn't the only one on edge, either. That morning Phineas had briefed the entire delegation under the strictest threats of secrecy because he needed everyone ready to run if things went poorly. There were fewer of us than usual in the library, and those present seemed to struggle to focus for any length of time. But admittedly I was the only one striding around the quiet shelves.

Eventually Julian accosted me, shaking his head in exasperation, and dragged me to Phineas's suite.

"I know this is where you really want to be," he said. "Leave the poor scholars in peace."

When Phineas finally arrived he looked weary and concerned, but he showed no surprise to see us. Lucas, Jasper, Jocasta, and Beatrice all followed him into the room, and my eyes flew to my brother. He had been there in the day's negotiation, and I didn't like the pale tinge to his face.

"Well?" Lucas demanded. I didn't know where he had spent the day since Phineas had insisted that only the usual negotiation team be present with him, and Lucas hadn't shown his face in the library, either.

Phineas shook his head. "They will honor a marriage alliance —but I'm not sure what good it will do us."

"What does that mean?" Lucas asked.

"I spoke in much clearer, more forceful terms than I have done previously, demanding that the exact details be laid out," Phineas said, in a grim voice. "I can't say that they exactly complied, but we did get one detail that I can only feel was intentionally withheld from us before. The emperor does not intend to honor Ardann with either his heir or his spare. They are offering his *youngest* daughter for an alliance."

Lucas drew back, horror on his face. "But she's only a child!"

"Yes, the Empire is in no rush," said Phineas. "And from the sound of it, you needn't fear their attempting to push a child bride on you—that is no more their custom than ours. No, it appears they are quite content for the negotiations to take years before everything is settled, and probably years more until the alliance is properly formalized."

A different horror filled Lucas's face. "Years? But..."

Phineas nodded, his own expression bleak. "This changes everything, of course. I think we can safely conclude that helping Ardann against Kallorway's current incursion is not on the Sekali agenda. I suspect there is only one thing in Ardann that Sekali has any real interest in."

His eyes sought me out and lingered on my face.

I flushed hot and then cold.

"What can we do?" I asked.

"I have informed Chen that in light of this new information, we must return immediately to Ardann to discuss the matter with our monarchs. He made no attempt to dissuade me from such a course of action."

Phineas paused and glanced at Jasper. "However, he did inform me once the meeting had formally concluded that you and your brother are Sekalis and will be remaining in the Empire."

"What did you say?" I asked, trying to keep my voice steady.

"Nothing," he said. "He didn't present it as a discussion."

Jasper stepped to my side.

"I don't think it has occurred to Chen or the emperor that you might refuse his offer," he said. "The emperor believes that given time and the chance to observe his empire, it will speak for itself. He truly believes that the ways of the Sekalis are vastly superior, and thus that you would inevitably choose them."

I knew in an instant Jasper was right. The emperor was as much shaped by the way he had been raised as his own people.

As we all were.

"So we have no choice," I said slowly.

"No!" Lucas stepped toward me, but Phineas blocked his way.

"The emperor has made it clear that you're a Sekali now," Phineas said. "What you do next is between him and you."

Lucas growled, thrusting Phineas's arm aside, but I kept my attention on the delegation head.

"But you think I should agree to stay? To ensure he allows the delegation to leave."

"I think you must do your duty to your prince, to your brothers, and to your people."

He met my eyes steadily. He might have just claimed I was a Sekali now, but I had no doubt which people he expected me to do my duty toward—and they didn't live in the Empire.

CHAPTER 17

*J*asper had dragged me from the room while Phineas whispered urgently to Lucas. But to my surprise, my brother made no attempt to discuss the matter with me, merely depositing me at my own suite before hurrying away himself.

I paced my rooms, my mind in turmoil as I tried to accustom myself to the idea of submitting to a life here in the Empire. Eventually I decided that I needed to talk to someone about it, or I would explode.

Since Jasper had disappeared somewhere unknown, I made my way to the suite of my other brother. To my utter surprise, I found Julian deep in consultation with Jasper. Neither seemed particularly surprised to see me.

"Phineas did everything short of order me to stay," I said, directing my question to Julian. "But what do you think I should do?"

"I think Father would prefer you come home than me, if it came to a choice," he said, nothing in his tone suggesting the words held any sting.

"I don't believe that's true," I said softly. "I've heard him talk about you all. Your father loves you. In his way."

Julian's mouth twitched. "In his way. Adroitly put."

"But in all seriousness," I said. "What should I do?"

I tried not to look toward Jasper, steeling myself for Julian's answer.

"I think you should say yes," he said. "I think it gives the rest of us the best chance. The emperor has no quarrel with Ardann. Chen has said we're free to leave, so I believe he will let us go—as long as he feels no need to keep us as tools to force your compliance."

"But what if he has no real intention of letting you go?" I asked. "He may wish to send a strong message to Ardann not to attempt to retrieve me. He knows we are weak, and already beset by Kallorway. We could not open up a second war front, no matter the provocation."

"Precisely why he will not bother with such a gesture," Julian said. "Ardann will have no choice but to let you go. I know Phineas fears for Lucas, but he has spent a lifetime imagining threats to the royal family, even where there are none. It is his job."

"You're in the Royal Guard too, if that gold robe is anything to go by," I said, nodding toward his garment.

He smiled broadly. "Ah, but I'm still young and less ingrained in my ways."

I glanced over at Jasper, surprised by his silence. He nodded at me gravely.

"Julian and I are in agreement. You should say yes."

An unexpected pain stabbed at my chest.

"You think I should stay? You think the Empire is what's best for our family?"

"What?" He stared at me in surprise. "No, of course not."

"We have discussed it at great length," Julian said.

"You have?" I looked between the two of them in astonishment.

"No need to look so surprised," he said mildly. "For once our goals are in alignment. He wants to save you, and I want to save myself." His hooded eyes laughed at me.

Jasper frowned at him before turning to me. "We think you should say yes and play along until the delegation is clear of the border. I will accompany them, ostensibly to retrieve the rest of our family. And then, you should make a run for it. With your strength, and with the element of surprise, they won't have a hope of stopping you."

"And, if they do, that's where I come in." Julian made an exaggerated bow.

"What?" I looked between them.

"I would come, but I'd be more hindrance than help." Jasper ground his teeth in frustration. "So Julian will be the one to slip away from the delegation and remain in Sekali. You'll watch each other's backs and head for Ardann as fast as you can."

I looked at Julian. "What happened to saving yourself?"

"You must be forgetting," he said. "Our father is most fearsome. I dare not return without you."

I rolled my eyes. "I'm beginning to think you just enjoy needling people, and you don't mean at least half the things you say."

"Perceptive, as always," he said, a laugh in his voice.

It took a moment for me to realize his implication, and I groaned.

"Naturally your previous comments on my brilliant perceptive skills were part of the truthful half of your pronouncements," I said.

"Naturally." He gave me a partial bow.

"Let's be serious," Jasper said. "We have a lot of planning to do."

The next morning, at my requested audience with the emperor, he evinced no surprise at my willingness to remain in the Empire. Just as Jasper had predicted. And at the same time, the Ardannian delegation departed Yanshin, with no attempt made to prevent their withdrawal. I had two highly intelligent older brothers, and together they had accurately deduced the emperor's mind.

Three days later, my confidence had dipped—a predictable consequence of three days of near solitude. I had insisted on remaining in the guest suite so Julian would be able to more easily find me, and I had barely left it other than to attend a daily instruction in the sealing composition.

I worked slowly, pretending confusion I didn't feel. They made no effort to rush me. I had insisted that I would not work the composition until my family arrived and could be sealed by it, but the Sekalis gave no indication that this precaution had been necessary. They seemed content to conduct a great deal of preparation and research first, discussing modifications and adjustments that might be possible for me alone and might perhaps prevent me from also being sealed.

This part of the training I followed with great interest, learning everything they could teach me about how the composition worked. In return, however, I gave them almost no information about how my ability operated, meaning they had little hope of arriving at any correct conclusions on their own.

But the problem occupied me day and night back in my suite as I attempted to solve it on my own. If I could work the sealing composition without sealing myself...

Given my difficulty in falling asleep, I had plenty of time to think. Even so, eventually, and with great regret, I put the idea aside. My powers had let me circumvent some things, but this consequence could not be avoided.

By the end of the third day, I had pictured the delegation's boat speeding downriver across the border so many times it appeared behind my eyelids even when I didn't call for it. Alone in my suite, I made no pretense of preparing for bed, packing the few belongings I had kept with me instead.

Every sound made me start, and every footstep sent me scurrying to the door. But the hours passed and darkness fell, and still there was no sign of Julian.

Until, at last, my door creaked open of its own accord, with no one in sight. I felt the arrival of power, however, Julian's shielding and invisibility compositions betraying his presence as clearly as did the ball of energy at his center. Thank goodness the Sekalis poured so much power into their palace and its decorations. No one would notice another clump of it, unless they had some particular reason to pay attention.

I worked my own composition, muttering the words as fast as I could, and watched my body fade before my eyes. As soon as it completely disappeared, Julian began to move, me trailing behind.

Lanterns shone throughout the gardens, despite the lateness of the hour, aiding the moon in revealing our path. I had traced the route several times on my way to and from my training, moving as casually and inconspicuously as possible, but Julian led us unerringly forward, without need of my guidance.

We met no one, and no one appeared to hinder us, despite the rapid staccato of my heart which sounded as if it could be heard throughout the palace. As agreed on previously, we made for a small side gate that would let us out into the eastern half of the city.

Three guards stood before it, their backs straight, and their eyes alert despite the lateness of the hour. I heard the faint rustle of parchment and risked a quiet whisper.

"No, don't. I have a better way."

Julian didn't know this part of the plan because he still didn't know about my extra ability, but Jasper had insisted I try it on him at least once despite my protests. With a single whispered word, I sent my power snaking out, tapping into each of the guards.

Their energy poured back into me, slamming into my body with such force that it might have overwhelmed me if I wasn't expending so much power on my own compositions as well as the one to drain their energy. My lost reserves filled to overflowing, and still their energy continued to fill me.

They stirred, swaying and glancing at each other in confusion. But I was pulling their energy too fast—they didn't have time to process what could be happening and react. Almost simultaneously they swayed and all toppled.

"Stop," I gasped instantly, cutting off the drain. With ragged breaths, I checked the lingering glow inside each of them. They were exhausted and would sleep for hours, but they would live.

A rattle sounded as the keys at one of their waists lifted into the air, carried by invisible fingers. Almost stepping on Julian's heels, I hurried to the gate, slipping through as soon as he opened it.

We had no sooner stepped through than the moon reflected off a strange flickering before me. Once, twice, and then a human form appeared in full sight. The power in his invisibility composition had worn off.

I had been waiting for it to happen, prepared to extend my own working to cover us both as soon as he appeared. But the words died on my lips, shock making me gasp and stutter instead.

"Lucas! What are you doing here?" My invisible hand reached forward to grasp his arm. "Where's Julian?"

"Never mind that right now." He was already thrusting his arm into his robe, diving for a fresh composition no doubt.

"No, never mind that. I'll do it. I have plenty of energy," I said. Hurrying to make up for my delay, I rushed out the words. But even as I said, "End binding", a shout rang out from further down the wall. Whirling, I saw a hand pointed in our direction by a guard standing at the top of the wall. Lucas had disappeared again, but I had taken too long.

"Time to run," said Lucas grimly.

He grabbed my hand and dragged me through the sleeping streets of Yanshin. We were still in hearing range when a shout went up at the gate behind us. They had discovered the sleeping guards.

Lucas ducked off the main road, pulling me through a maze of streets. I didn't know how he was finding his way, but I could sense power fanning out around him and could only assume he was using some sort of composition to guide him. I didn't waste breath asking.

My legs soon burned from the awkward run necessitated by our clasped hands, but I didn't let go. With both of us invisible, I didn't dare run the risk of lost seconds if we somehow got separated.

"They'll have sent riders ahead to the city gates," he said between panted breaths. "We'll have to fight our way out."

"Leave it to me," I said, and this time he made no speeches about sharing the burden of energy loss.

My blood thrummed, and my breath rasped through my throat, but I felt more relaxed than I had in those days of waiting, without word of my friends or family. Finally I could take action. Finally my power could do some good.

The warm hand clasping mine had something to do with the sense of surety as well. I didn't know why or how he was here, but he was. With Lucas everything felt right. We were a team again, and I believed we could do anything.

We slowed as we approached the gate, taking our time to scope out the situation. But before we could discuss a strategy, a loud gong-like sound rang out, and many heads turned in our direction. I looked down, but we were still invisible.

"We must have set off some sort of alarm composition," Lucas growled. "We need to move."

"Can you get us over that wall?" I asked, not waiting for him to respond. "I'll do the rest." I turned my attention inward, calling up the words I needed.

"Shield." I cast a bigger and wider net of security around us both. As soon as it settled into place, I whispered, "Incapacitate."

These guards were merely following orders. They probably didn't even know who they were chasing, merely that a concealed person had eliminated some of their guards. No one needed to die tonight.

My power punched toward the gathered group, immediately encountering a blockage. I poured more power into my assault, pushing harder and harder against their shields. I brimmed with energy, far more than any individual could usually carry, and I was willing to use every drop to smash through their defenses.

Even with my prestigious reserves, I began to feel tired as I pushed through layer after layer of shielding. Attacks rained down on our own shield, and my energy rushed from me even more quickly. The world spun, and Lucas gripped my arm.

"Don't take it too far," he said, his voice rough and worried.

I shook my head, forgetting he couldn't see me, and pressed on. I could feel the shields buckling, I was so close. My head whirled.

They broke, and my power rushed to each person, felling them in an instant, cutting off the strands of power that linked them like a web to the city.

"Drain," I whispered immediately, and a rush filled me as their energy poured back in my direction, clearing my head and strengthening my limbs.

"Stop," I said calmly, cutting it off well before draining anyone. With so many to draw from, and all of them already incapacitated, I had no need to cut it too close.

I glanced around and nearly screamed, clutching at Lucas

where I could feel the sturdy strength of his hand on my arm. Nothing but empty air lay beneath my feet. In my dogged focus, I hadn't even noticed the smooth movement of my own body.

Lucas had used a composition to send us floating up over the city wall. I didn't know what approach he had taken, but it must have used an outrageous amount of power. I locked myself into position, afraid to move my feet, despite knowing I had been moving before without affecting the working.

I didn't release my breath until our feet touched solid ground. And then we were off again, running across the empty ground between the city and the Abneris River.

We didn't clutch at each other this time, letting our legs fly freely across the rough dirt. Out here, in the open space, it was easy to keep track of each other from the glow of power that pulsed around each of us.

Lucas angled us south, so we would hit the river downstream from the ford. Julian and I had intended to use the ford to cross the river, but I didn't try to argue. Several attack compositions of unknown intent bounced off my shield as we ran, but still the ground flew by beneath my feet, my energy levels almost too high. I felt as if a too-long stride might send me soaring up into the air.

"Here," Lucas said, swerving in to approach the water at last.

A rough piece of brown material whisked into the air and then fell to the ground, discarded by invisible hands. A small but sturdy boat lay exposed, and when it began to push itself across the earth toward the river, I rushed forward and added my shoulder to the effort. Within moments it hit the water.

"Get in," Lucas instructed, and I didn't argue, jumping in as he pushed it the last small distance to float fully. The current tugged at the wood, trying to pull the boat out into the swiftly flowing river, but he held it steady. The side creaked and dipped lower into the water as I felt Lucas scramble into the boat beside me.

We shot off, riding the current, and I dropped the invisibility composition around us. Lucas sat at the stern, adjusting something I couldn't quite see in the darkness. I thought for a moment and then cut off all of my compositions, whispering a few words to extinguish Lucas's as well. I left behind only a warning trace, a lesser working than even a shield. Just something to let me know if any power approached us.

Lucas looked up, a question in his eyes.

"We need a different type of invisibility now," I said.

He hesitated for a moment and then nodded his agreement. My heart swelled. He trusted me.

Within moments he had the boat organized to his liking and faced himself forward, surveying the water ahead of us.

"Taking the river is a good plan," I said. "We can get off just before the forest starts and follow the edge of the trees all the way to the Overon. The forest will provide good cover, too, if we need it."

"We're taking the Abneris through the forest," he said, still not looking at me.

I frowned. "But we'll end up in the middle of the war. After the trees end, the Wall will prevent us from crossing into Ardann anywhere before Bronton."

The moonlight shone on his firm features, his eyes still set forward. "We're not going to Ardann."

CHAPTER 18

*T*he rush of the river beneath us, and the gleam of the moon overhead made the scene surreal. Winter crops soon sprouted on both sides of the bank. They loomed tall in some spots, short and fuzzy in others, their strange shapes thrown into odd relief by the moonlight.

"I don't understand," I said. "I don't understand any of this. What are you doing here? Where's Julian?"

He finally looked at me. "Did you really think I'd just walk away and leave you to the emperor like that? Without even a proper goodbye?"

He was right, I should have known better. I hadn't had the chance to see him after Jasper pulled me from Phineas's suite, the day before their departure, so there had been no opportunity to tell him my plan. I had just hoped he would forgive me when I turned up back in Ardann.

"So somehow you convinced my brothers to tell you our whole plan, and let you carry it out instead of Julian," I said.

"Does this look like your plan?" he asked.

"The boat is new," I admitted. "Also the not going to Ardann part. About that again…"

Lucas growled deep in his throat. "I was always coming back for you. I had my own plan. But your brother is extremely intelligent—"

"I'd noticed," I said dryly.

He ignored me and continued. "Jasper realized what was going on. He and Julian confronted me and told me everything. And then we made a new plan."

"They just agreed to let you return to Yanshin alone?" I asked. "And Phineas just continued on to the border without you? There's no way you could have got all the way there and back by now." I froze. "They did make it across the border, didn't they?"

"I received a composition from Julian approximately three hours ago," Lucas said. "They're across."

I relaxed again.

"Of course, you're right that Phineas would never have just let me go. So Jasper and I had to swap appearances. Phineas believes Jasper had second thoughts about leaving you all alone. He thinks that Jasper has returned to Yanshin to be with you, entrusting Julian with packing up your family and sending them to the Empire."

"Wait…are you saying?" I rounded on him so fast the boat rocked, and I had to stop and grip the wooden bench beneath me. "You're saying Jasper is currently returning to Corrin with your appearance? Are you mad? What happens when they arrive, and you disappear, and Jasper reappears? He'll be tried for treason!"

"You'll have to trust in your other brother to prevent that," Lucas said calmly. "I have left messages with them, and a truth composition will confirm their story. I didn't give them much of a choice. I was returning either way, this just ensured everyone else's safety."

"That's a big risk to take," I said.

"Like staying alone in the imperial palace with a half-baked plan to break out?" Lucas asked. "That sort of risk?"

I bit my lip. So he hadn't entirely forgiven me yet.

I struggled to even grasp the complexities such a composition would require, but I wasn't entirely surprised that as a royal he had such a working in his collection. Although no doubt it had been intended for use as a defensive measure and not to allow him to throw himself into danger.

"But where are we going?" I asked after a moment of silence.

"Kallorway," Lucas said grimly.

It wasn't exactly a surprise—if we weren't going to Ardann, where else could we be going? But I could still hardly believe it.

"What will the emperor do when he discovers you've fled?" Lucas asked. "Even if he doesn't blame Ardann, he may attempt to send his people after you. He has made it clear he has no respect for Ardann. And while the southern kingdoms are weak and divided, at war with one another and bleeding resources, we cannot stand as equals with his empire."

He clenched his teeth, his jawline tightening. "I have given it a lot of thought, and there is only one path open to me if I wish to protect both you and my kingdom. We must end the war with Kallorway."

I gulped. "I know my powers have increased, but I can't take on an entire kingdom with only you for backup. And anyway...I don't think..." I hesitated. Everything about him was grim and determined, but I couldn't not say something. "If we try to unite the southern kingdoms under Ardannian rule, we'll be almost as culpable as Kallorway."

"Ardannian rule?" he asked. "I have no desire to see my family rule in Kallmon. Any attempt to subjugate or occupy Kallorway would only serve to further weaken us both—the very thing I am attempting to prevent. No. Much as it galls me to say it, we must place our hope in Prince Cassius."

"You've changed your mind? You think he was telling the truth?"

Lucas hesitated, his silence speaking as loudly as words.

"I think that it is likely King Osborne found some ancient

history that told of his family's original domain," he said instead. "And I can see more clearly now the basis for his fear of the Sekalis and his insistence that we need a strong southern power to balance their empire—a position that previously seemed almost to border on lunacy. But he could not be more wrong in the way he has chosen to combat the threat."

The dark shape of a rock appeared before us, white water foaming around it. We had come upon it suddenly in the moonlight, and Lucas had to push the rudder hard to one side, nearly tipping us in his efforts to avoid it.

Neither of us spoke until the obstacle had been successfully navigated, and the boat was properly balanced again. Then he continued.

"Over four years ago now, the Sekalis invited an Ardannian delegation to Yanshin. King Osborne responded by unleashing an epidemic that killed hundreds and could have killed many more without the efforts of you, Beatrice and Reese. And now we learn that any alliance with the Sekalis—if such an alliance even eventuates—will not be for many years. With such a threat hanging over him, how will Osborne respond in that time? What new horrors will he unleash to decimate our kingdom? It took him two years to develop the epidemic and work out how to affect our weather without us realizing. We have time, but who knows how much?"

The moonlight made it hard to read the details of his expression, but his words still sent shivers up and down my spine.

"So," he said, "let us say rather that I hope Cassius was speaking the truth. Or some element of it, anyway." He hesitated. "And while my intelligencers have nothing concrete to report, their final message before we left Ardann did mention rumors of a rebellion. And it only makes sense. Kallorway cannot appreciate losing so many sons and daughters to the war, any more than Ardann does."

"But if he wasn't telling the truth?" I asked, barely loud

enough to be heard above the river. "If these rumors are false?"

"Then we will find another way." He sounded implacable, and I almost believed his determination would be enough to see us over any obstacle. Almost.

By the time daylight broke, we had passed into the forest, and I no longer had any great fear of pursuit. It would take time and skilled effort for the Sekalis to determine where we had gone. We had left behind no bodies for which they needed to seek vengeance, and so far they had demonstrated they preferred subtlety over speed. If they intended to retrieve me, I doubted it would be by sending soldiers into Kallorway.

The forest that pressed against the riverbank was old. Far older and wilder than the copses around Kingslee where I used to search for herbs a lifetime ago. The wide trunks told of unmeasured years, and the undergrowth grew thick and nearly impenetrable.

It was the same forest that pressed against the banks of the Overon. But somehow it had looked entirely different viewed from the railing of a royal barge as opposed to a small skiff tossed about in enemy territory.

No obvious landing places appeared, and neither of us spoke of taking a break in our wild journey, although longing thoughts of stretching my legs and moving freely had begun to fill my mind. Lucas had brought simple rations and several skins of water, and he insisted I sleep.

I didn't think rest in the small boat would be possible, but I had no sooner lain my head on the hard planks than I was asleep. When I woke, he showed me how to handle the basic rudder and bid me wake him if I encountered any trouble.

"Don't use your power to steer us," he cautioned, reading my face all too easily as I surveyed the boat's controls with discomfort. "There's no one out here to replenish your energy, and we might have need of it yet."

With a sigh I acknowledged the truth of his words and settled in for several solitary hours. A headache soon built behind my eyes from peering so intently at the sun dappled water ahead of us, but I didn't decrease my intent focus. I had nearly missed two patches of rocks already, the second one actually scraping against the hull of the boat.

It had been a near miss, rocking the boat wildly, but Lucas had somehow remained asleep. How much rest had he been getting the last few nights?

Eventually he woke, however, stretching in the small space. I watched the muscles of his shoulders and back bunch and strain. It hit me with sudden force that we were completely alone, and that no betrothal stood between us anymore.

Warmth heated my cheeks, and I spoke quickly to cover it.

"When will we leave the river?"

"As soon as we clear the forest," he replied, taking a long swig from one of the water skins.

"I've been trying to calculate the distance and the speed of the current, and work out when that might be," I said.

He raised an eyebrow inquiringly, but I shrugged apologetically.

"*Trying* being the key word, I'm afraid."

He grinned at me. "I'm hoping we'll be clear by nightfall. Then we can travel on in the darkness."

"Yes, about that," I said. "How exactly are we planning to get to Kallorway's crown prince?"

"I've brought us two robes," he said. "In wind worker blue. The Ardannian ones are close enough to the Kallorwegian robes to pass anything but a close inspection. If we keep away from any major centers, I don't think any of the locals will stop and question two mages."

"The prince of Ardann, pilfering his colleagues' robes," I said with a chuckle. "How the mighty have fallen."

"They'll thank me when I end this war, make a treaty with Kallorway's new king, and show the Sekalis that the south is not to be underestimated," he said.

I rolled my eyes. "Or probably they'll just forgive you because you're a prince."

A reluctant smile tugged at his lips. "That is also possible."

"What happens when we reach Kallmon, though?" I asked, my mind returning to more serious matters. "They're not just going to let us walk up to their crown prince."

"Fortunately for us we don't have to go that far," he said. "Cassius is two years younger than me, so he's still a trainee. And the Kallorwegian Royal Academy isn't in the capital. In fact, it's quite remote. We'll reach it long before we reach Kallmon."

"I always forget that they have an academy, too," I said.

"My father visited it once, in his own trainee days," Lucas said. "There was even talk of him doing an exchange year there. To foster ties between our kingdoms." He gave a grim laugh. "Obviously that didn't work out. Osborne ascended to the throne before it was more than a vague idea, and they attacked not long after."

He settled into a brooding silence, and I lay down to try to snatch some more sleep. Who knew when we would have the chance to rest again?

I woke with a jolt. It took me a moment to identify what had woken me. The rocking of the water had ceased. Lucas had pulled the skiff up on a small stretch of grassy riverbank, the trees barely visible in the gloom behind him.

"Welcome to Kallorway," he murmured, as I scrambled out of the boat.

Shivering, I looked around me. The air had a similar warmth

to Yanshin, and my thick cloak protected me from the night air, but it couldn't protect me from the dread that danced across my skin.

A few scattered trees could be seen to the south and the west, but mostly I saw level ground, lying cold and hard, ready for the planting that would soon begin as spring returned. Kallorway had fewer hills and more farming land than Ardann, but there were still stretches of our own kingdom that looked identical.

"It doesn't look so different," I said at last.

"It was all one kingdom once, remember," Lucas said, removing his bag from the bottom of the boat. As soon as he had done so, he pushed the boat back into the water, wading in far enough to ensure it got caught by the deeper current in the center of the river.

We stood and watched in silence as the water swept it away. How long before its careening path broke it against a patch of rocks? Long enough to confuse any attempt to track us, we hoped.

Lucas pulled out the two blue robes, and we removed our cloaks, pulling the robes on over our clothes before replacing the outer garment.

"It's a little big," I said, glancing down at myself.

Lucas regarded me. "It will pass at a glance. We just need to stay far enough away from anyone who might want to take a closer look."

I nodded and looked up to find Lucas's eyes locked on my face.

"I don't know if I've ever seen you in blue before," he said. "It looks nice."

"Not as good as healing purple will," I said, trying to defuse the charge that now seemed to fill the air between us, heating my cheeks.

He reached over and cupped my face in his hand.

"If we survive this," he whispered, "you'll never have to join a discipline."

His words made me tremble, conjuring up a future that made our current danger harder to bear.

"But I want to heal," I managed to say. "I like using my power to help people in such a tangible way."

He smiled, the expression tender and filled with admiration. "You'll be a princess, remember? If you want to heal people—or help them in any other way—you can. It just means you won't have to answer to Duke Dashiell. And you won't have to live at his estate, either—a good thing since I never want to be separated from you again."

I swayed toward him without thought, but he pulled back, the cold air rushing between us again.

"We need clear heads," he said reluctantly. "*I* need a clear head."

I licked my dry lips and nodded, looking quickly away. He was right, of course, although my treacherous body seemed more interested in being wrapped in his arms than anything else.

He hoisted his pack onto his back, and I did the same. At least whatever happened from here, we were in it together.

We traveled through the night without coming near another soul. We took small paths and minor roads where we could, encountering no one since the locals slept inside their homes, protected from the last hints of winter chill.

More than once Lucas called for a halt although he didn't seem tired. Constant combat training meant we were both in good shape, but the long hours of walking still took a toll. At least one blister was making itself known on each of my feet, and my legs ached in an entirely different way from how they had done in the boat.

When dawn began to lighten the air, I gestured toward a significant clump of trees, and Lucas nodded. We found a large bush, with an open space at its center, and crawled in to make a nest for ourselves.

After some debate, we agreed to leave only the most minimal warning composition in place while we both slept, concerned that using power would only attract attention.

We woke in the last hours of the afternoon and ate a quick meal mostly in silence. The branches of the bush pushed us close together, and my awareness of his presence made my movements clumsy and awkward.

Despite myself, my eyes moved constantly toward him, all too often catching his and holding us both in thrall until we started and continued on with our preparations. When I moved to repack my bag, my arm brushed against his, and he caught at it and held me.

"Elena—"

"No, you were right," I said quickly. "When this is over."

He hesitated before letting my arm drop and leading the way out of the bush.

"We'll reach their academy tonight," he said as we began to walk, my muscles protesting the renewed action.

I took a deep breath. "And what then?"

"We wait," he said. "We observe, and we look for an opportunity. If the trainees stay inside the Academy, then we need to work out a way to get inside."

I doubted we would get so lucky as to have Cassius come riding out and fall into our laps, but I knew nothing about how their system worked, so I said nothing.

Lucas drew a deep breath. "Our plans can only take us so far. Then it will depend on how Cassius responds." He looked over at me. "I trust you, Elena. We make a good team."

Somehow I managed a smile. We did make a good team, but my stomach still churned at his trust. There were far too many ways our fragile plan could go wrong.

"If it comes to it," I muttered, "if we end up hauled before Osborne, I only need the chance to work one composition."

Lucas threw me a sharp look.

"I didn't waste my extra three days in Yanshin," I told him. "I am now intricately familiar with the sealing composition."

Lucas stopped short. It took me a couple of steps to stop as well, and I turned back to him.

"It would be worth it to stop the war," I said. "If Osborne finds himself stripped of his power, he'll have enough problems to keep all his attention firmly on his own throne."

"Your abilities are too valuable to be sealed," Lucas protested.

I shook my head. "No. Life is too valuable. And this war has been bleeding us for too long. I'm not saying I *want* to be sealed, but if it comes to it, I'm ready to act."

Lucas looked like he wanted to argue, but after a silent moment he began to walk again. Neither of us spoke after that for several hours.

We stopped three times to rest and eat before Lucas pointed into the distance.

"There. Can you see it?"

The beginnings of dawn had lightened the darkness around us, but I could still barely make out a distant building. It loomed in the sky, its star-less outline all I could see.

Almost reflexively I said, "Shield," directing the protection to cover us both. Lucas glanced at me but said nothing.

"We need to find a place to hole up," he said. "One that will keep us in view of it."

"We need to get closer first," I replied.

He nodded and resumed our progress, although we moved more carefully now. Gradually the building grew clearer, the sun rising closer toward the horizon.

Just as I was about to whisper that perhaps we had gone close enough, he held up a hand to stop me. I froze, straining to hear what had startled him. A moment later I gave myself a mental kick and focused in on my ability to sense power and energy rather than my hearing.

Within seconds, I felt it too. Ahead of us, hidden by some

trees, two people moved in our direction. I stepped closer to Lucas, dropping my voice.

"Shall I hide us?"

He hesitated. "They might just be local farmers."

"And if they're not?"

"We might attract worse attention by hiding ourselves. They have most likely already felt our shields."

I winced. I hadn't asked him when I set the shield, and now I might have gotten us both into trouble.

"I'm sorry," I whispered, "I didn't think of—"

My words cut off when the two figures stepped from behind the shielding greenery. I had only ever met a single Kallorwegian, and he stood before me now, looking directly at us.

Prince Cassius lengthened his stride, hurrying in our direction, and Lucas tensed beside me. Every instinct told me to run or to hide or to fight, but this is why we had come.

"Elena. Lucas." Cassius regarded us without the least trace of surprise in his eyes, and every one of my nerves quivered. "I thought I might see you around here."

His dark brown eyes held the same excitement I remembered from the Battle of Abneris. But I had seen sincerity in them then as well. Now I saw only a disquieting pleasure.

"Cassius." Lucas gave him a curt nod.

"You were very easy to find," the Kallorwegian prince said.

I straightened. "Who said we were trying to hide?" The time had come to be bold. "We've come to end the war, just as you said."

"Excellent," he said with something like glee. "With your help my father will be ruling in Corrin within weeks."

I sucked in a breath, throwing a glance at Lucas. His eyes hadn't left the other prince.

"But what of the—" I began.

"The rebellion?" He laughed, a fanatical gleam entering his eyes. "All in Kallorway respect the power of my father and our rightful claim over Ardann. And now my father will be victorious —and I will be the instrument of that victory."

I swallowed and took a step backward. I should have known better than to ever consider Cassius might have been telling the truth.

"Lucas…" I knew my voice sounded panicked, and I wished we'd discussed in more detail what to do in this eventuality.

"Don't worry," Lucas said quietly, "there's only two of them."

Cassius smiled, his expression taking on a cruel hue that I hadn't seen the last time we met.

"Yes, indeed," he said. "I am not the fool here. I have not brought a legion for you to suck dry."

I gasped, my eyes flying to Lucas, and for the first time he faltered. We had feared discovering the rebellion was a lie, but we had never considered the possibility that Cassius could know my secret.

But neither of us had the chance to speak before the mage standing behind Cassius tore a parchment. A battering assault of pure power threw itself against my shield.

I tried to decide on the best composition to use, only to hesitate. Lucas usually wanted me to take the defense, holding as long as possible while he disarmed our opponents. And from the force of their attack, I might need every drop I had.

Lucas tore a composition of his own, and a tree tore itself from the ground and flew like a spear toward Cassius. The other prince didn't even flinch, a smile lingering on his face as his shield held.

His companion tore two more attack compositions, and yet more of my energy drained out as my power held our shield against him.

Lucas already had another composition in his hands, but his eyes had narrowed, jumping between Cassius and his companion. Cassius drew out several parchments from his robe and tore them one by one. Shield after shield flared into existence around them until the two of them stood behind multiple layers of shielding.

Meanwhile, the other mage sent yet another attack our way.

"So much power," I muttered, my knees wobbling.

My eyes lingered on Cassius. All those shields used up when they might not even be needed. So much strength thrown away. He didn't fight like other mages, attempting to preserve as many of their compositions as possible.

I reached out desperately. Perhaps there was someone else nearby, after all, who could lend power to my defense. But the land stretched away from me empty, the inhabitants of the Academy still too far away to reach.

Lucas caught me beneath the arm as I swayed again. I could see stark fear in his eyes as he looked at me, and I knew it wasn't for himself.

"We have to surrender," he muttered.

I tried to protest, but he shook his head.

"If these endless attacks keep up, they'll burn you dry. He said they plan to take Ardann with our help. I don't know what that means, but I'm fairly sure he doesn't mean to kill us."

Another composition hit my shield, and Lucas didn't wait for my agreement.

"We surrender," he called.

The second mage paused, another composition undamaged in his hands, and looked to Cassius for instruction.

"Then let your shield fall," he said.

Reluctantly, every part of me screaming in protest, I murmured, "Stop."

My power cut off, leaving us exposed and vulnerable.

Cassius smiled and took his time removing a small curl of parchment.

"See, there," he said. "I knew they would be sensible."

He ripped it, his power rushing toward us. Lucas's arms pulled me close, and then the world went black.

CHAPTER 19

*W*hen my consciousness returned, my body spasmed, gagging and retching. For a long moment I could make sense of nothing except my body's urgent need to clear my airway.

"Elena! Elena!" Finally Lucas's voice filtered through. "Stop and breathe," he called. "Just breathe."

I sucked in a desperate flow of air through my nose and forced my mind to take control over my body. *I can breathe. I can breathe. I can breathe,* I repeated to myself over and over, until the spasms and gagging subsided.

A wet, foul wad of material filled my mouth, held in place by a gag. But my nose was clear, and I continued to take deep calming breaths. My arms stretched back tightly, my hands bound behind my back, but my legs were free. Squirming, I managed to shuffle myself around and on to my knees, facing toward Lucas's voice.

He sat, his back against a large barrel and his face full of concern as he watched me. His own hands had been bound similarly to mine, but his mouth was free. Some sort of composition-fueled light source glowed on the wall near him, dimly illuminating our prison. I startled to shuffle on my knees toward him, but he quickly shook his head.

"No, stay where you are. Can you feel it?"

I paused and paid closer attention to the room. It appeared to be a subterranean storage room of some kind, several barrels scattered throughout it. No visible barrier stood between Lucas, on one side of the room, and me, on the other, but I could feel the telltale presence of power, extending like an invisible wall down the middle of the room.

"I've already tried everything I can think of," he said. "I can't get past it." He grimaced. "And it stings to try."

I looked around again, noting the only door—made of sturdy wood—stood on his side. He followed my gaze.

"Locked, of course. And I've searched these barrels too. Unless you can think of a use for hundreds of potatoes, they're not going to be much help."

I groaned, about the only noise I could manage clearly. Stretching out my senses, I felt people moving around above us, but none seemed to be coming in our direction.

I frowned questioningly at Lucas, letting my eyes rove around the room.

"As far as I can tell, I think we're being held in a basement storage room of the Kallorwegian Academy," he said. His tone turned wry. "I guess they don't have dungeons here."

I slumped down into a sitting position. No doubt we would soon be transferred to Kallmon and a real cell. Lucas might have been the one to lead us to that boat, but I had spent the first half of the year arguing that we should consider Cassius's assistance. I had been an idiot.

"The real question," Lucas said, continuing our one-sided conversation, "is what they intend to do next. It's all very well to keep a gag on you, but eventually they're going to have to let you eat and drink. We're not exactly easy prisoners to keep long term." His face looked white.

"So I can't help but wonder," he continued, "what method they have planned to force our speedy compliance."

I could feel any remaining color drain out of my own face.

"Obviously we need to get out of here," Lucas said. "And fast. But I'm afraid I'm drawing short on ideas. They seem to have done a fairly thorough job of clearing out my compositions—from what I can tell with my hands tied."

I looked up, my heart seizing. I had never known Lucas to be without a substantial number of powerful compositions on his person—it felt strange to think of him naked in such a way.

"Most of them are keyed to me, so they won't do them much good," he added. "But unfortunately they won't do us much good either. The best hope I can see is to conserve our energy until someone comes for us. Our best chance will be in transit, I imagine." He paused for a moment and lowered his voice.

"I think…I think I still have one composition. Right in the very toe of my boot. But it's only one to use as a very last resort, preferably when Cassius drags us before his father."

He looked at me, and I didn't need him to spell it out to understand what he meant. My eyes widened.

"You're not the only one who made use of your time in the Empire," he whispered. "It was a good idea—for a desperate circumstance. And so yesterday, while you slept, I wrote out a sealing composition of my own and stashed it separately to the rest of my workings. But I meant what I said about your ability, it's too important to lose. If it comes to it, better I do it. And you use every bit of power you can scrape up to shield yourself."

I shook my head stubbornly, and he growled his frustration. He looked at me, then away, then back at me again.

"Back in the emperor's library, when we discussed the idea of you sealing yourself, I said you were too important to Ardann. I told you that a ruler must think of the good of all. But the truth is I was only thinking about one person. You. I can't bear to see any part of who you are taken away."

He pinned me with his eyes. "I brought you here, this is all my fault. I don't care what happens to me, as long as you make it out unscathed." He paused. "But if the moment comes, and you're the only one who can get your hands on my composition, don't hesitate. My written composition will be a lot faster than you attempting to speak one. Use it, if you have to."

I shifted uncomfortably, almost glad my gag saved me from having to respond. He was right. I would prefer to be the one to work his composition—and seal myself in the process—than suffer whatever fate Osborne had in mind for me and my power. And if I could shatter Osborne's rule at the same time, so much the better.

I tried to settle into a more comfortable position, but I couldn't turn off my mind, and one thought burned stronger than the rest—the one thing Lucas had carefully avoided mentioning. And if he didn't bring it up, I had no way to do so. The frustration of that inability sat heavy in my chest, a tight knot of pressure that only grew tighter as time passed.

Cassius had been out looking for us. He had known we were coming. And much worse still, he had known of my new ability. So few people knew of that. And one of them had betrayed me.

My stomach surged, and only a supreme effort of will kept me from gagging again. I had told myself that not all the Stantorns were the same, that not all of them could be traitors. And I still wanted to believe that. How could Beatrice have sided with the Kallorwegians? She worked day after day, month after month, to reverse the damage they did to our soldiers. She had been the one to break the power of the green fever epidemic. I couldn't reconcile anything of her character and actions with such a despicable betrayal.

I could see her now, sitting beside me in the Sekali garden, and I remembered who else had been there. I hadn't told Jocasta my secret, but she had come upon Beatrice and me...What if she had arrived at the beginning of the conversation and heard the whole thing before making her presence known? And yet that thought didn't bring much comfort. Jocasta might be gruff on occasion, but I would never have picked her as a traitor.

The idea that I might know her even less than I had thought, sat heavily in my stomach. She wasn't a Stantorn, but she had no allegiance with any of the other great families, either. And I had no actual evidence the treachery was limited to the Stantorns. Perhaps they had recruited others to their cause? The thought only made me feel more ill.

Lucas didn't speak again, and time stretched out, impossible to measure in the windowless room. The wad in my mouth only grew more rank, and I desperately tried to keep my mind from fixating on it. Unfortunately my second strongest sensation was thirst, soon followed by hunger. My hands had burned for a while, but they had now lost sensation, another thing I was trying not to dwell on.

I entered an almost stupor-like daze for an unknown length of time. Only the sense of a single person approaching our storage room jerked me out of it. With a surge, I pushed myself onto my knees, managing to scramble to my feet, despite a dangerous wobble.

Lucas started, looking from me to the door as he also got to his feet despite his bindings. I had no real way to tell who it was that approached, but I fully expected to see Cassius's face when the door opened.

It took me a moment to reorient when an unfamiliar man appeared. He was alone, the only one on the whole basement level, apart from us, but he didn't look like a guard, or even a powerful mage.

His hair—mostly white, although his face only bore the lines of middle age—stuck up in all directions, and one of his eyebrows grew larger and bushier than the other, giving him a lopsided, almost perplexed look. He wore a robe, but it was so faded and worn it was hard to tell its original color. If pressed, I would have guessed purple. But what was a disheveled healer doing in our prison cell?

For a silent moment we all stared at each other. And then he spoke.

"Drat! I was hoping Elena would be the one on the door side. You'll have to give me a moment, this complicates things." He strode straight back out the door, leaving it swinging open behind him.

Lucas, clearly shocked and suspicious, stayed in place for several breaths before rushing toward the open door. He hadn't made it all the way when the strange man reappeared, almost colliding with him.

"Oh! Oh goodness! Steady on there. There's no point rushing off until we can get that shield down and Elena out."

Lucas, who looked as if he had been about to headbutt the mage, paused.

"What do you mean?" he asked. "Who are you?"

"I'm Declan," the man said, fumbling with several pieces of parchment and a pen which he thrust out to Lucas. "I'm afraid the prince burned all your compositions when he found he couldn't use them, so you'll have to write a new one."

Had this strange man come to free us? And was he not a mage at all then? My head rang with questions that I couldn't voice.

Lucas raised his eyebrows, lifting his shoulders awkwardly.

"Oh, of course. Foolish me." The man dropped the parchment and pen to the ground and pulled a knife from his boot. Circling around Lucas, he cut his bonds.

Lucas groaned softly as he was released, pulling his hands around to the front and shaking them.

"That's going to hurt," Declan said, sympathy in his voice. "Until the blood starts flowing freely again."

Lucas bent and attempted to retrieve the pen, but his hand spasmed, and it slipped through his fingers.

"Just give it a moment," said Declan.

"Why don't you do it?" Lucas asked, eyeing him suspiciously.

"Not my area of expertise," Declan replied.

"Are you only a healing assistant, then?" Lucas asked.

"No, I'm a true healer. Of sorts." Declan shook his head. "There will be time to exchange stories once we're free of this place. Try again now."

This time Lucas's fingers obeyed him, gripping the pen firmly, although I could see from his face that it hurt to do so. He paused for a moment to think and then frantically began to scrawl words across the page.

I waited, trying to contain my impatience as he wrote for what felt like forever. But at last he straightened again and ripped the parchment neatly in half. His power didn't attack the wall with full force, as I had expected, however. Instead a soft crunching noise sounded, and several of the stones not far down from the door pushed themselves away from the wall, creating a hole on my side of the room into whatever corridor or antechamber the room opened off.

"Good thinking!" Declan said, moving for the door in Lucas's wake.

A moment later Lucas reappeared, crawling through the hole, Declan's knife in his teeth. Rushing to my side, he cut first my gag and then the rope around my hands. My arms swung free, every muscle screaming in protest. Painful stabbing pricks sprung to life within my hands, racing up my wrists. Tears sprang to my eyes.

I spat the wad of material out of my mouth and then spat several more times for good measure, trying to clear my mouth of the taste. A hand thrust through the hole in the wall with a water skin, and Lucas retrieved it, holding it to my mouth. After several deep gulps, I gasped and managed to rush my way through a healing composition.

The pain subsided, full mobility returned to all my limbs. A soft sigh beside me told me Lucas had also received the benefits of my working.

"Best not to linger," Declan called softly through the opening.

"What is going on?" I whispered to Lucas.

"I have no idea," he said. "But I much prefer it to being tied in a storage room."

He led the way out into what turned out to be a larger storage area with piles of crates in all directions.

"This way," Declan said, gesturing into a dim corner.

"And why should we go with you?" Lucas challenged.

Declan looked back at him, confusion on his face. "Would you prefer to go back into that room?"

"We need him to get out of the Academy, at least," I said to Lucas.

"And you might want my help beyond that," Declan said. "It's remote out here. You won't get far without power, and that power will pinpoint your location like a beacon."

Lucas grimaced, unable to refute his words but clearly not liking it.

"Very well," he said. "Let's get moving then. But once we're clear, I want answers."

Declan nodded and led the way, hurrying into what looked like a dead-end corner of the vast basement. But stepping behind a particularly large stack of crates, we found a rickety set of wooden steps.

"An old servants' way," Declan said. "Rarely used now. And it's past bedtime for the trainees, so there shouldn't be anyone much about anyway."

I exchanged a glance with Lucas. So we had spent a whole day down here. Had Cassius planned to starve us into submission?

The stairs creaked menacingly, and I wasn't sure if I was more in fear of discovery or of them collapsing beneath us. But they held solid, taking us up out of the basement and into a passageway that appeared to run within a wall.

"The mages don't like servants using the same passages as them," Declan noted.

Clearly the Kallorwegian Academy had a vastly different take on formality and hierarchies compared to our own.

Eventually the path led us to a small door which Declan opened with a key from inside his robe. Outside clouds hid the moon, only the stars providing faint illumination. Somehow we had emerged outside both the building and the wall surrounding it. Declan carefully locked the door behind us before hurrying off across the open ground.

When he realized we weren't following, he stopped and gestured for us to hurry.

"We need to get somewhere safe," he said. "Somewhere hidden."

I made a split-second decision, starting after him without comment. Lucas hesitated a moment longer and then followed me.

We walked quickly, almost jogging, and it took everything in me not to set up a shield around us. But it had betrayed us last time, and I didn't want to make the same mistake again.

Eventually we crossed a minor road and approached a small cluster of dwellings, more a hamlet than an actual village. Declan led us to the one that straggled furthest from the group, a small, sturdy looking cottage. It didn't look like much of a hiding place.

Declan knocked once on the door, paused then knocked again, three times. It creaked open, and an older woman ushered us in. Unlike Declan, she wore no robe, and her face looked prematurely aged, lined with grief. She paid no special heed to Lucas or me, merely closing the door firmly behind us.

Crossing the room, she pushed a chest to the side and rolled up a rug, exposing a perfectly ordinary looking floor. Before I could even formulate a question, however, she knelt down and pressed hard on one section, simultaneously reaching across to press on another. A whole section of the flooring lifted, revealing stairs leading down into darkness.

I backed up several steps.

"I'm not walking myself into another prison." I shook my head vehemently.

She shrugged. "Then the front door is open to you. But if you wish to stay, it must be down there. And it must be quickly. They will search the hamlet when they find you gone."

Lucas stabbed a finger in Declan's direction. "You're coming too, and we're getting answers as soon as we're down there."

"Of course," he said.

Lucas gestured for him to precede us, and he did so without hesitation, the woman handing him a lantern as he passed her. Lucas and I filed in behind him.

To my astonishment, the steps led us not into a small basement hiding hole, but into what appeared to be a complete house, much larger than the one above us and lacking only windows.

"What is this place?" I gaped around me.

Declan bowed with a dramatic flourish.

"Welcome to one of the headquarters of the Kallorwegian rebellion," he said.

CHAPTER 20

"We've heard that before," Lucas said.

"Yes." A look of disgust transformed Declan's odd features, wiping away the bumbling, incompetent air he had previously worn. For the first time he looked dangerous. "I had to spend the afternoon lingering near our princeling, waiting to hear where he had stashed you and with what defenses. I heard him laughing with his cousin about how well his plan to lure you here worked."

He shook his head. "It should be no real surprise, though. The best lies are always built on truths that have been twisted to deceive. You let yourself believe him because it was so evident that there must be those in Kallorway who oppose such a sense-less and wasteful war."

"Wait," I said. "We want answers, but I'm sure you'll under-stand that our trust is low. Will you submit to a truth composition?"

I had expected at least a token protest, but he didn't seem in the least offended by my request.

"Of course," he said. "An excellent idea, in fact. My compa-triots frequently make use of them."

I frowned, noting his choice of words. He had claimed to be a mage, but we had yet to see any sign of his using power, and now he did not include himself among those who used truth compositions.

Pushing the matter to the side of my mind, I hurried through the binding words, making the composition as powerful and as ironclad as I could make it. Declan watched the whole process with interest, his eyes dwelling on the glow that appeared in front of me.

"It looks just like the ones I've seen performed before," he said. "Although I can see you are both strong and skilled for a trainee—just as the rumors say."

"Never mind that," Lucas said. "Tell us more of this rebellion."

"I suggest we make ourselves comfortable first," Declan said, gesturing to a polished wooden table surrounded by chairs. "Your Highness," he added, and the title made Lucas unbend and take one of the offered seats. The table held a bowl full of apples and a tray with a loaf of bread.

Once we were all seated, Declan cut several slices of the bread, placing them in front of us while Lucas and I both fell on the fruit. When our mouths were full, Declan began talking without being prompted.

"For years now, many of the mages of Kallorway have felt unhappy with the king's policy of war. He claims we must unite for protection against the Sekali Empire, and his paranoia where they are concerned seems to be genuine, if not exactly rooted in reality."

My eyes flickered to Lucas, my mouth full of apple. Nothing in his face suggested he shared some of the Kallorwegian king's concern. The last thing we wanted to do was undermine a rebellion, if one did indeed exist.

"But," Declan continued, "it goes beyond that for him. It has been clear for many years now that the king is driven by pride and a sense of grandeur. He wants a southern empire, like the northern one, with himself as the emperor."

He sighed. "Some of the families buy into his vision, of course, lured by the promise of power and riches. They are the most powerful among us, the ones whose children rarely face the front lines and have little to fear there. But others exist."

He glanced up at the ceiling. The woman who guarded the entrance to this secret house had not been a mage, but her face had borne the ravages of grief. Had she lost a child to the war?

"As the years pass," he said, "more and more come to our side. The very strongest still support him, but the numbers are now overwhelmingly with us. And that's why Osborne and his son grow desperate. Rumors of a new and terrible weapon in Ardannian hands reached us nearly four years ago." He bowed slightly in my direction. "And all his efforts to acquire this weapon have failed. Then this marriage alliance with the Sekalis. He is afraid, and now his own kingdom is turning against him. He needs a decisive victory, and he needs one fast."

"You are saying Kallorway is weak. That King Osborne is weak," Lucas said.

Declan looked him directly in the eyes. "I am saying he is desperate and cornered—or feels himself so. A rat on a sinking ship, who will not hesitate to strike out with tooth and claw. I am saying that if we cannot overthrow him soon, he may yet bring us all to ruin."

"So overthrow him," Lucas said coolly.

Declan sat back, sadness in his eyes.

"Many at court now openly oppose the war. Many talk more and more openly of opposing the king. But fewer are the number actually willing to move against him. Those of us who have stood against the war from the beginning have had decades now to hone our network, to bring others to our cause, but we haven't had the numbers or strength to act. We know once we do, we will be exposed and mercilessly hunted down. We will only get one chance, and we must make it count."

"A convenient excuse never to act," Lucas said.

"The time is fast approaching," Declan said. "As our numbers have grown, inevitably word is leaking out. The king has heard rumors of our existence. We are all on high alert. For years we have worked to place our people in key locations and positions around the kingdom, so that we may be ready when the moment arrives. I myself have been at the Academy for two decades now and working with Mabel up there for ten of those years. This safe house has become one of our main hubs because of its accessibility to the front lines and distance from court."

His eyes gleamed as he watched us continue to shovel food into our mouths.

"And here I was, perfectly placed, when whispers spread through the Academy that Cassius had left in the early hours of the morning and returned with two prisoners. When I heard who you were, I knew the time—at least for me—had come."

A slow smile spread over his face. "After two decades, it is good to finally act. We cannot afford for Osborne to get his hands on the two of you."

"Thank you," I said, my eyes straying to the light of my truth composition, brighter than that of the lantern. It had never once darkened. "I don't think we've thanked you yet, for rescuing us."

"It was my honor." He gave a little bow from his seat.

"And what is your plan now?" Lucas asked.

"I'm afraid I'm neither the leader nor the brains of our rebellion," he said. "I have sent word to those who are, but we may have a wait on our hands."

A muffled banging made us all pause, looking up toward the ceiling. No one spoke or even moved as we heard Mabel's footsteps slowly cross to her front door.

Voices came next, crisp, angry voices, and her cold, sullen

one. But I couldn't make out any of the actual words. Lucas stood, slowly, but Declan gestured for him to retake his seat.

"They will not find us here," he whispered.

Lucas sank back down, but he looked at me as he did so. His expression instructed me to be ready. I could only imagine how impotent he must feel, stripped of all his compositions.

Boots stomped through the house above us, and the scrape and bang of furniture, roughly moved around, came deafeningly through the floor to us. But no shout of discovery sounded, and no crack of light denoted the opening of the door above our heads.

At long last, when I felt I couldn't take the tension of hidden waiting anymore, the footsteps retreated, and the door closed. Some more dragging and banging sounded, presumably Mabel, straightening her house, and then everything fell silent again.

"Should we...check on her? Or something?" I asked.

Declan shook his head. "There is no need. She's watched over this house for years without flinching. She is made of iron, that one."

"Don't you need to get back to the Academy?" Lucas asked. "They've obviously worked out we're gone. Won't they be wondering where you are?"

Declan shrugged. "To be honest, I'm not sure they even remember I work there half the time. I'm neither commonborn servant nor proper mage instructor. Officially I'm a sort of groundskeeper, I suppose, but in reality, they just wanted me out of sight and out of mind. A state of things that I encourage, for obvious reasons."

He grinned, his lopsided eyebrows giving him a crazed look. I tried to imagine how he might fit among the mage families I knew back home. It didn't take much consideration to see why they had shoved him into some remote corner to forget about him. He reminded me rather forcibly of Coralie's stories about her eccentric great-uncle who had chosen to sell compositions to commonborns rather than join a discipline.

"Why did they feel the need to give you a position at all?" Lucas asked, faint traces of suspicion still lingering in his voice.

Declan's expression changed, something in the tightening of his features giving me the impression it was a topic he didn't want to discuss. I looked down at my composition glow as he spoke, but it never wavered.

"My family were long ago granted honorary positions as the king's personal healers. In perpetuity," Declan said. "We were given special privileges in exchange for our services, including the right to train our children at home rather than send them to the Academy."

Lucas raised both eyebrows. Even I knew that Kallorway operated the same way as Ardann—every mageborn was required to attend the Academy at age sixteen.

"I believe the intent was that we would always be able to remain near the king. But my grandfather chose to turn his back on court and move his family down to the southern forests. They lived in relative isolation and became...well, they became a little eccentric, I suppose, for lack of contact with the outside world."

His eyes grew distant. "Eventually only my mother and I remained of our family. She refused to leave her home, and perhaps it was for the best. She had built up quite an...odd reputation. But when she passed away, I made my way north and presented myself to the king. I have always believed it to be a gesture of irony that he chose to place me here, at the Academy, where my family have not attended for generations."

It was an odd story, by far the oddest I had heard of any mage family, and I sensed there was more to it, despite the glow of my composition remaining steady. I tried to think of a question I could ask that might draw out some answers, but the sound of the front door of the house above us drove all such thoughts from my mind.

There had been no knocking this time, and no urgent voices. Just the sound of the door thrusting open, and then a thud almost directly above my head. Footsteps hurried across the floor, and then we heard the door close.

"Declan! Declan get up here," called a voice I thought was Mabel's, the words coming to us only faintly through the floor above our heads.

Declan jumped up, Lucas and me with him, and the three of us hurried to the steps and the trapdoor above them. Emerging into the small cottage, we found Mabel crouched next to a young man who lay stretched out on the floor.

Declan dropped to his knees, gently rolling the man over and checking his pulse. Puddles pooled on the floor from the man's wet clothing, and an ugly looking raw burn ravaged the right side of his face.

I waited for Declan to pull out a healing composition, but he made no move to do so. The man groaned in pain, although he appeared unconscious, and I pushed my way forward.

First I spoke a pain relief composition, and then when Declan neither rebuked me nor commented at all, I continued on to heal the newcomer's burns. He stirred, groaned again, and then as the skin healed itself, he opened his eyes. For a moment, they held nothing but confusion. Then sudden alertness returned, and he sat up fast, clutching at Declan's dirty robe.

"I don't know what happened, but there were king's mages everywhere searching the fields." He sounded panicked and distraught despite now being free of pain.

Lucas shifted uneasily beside me. We knew why the area was currently full of searchers.

"We were separated, and I only just escaped and made it here unseen. But Felice is the one who had the information. I got her safely across the border, but we weren't expecting to run into trouble out here, and they caught us unaware. I couldn't protect her."

Mabel turned matter-of-factly to Lucas and me.

"You'll have to go and rescue her."

"I'm not so sure that's a good idea," I said uneasily.

Mabel gave me an icy look, so I hurried to clarify.

"Not that I don't want to rescue her, of course. But I'm not sure us wandering around out there is going to help anyone right now."

The man seemed to finally see us, frowning as he looked us up and down.

"I don't know who you are, but if you're with us, saving Felice is vital to everything. We've been working for a year to get her into the right position to find out their plans, and she's finally done it. We can't lose her now."

"Their plans?" Lucas asked, stepping closer to the man. "Whose plans?"

"The traitors, of course."

Lucas's expression didn't change. "Officially speaking, aren't you lot the traitors?"

The man shook his head impatiently. "Not Kallorwegian traitors. The Ardannian traitors."

$\mathcal{L}$ucas stiffened, but I leaned forward.

"The traitors? Do you have names?" I didn't bother to hide the eagerness in my voice.

He shook his head. "Felice has the names. There was no time for talk, and they wouldn't mean anything to me anyway. I was there to get her over the border."

"Over the border?" Lucas's voice sounded sharp. "So you've come from Ardann?"

The man peered at him uneasily, perhaps finally noticing our accents.

"From Bronton, of course. She's been there nearly a year." He turned to Declan with a frown. "Who are these people? What are they doing here if they're not here to meet Felice?"

Declan's eyes glowed. "This is Prince Lucas of Ardann and the Spoken Mage. They're going to free Felice, stop this war, and depose King Osborne."

The man recoiled before recovering and examining us more closely.

"Are you sure?" he asked dubiously. "Maybe they'll just drag her straight back to Ardann for an intelligencer's execution."

"It seems we have similar aims," Lucas said. "I can't end this war on my own, and it sounds like you can't either. For the moment, it would appear we are in this together."

"We need to move fast," the man said, striding toward the door.

"Hold on there," I said.

I didn't know what he had needed to do to get their intelligencer agent across the border, but he had been seriously wounded, and my healing hadn't been able to restore his energy levels. I could feel the core inside him, concerningly low. He needed to rest, and he certainly wouldn't be able to run far.

The man turned to glare at me. "She could be being captured or killed right now!"

"We'll go," I said. "We'll go immediately. But you need to stay here. You've just been healed, but you're on the verge of collapse, and you'll only be a liability."

He swore under his breath, not letting go of the door, but Declan stepped in, pulling him to the side.

"Mabel will get you below to one of the beds, you'll be safe there," Declan said. "I'll go with them."

Lucas had already eased the door open and was carefully checking if the immediate vicinity was clear. His face twitched at Declan's words, and he looked back at me, a question in his eyes. I shrugged. The old man didn't look like a fighter and had yet to produce any sort of composition, but he knew the local area. And although his energy felt like he could do with a good sleep, he wasn't about to keel over.

"We're clear," Lucas said. "Let's go."

The three of us filed quickly from the house.

"They were coming from the border, so we should head that way." Declan pointed east, toward Bronton.

Lucas took off at a jog, and I raced to catch up with him. The darkness kept our progress slow enough that we could talk as we went, the moon sliding in and out of the clouds to provide patchy illumination.

"They might already have her," I said. "What if they've taken her back to the Academy already like they did with us?"

Lucas shook his head. "The rebel said there were king's mages everywhere. They must have left us in that storage room for so long because Cassius was waiting for reinforcements to arrive from the capital. If they catch her, they'll haul her straight back to the king."

"We can't let that happen," I said. "We have to know who the traitors are."

I didn't look at him as I said it. The traitors had always been a touchy topic between us. His mother was a Stantorn, and he felt the same way about his relatives betraying us as I did about Beatrice: unthinkable.

"We don't even know how many of them we're up against," he said. "And if we use any compositions, we might attract them straight to us. But we do have one advantage. Can you tell where they are?"

Declan regarded us with confusion, but Lucas ignored him, clearly having decided that speed now overrode secrecy. And since our enemies now knew about my ability, he was probably right.

I had been monitoring our immediate environment, trying to ensure no one surprised us, but I pushed my awareness out as far as it would go.

"There are two of them moving away from us northward," I said, pointing to our left.

"That doesn't sound like Felice," Declan said.

I growled in frustration. "I can only feel them when I'm close enough. Maybe I should work a searching composition? The power won't be centered around us, so—"

I stumbled to a halt.

"Wait!" I closed my eyes, focusing on my other senses. We had been moving closer to the border as we talked, and something else had come into range. "I can feel a whole group, it might be… Yes, it must be!"

I opened my eyes and pointed ahead of us a little and to the right. "That way. Come on!"

Lucas didn't hesitate, racing in the direction I had pointed, Declan and me at his heels.

"I felt a group of them clustered together," I panted as we ran. "It makes it harder to differentiate when there are more people closer together, but I thought so many out in the middle of the night must be them. And I'm sure now because I just felt a fifth person. I missed them at first because their energy is so low, and they're just slightly behind the others."

"Not with the others?" Lucas asked. "So perhaps they haven't caught her yet?"

"Let us hope so!" Declan said, somehow moving faster despite his age and the poor lighting.

"I only managed to scribble a couple of compositions while Declan was talking earlier," Lucas said. He glanced at the Kallor-wegian. "What is your arsenal like?"

"Empty, I'm afraid." Declan spread his arms apologetically.

Lucas and I shared a confused glance, but we didn't have time to explore the strangeness of our guide.

"It's up to you then, Elena," Lucas said. "But you can draw from Declan and me, at least, even if the enemy are shielded against you."

"Draw from us?" Declan asked.

"She knows what she's doing," was all Lucas said in answer, and my heart swelled at his praise, despite the situation.

I held up a hand, and we all slowed. We had reached a large clump of trees, almost a small wood. The others I sensed were among the trees. Now that we were closer, I could feel them more distinctly. I focused on the weaker, separate one.

"I think she's climbed a tree," I whispered to Lucas and Declan.

We heard a shout and the sounds of someone moving through the trees.

"Sounds like they know she's in there, and they're searching through the trees for her," said Lucas.

"I'll take them," I said. "You two find her. Declan, stay close to Lucas and make sure she sees your face first." I pointed toward the western edge of the trees. "She's in that direction." I took off running.

Thankfully the other four had remained together rather than spreading out among the trees, and when I got even closer I could hear why. They thought it was me they had cornered and were therefore approaching her with due caution and strong shields. Although they had been here long enough without any sign of my attacking or defending myself that several of them had concluded I must be weak, possibly even unconscious. And they had gotten sloppy as a consequence.

"Drain," I whispered, making sure to send my power toward Lucas and Declan rather than the shielded mages of the king or the weakened Felice.

When I felt full of more energy than I could hold, I whispered, "Stop," and then, "Shield." The comforting sensation of my power wrapped itself around me.

"Hey! Do you feel that?" one of them asked, turning in my direction.

I stepped out of the trees.

"Evening," I said. "Were you looking for me?"

All four of them started fumbling at their robes for new compositions. I could feel the strength of their shields, but I was willing to bet they weren't as equipped as their crown prince. Kicking at a small pebble at my feet, I sent it sailing toward them. It passed through the first layer of shielding around them—the strong one—without pause, only bouncing off the second layer

259

underneath. I grinned. They had heard of my power and put all their strength into shields that would prevent my power from reaching and draining them. But I didn't need their strength.

"Attack them," I said, sending a whip of my power toward a nearby tree. It tore itself from the ground and began to slam against their shields like a battering ram.

"Rocks," I added, and every boulder around us, large and small, lifted into the air and joined the assault.

Their shields crumpled and collapsed, but two of them had released new ones. My attack didn't let up, wearing these ones down as well. The other two had ripped assault compositions, one sending what looked like lightning bolts in my direction while the other bombarded me with pure power. My own shield didn't even flicker.

Energy drained out of me at my enormous output of power, but I had extra to spare. When I felt their final layer of physical shields waver, I took a preparatory breath.

They fell, and the next wave of rocks hit the mages, knocking three to the ground. The remaining mage was swept up by the tree trunk and slammed against another tree, sliding down to slump onto the ground.

"Stop," I said quickly.

A quiet groan told me one at least of them was alive. I knelt beside each mage one by one, my hands slipping in and out of the various pockets of their robes even while I checked their breathing.

Somehow they had all survived. Gratitude filled me even though they were my enemies. I already had enough deaths haunting my dreams, I had no desire to add more to their number. Only one was still conscious—the source of the groans. A broken arm, a severely broken leg, and what looked like several crushed ribs kept him immobile on the ground.

"Next time, come better equipped if you want to take me down," I said as I divested him of his compositions. "And you can let your king know that the Spoken Mage isn't a weapon he's ever going to wield."

I could see fear in the man's eyes as well as pain, but I made no further attempt to reassure him that I didn't mean to finish him off. Let him sweat.

"Elena?" Lucas emerged from the trees, surveying the fallen mages.

"Did you find her?" I asked.

He nodded, a dark woman in her early thirties limping into view behind him, supported by Declan. Her wide eyes stood out in her dirty face as she regarded the destruction around me.

"She needs healing," Lucas said.

I thrust half my gathered handfuls of parchment at him, giving the remaining slips to Declan.

"Here, fresh supplies," I said. "I bet there's a healing composition in there. One that will last to get us out of here at least."

Declan immediately began to flip through the pieces, muttering to himself, but Lucas frowned at me.

"You can't do it?"

"I don't want to run lower than I need to," I said softly.

"But..." He looked around at all the downed mages.

I shook my head. They might be unconscious, but the stored power from the shields they had released still hung around them. It had been designed for my power, not for stones or trees or my thieving hands, and it had not kept them from injury. It did, however, still keep my power from connecting with them and draining their energy.

"Got one!" Declan announced. "And it doesn't look like it's keyed to anyone in particular. I'll try it."

He ripped it cleanly in half, flicking his fingers toward Felice. She sighed and then straightened, her stance steadying.

"Good." Lucas thrust the compositions he held into his cloak without reading them. "Let's get out of here."

The four of us left the cover of the trees and hurried back

toward Mabel's house at the steady jog we had first used. When I saw that Felice struggled to keep up, her energy levels near to collapse, I met Lucas's eyes and gave a nod in her direction.

He fell back and pulled one of her arms over his shoulders, supporting her as they continued to hurry forward, although slower than before. Declan and I led the way, my senses alert for anyone else in the vicinity.

"I knew there was something different about you," Declan murmured as we strode along side-by-side.

I kept my attention on our surroundings.

"Yes, of course," I said. "Spoken Mage, remember?"

"No, something more than that," he said. "You drained my energy. It's supposed to be impossible, but you just did it."

I almost tripped, and he put out a hand to brace me.

"Is that what the prince was talking about earlier? Can you sense the energy of others?" He sounded breathless and excited.

"How do you know that?" I asked. "You can't have felt it."

"But I did." He turned to me, and his eyes glowed in the moonlight.

"I confess, I have been longing to meet you ever since I first heard rumors of your existence. Another mage whose power doesn't follow the normal rules."

"What do you mean *another*?" I nearly tripped again, too distracted now to watch for pursuers and still keep track of the ground beneath my feet.

"I mean myself," he said. "You might perhaps have noticed I'm a little odd." He smiled, apparently reconciled to the epithet. "But what no one still alive in Kallorway today knows is that there's a reason for it beyond my isolated life."

My pulse quickened. "You can speak compositions?"

He quickly shook his head.

"How can you take energy then?" I asked, disappointed but also intrigued. "No one has ever been able to do it with written compositions."

"I can't take energy," he said calmly. "But I can feel it because I can give mine away."

"You can give energy?" I asked. "To anyone?"

He nodded. "Yes." He paused. "But it's permanent." The moon sailed from behind a cloud and illuminated a wry grin that somehow lent gravity to his mismatched face.

"Permanent?" I whispered, trying to grasp what that meant.

"We know that only some families have the ability to control power," he said. "It's been like that since before our records began. And we know that they pass that ability on to their children. But my family has always passed on a different sort of ability."

An extra dark patch in the far distance told me we were approaching the collection of houses. I tore my mind away from his words long enough to do another sweep of the area.

"What sort of ability?" I asked once I was sure we remained safe.

"There is something different about our energy," he said. "Or, perhaps more accurately, our ability to use it to access power. Unlike everyone else, we cannot access power at all—not in a controlled way, like the mageborn, or even an uncontrolled way, like the commonborn."

I stared at him. That sounded like the Sekali sealing, but I felt no shadow over his energy. From my perspective, it felt entirely normal, if a little low.

"That's why your family was excused from attending the Academy," I murmured. "But why royal healers? Why let you wear a purple robe?"

"King Osborne has no idea why," Declan said. "Apparently his father did not think to tell him. Or perhaps it was his grandfather who did not tell his father. We have been gone from court life for a long time. He—like those at the Academy—simply assumes I am weak and choose not to work compositions."

"So, you're a sham mage?" I asked, utterly confused. Not that it would do any harm in his case, if he couldn't cause any damage by writing.

"Well...that's a worthy question," he said. "I suppose you could say that. But, on the other hand, I can do compositions of a sort. The same ones—the only ones—all my other family members could do while they were alive. And if Osborne knew the truth of our ability, he would have never posted me out here and forgotten about me."

"You mean the power to give away your energy?"

He nodded. I could see Mabel's house now—still distant, but its shape distinct against the night sky.

"Members of my family have always been able to work only one type of composition: healings. But we can work any healing, almost without limits—except for one, all-important, limit. Our healings don't work like normal healings. They don't use power to accelerate the healing process of the body, or to regrow what can't naturally be regrown. Our healings use our energy directly, transferring a part of it permanently into our patient. Healing them, yes, but also making them stronger and us weaker. Once that energy is gone, no amount of rest will ever replenish what we have lost."

He sounded unutterably weary now, beyond our actual exertion. "And that is why the kings of the past gave us honors but kept us close and kept our ability a secret. Each of us has the capacity to complete only a very limited number of healings before we reduce ourselves to the point of death. They wanted our power kept for them and their families alone."

My eyes widened, and I swallowed, my mind racing through the various ramifications of his story.

"But no one can take it from you?" I asked, suddenly alarmed. "I mean, the energy I took will replenish?"

"Oh certainly," he hurried to reassure me. "We can exert ourselves like any commonborn, wear ourselves out, rest and recover. It is only when we work our own compositions that we give a part of that energy away forever."

I looked at him sideways. I could now understand why he felt perpetually tired, although he had done nothing of particular exertion, nor worked any compositions. Who had he chosen to use part of his precious energy on?

"It must be hard," I said tentatively. "Seeing need but knowing what it will cost you to meet it."

He smiled a little wistfully. "You see straight to the heart of the problem. And that is why my grandfather decided to take action. When he was still a young man, he healed the wife of his king. But it was not the first time he had been called upon to serve, and the working cost him greatly since the queen was pregnant at the time, and so there were two patients draining his energy."

The moon reappeared, showing sadness lurking in Declan's eyes.

"The composition weakened him near to death," he continued. "He had grown up alongside the king, and the two were close friends. I suppose when the king saw the cost, his heart must have softened because he was convinced to release my family to go and dwell in isolation."

"Away from all temptation," I whispered.

He nodded. "But even then, we had those we most loved with us. And everyone falls sick eventually. You can either choose to watch them suffer, perhaps die, or eventually give so much of yourself away that you might as well gift them the rest before you fall into permanent slumber."

"You said in the end, only you and your mother remained," I said, the house now looming before us, our goal nearly reached. "Is that what happened to her?"

His eyes grew soft, and a smile lingered around his mouth. "She was...eccentric. She believed that her energy was meant to bring good to the world, and that she would always know when she saw someone in need of it."

"And did she?" I asked.

"She seemed to think so. She knew how much she was giving away, but she didn't care. She just made me promise that when I was the only one left, I would leave the forest and return to the world. And one day—when her energy was already so depleted that she barely had the strength to get through a day—a young couple found us. They had heard rumors of my mother's miraculous acts."

My heart seized, my mind freezing and my stomach churning. He kept talking.

"She said she knew as soon as she saw them that they were the ones. She never hesitated when she wrote out the compositions for them. Two—so extravagant. And she didn't want them to know the ultimate price she paid. She said farewell to me before she bound her energy into those two rolls of paper, and she insisted I not tell them her fate when I met them to hand over the completed compositions."

Tears sprang to my eyes and choked my throat. Was he saying what I thought he must be saying? We reached the house, and he pulled open the door, stepping aside so Lucas could maneuver Felice inside, giving me a strange look as he passed. But now that I had stopped, I couldn't seem to move again.

Declan paused and looked at me.

"When I heard about your ability…And then about your brother. When I calculated your age. And now…you can manipulate energy…"

I looked at him, my eyes awash with unshed tears.

"Our compositions cannot grant a commonborn the ability to control power," he said. "It makes no sense. And yet…I never heard of anyone else in my family using their ability to shape a child not yet born. Perhaps, perhaps somehow…"

I nodded, unable to find the words to confirm his hope. I bore my parents' blood, as all the tests had confirmed, and yet apparently I also carried a mage's energy, transferred directly into my very moment of creation. And that energy must somehow have mingled with the seed of control passed down in my father's blood from his Sekali ancestor—the seed he had apparently passed to me and not my brother.

In some strange way, it felt almost as if Declan was long-lost family. But, at the same time, I knew now without any further doubt that the circumstances that had led to my gift had been unique. I wouldn't stumble on another spoken mage. And the knowledge made me lonely, in a way I had never felt before.

"Elena?" Lucas reappeared in the doorway. "Is everything all right? We need to get below."

And just like that the strange loneliness dissipated. I was not alone.

"Felice says she has important news," Lucas said as Declan and I entered the house, the old man still darting me hopeful looks. "But she's refusing to tell it to me."

CHAPTER 22

"My instructions were clear," Felice repeated stubbornly. "I am to report only to General Haddon." She looked over to Lucas and me. "And while I'm more than grateful to you for rescuing me, you're Ardannians. I'm waiting for the general."

Lucas stood, his hands balling into fists, and his frustrated breaths coming fast. I put a hand on his arm, and he looked down at me, deflating.

"In that case, I can't remember the last time I slept," he said. "Wake me the second the general arrives."

He disappeared in the direction of the beds that Declan had been trying to coax us into for the last half hour.

"I think I'm going to sleep too." I paused as I walked past Felice. "I highly recommend you don't *forget* to wake him when your general does arrive. I suspect you're going to need us again before this is all over." I didn't bother mentioning myself. Lucas wouldn't let me sleep through anything important.

Not that I thought I would be able to sleep. I had used the extra energy I had taken from Lucas and Declan, but my mind buzzed with the news of Declan's strange ability, and the part it had played in shaping me.

The feeling that he was family lingered, sitting strangely beside the hatred of the Kallorwegians that had been the background of my life growing up. Despite the revelations I had already received about my origins, I had left for Yanshin feeling fully Ardannian. And yet now, only weeks later, I had to acknowledge that both the Sekali Empire and Kallorway could lay claim to a piece of me. And I didn't entirely know how I felt about that.

I tossed on the pillow, despite it turning out to be deceptively soft given the rough appearance of the small bedroom. I had chosen Ardann over the Empire, but did that mean I had to reject everything of the Sekalis? They had found a way to release their commonborn, and I would emulate them if I could. And Kallorway had killed my friends...yet I couldn't blame Declan for that, or Mabel.

Despite my churning thoughts, my consciousness faded, slipping into sleep in spite of everything. My body had been alert for too long now, and my mind couldn't win the fight.

When someone shook me awake, I couldn't place the passage of time, the windowless underground house looking exactly as it had when I went to sleep.

"The general is here," Mabel said. "If you want to hear the talk, I suggest you hurry."

"What time is it?" I asked.

"Just gone dawn," she said.

"Thank you," I called as she left the room.

She paused and looked back, a shade of surprise on her face. "All who serve our cause are welcome here."

"Who did you lose?" I asked.

Her worn hand tightened on the door frame.

"My sons. All of them."

I sucked in an involuntary breath, my stomach contracting. All of them?

"We do not have your policy here of one per family," she said. "Things are not so evenly spread."

I winced. "And you don't hate me? For being Ardannian?"

"My hate is directed where it belongs," she said firmly. "At the person who started this war, and the one who commanded my sons must fight in it. Anyone who opposes King Osborne is welcome in my home."

She disappeared out the door, and I rushed to follow. Out in the main room, I found the chairs around the wooden table had been filled but for one beside Lucas. Mabel was already making her way back up the stairs toward the open trapdoor, so I slipped into the empty seat.

Lucas nodded at me, and Declan smiled and murmured a good morning. The man at the head of the table, a tall and imposing older mage who carried himself as if he knew his own worth, regarded me with undisguised interest. General Haddon, I assumed. Head of the Kallorwegian Royal Guard.

I shook my head. Learning he was the head of the rebellion had left even Lucas taken aback. It made their organization seem real in a way it hadn't before with only Declan, Mabel, and the injured intelligencers as its face.

"I came in response to Declan's summons," the general said. "Though it wasn't easy to get away without raising suspicion. It is fortuitous indeed that Felice has returned at the same time. We shall hear your report first, Felice, and then discuss what is best to be done with our...new arrivals."

Felice stood.

"It took us years to embed her deeply enough in the ranks of our intelligencers that she was given a prime assignment," Declan whispered to Lucas and me.

"So she has spent the last year spying on Ardann," Lucas said, his voice tight.

270

Felice caught his words.

"Ostensibly, yes," she said to us. "But in reality, I was there to serve the rebellion. We have long known that someone from your kingdom is colluding with King Osborne, but he keeps their identity extremely close to his chest. The ancient historical tome that sparked his obsession over ruling a southern empire came from an Ardannian library, not a Kallorwegian one. We knew that if we could get an intelligencer sent to Ardann, the information would eventually come to light."

"And a year ago we succeeded," General Haddon said.

She nodded respectfully in his direction.

"Our Armed Forces conducted two simultaneous raids as an opportunity to get two intelligencers across the border. The other agent was truly Osborne's man, and he was sent across the Wall. I don't know his mission. I was tasked with infiltrating Bronton and taking up residence in the Kallorwegian safe house there. Osborne already has an intelligencer manning the house, but they wanted back up for him."

"And obviously you succeeded," the general said.

She nodded. "He has a house against the wall with a secret way in and out, so that our agents don't have to get past the gates. Getting in was laughably easy once I made it to Bronton. Osborne's intelligencer does a perfect Ardannian accent and has passed as a local for many years. I posed as his niece, arrived to stay after losing my family to the green fever the year before and bouncing from relative to relative."

She shook her head. "No one suspected a thing."

"We had hoped to hear from you before now," the general said.

"I'm sorry. My supposed uncle was reticent, to say the least, and I had to tread slowly, at risk of being exposed by both sides. In terms of Ardannians, he dealt mainly with a young lieutenant."

She grinned. "One who thankfully turned out to be rather susceptible to my charms. He assumed I knew more than I did, and I was able to get him talking. I planned to gather just a bit more information before returning—but he appeared at the house, full of excitement. He told me it was all finally happening, and the plan was at last in motion. Something had happened to trigger it earlier than planned." She glanced toward Lucas and me. "That's when I sent out the message to send someone to help me across the river."

"The plan?" Lucas leaned forward. "What plan? What did he tell you?"

She looked to the general for confirmation, and after regarding Lucas for a moment, he nodded.

"The royal family are to visit the Academy for some sort of grand gala."

Lucas frowned and nodded. "The anniversary of the Academy's construction."

"They are to be assassinated at the Academy," she said. "And in the chaos that follows, Kallorway will push across the border and take the kingdom."

Lucas's muscles tensed, his face going pale.

"Impossible," he said. "These days the Academy is an even safer place than the palace. No Kallorwegian assassin could penetrate its layers of protection."

"Lucas." I gripped his arm, my voice coming out small and strangled. But I didn't look at him. A horrible realization had held me silent as Felice's story unfolded, and I directed my question at her.

"The traitors! Who are the traitors?"

I could feel Lucas's arm tense beneath my fingers as Felice stared at us.

"The Ellingtons," she said at last. "Or at least some of them."

My stomach turned, surging so strongly I had to clamp my lips closed and fight to keep it in its place. The Ellingtons? A parade of faces flashed through my mind. Walden. Dariela. Acacia. Finnian's mother. Duke Lennox. Duke Magnus. Martin.

After a moment, in which everyone at the table stared at us, I managed to gasp out some words.

"It was Martin, wasn't it? The young lieutenant you charmed?"

She nodded, hesitated for a moment, as if trying to decide whether to speak, and then said, "I was there you know. In a back room when Martin led you through the wall last year. He came barreling in, said to open the wall and get a message to the breach team that he was bringing both of you out to them. Said to tell them that he'd circle around and come between the rocks and the trees from the west. I hadn't had much of a chance to get to know him at that point, so the agent instructed me to stay out of the way and leave everything to him."

"We were trying to keep our mission quiet," Lucas murmured, his voice flat. "I assumed that was why he didn't take us through the gate. But he just needed a chance to get a message out, to let the breach team know to set up the ambush." He shook his head. "We were fools."

"How could we have known?" I said softly. "And with everything that happened, it never occurred to me to mention to anyone how we left the town. If I even thought of it at all, I would have assumed it was a bolt-hole of our own."

Lucas laughed bitterly. "We weren't supposed to come back, remember? No doubt he didn't think it mattered what we saw."

But as foolish as it made me feel, it wasn't the thought of Martin that had nearly made me lose what little I had eaten in the last day.

"The book," I said. "The ancient history from an Ardannian library. And the gala."

Lucas met my eyes, his face draining of all remaining color.

"Walden."

"He boasted to me once about how much time he has spent in the Academy library," I whispered. "About how well he knows it. What if he found some remaining true history and sent it to

273

Osborne? If he had heard rumors that the king favored the idea of aggressive expansion, he might have guessed it was just the spark needed to propel him to action."

I swallowed. "And then he acted as Academy Head in Lorcan's place the whole time we were at the front last year. Who knows what he might have done to sabotage the protections—what entry points he might have hidden in them?"

Tears slipped unheeded down my cheeks. Walden had pretended to be my friend. He had helped me train, and I had confided in him, had told him my secrets.

"Now we know how Cassius knew of your ability," Lucas said grimly.

I felt a new stab of anger, alleviated only by a background relief that Beatrice and Jocasta at least were innocent as I had longed for them to be.

"So it's true?" General Haddon leaned forward. "When Osborne warned me of the measures I might be called to defend him against, I wondered if his sources had turned against him and were feeding him fanciful stories."

"It's true," Lucas said shortly. Any question of keeping my secret was long gone.

"The potential…" Haddon said with a speculative gleam that made me straighten my back and re-engage in the conversation.

"Yes," I said. "I am possibly the strongest mage who has ever lived." I suppressed the urge to glance toward Declan. My origin wasn't important in this moment. "And that is why Lucas and I will be going to stop the assassins. Alone."

These people appeared to be genuine in wanting to end the war and maintain the separate sovereignty of Kallorway and Ardann. But that didn't mean I was going to walk any of them past all our defenses and into the heart of our kingdom.

"We will save my family," Lucas said, his voice implacable, "and then we will crush the Ellington traitors and remove their blight from Ardann."

The general stood. "In light of all that is happening, I must return quickly to my post. But I promise you this. If you do your part, we will do ours. If you defeat the assassins and expose the traitors, you will cripple Osborne's war plans. In that opportune moment we will strike. Osborne will agree to peace with Ardann or he will lose his throne."

Lucas stood also. "We will not fail."

Mabel gave us a small bag of food and two skins of water which would last us to the border. The group had dispersed quickly, and only Declan remained to see us off, providing basic weapons to go with Mabel's offerings. He must have stayed up with Felice, rather than sleep as we had done while waiting for the general's arrival since he hadn't regained the energy I took from him. I pushed down a brief surge of guilt as he pulled me aside just before we left.

"You have become everything my mother could have wanted," he said. "I know she wouldn't regret her decision to help your parents."

"Thank you." My emotions had been pulled in so many different directions in the last few days, that I felt strangely numb.

"I feel we are connected," he said. "Although we don't know each other. Part of me wishes I could accompany you, to see you in action, but I know my place is here. I need to see Kallorway on the right path again. But I want to give you a gift."

For a moment I thought he wanted to offer me some of his energy, and I nearly recoiled. But he handed me instead a small yellow silk pouch. I took it tentatively, but Lucas called my name impatiently from the door.

"Thank you," I said again, tucking it safely inside my clothes. "I hope we will meet again when our kingdoms are at peace."

Lucas and I stepped out of the door into full daylight. We had discussed waiting for night, but we couldn't risk losing any more time. Spring wouldn't officially start until the next day, and I seemed to remember the plans for the gala placing it several weeks into spring in the hope of warmer weather. But Felice had said something had happened to trigger the plans. We couldn't risk being too late.

And so we braved the brightness of day, taking advantage of the light to move as fast as possible, alternating between periods of walking and periods of jogging. The mages searching for us must have assumed that we made for the border after freeing Felice because we saw no sign of them in the immediate vicinity.

We barely talked, pausing only briefly to eat the cold rations Mabel had sent. Tension radiated off Lucas, and I could tell he had to constantly restrain himself from setting a faster pace. He wanted to be in Corrin already, but he knew we couldn't maintain greater speed for long.

"I keep running over and over it in my mind," I burst out eventually. "All the little things I didn't see. The way Walden kept secrets from Lorcan and the other instructors. I appreciated it at the time, I thought he was doing it for me, but I feel so naive now. Why would he keep secrets from the head of his discipline for me —a first year trainee he barely knew?"

My pace increased, my frustration lending me speed, and Lucas matched it without comment.

"For a long time I was convinced General Griffith was the traitor," I said. "You tried to tell me he wouldn't betray you and neither would the Stantorns. But Walden, on the other hand, pointed me straight in the general's direction. And even when I discovered for a fact it wasn't the general, I didn't suspect Walden. And the Sekalis! Your parents wanted to keep me away from them, and who introduced me? Walden!"

"I never liked him," said Lucas quietly.

"I knew you weren't happy I was considering training with

him with my energy ability," I said. "You talked me out of continuing, in fact. Why didn't you say anything more specific?"

Lucas shrugged. "Because I didn't have anything more specific to say. I didn't think he was in league with Kallorway or heading up a conspiracy to overthrow Ardann. I just didn't like how friendly he was to you from the moment you arrived."

My brows drew together, and despite everything, I couldn't resist a wry smile. "You thought he should have been more like you? Cold, arrogant, and suspicious?"

Lucas winced slightly. "What they claimed about you was impossible. I was convinced you were a Kallorwegian agent, skilled enough to fool Lorcan and worm your way into the Academy. I was in class and didn't hear the briefing Lorcan gave my parents. I didn't know how hard he'd tested you. It was only when I witnessed the truth composition and then saw your power for myself that I really believed you could be who you said you were."

I had never thought to ask him what he had been thinking when I first arrived at the Academy. So much of his behavior then made sense now. But it didn't explain why he had suspected Walden just because of his kindness.

"Coralie was kind to me when I arrived," I said. "Do you suspect her of being a traitor as well?"

"Of course not. But…she's a Cygnet. And a trainee. Walden, on the other hand, is a member of one of the great families and a senior mage in the Academy discipline. It never sat well with me how well he wore his jovial mask—not for someone I knew had the cunning to keep up with the power plays of the top mages. He acted as if he had no agenda of his own—but in the world I'm used to, everyone has an agenda."

I extended my arm across his middle, forcing him to a sudden halt along with me.

"There's someone there," I whispered. "In that group of trees."

We had crossed the main road some time ago, aiming to hit

the Abneris just south of the main conflict zone. We were relying on the Kallorwegian side being much less heavily patrolled, since Ardann had no interest in pushing the fight across to them.

"I feel them too," Lucas said. "They're using power for something. Probably shields. Soldiers, do you think?"

"Could be. But there are only two of them."

"Let's go see."

We circled around and approached the trees from the far side to the other people, moving as quietly as we could across the mostly level ground. Once among the trees, we could hear quiet words, the conversation covering the small sounds we made.

To my astonishment, I recognized one of the voices. I looked wide-eyed at Lucas, but his focus didn't leave the two mages in front of us.

"I still think your father is right," said the one who had stood behind Cassius when he captured us. "They'll be back over the border by now easily."

"Perhaps." Cassius sounded dismissive. "But as I've told you already, I'm not so convinced. They came here in the first place, didn't they?"

"Because they thought you were going to help them," his companion muttered, clearly a fellow trainee from the Academy by his age. Perhaps even the cousin Declan had mentioned.

"What was that?" Cassius asked coldly.

"Nothing," the other trainee said quickly. "I'm just not sure what my father will think if he hears I went against the king's orders. Even for you. I heard the duke telling his men that His Majesty didn't want us alerting the Ardannians that anything unusual was going on."

"We'll keep searching until we find them. They were like a beacon last time. And when we do, and I drag them before my father, he'll be grateful," Cassius said. "He'll forget all about the failed attempt at Bronton last year."

"They're shielded, but they might not have activated strong ones yet," I whispered. "I could—"

Before I could finish the thought, Lucas erupted from the trees, launching himself at the Kallorwegian prince. He took me by surprise, but them more so. By the time Cassius's friend reacted, and attempted to go to his prince's rescue, I had caught up. The dagger Declan had supplied slid free of its sheath in my boot. I swung it, hilt downward, and connected with his head. He crumpled to the ground.

When I looked up, Lucas stood over a prone Cassius, his fists clasped and his chest heaving with ragged breaths.

"Is he still alive?" I rushed over to check on the Kallorwegian prince.

"Yes. Although it's more than he deserves."

I looked up at him. "How did you know that would work? How did you know they didn't have a physical shield as well as their shields against compositions?"

He shrugged. "I didn't. Not for sure. But I guessed it. You heard what they said. This wasn't a sanctioned mission, like the last one. And I was betting they were saving their strongest compositions until they had eyes on you."

I shook my head. "That was a big risk to take."

He didn't say anything, but I could see from the way he held himself that he had exploded out of anger and frustration as much as instinct and strategy. He had needed an outlet, a way to express his rage and betrayal, and Cassius had provided one.

"You showed me their strategy, yesterday," he said, speaking a little more calmly, "putting all their strength into their magical shields. I was just relying on their not having had enough time to change strategies after it failed to stop you last night."

Perhaps there had been a little more thought than I had given him credit for.

"Well, it worked," I said. "But what are we going to do with them now?"

"Can you break through their shields and drain them?" he asked.

I nodded. With only the two of them, and without attacks coming at me as well, I was confident I could break through.

"Attack," I said, and my power poured out, slamming against their shield. It kept going, burning through it, until at last it collapsed. I drained them both, leaving just enough to keep them alive. The same fury that had driven Lucas gave me the nerve I needed to push my working to the edge.

"They won't die," I said when I was finished. "But they'll sleep for a very long time."

"Good." Lucas said. "From the sound of it no one knows they're out here. But we can soon change that. I suspect when we get across the river your adoptive father might be interested to hear that Kallorway's crown prince is lying just across the water, unconscious and unguarded."

CHAPTER 23

The worst part of crossing the river was the cold. We easily evaded the few Kallorwegian patrols, but when we emerged from the water, we must have triggered an Ardannian alarm composition.

A patrol converged on us with commendable speed. When they saw there were only two of us, and that we looked more bedraggled than dangerous, they hesitated, and the extra second gave the young lieutenant a chance to see our faces. I vaguely recognized him as a trainee from two years above us. He told his soldiers to stand down, approaching us with caution.

"Your Highness? Spoken Mage?"

I frowned at his wary posture and then realized he must be wondering if we were some sort of Kallorwegian ruse.

"Yes, it's us," I said. "Would you like a demonstration as proof? Dry," I said clearly, pointing my finger at my own clothes and then Lucas's. The water evaporated off us, steam rising from our now pleasantly heated clothes since I had added a layer of warmth to the composition.

The lieutenant's face relaxed.

"What are you doing here?" he asked.

"Never mind that," Lucas said. "We need to speak to the general. Now."

The patrol formed up around us without prompting from their supposed leader, and we jogged the whole way into Bronton. It all looked so strange—on the one hand familiar from the many months we had spent here, and on the other startling and different. The front was its own world, and I had gotten used to no longer being part of it.

A mage tried to accost us at the doors to headquarters, but Leila was passing through the entranceway and roundly took him to task. He accepted her reprimand and stood aside. I hid a smile as I greeted her. She had clearly only solidified her position here. Seeing a commonborn berating a mage was beyond unusual, and yet somehow she managed to carry it off. Either that or she knew that Lucas's presence would protect her.

She bowed extra low to him, murmuring his title before grinning cheekily at me.

"The general's in the main room." She pointed down the corridor.

We hurried off toward him, and she followed unabashedly behind. Her curiosity would have to wait, though, because the general took one look at us and cleared the room.

"What are you—"

"We need two horses," Lucas said with authority. "And for you to send a message ahead of us to Corrin."

"What's going on?" Griffith asked, looking between us. "I could have wrung Julian's neck when I heard he had helped you both break out of the Empire and run for Kallorway of all places."

"We don't have time for explanations," Lucas said. "We need two of your strongest horses. And you need to prepare for an attack. We're hoping it won't come, but best to be prepared. Send one company after us to Corrin, though. We might need the extra back up before this is all over."

"I don't understand," the general began.

"Do you need to?" Lucas asked sharply.

"Father," I said, using the term for the first time. "This isn't the time to show disrespect to the crown."

His eyes latched onto me, and to my relief he accepted the warning I was trying to signal.

"Of course, daughter," he said with a respectful bow. "No disrespect was intended. Devoras loyalty is absolute, as always."

"Excellent," Lucas said. "Those horses, then, and the soldiers to follow behind. And I need a message composition, one directed to the palace."

General Griffith sorted through a pile of parchments that had been left on the large table in the middle of the room.

"Here," he said, ripping one and holding the resulting ball of power out to Lucas.

"This is Prince Lucas," he said into it.

"Your Highness?" The disembodied voice that replied didn't need facial expressions to communicate its owner's astonishment.

The general leaned in.

"It's him, soldier. Be ready to take a message."

"Yes, sir!"

"Tell my parents to stay away from the Academy at all costs," Lucas said.

"The Academy, Your Highness? But they're already there."

Lucas and I exchanged a panicked look.

"Already there? For the gala?" Lucas asked.

"No, the gala's not for two weeks," the voice said. "But they're holding some sort of...dress rehearsal, or something, for it. No one told me the details, but I saw them leaving the palace myself just before my shift started."

"Send a messenger after them," Lucas said.

"The Academy is shielded against—"

"Not a composition," Lucas said. "An actual messenger. Have

him warn them to get back to the palace immediately. And send two squads of royal guards with him."

"Two squads? Could you confirm that? Their Majesties already have their usual guards with them."

Lucas hesitated. "All right, scratch that. Just send the messenger. Move fast."

He squeezed his fist together, as if he could snuff out the ball of power, and it responded to his signal, shrinking and then disappearing. He looked at me.

"Their guards know what they're doing, we'll have to trust in them. Sending more risks creating chaos that will only play into the assassins' hands."

"Assassins?" The general sounded alarmed.

"Not if we can get to them first," said Lucas.

"Go to the stables attached to this estate," Griffith said. "Ask for my two personal mounts. They can carry me into battle and ride all day. They're the strongest we have."

Lucas nodded acknowledgement. "And General? I recommend you find and detain Lieutenant Martin as soon as possible. Probably best to do the same to any other Ellingtons you have in your ranks, just to be sure."

Shock crossed the general's face. "The Ellingtons?"

Lucas didn't take the time to answer, heading straight out the door, but I paused on the way. The general's eyes latched onto me, clearly hoping for an explanation, but I had remembered something else.

"Oh, one other thing. If you send a squad quietly across the river, you'll find someone interesting waiting for you on the other side." I quickly outlined where he could find Cassius.

The shock on his face grew, only to be replaced by a spreading grin as he grasped the opportunity I was offering him. Hopefully acquiring the enemy's crown prince would soften the sting of his officer's betrayal.

As soon as he had grasped the information, I took off after Lucas.

When we stood in front of the horses, I gulped. I had never ridden before, and now didn't seem like a great time to learn.

"Don't worry," Lucas said. "You'll be riding in front of me."

I almost melted with relief. "Why two horses, then?"

"You don't weigh much compared to the general, but two adults is a heavy burden for a horse, and we'll be pushing them hard. The second one is for when the first one tires."

He vaulted onto the horse's back, and a groom threw me up and helped me position myself. Lucas's strong arms encircled me, gripping the reins. He spurred the horse forward, and it leaped into motion, nearly unseating me but for Lucas's steadying hold. The second horse followed behind on a lead rein.

Both Bronton and the camp around it quickly fell away. Lucas slowed for no one, and those who found themselves in our path threw themselves aside rather than be run down. We soon settled into a rhythm, Lucas's close steadying presence the only thing keeping me from giving in to fear and panic about my friends and his family. But as many times as my mind leaped ahead to the Academy, it kept circling back to the past.

"Duke Lennox must be in on it, too," I said into an extended silence. "The more I think about it, the more foolish I feel that I didn't put it together. My attackers in first year were all killed in prison or managed to escape. I got a glimpse of one in a crowd of Stantorns and was sure he must be working for them, but it never occurred to me to question that the Head of Law Enforcement is an Ellington."

I paused and shook my head. "That attacker was probably never a Stantorn at all. And no wonder the Ellingtons felt free to attack me at will, knowing Lennox could clean up their mess. I was training with Walden at the time, too, and he knew I wasn't making progress. I think both those early attacks were them.

They wanted to see how I would respond to a dangerous situation, if it would bring out my powers as it did that first time."

"And it worked," Lucas said quietly. "So I guess you could say he was a good teacher."

I didn't bother replying to such an obviously facetious remark.

"And Dariela," I said. "She's an Ellington. I can't make much sense of her behavior, but I suppose we were never friends at all."

Lucas's arms tightened around me.

"I'm sorry, Elena. I wanted you to be more suspicious of others, more reticent, but now that you've learned the lesson, I wish I could wipe it away for you."

Lucas pushed the horses as hard as he dared, and the road flew past at a pace that made our previous journeys on it in carriages seem ludicrously slow. But it still took us hours to reach Corrin. I had been skimming drops of energy from everyone we encountered and held so much that I almost wondered if it would come bursting out of me as uncontrolled power.

So when we reached the city streets, I didn't hesitate to compose a working that swept the streets clear in front of us, allowing us to keep up the headlong pace. The city didn't seem to be in the type of chaos that an assassination of the king and queen would create, but it was possible word just hadn't gotten out yet.

As we made the final approach toward the Academy, we could see something, at least, was wrong. A mass of people milled in the streets outside the gates, a mix of red and gold, gray and silver, as commonborn guards and soldiers crowded in close around their mage officers.

A shout went up as soon as we drew close enough to be recognized.

"The prince! The prince!" sounded on many voices, but almost as many cried, "The Spoken Mage has returned!"

The crowd parted for us, and Lucas swung down before the gates, lifting me down after him.

"Where are my parents?" he asked General Thaddeus who we found at the center. "And my sister?"

The Head of the Royal Guard looked shaken and older than I had ever seen him, his Stantorn confidence evaporated.

"Thank goodness you're alive, Your Highness."

"Never mind me," said Lucas crisply. "What about my family?"

"They're inside," the general said, gesturing at the gates. "Their health is unknown."

"What happened?" Lucas asked.

"The messenger was sent immediately as you commanded. He never returned. When a second one was sent, he found the Academy secured against him."

I looked around at the number of mages in the crowd.

"Surely you can open a gate!"

"It's not the gate," the general said stiffly. "There is a second layer of workings built into the perimeter of the Academy, for use only in emergencies, and they've been activated. Only the Academy Head can do that."

"But have they been raised to keep my parents safe or to keep help out?" Lucas asked.

"That is a question we cannot answer," said the general. "And it's the reason I have hesitated to batter the workings down with every power I can call to my command. Especially since it would no doubt take a great deal of that power—if it could even be done —leaving little protection for what might come after." He frowned. "Do you have reason to think they might have been raised against your family? Do you doubt the loyalty of Lorcan?"

"Not Lorcan, no," Lucas said.

Our eyes met. What composition keys might Walden have been able to access while acting as Academy Head?

"Elena!" Julian pushed through the crowd. "You're alive! How did you get here?"

Thaddeus glared at him. "You, young man, are only here because I need every mage at my disposal. But you have proved you can't be trusted with the care of His Highness."

I winced.

"We're going in, Julian," Lucas said. "If we can, we'll send word out."

"But—" The general began to protest, but Lucas turned to me.

"These protections were designed for the trainees not the royal family. Lorcan described them to me once. It's a sort of net of power, woven from a vast number of compositions to give it strength. It's designed to keep anyone who is not a trainee or instructor from passing in or out. Officially we are still trainees."

Thaddeus looked torn, and I could almost hear his mental dilemma. Did he let the only member of the royal family who he knew for sure was safe walk into danger if it might mean rescuing all the others?

"I'm not asking your permission, General." Lucas pulled on my hand only to pause. "Oh, and I suggest you weed through these officers immediately. Place any who are Ellingtons into custody. And send men after Dukes Lennox and Magnus and their families. In fact, round up every Ellington you can find. We'll sort them out later."

"Your Highness?"

"They're traitors, Thaddeus," Lucas said. "I've just come from Kallorway, and my information is certain, although I don't know how far the rot spreads."

Julian swore under his breath but met our eyes with determination.

"We won't fail you," he said.

Lucas grabbed the gates, and for a moment I held my breath, wondering what would happen.

They swung open in the most normal way possible, and he walked through, with me almost tripping over his heels. The gate swung shut behind us, although we didn't touch it, the only visible sign that anything unusual was going on. But I didn't need my eyes to sound an alert when I could feel the suffocatingly strong press of power around us.

Lucas arced a path around the central fountain, heading for the front doors which were firmly closed. This time, however, although he tugged at them, they refused to open. He looked at me, eyebrows raised.

I shook my head. "There's so much power on that door it would take an immense working to get it open. And apparently it's not the kind of power that recognizes us as trainees. I could batter our way through, but we may not like what we find on the other side. We need to find another way in."

"The library," Lucas said. "It has the largest windows."

As we ran around the side of the building, I could see a gleam in Lucas's eyes. He hoped we would run into Walden, holed up in his sanctuary, but I felt sick at the thought of seeing my old mentor.

Power coated the building's walls and windows, but not like the power on the door.

"Let me," I said.

I used the binding words this time to allow me to craft a more complex working. I took my time to build up a composition that combined pure power with a physical element. When I said, "End binding," a stone bird bath lifted itself from one of the garden beds and flew, faster by far than either of us could have thrown it, at one of the windows. Alone it might have bounced back off, but the power I had coated it in propelled it forward, smashing the glass which shattered back into the room. The final shreds of my power smashed out the shards that remained in the sill, leaving us a safe entry point.

"Very neat," said Lucas with an approving smile. He seemed to have entered a place of utter focus, his fears and doubts stripped away and buried beneath the need to act.

We climbed inside. The library appeared completely deserted, as I would have expected it to be at this hour when all the trainees should be in composition class.

"Let's see what's going on in—" I said, at the same time as Lucas said, "Let's find Lorcan." But both of us cut off, swinging to a halt near the entrance of the library.

The huge room wasn't empty after all.

A smear of blood trailed from the door back toward the huge front desk. At the end of it we could just see a pair of legs, sprawled at an awkward angle on the floor, the rest of the body hidden by the desk.

I gagged. He must have entered the Academy some time ago. How long had his body been lying discarded here?

A sound from deeper in the library made us both stiffen just as Walden stepped into view. He froze, his eyes racing between us and then down to the partially concealed body. He had washed his hands and face, but he had missed a streak of red almost on his hairline and a splatter across the front of his robes.

No part of his usual geniality remained on his face. His shock at seeing us transformed quickly into anger.

"Those Kallorwegians can't get anything right." He spat the words at us. "I suppose you were the ones to send the messenger." He gestured at the man. "And now look what I've been forced to do. Desecrating the library, no less!"

"Desecrating...the...library?" I took a step toward him, rage burning away the sense of sorrow and loss and awful defilement that came from knowing I had shared my inner self with him.

But Lucas grabbed my arm, pulling me back.

"Don't waste your time and energy on him. We need to find my parents and sister."

Walden swelled, the image of the jovial, slightly rounded librarian jarring with his contorted features.

"Always those in power overlook the true value of us scholars. I am the one who discovered the true authority that belongs to the southern throne. And it is I who first saw that Stellan was no more fit to wield it than Osborne. After hundreds of years, only I had the true dedication to this library that was necessary to discover the hidden treasure my ancient predecessor carefully preserved."

He took a step toward us, his eyes alight. "In the secret storage space my explorations uncovered, I found the explanation he left for those who would follow. As a true librarian, he could not stand by and watch the destruction of history, and so he secreted copies of the books and scrolls King Stellan's ancestor destroyed. He did not explain why he allowed the knowledge of these hidden records to be lost, but I know I was meant to be the one to find them."

His eyes narrowed. "And in that act of destruction, both the Kallorwegian and Ardannian royal lines showed they were never fit to rule in the first place. They allowed the truth to be lost even by the crown itself! They did not value the power of knowledge wielded by the proper hands, and they will realize their mistake too late. You'll regret underestimating me, *Your Highness*. You may think the Ellingtons are the weakest of the great families, but we have strength none of you ever imagined. And we will finally take our place ruling over you all."

He tore a parchment I hadn't even seen him retrieve, and a shield of both power and smoke sprung up between us. I heard his feet hurrying away, deeper into the library, his shield protecting his escape.

I wanted to go after him, but Lucas's arm tugged me back toward the door, and I followed him. We ran down the quiet corridor, bracing ourselves for what we might find in the entrance hall, but it stood empty. Lucas sprinted for the stairs, and I followed close behind.

We took the stairs only one level, and I realized Lucas was making for Lorcan's office. It was the logical place to find important visitors. But our thundering steps must have drawn attention because the head of a first year poked out of a classroom door.

"Prince Lucas? Elena?" she asked. "You're back? What's going on?"

"Stay inside," Lucas snapped. "And bar the door. Check it's a trainee you recognize before you open it again."

She stared at him in surprise.

"Go!"

Starting, she disappeared back in and slammed the door behind her.

"Stop. Wait," I said. "We need to get them out. All of them. Who knows what could happen? And they might know what's going on, too."

Lucas pulled himself to a stop beside our composition classroom, punching the wall once before wrenching open the door and stepping inside. I closed it again behind us.

For a moment, nine pairs of eyes blinked at us. And then my friends shrieked my name, pouring out of their seats to crowd around us.

"Stop," said Lucas, and they all froze. "Have you heard anything of what's going on? Seen anything?"

"What exactly is the meaning of that?" asked Redmond coldly from the front of the room.

Lucas met his eyes, not backing down.

"The Academy's defenses have been raised. My family is somewhere here, and we are all in danger. Even now there may be Kallorwegian assassins present inside the walls with us."

Lavinia gave a quickly stifled shriek. I looked around the room.

"Where's Dariela?"

"She chose not to attend today's class it seems," said Redmond, somehow managing to sound offended by her absence despite Lucas's news.

"I'll bet she did," said Lucas grimly. "If you meet an Ellington on your way out, apprehend them if you can, run the other way if you can't."

Weston surged to his feet, his seat falling to the ground behind him.

"Are you saying the Ellingtons are in league with Kallorway?"

"I'm afraid so," I said. "Lucas sent a messenger ahead to warn his parents, and we just found Walden standing over his body."

"Walden?" This time Redmond's calm failed him, and he reached a hand back to steady himself against the desk behind him.

Lucas looked from Weston to Calix. "Thaddeus is outside the gates, but the front doors are barred by we don't know who. Secure another way out that can be used to evacuate the trainees and servants. Get them out to the safety of the Royal Guard, but give the library as wide a berth as possible."

Both of them nodded, their faces grim, and exited the room.

Lucas scanned the remaining group.

"Natalya and Lavinia, go pass the word to the other class-rooms. Tell the junior instructors to accompany the trainees out." He looked over at Redmond. "Redmond will hold whatever path Calix and Weston find until all of them are out."

I half expected Redmond to protest, but he made no demur, merely pulling a number of parchments from his robes. He ushered the two girls out of the room ahead of him.

Only our friends remained.

"Don't even try to tell us to leave." Finnian sounded far grimmer than I had ever heard him. "We're going to help you." His hand hovered protectively behind Coralie's back, but he didn't attempt to convince her to run for safety.

Lucas met Finnian's gaze measuringly and then nodded once.

"I've been sick with worry for you." Coralie threw her arms around me briefly before letting go and stepping back to Finnian's side. "We won't let you down," she added.

I turned to Saffron and Araminta. "I don't doubt your bravery and willingness to stay, but we need you to get the servants out." I looked from one to the other. "I don't trust that anyone else would care enough to put the effort in to be sure they're all out."

Saffron looked torn, but after only a moment she nodded.

"I understand." She also gave me a quick embrace. "Just don't die."

"And same to you." I managed a weak smile before she and Araminta slipped out of the room.

"How long do we give them all?" I asked. I could already hear feet in the corridor.

"No more waiting," Lucas said. "My family needs me."

CHAPTER 24

"Where are we heading?" Finnian asked as we joined the throng in the corridor, moving against the flow of trainees.

"Lorcan's study," I answered. "We received information that Kallorwegian assassins were planning an attack on Lucas's family while they're visiting the Academy today. Walden encountered our messenger, and he must have raised the Academy protections to prevent anyone else getting inside. That means the assassins must already be here. Walden may have still hoped to be able to leave them to carry out their plan—whatever it is—but he knows Lucas and I are here now. So I suspect they're about to abandon subtlety and go for a direct approach."

"What are they doing here today?" Finnian asked. "We've all been preparing for them to visit for the gala, but that's not for—"

"Walden lured them here." Coralie sounded sick. "I heard him three days ago in the library telling Jocasta how he had discovered an urgent issue that needed Their Majesties' personal attention as soon as possible. I guess when you're a monarch, as soon as possible means in three days. I thought it had something to do with the gala, but I was only walking past, so I didn't hear everything."

She squeezed Finnian's hand. "Is it really true? That he's a traitor? And...Dariela too?"

"That depends," said a voice from the corridor ahead of us, "on where your first loyalties should lie."

"With your crown and your kingdom," snapped Lucas, stopping and facing off against Dariela.

"Or with your family?" she countered.

I stepped forward, pushing Lucas behind me. Looking Dariela in the eye was difficult, all my feelings of betrayal flooding back. But I forced myself to do it, and to keep my face as open as I could manage.

"I've learned a lot about family in the last few years," I said. "I've learned that family will sacrifice for each other—they'll put their own needs aside."

Something subtle shifted in her face. It was a fleeting expression, gone in an instant, but it gave me hope. Some part of her was disappointed at my talk of sacrifice for family—she wanted to be convinced to do the right thing. I pressed on.

"But that goes both ways." I took a step toward her, and she didn't move. "Does your family sacrifice for you, Dariela? Are they willing to put aside their pride—and even their future—for you? Do they encourage you to do the right thing, no matter what?"

She flinched. Emboldened, I continued.

"Because if not, maybe your loyalty doesn't belong with them at all. I've learned another thing about family. It isn't static. It can grow and change. You can find new family." I gestured at myself. "Who knows better than me that you aren't bound by your blood?"

Lucas stepped up beside me, his manner softened.

"At the end of the day we're all responsible for our own choices," he said. "It's not too late for you, Dariela. You can still make the right choice. If you help us turn back the tide of death and destruction, I give you my word the crown will protect you."

Something cracked inside her. I could see it written clearly across her face, but her shoulders didn't slump, her posture didn't change.

"I have no wish to sit as queen on a throne drenched in blood," she said. "I will help you."

"Queen?" Finnian and Coralie stepped forward to join us.

She glanced back over her shoulder. "The treachery of my family goes further than you know. Kallorway think we aid them in exchange for positions of power within their empire. Osborne has sworn that an Ellington will govern Corrin when it's a subject of Kallmon."

Lucas shifted, anger radiating off his body, but he said nothing.

"But the Ellingtons have had enough of being secondary to those who believe themselves stronger. They play a deeper game than anyone knows."

Lucas glanced at me, and he didn't need to spell out the request in his eyes. I spoke quickly, but clearly, speaking a truth composition. When I had completed it, I asked Dariela only two questions.

"Is everything you've said to us true?"

"Yes," she said firmly.

"And you will aid us?"

"Yes," she said again, though her voice sounded weary this time.

I balled my fist, cutting off the composition, as my friends exchanged relieved looks. Lucas stepped slightly forward.

"My family," he said. "What of my family?"

"Walden intercepted the messenger," she said. "He realized something must have gone wrong and that more would follow, so he raised the external protections." She looked at Lucas and me with a wry gaze. "The two of you were supposed to be in Kallorway. No one was supposed to be able to get in."

"I should have sent the squads of guards with him," Lucas muttered. "I signed his death sentence by sending him alone."

I took his hand and squeezed it.

"And the front doors?" I asked. "Was that Walden, too?"

"The front doors?" Dariela frowned. "I know nothing of that. Your family are meeting with Lorcan in his office. When they finish and leave the Academy, they are to be assassinated on the front steps, viewed through the gates by the law enforcement guards conveniently summoned by Duke Lennox just in time to see—but not prevent—the spectacle. Kallorway wishes to send a message. And the Ellingtons wish that message to be received by the people of Ardann. The external protections won't interfere with any of that. In fact, they'll assist to keep the guards back."

Finnian frowned. "Then who secured the doors?"

"Lorcan," I said. "It has to be. When he realized no one else would be able to get through, he must have hoped to raise as many barriers between the assassins and their targets as possible —force them to burn compositions before ever they get near their intended victims. And he's retreated into the Academy's inner sanctum to keep the royals safe until help arrives."

"But if he knows the external protection is up, then he knows there is no help coming," Coralie said.

"But there is help coming." I looked first at Lucas and then my friends and last at Dariela. "We came, didn't we?"

Coralie gripped her bottom lip between her teeth, looking equal parts determined and terrified.

"We have to get to them," Lucas said. "Before the assassins decide it's time to switch plans and forget the steps."

He moved first, but the rest of us were right behind him, rushing toward the door to Lorcan's office.

"How many assassins are there?" Lucas asked Dariela.

She shrugged helplessly. "That was the Kallorwegian part of the plan. I never heard the details."

As we approached the external door to Lorcan's waiting room, we could hear no fighting, nor any screams or cries. Cautiously Lucas inched it open, peering inside before swinging it wide and entering freely.

"Thornton?"

Our combat instructor stood in front of the closed door to Lorcan's study, a drawn sword in one hand and a curl of parchment in the other.

"Thank goodness," I said. "So they're still safe? They're inside?"

Instead of answering, Thornton's eyes narrowed into slits, his gaze roaming over us to settle suspiciously on Dariela.

"She's with us now," said Lucas. "I take it you know about Walden, then?"

Thornton relaxed, but only slightly.

"I saw him kill that messenger with my own eyes. To be honest, I didn't think he had it in him." Thornton looked disgusted rather than impressed, however. "By the time I got to Lorcan and Their Majesties, Walden had somehow managed to raise the border protections—and to lock them in place so Lorcan couldn't remove them. Which means Their Majesties and the princess can't get out. Other protections, however, are down. Such as the one that should have notified Lorcan of intruders on the premises. Except the one limiting communication via composition." He sounded grim. "That one is still in place."

"So Lorcan secured the building and retreated in here." Lucas nodded. "A sound plan. But you're going to need some help if you're going to hold that door. That's what we're here for."

Thornton looked us up and down measuringly, an uncertainty lingering in his eyes. Was he thinking of Clarence?

"You've trained us for this," I said softly. "We won't fail you. Shield." My power sprang up in individual bubbles around each of us. I hadn't placed a single limitation on my working. I would keep us all alive if it killed me.

Something like relief washed over Thornton's face. Had it been our identities he questioned?

"Actually," he said. "That's not what's going on. You need to—"

An explosion rocked the room as the wooden door we had closed behind us blew off its hinges, catapulting into the room with a wall of flame. What would have happened to Thornton without our presence I didn't know, but my shield held firm, not so much as a breeze rustling anyone's hair.

Coralie looked at me in concern, and I smiled at her reassuringly. I overflowed with energy already, and I could feel the trainees and servants who still remained in the building, an untapped source of more power.

Every one of my friends withdrew a parchment as five mages in black robes barreled through the smoking doorway, their own shields firmly in place. I drew a breath, my mind racing through the possibilities, when a hand grabbed my arm and pulled me back two steps.

Thornton leaned over to speak quietly into my ear.

"They're not here. This is a diversion."

"What?" I stared up at him, my attempts at a composition entirely derailed.

"I will hold this door to my death to convince the Kallorwegians otherwise, but Lorcan had somewhere stronger to go. He took them to the dining hall. After your first year exams, he set up extra protections there so it could be used as a gathering place for the trainees in an emergency. He's hoping Walden doesn't know about those."

I swallowed. If Walden did, then he would know Lorcan would go straight there. If he had enough assassins, he might have decided to send attackers to both places, just to be sure. My friends had entered battle, but I couldn't follow the action or assist them. My mind seemed at once frozen and scrambling too fast to be of any use. I couldn't pull up a single word in front of my eyes.

"You need to go to them," Thornton said. "Protect them. I'll remain here."

I shook my head. "Alone? You'll be killed."

He raised his sword and stepped to the side to engage one of the Kallorwegians who had made it past my friends. Looking back over his shoulder, he actually smiled.

"Don't underestimate me."

Finnian grabbed at my shoulder, spinning me back around. From the look on his face, he had gathered the gist at least of Thornton's words.

"If we all leave it will be too obvious," he said, his words slurring together in their speed. "They might follow us and make things worse. We'll stay here to help Thornton. With four of us we should be able to keep them distracted while you and Lucas go."

I hesitated. If I left, I would have to drop my shields around them. I couldn't keep them up from such a distance in the chaos of whatever fights I would encounter. It would mean leaving them potentially to die.

"Go!" hissed Coralie, dashing past as she tore a parchment and sent a wind sweeping through the room. It broke against the assassins' shields, but succeeded in pushing them to one side, clearing my way to the door.

And in that moment, I knew Lorcan was right. I had to trust my friends to stand on their own—as they trusted me. Too much rode on us now for me to think I could carry this whole load on my shoulders.

With a nod, I ran forward, ducking beneath a fire ball that sent a nearby sofa into flames. As I passed Lucas, I grabbed him around the forearm, yanking him away from his opponent and out the empty doorway before he realized what had happened.

"Elena, what are you—" He struggled to free himself from my grip.

"They aren't there," I said, and he instantly stopped struggling. "Come on!"

He raced beside me as I barreled down the long corridor toward the entrance and the dining hall on the other side of it. His trust touched me, and I panted out an explanation as we ran.

"He's a diversion. They aren't there. Lorcan has them in the dining hall."

"But, Finnian and—"

"They know. They're staying to keep those ones busy."

"Maybe the Kallorwegians don't know," he panted out as we slid through the now empty entrance hall, all of the trainees having passed through to whatever exit Calix and Weston had managed to clear.

"Maybe." I could hear the disbelieving note in my voice, and Lucas didn't press the point.

He had his hand on the handle of one of the dining hall doors when running feet came thundering from the direction of the library. He let it go and stepped away, but the Kallorwegians had already seen us. If they had been unsure where to look for the royals before, they had a good idea where they might find them now.

"We keep them here," he said to me. "They don't get through this door."

His voice must have carried further than I thought because the door behind us cracked open.

"Lucas!" His sister's face appeared, astonishment and relief competing for prominence.

"Get back inside," Lucas snapped. "And stay there!"

He stepped forward, placing himself in front of me, where his bulk blocked the slim opening from view of the mages who were pouring into the entrance hall. I glanced back in time to see a flash of red and gold before the princess disappeared as if pulled away by someone. Lorcan took her place.

"Elena!" Horror was replaced with relief.

"They're coming," I said. "Get that door closed."

Lorcan hesitated.

"We've sent the trainees out," I said. "And the servants. Everyone we could. We'll hold the Kallorwegians here. If we can't, it will be up to you and whatever guards you've got with you to get the royals out. If you can make it past the gate, Thaddeus is waiting."

Lucas had drawn his sword and already ripped two compositions with the aid of his teeth. I turned back toward him, ready to help, but Lorcan called to me again.

"Elena! Walden, he—"

I threw a final glance over my shoulder. "I know! Now get that door closed!"

The thud of wood against wood sounded, and then power blossomed at my back. I nodded with satisfaction and surveyed the scene in front of me.

I had withdrawn my shield around the others, but it remained around Lucas, and from the jolts I had felt it had already seen use. The black-robed assassins caught sight of me, and a ripple of movement spread through them as all of their hands dived for their robes. They hadn't been expecting me, so perhaps they had run the risk of lighter shields, holding their stronger compositions back in case of need.

"Drain!" I screamed, and my power raced against the speed of their hands. Most of them managed to rip their compositions in time, but one was a beat behind the rest.

My power caught him before he could release his shield, ripping the energy from him so fast that his body jerked, his composition slipping from his fingers. The speed had kept me from setting any limitations, and my power drained him before I had time to think about what was happening.

My own body jerked at the horrible feeling of my power ripping the last breath from his body. He swayed in place for the briefest second, and then his body crumpled to the floor. I wavered, a brief and violent sickness sweeping through me before I forced it back.

My power still beat against the others' shields, and I let it. Filled with their companion's energy, I could afford to weaken them. But as fast as my power drained their shields, they ripped new ones, overlapping them so that they were never left unprotected. Six of them still remained, and even with my vast stores of energy, I could feel myself slowly draining.

Lucas darted to my side, his sword dripping red. Following his trajectory, I saw an assassin lying face down, blood pooling around him. I cut off the power that beat against his now pointless shield.

"They have limitations," Lucas said. "Their shields, I mean. They've put all their power into protecting against your attack, and their protections against physical attack are weak."

Lucas had still had no proper opportunity to replenish his own compositions, although he had used several of the ones I collected in Kallorway for him. I knew they wouldn't have the strength of his own, though.

He didn't hesitate, however, wielding his sword as if he considered it an equally satisfactory weapon. I would have to be his power, and he would be my arm.

"Her," I said, pointing at one of the attackers at random.

Lucas didn't need an explanation, racing straight for her as I whispered, "Attack." An ornate lantern tore itself from the room and flung itself at her, beating against an invisible shield. I could already feel how much weaker this layer of shielding against physical attack was. It crumpled just as Lucas reached her.

She tried to tear another composition, but her hands trembled, and she didn't manage it in time to save herself from his blade.

We had reduced their numbers to four, but the remaining assassins had realized our strategy. When Lucas approached the next of them, not only had he already set a third layer of shielding around himself, but he had his sword drawn and ready. One of the others approached close, ready to back him up, and I pulled my sword free, ready to fight beside Lucas if needed.

Before I could move toward him, however, a fresh assault hit both of our shields. Lucas didn't even pause, his sword flashing as he attacked the two assassins near him. But I staggered from the sheer force of the power hitting us and the resultant speed of the energy drain.

I had barely regained my balance when a sword flashed past my face, deflected by my shield. The remaining two attackers had come for me. Out of the corner of my eye, I thought I saw one of Lucas's attackers fall before his blade, but I didn't have time to check.

The clatter of feet on the stairs sounded above the ring of blades and the whoosh of a wind someone had unleashed. I looked up in time to see a group of at least ten servants frozen on the lower portion of the stairs. My eyes just had time to meet Saffron's at the back of the group before I heard a ripping sound beside me.

"Shield!" I screamed. My power sped across the room, racing the power released by the assassin beside me.

But his outpaced mine, staying just ahead. I could do nothing else to protect the servants from this distance, but my body reacted instinctively anyway. I careened past my attackers, saved only by my shield which shoved them out of my way. But I had only made it a couple of strides when the assault composition hit the huddled commonborns.

The assassin's power burst against a solid shield, however, and Saffron pushed to the front of the group, two parchment halves slipping from her fingers. I breathed a sigh of relief as my own shield enclosed them just as Saffron's protection cracked.

"Get them out of here," I called to her.

Her eyes flew behind me, to the closed and shielded dining hall door, and then across to the closed and shielded main doors. Desperately I saw her look up the opposite corridor toward Lorcan's office.

Two black-robed shapes appeared blocking the gap, and my stomach dropped. Where were Finnian and Coralie? Had the attackers realized the ploy and given up?

But there was no sign of my friends chasing them down, coming to join the fight.

The two new assassins immediately began to pull out composition after composition, making no effort to reach for their swords. Their appearance allowed the two near me to resume their physical attack, one running to the new group while one remained near me.

My shields protected everyone, holding back the swords, but each new composition and each new sword blow drained more of my energy. Lucas had managed to disable one of his attackers and sparred with the second, keeping him from joining the drain on me, but it wasn't enough.

Saffron began to usher the servants back up the stairs, but the Kallorwegians continued to hurl compositions after them, forcing me to keep my shielding going. I swayed, my mind racing frantically as I tried to work out how to best use my remaining energy. But exhaustion pulled at me, making it hard to think.

I needed to replenish my energy from the servants. The further they got up the stairs, the harder it would be for me to do so. I needed to act now.

The letters that would spell out the single word I needed—drain—struggled to form in my tired brain. I pulled them into line, only for them to shatter as Dariela came charging past the assassins at the entrance to the corridor. I felt the power shielding her, and I felt it flicker. Abandoning my letters, I pulled up new ones.

"Shield," I said, yet again, extending my protection over her too.

My knees buckled, and I dropped onto them, only barely keeping from keeling over completely. Dariela nearly collided with me, my shield recognizing that she wasn't a threat. She tried to pull me to my feet.

"He's coming," she panted.

"Who?" I gasped out, but she didn't need to answer.

Brushing past the assassins, who still continued their attack with what seemed to be endless compositions, Walden hurried into the room.

He paused and took in the situation in an instant. His eyes latched onto my pale, sweating face, and he smiled. His hand thrust into a pocket, and I reformed the mental letters I needed for a draining composition. I needed energy, and I needed it now.

He tore his working before I managed to speak mine, although only just. His power surged, racing toward Lucas, Dariela, and the servants simultaneously. When it reached its destination, it took me by surprise, shaping itself into a shield, a second layer encircling the shield of my own that already protected them.

Then my draining composition smashed into his barrier around the servants, and I understood the purpose of his working. He had blocked me from accessing their energy—no doubt while leaving them open to physical attack, forcing me to maintain my own shields around them. With the rest of the Academy evacuated, and those in the dining hall protected behind their own shields, I had no one left to drain.

The Kallorwegian attackers took only seconds to comprehend the new state of affairs, and they shifted their attacks, aiming swords toward my friends but power toward me. One of them collapsed an upper section of the stairs, trapping the servants and Saffron within their reach.

And, worst of all, two of them had now begun a steady assault on the dining hall door. I considered throwing another shield across it, but I was already stretched dangerously thin.

Walden withdrew a parchment, moving slowly this time, smiling across the distance at me. My stomach turned. Nothing about him proclaimed the fighter, but in a war of words, his cunning mind was the most dangerous thing present.

I could tell from the way he took his time that this was his strongest composition, the battle-winning one. And something in his eyes told me it was coming for me. Like the snow blossom he had uprooted months ago, I had no further purpose, and he would have no qualms about discarding me. I was depleted enough that if his attack had enough force it would break through my shield. I cast a desperate look around the room. Did I drop the other shields and focus all my remaining energy on my own? But the other assassins still fought on, their swords flashing, held back only by my power.

One of them had ripped up stones from the floor and walls and even ceiling, setting them to batter away at my shields. Sweat dripped down my forehead, my breathing ragged despite my lack of physical exertion.

Lucas could hold his own with his sword, and he must have shields in his small, stolen store. I met his eyes across the distance and read permission in them.

"End Lucas," I whispered, almost silently.

But would it be enough? Should I drop my other shields as well? Dariela drew her sword, and I stared at her, my confused and exhausted brain struggling to decide.

The tearing of Walden's parchment seemed to echo despite the sounds of battle. I had taken too long. My imagination told me I could physically see his power rushing toward me.

A battle cry rang out above it all as a flying figure leaped in front of me, taking the full brunt of deadly power Walden had unleashed.

I screamed and dropped to my knees beside Lucas's prone

body. The shield we had raided from the Kallorwegians across the border had failed, and he lay there, exposed and still. My own shield stretched to cover him.

Looking up, my gaze focused on Walden. Lucas's sacrifice had brought clarity to my foggy mind. I had to end this, and I had to do it fast. But Walden stood comfortably behind a strong shield, and my energy was dangerously depleted. For a moment anger flashed in his eyes at Lucas's intervention, but satisfaction replaced the emotion as he examined Lucas's body.

Dariela dropped to her knees beside me. "I'm so sorry. I'm so sorry. I'm so sorry." She murmured it over and over again, her usual strength broken by everything that had happened.

Across from us Walden pulled out a parchment. What new horror did he mean to unleash? But instead of ripping it, he pulled out a pen, and crouched down to rest it on the ground, oblivious to the battle raging around him.

Cold surged through me. His shield and my weakness bought him the chance to use the one advantage that was usually mine. He could shape his working to the situation, giving it finesse and targeted strength. And Walden might not be able to wield a sword, but I didn't doubt the sophistication of his composition skills. We couldn't allow him to unleash whatever horror he was writing out on that page.

Every second I weakened further, and there was only so much I could do at once. Lucas's words from Kallorway sprang into my mind. He had said a time of desperation might come when my own compositions wouldn't be enough.

I kept my eye on Walden who was taking his time. And why not? The longer he waited, the weaker I became. I had to find another way to stop whatever battle-winning composition he was concocting.

"Dariela," I hissed. "Take off Lucas's boot."

To her credit, when issued a direct instruction—even a strange one—she didn't hesitate.

"Which one?"

"I don't know. Both. There's a composition in one of them."

She crawled around his body, gripping the closest boot and yanking hard. I took a deep breath and summoned the words I needed in my mind's eye in order.

"I'm going to put everything I have into breaking their shields," I said. "If I drop my shields, can you replace them around you and Saffron and the servants? You shouldn't need to hold for long."

She nodded, pausing in her efforts to remove Lucas's second boot to withdraw two small slips of parchment and rip them. They looked short, and I doubted they would last long. She resumed her efforts on the boot as I whispered, "End."

All of my shields dropped. I gave myself a single second of sweet relief, and then I said, "Attack."

All of the Kallorwegians, as well as Walden, looked up, but my force focused on the closest black robe, battering at the assassin's shield. The room whirled around me as the last of my power drained away. But I had been focused on defense for some time, and none of them had renewed their shields. I held on, clinging to my consciousness with every ounce of willpower in me.

I felt the mage's shield crack as I held onto the image of a final five letters.

"Drain." The word fell from my lips, more breath than spoken word.

As this final burst of power left me, I slumped forward to lie beside Lucas. But I was still half-conscious as it found its mark, energy pouring back across the room and into my depleted body. Sight returned and sound. I pushed myself back into a sitting position as the mage I drained managed to activate another shield, cutting me off.

But I hadn't limited my composition, and it had already found another mark, filling me with even more energy until that source was also cut off. But with each fresh burst of energy, I was able to strengthen my attack, breaking through again and again in a cycle that left me a little stronger with each passing moment.

Walden looked worried now and began to write faster, his shields the only ones that hadn't broken.

Dariela's shielding efforts wouldn't last much longer either.

I worked another assault composition, using my regained energy to pour power at all of them, but focusing on Walden. Two of their shields dropped, and I sucked up more energy. I felt Walden's protection falter, fear flickering in his eyes for the first time.

His pen paused, and his other hand reached for an already completed composition. I held out my hand to Dariela, sure she must have found Lucas's sealing composition by now. The second Walden's shield cracked, I would unleash it, throwing everything I had left into a shield that would enclose me in a bubble with Walden and the servants. Someone at least might still benefit from my desperate act.

I just hoped the shield would hold long enough to keep everyone else safe. Surely by the time the sealing blocked my power—thus cutting off my shield—it would be too late for it to seal them too?

But nothing was placed into my fingers. Turning my head, I saw Dariela finish reading the words on the paper in her hand. She looked up at me, comprehension on her face. She made no move to hand it over.

"No," I said, as she gripped it in both hands and began to tear. It was too late to intervene. All I had time to do was shout out my prepared shielding composition, adjusting the layers in my mind to change slightly who I protected.

All of Walden's accomplices now lay prone around him, too drained to respond to the new threat. As Walden's shield fell, I poured every remaining drop of their energy into holding the shield around Dariela, Walden, and the servants. I only wished I could shield Dariela from the sealing as well. Did she know the sacrifice required of the mage who worked a sealing composition?

Power flared as the sealing composition was unleashed, drawn from Dariela as well as the parchment she held. But even as I felt it, safely contained within my shield, I realized my mistake. When Walden lost his ability to access power, the power he had already unleashed into his unfinished composition would rebound—just as it had once done for Clarence in our composition class. Walden would inadvertently destroy those within my shield at the very least—if he didn't bring half the building down as well.

"Dampen!" I yelled, dropping the now unnecessary shield to pour power into my new composition.

An explosion of light and noise emerged from the parchment in front of Walden, expanding upward for at least a foot before suddenly reversing and sucking back into itself.

It was over.

CHAPTER 25

*W*alden's scream cut through the breathless silence. His hands and lower arms had been too near the parchment and had been mostly destroyed by the contained explosion—blackened and burned almost past recognition.

Now that it was safe to do so, Saffron urged the servants down the stairs and into the entrance hall. Several of them hung back, clearly terrified and traumatized, but Damon boldly led the way. I hadn't seen him in the crowd before, and I managed the ghost of a smile. I was glad he had been one of those present.

"Gather their compositions," Saffron said to him. "I don't want any nasty surprises catching us from behind if one of them wakes up."

She turned to me, her face stricken as her eyes lingered on Lucas's body. I shook my head at her.

"Coralie and Finnian. We left them in Lorcan's office with Thornton. I don't know…"

She didn't need me to finish, sprinting off down the corridor while Damon rallied a couple of the other servants to his task. I didn't bother to warn them about not looking at the words. They would find out soon enough that they no longer posed a risk to themselves or anyone else.

But I knew that I was only delaying the inevitable moment. Forcing myself to confront reality, I looked down at Lucas, lying next to where I knelt. His body was unmarked, but he lay still, half rolled away from me.

Tears blinded me as I reached out trembling hands to turn him onto his back. I could see no signs of life, but I had to at least try.

Dragging a rough arm across my eyes, I tried to say the beginning of the binding words that would allow me to compose a diagnostic working. Perhaps life still lingered inside him, although his chest no longer moved up and down.

"No!" Dariela pulled at my arm, breaking my concentration before I could gather any power to begin. "It's too late. You'll only kill yourself trying. I'm so sorry, Elena. It should have been me."

I needed to tell her that I didn't care what it cost me—that I had endured too much to forever be separated from him now. But I couldn't seem to find any words. I knew, though, that I couldn't live with myself unless I tried. I would gladly give up every last drop of my power to bring him back.

The thought lodged in my brain, calling up an image of Declan's lopsided eyebrows. But it was his words that made me jerk into motion.

We can work any healing, almost without limits, he had said. And then he had given me a gift. I had even noted that he felt tired as he handed it over.

I pulled out the silk pouch, my fumbling fingers almost dropping it in my haste. I had forgotten all about it in the frantic hours that had passed since I received it. Ripping it open, my fingers found the smooth surface of a piece of parchment.

I pulled it out and read the words as fast as my eyes could go. My fingers began tearing it before my eyes had even reached the bottom, ripping all the way through a mere second later. I flicked my fingertips in Lucas's direction.

Just as Declan had promised, the rush that it released felt like energy rather than power. A small piece of him—far more powerful than any healing composition fueled by power, settled over Lucas, sinking in along his long frame.

If there was any lingering remnant of life in Lucas, any hope of resuscitation, Declan's healing could retrieve him. My own heartbeat thundered in my ears, drowning out the sounds around me. One beat. Two. Three.

He sucked in a violent breath, his body spasming. Another breath, and another. Then he was moving, surging to his feet before I could prevent him. I jumped up beside him, searching his face in disbelief.

He looked around wildly. "What's going on? What happened?" He took in the servants, still stripping our enemies of their compositions, and Walden's slumped body lying where he had passed out—from pain or shock, I didn't know.

"Where are my family?"

I had been too terrified for him to think of them, and even now, I couldn't pull my mind away from the miracle of his recovery. Tears streamed down my cheeks.

He looked back at me, his attention caught by my appearance. Alarm sprang into his face, and he gripped both of my arms.

"What is it? What's the matter? Are you injured?"

"You're alive! I can't...I can't believe it."

He frowned. "I remember jumping in front of you, but then everything is blank."

"Declan saved you." I couldn't seem to stop smiling at him.

He stared back at me in confusion before sweeping the room with his eyes as if looking for the Kallorwegian, and I remembered that in the midst of everything I hadn't yet told him Declan's news.

"Finnian!" Still looking around the room, Lucas was the first to see the new arrivals limping down the corridor.

Finnian had a heavy gash in one leg, and one of his arms hung at a strange angle. His pale face was half covered in blood from a wound that must have been healed because I could see no trace of it now.

Saffron supported him under one shoulder, and Coralie the other. We rushed forward to meet them half way, helping them to lower Finnian to the ground. He made only a strangled groan, but he swayed, his pale face suggesting he was close to passing out.

Coralie's energy felt low, and I guessed she had written compositions on the spot to save him from whatever wounds had caused all that blood. I turned to Saffron instead, and she offered before I could even ask.

"Take as much energy as you need to heal him." Her worried eyes stayed trained on her cousin.

I did so without argument, healing him while the others all watched on. When I finished, he smiled up at me.

"You know, you're a handy friend to have around, Elena."

I laughed out my relief.

"How about you boys see if you can minimize this nearly dying thing next time?" I suggested.

"Next time?" Finnian shook his head. "I promise to be ever ever so good if only you can please make sure there's never a next time."

He tried to smile but was too exhausted to quite pull it off.

The door to the dining hall shrieked as it opened, attracting all of our attention as Lorcan exited first, surveying the mess and chaos of the entrance hall. His eyes eventually latched onto us, and he called something over his shoulder.

Several guards appeared next, compositions and swords still gripped in their hands. It was galling to see them so fresh, but I knew why they had stayed as a last defense.

Princess Lucienne preceded her parents into the entry, but Queen Verena saw us first. She called for her son, and he hurried across to her, weaving his way past bodies and gaping holes in the floor.

I looked back at Coralie before glancing down the corridor behind her.

"I'm sorry," she said quietly. "They got past us and realized the royals weren't there. Dariela went after them, and I should have come too, but..." She looked at Finnian who had regained his feet.

He said nothing, his arms snaking around her stomach and tucking her back in against his chest, leaving her still facing me, guilt on her face.

"You did the only thing you could do," I said. "I understand." I looked down the corridor. "But what of Thornton? Is he in need of..." My voice trailed away at the stricken look in her eyes.

"He did everything he could. I wish you could have seen him fight. But there were five of them, and they had so many compositions."

My tears welled again, and I pushed them down. Thornton had done so much to keep his trainees alive over the years, and now he had been the one to pay the ultimate price himself. But I knew he would have been pleased with me. I had saved as many as I could, and that would have to be enough.

Together we all crossed back into the center of the room. Dariela stood there, her eyes fastened on two torn pieces of parchment still in her hands.

"Why did you do it?" I whispered to her. "Didn't you know it would block your access to power too?" I could feel the shadow over her energy, and it felt unutterably strange on someone I knew and had trained beside.

"I knew," she said. "All of the Mage Council knew about the delegation's discovery, and Lorcan told Walden..." She looked up at me. "But it had to be me. This was my mess, not yours."

317

"I'm sorry," I said.

"Elena!" Lorcan called my name, pulling me from the moment. He stood over Walden's unconscious body, staring down at him with shadowed eyes.

I picked my way across to him.

"Lucas tells me you're responsible for all of this." He gestured at the bodies that littered the floor around us.

"Well, not all of it," I said.

He raised an eyebrow. "And now he tells us that he thinks you'll be able to use sheer force to single-handedly batter down the protections that are still raised around this Academy. In fact, he seems to think you limitless."

I bit my lip. "There might be something I never told you."

"Evidently." He paused. "But now is hardly the moment for recriminations. I understand you'll need some energy?"

It turned out the servants Saffron had been gathering from the top floors weren't the only ones still trapped in the Academy. Araminta had the rest of them hiding in the gardens after the protections failed to let them through like the trainees and instructors. Something I would need to have a word with Lorcan about in the future.

It turned out to be fortunate, however, since I had to drain more than half the energy of every person left standing to create enough power to smash the protections with the single strong blow required. They cracked at my onslaught, coming down in a sudden rush. Thaddeus had the gates pulled open before any of us could move, and squads of royal guards poured in to form a protective circle around Lucas and his family.

The jostling guards tried to pull Lucas away from me, but he kept a firm hold, refusing to let us be parted. They gave in, sweeping me into the bubble of stillness they had created. Tired, dirty, strained, and with a tear-stained face, I found myself face-to-face with Lucas's parents. King Stellan and Queen Verena.

"That was an…interesting display," the queen said.

318

I didn't like the concern flickering behind her royal mask.

"You have nothing to be afraid of, Mother," Lucas said, gripping my hand tighter. "Like I already told you, Elena just saved all of our lives."

"For which we must thank you," the king said.

"You're welcome, Your Majesty," I replied.

"I hope you won't be offended," King Stellan said, "but I think it might be best if you remain here for now. Just until we have all this sorted out."

"I've told you, you can trust her." Lucas's voice grew heated.

"So much power in one person," Princess Lucienne murmured, her eyes locked on me consideringly.

"If she stays, I stay." Lucas straightened and slipped his arm fully around my back.

"Very well," said the king. "We cannot tarry here, but stay if you must."

"I'm going to marry her, Father," Lucas said in a serious tone. "So you'll have to accustom yourself to her presence eventually."

A thrill ran through me at his bold declaration.

"Lucas!" His mother reached out for him, but he ignored her, keeping his eyes firmly on his father.

"I'm not asking for your permission. I'm stating a fact. I will give everything for this kingdom except for this. I will not give up Elena."

Lucienne stepped forward when her parents said nothing, and unlike them her face held no shock. If anything, her eyes gleamed appreciatively.

"What my parents mean to say, Elena of Devoras, is that we will be more than delighted to welcome you into our family." She glanced at her father. "But perhaps it will be best if you both stay here for now. Who knows what rumors will be swirling, and—"

"We will gladly stay," Lucas said. "I think we've done our part."

"Your Majesty! Your Majesty!" A mage I didn't recognize

squeezed his way into our circle. "We've just had word from Kallmon."

"From our intelligencers?" The king frowned.

"No." The man shook his head, looking astonished. "From General Haddon, Head of their Royal Guard."

"What did he say?" asked the queen.

"King Osborne has been assassinated by a rebellion led by the general. He says that Prince Lucas and the Spoken Mage promised him our support. He wants that support in exchange for a peace treaty."

Peace. It was a hard concept to imagine. No more conscription. No more soldiers sent off to die.

But the royals looked concerned rather than pleased.

"Lucas?" The king looked disapprovingly at his son.

"No one said anything about assassination," Lucas said. "You know I would not lend Ardann's support to regicide."

Suddenly I understood their concern. I imagined regicide was a worrying precedent when you sat on a throne yourself. And no doubt General Haddon was aware of that and had chosen his words wisely. I had gazed into Mabel's eyes, and I couldn't believe the rebels had ever intended anything but death for Osborne. There had been too much blood shed.

"We did get a report from one of our intelligencers as well to confirm it," the man—who must be a trusted official—said tentatively.

"What did they say about the succession?" Lucienne asked.

"She said that the rebels conducted a coordinated attack against every member of Osborne's family. But the crown prince has disappeared without a trace. They think he might still be alive."

"Ah, about that..." I said, his words reminding me of yet another thing I had forgotten in the chaos. "I believe we'll find that General Griffith has him in custody in Bronton."

"General Griffith has Prince Cassius?" King Stellan stared from me to his son.

"It's a long story," Lucas said.

"We don't have time for it now," the king said, "but I shall expect to hear it very soon."

"This could be just what we need to salvage the situation," Lucienne murmured. "Tell the rebels we will sign a peace treaty with Kallorway on the condition that we sign it with the rightful king—King Cassius. And tell them if they don't agree, we might decide it's finally time we took the fight to them."

The queen frowned. "Put Cassius on the throne only to find ourselves in the same position in five years' time when the son decides to continue his father's dream?"

A thought had been circling my mind, trying to get my attention ever since Dariela's sacrifice and Damon's unexpected good fortune. But only now did it properly land.

"Excuse me," I said. "I might have an idea about that."

All four of them looked at me inquiringly, and I swallowed. But it wasn't an idea I could let go, so I continued to speak.

"I understand you've heard about the sealing composition we learned from the Sekalis. What if you gave Cassius back his throne on the condition that he seal himself? Along with all the key mages who supported him. It should pacify the rebels, and it will ensure Cassius remains weak—it will take everything he has just to keep his own throne, I imagine." My voice grew excited at all the possibilities.

"And we could make sure they use the opportunity to seal some key members of their commonborn population as well. Some of them have been supporting the rebels, so perhaps they could be chosen. I think we would find in five years that Kallorway was an altogether different sort of kingdom."

The king and queen exchanged a long look.

"It's actually an excellent idea, Elena," the king said.

I licked my lips. I might be pushing my luck, but I had to take the opportunity presented to me.

"And we could do the same," I said. "We have to do the same."

Even Lucas looked shocked, so I hurried to clarify.

"Not you, of course. I didn't mean that. But we have mages incarcerated right now because they proved themselves unable to control their power—or they chose to abuse it. Why not offer them a choice? Remain in prison for the rest of their days or lock their power forever. We couldn't seal all of our commonborn that way, but we could seal some."

The royals exchanged another look.

"An idea that bears serious consideration," Lucienne said slowly.

"When our immediate troubles are past," the king said firmly. "For now, we must get back to the palace."

I nodded, ecstatic that they had taken me so seriously and would even consider the idea. From the way Lucas's arm tightened supportively around me, I knew he wouldn't let them forget it, or try to brush it aside.

When his family left, a detachment of the guards remained behind, still providing us a circle of quiet amid the new busyness of the courtyard as soldiers and more guards poured in to comb the building and grounds for any sign of further Kallorwegian activity.

Lucas immediately took me properly into his arms. "You're brilliant, do you know that?"

I smiled up at him, soaking in his presence and the wonderful fact that he was alive.

"They'll get used to you, I promise," he added. "It's just a lot to take in all at once. My family isn't used to knowing that someone else is stronger and more equipped than them."

He brushed back a strand of my hair that had fallen across my face.

"But that's exactly why I know they'll accept you." He didn't exactly sound happy. "Royalty is supposed to marry strength."

I smiled up at him. "I let General Griffith adopt me so we could be together, remember? I don't care why they agree, just that I never have to be separated from you again."

He pulled me still closer, the heat in his eyes making me shiver.

"I have promised you so much, Elena, and failed to deliver. But this is one promise I don't mean to break. If you will become my wife, I will never stop fighting for us again. Every day for the rest of our lives. Because you are everything I need and more. Your passion, your determination, your integrity—even your maddening stubbornness. I need it, and our kingdom needs it. Together we're going to build a new world." His voice dropped low, delicious shivers springing up everywhere his whispered words brushed against my skin. "I love you, Elena."

"I love you too," I whispered back.

His kiss cut off any attempt I might have made at listing the reasons why, and so I leaned into the embrace and let my lips tell him in a different way.

CHAPTER 26

*L*ater, when the building had been cleared by the Royal Guard five separate times, we were allowed back to our suites. After everything that had happened, I wanted sleep. But I wanted answers more.

No doubt Lucas's parents were using compositions to pry them out of Lennox, but we had our own source right here. Lucas and I found Dariela in her suite, packing. She didn't seem surprised to see us and gestured for us to take seats. We did so, and I glanced at Lucas before launching straight in.

"You said before that the actual assassination was the Kallorwegian role in the plan. What was the Ellington role?"

"Our part was supposed to be to sow confusion and chaos in the wake of the assassinations," she said, "preparing the way for their army to sweep through the kingdom." She continued to pack.

"And the real plan?" I asked.

She glanced over and swallowed. "The assassins were supposed to kill the king and all his family. But Walden and Lennox had planned to arrange it so that you were absent, Lucas. They had Ellingtons ready in key positions to seize power in the resulting chaos. And then you would have been offered a choice. Marry me and ascend the throne with their full support or be executed like your family before you."

"I would never—" Lucas started to growl, but she cut him off.

"Wouldn't you? Remember you were meant to believe Kallorwegian assassins just killed your family." Her eyes flicked to me. "And if you had suspicions about my family's involvement, there would have been other inducements..."

Her family had planned to make her queen. But even speaking the words seemed to disgust her, and bitterness tinged her voice as she spoke of her relatives.

"They wanted legitimacy for the reign and as smooth a transfer of power as possible," she continued. "Naturally you wouldn't actually have been left to rule, Lucas, but they had plans for you in the immediate aftermath. Plans for all of Ardann while the kingdom remained united behind the true heir."

"Kallorway," I murmured, the breadth of their plan only now becoming clear.

She nodded. "While Ellingtons seized power in Corrin, agents of our family were poised to assassinate King Osborne and his family. A deep division already splits Kallmon. In the confusion that would follow, with neither side claiming responsibility for the assassination, it wouldn't have been the Kallorwegian army that swept across the border. Instead it would have been an Ardannian one heading the other way—an army bent on avenging not only their king, slain by Kallorwegian assassins, but the countless deaths of the last thirty years."

I stared at her open-mouthed, and she met my eyes steadily.

"If the Kallorwegians succeeded in their assassination, is there a town or family in Ardann that would stand against such a plan? That would protest against strong leadership that promised to lead them into Kallorway and end the aggression once and for all?"

I said nothing. There was nothing to say.

"And when the dust settled," she said, "Osborne would have his united southern empire. Only he wouldn't be alive to see it. An Ellington dynasty would rule over the south, with a strong young queen left to lead alone—in mourning for her king, killed in battle against the Kallorwegians."

"Only I don't suppose they ever meant for you to rule alone," I said softly.

She gave a humorless laugh. "Perhaps I should have said a puppet queen, bound by loyalty to her family and crippled by guilt over the blood shed to give her a throne. No, I don't imagine they ever intended for me to rule in anything but name."

"I'm sorry, Dariela," I said.

"I knew nothing about any of it," she said. "Up until last summer when they finally decided I was old enough to be told the truth of their plans. All I knew growing up was that I must always train harder, must always be the best. But now I know that even my parents' marriage was arranged by Duke Lennox, strategically planned to produce the strongest possible children —since the Ellingtons needed a child of the correct age to embody the perfect image of a ruler."

She gave a tight smile. "They waited to have children until Princess Lucienne was born—they needed our ages aligned after all if they wanted one of their children to marry a prince or princess—only then it took them years to fall pregnant. Imagine the irony if the perfect breeding pair had been unable to produce a child. But then, just after Lucas was born, they fell pregnant with me."

She paused.

"It still seems ironic to me, though. For twenty years I was pushed to be the best—and now it turns out they always intended for me to marry into power. I fought for so long to prove I was good enough on my own, stronger than all the Ellingtons who had come before and failed to win our family prominence." Her voice dropped. "Perhaps all they really wanted was to break my spirit. To prove I wasn't good enough so that I would make no protest when they took control of my reign."

"Perhaps," said Lucas, his voice showing no sign of the tears that clogged up my throat and prevented me from speaking. "But they didn't, did they? Because here you are standing when they are falling. It is my sister who will rule as queen one day, not you, but right now you're proving that you would have made a far better and stronger ruler than your parents ever intended."

His words seemed to do more than any sympathy from me could have done. Her back straightened, and a determined look came into her eyes.

"And you succeeded, you know," I said. "You were the best in our class."

She laughed dryly. "Except for the two of you, you mean. The Ellingtons have been planting the seeds for this plan for decades. And then you came along, Elena, and upset everything. They've been trying to work out how to deal with you for nearly four years now."

"I thought you didn't know anything about it back when Elena arrived," Lucas said.

"I didn't. But I made my parents tell me everything last summer, once they broke the news. There has been ongoing disagreement among the broader family on the correct handling of the Spoken Mage. At first Walden was convinced he could befriend you and turn you against the other families. He thought he could unlock your powers and shape you into the Ellingtons' greatest weapon." She shook her head.

"The balcony collapse? That was him. All those attacks on you? Him. Well, except for the last attempted abduction during exams. That was only partially him."

"So it really was the Kallorwegians?" I asked.

She nodded. "They demanded he help them abduct you as proof of loyalty. When the abduction failed, Duke Lennox insisted that Walden pull back from interaction with you. He was becoming concerned that it might raise someone's suspicions. They always walked on a knife edge, their true plans at danger of discovery from both sides."

She turned back to her packing. "But Walden always held out hope he could sour you against the other families and win your outright loyalty. I think only your relationship with Lucas finally disabused him of the notion. And by then my family had settled on a new plan of action. They had decided that letting the Spoken Mage loose in Kallorway would be exactly to their liking. They did their best to help the Kallorwegians capture you on the front lines."

"But they nearly killed you, too," I exclaimed.

"My patrol wasn't supposed to be there, remember? And when we did stumble into the trap, those attacking mages and soldiers didn't know who I was—or care either, I imagine."

"But even that plan didn't work," Lucas said.

"No, you constantly eluded them," she said, "growing past their expectations. You showed no sign of siding with them, and they couldn't risk pursuing such a connection more openly without risk of being exposed. You resisted capture by Kallorway, but equally showed no inclination to storm Kallmon on behalf of Ardann. I'm not sure what they would have done next if Walden hadn't acted on his own."

Something in me didn't want to hear her words, but another part couldn't stop listening, desperate to understand everything that had happened to me since my powers were unleashed.

"While we were away," she continued, "Walden had access to all of Lorcan's records. He stumbled on some information about you. Something about your parentage?"

She frowned. "I didn't entirely understand that part, but apparently he spent months combing through the library, researching some connection you have with the Sekalis? He'd been to the Empire before you arrived and understood something of their culture. He'd even kept a Sekali contact that he could use for clandestine communication. He informed the emperor of your ability to speak compositions and of your connection to the Empire, thinking it was time you were removed from the equation altogether."

She got a distant look, as if remembering something. "Lennox and my parents were furious with him for months after the Sekali delegation arrived with the proposal of a marriage alliance." She looked at Lucas. "My family needed you here for their own plans."

"I don't think an alliance was really the Sekalis' primary motivation," I said.

"No, and that's what Walden always claimed," she said. "He maintained it was only you they wanted, and I suppose he proved himself right. And when the delegation returned with Lucas in tow, and the rumor spread that you had run to Kallorway, he triumphantly pointed out that things couldn't be more perfect."

She stopped and shook her head.

"He knew you would head for Cassius, so he sent word ahead about your new ability. He wanted you captured and taken to Kallmon. Once there, the Ellington agents would have freed you and, one way or another, sent you straight into a final showdown with Osborne. What more perfect way to ensure Kallorway devolved into chaos?"

"But I was with her," Lucas said. "I thought they needed me here, safe—at least for the moment?"

A grin inched across her face. "Yes, but unfortunately for Walden, the news that the you who returned wasn't actually you didn't reach him until after he'd sent the message. And by then it was too late. Things were in motion, and we had to move the whole plan forward to keep pace with them. Lennox descended on the Academy in person to berate him. It would all have been quite entertaining if I hadn't been convinced my silence had sent you both to your deaths."

"So you meant your efforts at friendship at the end of third year?" I asked.

She nodded. "I felt like a whole new aspect of life had opened up to me—the possibility of friends and laughter and something other than constant training. And then I went home, and my parents sat me down and told me everything. I didn't know how to face you when I came back to the Academy. I was terrified and angry, but I didn't know how to betray my family. I turned to Acacia for reassurance that what they were planning was somehow justifiable—she's an Ellington and a good person, I thought she must have come up with some compelling argument to show me that my doubts were unnecessary."

"And?" I asked, almost afraid of the answer.

Dariela sighed. "All I did was throw her into the same conflicted situation as me. She turned out to be one of the family members who didn't know anything about it. Like Finnian's mother and aunt. And Duke Magnus."

Lucas and I exchanged a look.

"Duke Magnus wasn't part of the conspiracy?" he asked. "We should probably let someone know that."

Dariela frowned but then seemed to catch on quickly.

"I suppose you've rounded up all the Ellingtons you could get your hands on. A wise move. We're a large family, though. I don't know where every single person stands."

"A truth composition will soon sort them out," I said. "Anyone who refuses to submit to one will no doubt be treated as a traitor, so there will be inducement enough to participate."

"It's a good thing one of the dukes remains loyal," Lucas said. "This will wreak havoc on your family. And those who are left— those who did nothing wrong except to possess the wrong relatives—will need leadership in the coming days."

"With all of this, plus the new sealing composition from the Empire, I imagine we'll all need strong leadership in the coming days," Dariela said. She looked at Lucas and my clasped hands. "So it's a good thing we have the two of you."

EPILOGUE

I stood beside Lucas at graduation, our hands entwined. The summer sun warmed the crowd gathered in the Academy grounds. The exams had been as easy for both of us as Jocasta had predicted months ago, and our days at the Academy were now officially ending. In reality they had ended a couple of weeks ago, but our families and friends had all gathered inside the Academy grounds for the official graduation ceremony.

I surveyed the seven year mates who stood with us, giving myself a moment to acknowledge the bittersweet nature of the day. We should have had three more standing with us. My eyes roamed out over the audience, picking out Araminta's diminutive frame sitting close to my own family. A tall man and a short woman sat beside her, beaming as broadly as if their daughter was indeed graduating alongside us—as she should have been.

The proud faces of her parents only confirmed my suspicion. Lucas and I weren't the only ones to have graduated with ease. Araminta had come too far to fail the Academy—unless she had done it on purpose.

She had been quiet and withdrawn the entire week leading up to exams, starting from the day Lucas's parents announced the

331

change in the law regarding anyone found to have insufficient control over their power. And the day after exams, while the younger trainees returned to their families for summer break, a quiet ceremony of a different sort was held in the Academy arena.

It had already seen use a number of times, as the mageborn prison cells were emptied. The royals had forced the arena into service until the palace had time to properly shield a large enough room elsewhere for sealing ceremonies to take place.

Jasper had been in the first batch of commonborns to be sealed, along with every other commonborn university graduate currently alive. Each town and village across Ardann had been permitted to select representatives to be sealed along with their schoolteachers. In time there was talk of those teachers selecting promising students for the same honor.

But Araminta's case had been a little different. Not guilty of any crime, she had been permitted to select ten of the many commonborns her power would seal. And alongside her mother, she had done the greatest possible service of friendship and chosen my parents and Clemmy. Even as I watched, my little sister leaned forward and waved at Araminta, beaming.

Coralie's family sat behind them, their eyes locked on Coralie and Finnian with pride, excitement, and delight. I noticed Finnian's family, sitting in the front row, looked a little less enthused as they eyed their son.

I wasn't too worried, though. Once everything calmed down, Coralie had filled me in on events in Torcos after we left. Apparently, Finnian had begun talking about how he should take his small fishing boat onto the Overon and make his own way upstream to check out the Empire for himself—since the border was now open.

Saffron had described the resulting scene with bubbling laughter, telling me how our usually sweet friend had transformed into a terrifying creature who utterly forbade him from even thinking of such a thing.

"Aunt Helene was watching the whole thing, thank goodness," she had said. "She wouldn't even speak to Finnian for three hours afterward, but Coralie she immediately took under her wing."

She had paused and shaken her head. "Knowing Finnian, I rather suspect he knew his mother was there all along and came up with the planned boat trip as a way to unite her and Coralie. If that was his plan, it certainly worked."

Saffron's explanation turned out to be the first Coralie had heard of this theory, and she immediately stormed off to confront Finnian. Since the end result of this effort was that she dragged him back to join us, his arm firmly wrapped around her waist, I wasn't sure how much confronting had actually gone on.

But since Lucas sat in an armchair only an arm's reach away from me, I watched my friends' happiness with unalleviated joy. Fourth year had finally become what I had dreamed it could be.

I glanced down the row of graduating mages, my eyes picking out my friends. I knew I would look back on the last few months as some of the best of my life. Finnian had even managed to get Lucas to laugh on three separate occasions in the one conversation. Despite the various important happenings going on in the kingdom, for that short time we had been able to be no one but ourselves, safe within the Academy walls.

But all of that was changing now. Tomorrow I would move into the palace, into a set of apartments officially granted to the Spoken Mage. My betrothal to Lucas wasn't to be formally announced until the Midsummer Ball, but it wasn't going to be a surprise to anyone when it happened. The thought of becoming royalty still daunted me, but with the pace of change happening all around us, I knew there wouldn't be time for me to worry about where I might fit in.

General Griffith watched three of his children graduate from beside Finnian's parents. He had returned from an extended sojourn in Kallmon—along with a large number of his Armed Forces officers and soldiers—just in time to be in attendance. Lucas and I, our exams already completed, had been present to hear his report.

The rebels had agreed to honor Cassius's crowning in exchange for peace with Ardann and the choice of who was to be sealed—both mages and commonborn. Any surprise that the rebels had so easily acquiesced to keeping Cassius on the throne evaporated at the news that his coronation had been followed immediately by his marriage to General Haddon's daughter—a graduated mage several years the prince's senior.

General Griffith had looked almost gleeful as he spoke of the years of effort that would be required to remake the Kallorwegian court and heal the cracks that now tore it apart. He was clearly more than happy to let the new King Cassius spend his days struggling with the Head of his Royal Guard—now also his father-in-law—over who wielded the true power of the throne.

"I doubt the Kallorwegian throne will be strong again until Cassius's future unsealed child takes the crown," he had said.

Celebrations had broken out across Ardann as the conscripted soldiers returned to their homes with news of the peace treaty. A more restrained jubilation had been felt in the palace when the missive taking the news to Yanshin resulted in Chen's arrival as a permanent ambassador.

It seemed the emperor had recognized that he could not undo what had been done. The border was now open, the Empire's secret was revealed, and the southern kingdoms once again stood united and at peace—a force to be reckoned with.

And though nothing was stated outright, it seemed he recognized that no good would come of trying to lay claim to Prince Lucas's betrothed, even if I did contain a drop of Sekali blood. Reading between the lines, it seemed that an increasing commonborn population combined with the beginnings of dissent among the sealed mage clans were indeed responsible for the emperor's unexpectedly forgiving attitude. He had heard of the new approach being adopted by Ardann and Kallorway, and he wished Chen to observe the process and its ramifications.

He had even agreed to welcome ambassadors of our own in his court. Nothing had been announced yet, but as immediate family of two of King Stellan's choices, I already knew exactly who was to be sent. And I couldn't be prouder of either of my brothers—although I would miss them both.

I was glad they were to go, especially Jasper. He would have the chance to learn and grow in a place where his intellect and capacity would be truly valued and respected. And perhaps one day I would have the chance to visit him there. Because if I could claim both Jasper and Julian as my brothers, then surely I could also lay claim to the Sekali and Kallorwegian parts of me without rejecting the fact that Ardann would always be my home.

When the ceremony was completed, a parade of people came past to congratulate us. Lucas's parents and sister, of course, as well as my own family—both the original and adoptive members. Even Declan—who fit neither of those categories, and yet was somehow part of my strange patchwork family anyway—had traveled to Corrin to attend. After what he had sacrificed for Lucas, he would always be welcome in Ardann.

Jasper had Clara by his side, the two of them engaged and busy planning their wedding. As a graduate, Clara had been sealed alongside Jasper, and already she was turning around her family's fortunes. In the face of such a gesture, some at least of her family's bitterness toward the mages had faded away. Or perhaps they had decided that a son-in-law who was brother to a future princess would bring sufficient value to the family. Whatever the reason, they had thrown their full support behind Jasper and Clara, and my brother's joy brightened my day. I didn't doubt for a moment that any children he and Clara produced would win themselves a place at a sealing ceremony.

Beatrice came to congratulate us as well. She said she had

seen so much of us all in the past three years that she had started to feel invested in our year level. I had confessed to her my brief suspicions about her loyalty, and she had forgiven me freely. She had even promised to teach me healing, in whatever time my royal responsibilities would allow.

Knowing she would stand beside me had given me confidence, and also led me to think of who else I wanted around me in the challenges to come. When Beatrice stepped away and Araminta took her place, I turned to Lucas.

"As a princess, will I be permitted to employ my own officials?"

He looked surprised. "Certainly, if you wish to do so."

I turned back to Araminta. "Then I'd like to offer you a job, if you'd like one."

She frowned. "But I can't compose anymore."

"And that's exactly why I need you," I said. "A commonborn with power, and a mageborn without. A new princess and someone who's a child of both worlds. Together we will have to be the ambassadors of a new way."

I smiled at Lucas. "And I want Leila, too. I don't know what's happened to her now that the conscripted soldiers have been released, but she has the sort of skills I need by my side."

Coralie, who had wandered over to join us, laughed at that.

"You're not wrong there. Can you imagine her unleashed on the palace?" She shook her head.

I pulled my first mage friend into a tight hug.

"I'll miss you, Coralie." My voice sounded thick from unshed tears. "Thank you for everything."

She hugged me back. "I'll miss you, too. I might miss you so much I have to come and stay regularly at the palace."

I chuckled. "You'll be more than welcome whenever you want to come."

Saffron walked over, and I pulled her into the hug.

"You, too, Saffron."

"If Coralie joins the healers like she's threatening, I might have to," Saffron said. "Otherwise she'll move into uncle's estate with the other healers, and I'll never get a break from her and Finnian."

Coralie snorted and shoved her away playfully, but I just grinned. I would gladly welcome Saffron to court. I had once joked that I would put in a good word for her with Calix, but for the last month I had been noting how well-suited she would be for my other adoptive brother. Growing up with Finnian, she seemed well-equipped to keep Julian in line. I just needed some time to help both of them see it.

Dariela approached tentatively, and I detached from my other friends to welcome her. I hadn't expected her to attend, so it meant a lot that she had come despite how painful it must be for her.

"I'm sorry you weren't up there with us," I said.

A small confused frown crossed her usually confident face. "The strange thing is that I'm not. Not completely."

I examined her face. It held a calm acceptance that made her look older and wiser.

"But what will you do now?" I asked.

She shrugged. "Discover who I am, I suppose. Everything I used to be has been stripped away, and now I'll have to learn what sort of person is left."

"A good one," I said. "And when you've worked that out for yourself, you'll have one friend waiting for you—regardless of your new status. And a job, too, if you ever want one. Being sealed hasn't diminished your brilliance, and Ardann will need brilliant people in the years to come."

Over her shoulder, I caught Lucas's eye. He had drifted apart from the crowd while I talked and stood near the corner of the building, his face inviting me to join him. Dariela saw my distraction and managed a smile, waving me away. After a moment's hesitation, I slipped away to his side.

He took my hand and led me around the building and through the grand Academy entrance. We walked slowly as I took it all in, letting the memories wash over me. Together we walked down the long corridor and through the library doors.

I stood there for a moment, my eyes on the desk, memories of Walden and Jocasta competing for prominence. I kept my gaze firmly averted from the floor, although it had been cleaned and polished months ago.

"You couldn't have known," Lucas murmured against my hair.

I took a deep breath and let his words sink in. He was right, and I needed to let my guilt go. Walden had meant me harm, but circumstances had turned out in my favor. Like the physical attacks from first year that had succeeded in freeing my power. And in the end, I had used that power for good.

As we moved deeper into the library, strolling between two long shelves, I ran my hand along the books. So many words. So much still to learn. A different sort of power lay here, and it was going to change our world as inexorably as my own. Already I had received word of at least two books about the experiences of commonborns—written by commonborns—currently being drafted.

And Jocasta had also begun a book on the Sekali Empire, while a team of mages and sealed commonborns at the University were carefully studying and creating copies of the history books Walden had been keeping hidden away. They even had a Sekali history book brought as a peace offering by Ambassador Chen. Future mages would not have the same gaps in their library that past mages had faced. They would not have the same excuse of ignorance that had nearly crippled us all.

Deep in the library, Lucas stopped and wrapped his arms around me.

"Do you think we should frame a copy of that old news sheet you found in Kingslee?" he asked, gazing down at me with a distracting smile. "Without it, we might never have found you."

"I don't know that I want a daily reminder of that," I said. "I can't even imagine my life without you or words."

"Good," Lucas said, "because I'm never letting you go."

"I love you, Prince Lucas of Ardann," I said softly.

"I love you, Elena, the one and only Spoken Mage."

I gripped the front of his robe and rose onto tiptoes, bringing my face as close to his as I could. For a moment he stayed tantalizingly out of reach, his eyes teasing me. Anticipation spread through me, and then he leaned down and brought his lips to mine. They tasted strong and sure, and full of promise for our future.

NOTE FROM THE AUTHOR

Thank you for joining me for Elena and Lucas's adventures! I hope you've enjoyed the journey. I'm already dreaming up more stories in the Spoken Mage world, so if you would like to be informed of future releases, as well as Spoken Mage bonus shorts, please sign up to my mailing list at www.melaniecellier.com. You'll find an exclusive bonus chapter of Voice of Power—retold from Lucas's point of view—in the welcome email.

In the meantime, for more fantasy, romance, adventure, and intrigue try *A Dance of Silver and Shadow,* the first book in my *Beyond the Four Kingdoms* series in which twelve princesses must do a lot more than just dance when they get caught up in a dangerous and magical competition.

And if you enjoyed my Spoken Mage series, please spread the word and help other readers find it! You could start by leaving a review on Amazon (or Goodreads or Facebook or any other social media site). Your review would be very much appreciated and would make a big difference!

ROYAL FAMILY OF ARDANN

King Stellan
Queen Verena
Crown Princess Lucienne
Prince Lucas

MAGE COUNCIL

Academy Head (black robe) - Duke Lorcan of Callinos
University Head (black robe) - Duchess Jessamine of
Callinos
Head of Law Enforcement (red robe) - Duke Lennox of
Ellington
Head of the Seekers (gray robe) - Duchess Phyllida of
Callinos
Head of the Healers (purple robe) - Duke Dashiell of
Callinos
Head of the Growers (green robe) - Duchess Annika of
Devoras
Head of the Wind Workers (blue robe) - Duke Magnus of
Ellington
Head of the Creators (orange robe) - Duke Casimir of
Stantorn
Head of the Armed Forces (silver robe) - General Griffith of
Devoras
Head of the Royal Guard (gold robe) - General Thaddeus of
Stantorn

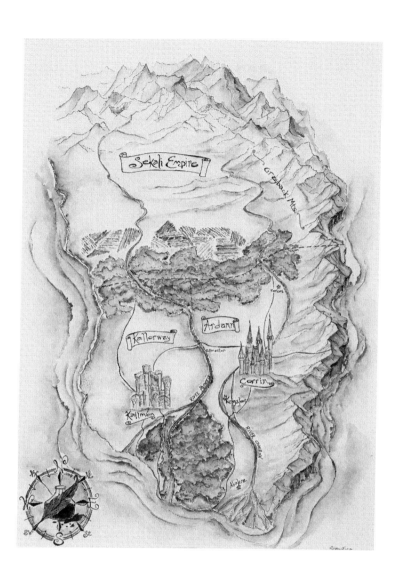

ACKNOWLEDGMENTS

After writing interconnected stand alone fairytale retellings, the Spoken Mage series was a new adventure for me. It is with a great sense of satisfaction and accomplishment that I finish Voice of Life, the final Elena book. That doesn't mean it was easy, of course—far from it. But it has been an incredible encouragement to know so many readers have embraced Elena and her adventures and have been waiting eagerly to see her overcome all obstacles and find her future with Lucas.

And, as always, my team have been instrumental in helping me create and hone this final story. From my wonderful, long-suffering family—Marc, Adeline, and Sebastian—to my beta readers, editors, and author friends, I couldn't do any of this without your support.

My developmental editor, Mary, has been with me for the whole series and has provided so much insight and assistance. Thank you for your flexibility and commitment.

The same thank you needs to go to my beta readers—Rachel, Greg, Ber, Katie, Priya, Marina, Casey, and Aya. You all once again impressed me with your speed and insight. And a special thank you to Aya for jumping onboard at late notice to help bring a new perspective to the completion of this story.

I want to give an extra thank you to my dad, who supports all the aspects of my writing life, from helping with technical elements like my website, to beta reading and copy editing. And I'm also more than grateful to have Deborah on the team for proofreading. Your eye and memory for technical detail when it comes to words and grammar astounds me with every book.

I love this cover and am so grateful to my designer, Karri, for the care she has put into this series. I'm thankful to have a creative team around me to make up for my areas of weakness—visual design definitely being one of them!

To my author friends—you know who you are!—thanks for walking through this Spoken Mage journey with me. The writing life can be a crazy one, but the people make it worth it.

And I want to give an extra thank you to every one of my readers. My writing worlds couldn't come to life without you—thank you for your passion and dedication.

Through every doubt, uncertainty, difficulty, pain, joy, triumph, and encouragement, one constant always remains. Thank you to God, my steady rock.

ABOUT THE AUTHOR

Melanie Cellier grew up on a staple diet of books, books and more books. And although she got older, she never stopped loving children's and young adult novels.

She always wanted to write one herself, but it took three careers and three different continents before she actually managed it.

She now feels incredibly fortunate to spend her time writing from her home in Adelaide, Australia where she keeps an eye out for koalas in her backyard. Her staple diet hasn't changed much, although she's added choc mint Rooibos tea and Chicken Crimpies to the list.

She writes young adult fantasy including her *Spoken Mage* series, and her *Four Kingdoms* and *Beyond the Four Kingdoms* series which are made up of linked stand-alone stories that retell classic fairy tales.

Printed in Great Britain
by Amazon